METSY HINGLE
DEADLINE

ISBN 0-7783-2096-0

DEADLINE

Copyright © 2004 by Metsy Hingle.

MIRA and the Star Colophon are trademarks used under license and registered in Australia, New Zealand, Philippines, United States Patent and Trademark Office and in other countries.

www.MIRABooks.com

Printed in U.S.A.

In memory of my beloved aunt Doris Hingle,
whose love lives on in the hearts
of all who knew her.

ACKNOWLEDGMENTS

While writing this book, I relied on both the technical and emotional support of many people to bring it to fruition. Without them, I would have been lost. My heartfelt thanks go out to the following people for their help in bringing life to *Deadline:*

Valerie Gray, my editor and friend at MIRA Books, whose insight and help truly make me a better writer.

Dianne Moggy, Editorial Director of MIRA Books, for her trust in me and support.

Karen Solem, my agent, for her unending support.

The amazing MIRA staff, who continue to astound me with their support.

Sandra Brown, my dear friend, for her friendship, love and for allowing me to bounce my story ideas off her.

Hailey North, my dear friend and fellow writer, for her friendship, support and e-mails.

Bill Capo, TV investigative reporter for Channel 4 News in New Orleans, for his friendship and support, and for answering my questions about the inner workings of the newsroom.

Marilyn Shoemaker, my fan and researcher, for digging out all those tiny details that helped me create the town of Grady, Mississippi.

Bill Greenleaf, press communications specialist with the Mississippi Department of Corrections, for answering all my questions about the inner workings of the state prison systems.

A special thank-you goes to my children and family, whose love and support enable me to spin my tales of love, hope and happily-ever-after.

And, as always, to my husband, Jim, who is my love, my family and all things to me.

Dear Reader,

Thank you so much for picking up a copy of *Deadline*. I hope you find it to be a real page-turner, and that it keeps you on the edge of your seat.

If this is the first time you've read any of my work, I do hope you enjoy it. For those of you who are familiar with my books, you won't be surprised to find that *Deadline* is set in the South. This time I've moved the setting from my hometown of New Orleans to my neighboring state of Mississippi in the fictional town of Grady.

As always, one of the greatest joys for me as a writer is hearing from readers, and I'd love to hear from you. Your comments, opinions and feedback on my books mean a great deal to me. So please keep those letters, cards and e-mails coming.

In fact, as a special thank-you I've created two gifts for you—a commemorative bookmark for *Deadline* and a recipe card for the mint julep that's mentioned in the story. While supplies last, I'd be happy to send both the bookmark and the recipe to each reader who writes and requests them. Simply either write or e-mail me and say that you'd like one of my commemorative *Deadline* bookmarks and the mint julep recipe used in *Deadline*.

Until next time, happy reading!

Metsy Hingle

P.O. Box 3224
Covington, LA
U.S.A. 70433

www.metsyhingle.com

Prologue

"It wasn't a suicide."

Skimming over her notes for Channel Seven TV's noon news report, Tess Abbott barely registered the caller's comment. Instead, she shifted the telephone to her other ear and underlined the alarming statistics that she'd uncovered in her investigation on plastic surgery being performed on teenage girls.

"Did you hear what I said? It *wasn't* a suicide," the woman repeated, her Southern drawl even more pronounced. "He was murdered."

Suddenly Tess jerked her gaze away from her notes and gave her full attention to the caller. "Who was murdered?"

"Jody Burns."

Every muscle, every nerve in Tess's body went still at the mention of her father's name. Two months ago when the news broke about her father's suicide in prison, the media had been all over the story—especially the tabloid bottom-feeders. They'd come out of the woodwork, dogging her at the news station, pestering her grandfather at the Capitol. They'd even staked out her apartment on the outskirts of Washington, D.C., in an effort to get some reaction from her. As an investigative TV reporter, she had understood the media's frenzy over the story. After all, the death of the man who had killed the only child of the powerful senator from Mississippi twenty-five years earlier was news in itself. Coupled with her grandfather's outspoken views on stronger penalties for criminals, the suicide of Jody Burns was all the more newsworthy. While the reporter in her had understood the hunger for a juicy story, the child in her who had lost both her parents that long-ago night had resented the intrusions. She resented it even more now, she realized, her jaw tightening, because she'd thought all the hoopla over Jody Burns's suicide was finally behind her. "Listen, I don't know who you're working for and the truth is, I really don't care. But I'll tell you the same thing I tell everyone else. No comment."

"But—"

"And unless you want me to file harassment charges against you and whatever outfit you're working for," Tess barged ahead, "don't call me again. Ever."

"Wait! Please, don't hang up! I'm not a reporter. I swear it!"

There was just enough desperation in the woman's voice to pique Tess's interest. She hesitated a second, then said, "All right. Then who are you and why are you calling me?"

"I am…was a friend of your father's," the woman corrected. "And I'm calling you because Jody didn't kill himself like they said. They murdered him and made it look like a suicide to keep him quiet."

Tess squeezed her eyes shut a moment, fighting back the images that flashed through her mind—images of herself awakening from a bad dream, of entering the den and seeing the father she adored kneeling over her mother's body, covered in her blood. Shaking off the memory, she said, "How Jody Burns died is of no concern to me."

"But he was your father."

"He ceased being my father the night he killed my mother," Tess informed her, making her voice as cool as her heart for the man she'd once called "daddy."

"But he didn't kill her."

Tess started to tell the woman that she was wasting her time, that Jody Burns was no innocent. After all, she should know, Tess reasoned, since she was the one who'd found him still holding the bookend in his hand that he'd used to smash in her mother's skull. But before she could get the words out, a knock sounded at her office door.

"Hey, Tess," Jerry Wilson said, sticking his head inside the door. "You're up in fifteen."

"I'll be right there." When the door closed behind him, she said, "I have to go."

"But what about your father? Don't you want justice for him?"

"Some would say he got the justice he deserved—even if it came twenty-five years late," Tess countered, recalling her grandfather's words when they had first learned of Burns's death.

"Then they would be wrong," the woman insisted. "Jody Burns didn't belong in that prison. He was not the one who killed your mother."

"A jury thought otherwise."

"The jury was wrong. And your father was going to prove it, too. That's why he was killed and it was made to look like a suicide."

Jerry tapped at the door again. "Tess."

"Coming," she said.

Regretting that she'd allowed the conversation to even get started, and aware that she needed to get to the set, Tess said, "Listen, I have to go."

"That's it? Aren't you going to do anything?"

"No."

"I would have thought you would want justice."

"I'm all for justice. But there's nothing I can do." Softening, she said, "Listen, if you really believe what you've told me, then you should contact the police."

"The police! They're the last ones I can go to. Oh, God, this was a mistake. I never should have called you."

"Wait!" Tess had been an investigative reporter long enough to recognize panic in the woman's voice. "What do you mean you can't go to the police?"

"Because I can't risk it. If he was to find out that I knew… No, I can't take that chance."

Oh, what she wouldn't have given to see the woman's face, Tess thought, to be able to look into her eyes, read her. "Listen, if you're in some kind of trouble—"

"I'm not. At least not yet. But if he finds out that I know and that I called you, God knows what'll happen to me."

Tess could practically taste the woman's fear. "If who finds out? Tell me who it is that you're afraid of."

"I can't. I've already said too much."

"Then tell me who you are, how to reach you," Tess said. "I'll help you."

"The only way you can help me is if you finish what your father started. Don't let him get away with murder again."

"Again?" Tess repeated.

"God, don't you understand? The person who had Jody killed is the same one who killed your mother. And unless you do something, he'll get away with it this time, too."

But before Tess could demand more information, the connection was severed and a dial tone buzzed in her ear.

Chapter One

"Good afternoon. This is David Rabinowitz with the noon report for Channel Seven News. At the top of our news is this morning's emergency landing of an American Airlines 747 at Reagan International Airport following reports that a bomb was on board."

Veronica "Ronnie" Hill sat back in her chair in the control room at Channel Seven News and studied the studio monitors. As the show's producer for the past ten years, she watched the broadcast with a critical eye. The new anchor was a good choice, she decided, satisfied with his delivery. While his boy-next-door good looks would certainly appeal to the female viewers, the fact that he'd reported sports for a rival network would draw in the male viewers. All in all, they were counting on seeing a jump in the ratings with the new guy on board.

"To give us an update on the situation, we'll go live to Reagan International Airport where Tess Abbott is standing by," David said.

Ronnie frowned when it took an extra two seconds for the monitors to do a split screen. Then the screens split in two with a view of David seated at the studio news desk on the left, and a view of Tess standing outside the airport complex on the right. But it was Tess on whom Ronnie focused. She made a dramatic image, Ronnie thought, with her booted feet planted firmly on the ground. An early-October wind whipped her mocha suede skirt against her legs and her dark hair swirled about her face and shoulders. Behind her, crash trucks zoomed by, followed by a swarm of military vehicles and more cars with flashing lights. To her left a jumbo jet bearing the American Airlines logo sat idle and detached from the jetty. Hordes of personnel flocked around the plane.

"Tess, this is David in the Channel Seven studio. Can you give us an update of what's going on out there at the airport?"

"Well, David, as was reported earlier, an American Airlines flight that was en route to La Guardia Airport in New York made an emergency landing here at Reagan International around nine-fifteen this morning after a passenger on the plane informed a member of the airline's flight crew that there was a bomb aboard the aircraft," Tess began her report.

"All right, go to a full screen of Tess," Ronnie whispered.

As though the cameraman could hear her, the monitor switched to a full-screen view and zoomed in on Tess. Holding the microphone in front of her, she ignored the noise and activity behind her and looked directly into the camera. "My sources tell me that it appears that the bomb threat was a hoax. No bomb or any explosives were found on board the plane. I'm also told that the passenger has since confessed to being despondent, having recently broken up with his girlfriend. He now says he claimed to have a bomb on board in order to get his estranged girlfriend's attention."

"That's some attention getter," David remarked.

"Unfortunately, it's probably going to get him the wrong kind of attention," Tess replied. She pushed the hair that blew across her face out of her eyes. Without missing a beat, she continued. "Because the federal authorities now have him in custody and will be charging him."

"Do we know who the guy is?" David asked.

"The authorities haven't released his name yet," Tess said, her voice strong and sure above the scream of the wind and the noise around her. "But according to an unnamed source, the person in custody is a thirty-two-year-old male who boarded the flight in Virginia."

"What's it like there inside the airport, Tess?" David asked.

"I'd call it controlled chaos, David. As a safety precaution, two of the terminals were vacated before the American flight landed, and all incoming and departing flights were suspended."

"There must be a lot of unhappy travelers, not to mention some crazed ticket-counter agents," David commented.

"Well, as I said, it's chaos, but it's controlled. In addition to the displaced passengers from the American flight that was deplaned, we have a lot of passengers whose scheduled flights have been suspended. So there are a lot of people waiting inside the terminal," Tess explained with a nod of her head to the airport complex. "And they're unsure if, or when, they'll be able to continue with their travels."

"Are tempers running high?" David asked.

"Surprisingly, no. Most of the people that I spoke with were concerned, but very understanding. I think the feeling is that they would rather be safe than sorry."

"Any idea how long before flights will be under way again?"

"The last report I received said that all flights were still suspended, but…just a moment, David."

While Tess pressed her free hand against her headset and listened, Ronnie studied the young woman she'd worked with for the past three years. Despite her initial misgivings when Tess had been hired, the girl had proven herself to be more than just another pretty face. She was bright, hardworking and easy to get along with—something that Ronnie couldn't say about all of the reporters under her direction, or even the news anchors for that matter. No, Tess Abbott was a good one, she mused. While very little impressed her in this business, Tess had. Somehow the girl had managed to keep her cool and do a good job even during the circus atmosphere following her father's suicide and her grandfather's appearances on Capitol Hill. Never once had she brought anything personal into the newsroom. In short, Tess was a real pro. That's why seeing the shadows under Tess's eyes now, and remembering her distracted demeanor all week at work worried her. Something was wrong.

"David, I've just been told that the airport has been cleared for incoming flights again," Tess reported. "And all other flights will resume within the hour. It's suggested that anyone who is either meeting an incoming flight, or scheduled to fly out this afternoon, check with the airlines first for updated arrival and departure times."

"Thanks, Tess."

She nodded. "Reporting live from Reagan International Airport in Washington, D.C., for Channel Seven News, this is Tess Abbott."

The screen switched from Tess back to David in the studio. "In other news today, the president addresses the nation tonight. Among the key topics will be the nation's economy."

Tuning out the rest of the news report, Ronnie drummed her fingers on her desk and considered the best way to approach Tess. She liked the girl, considered her a friend. And because she did, she needed to get Tess to open up and tell her what was wrong so they could fix it. Never very good at mind games, Ronnie picked up the phone and dialed Tess's cell phone.

"Tess Abbott," she answered on the third ring.

"Tess, it's Ronnie."

"Hi, Ronnie. Hang on a sec, will you?" she said. "Eddie, I'm going to head over to the theater to do the interview with that playwright. I'll just meet you there."

"Do I have time to grab some lunch?" the cameraman asked.

"As long as it's a quick one," Tess replied. "Okay, sorry about that, Ronnie. What's up?"

"Tell Eddie to take a long lunch and see if you can push your interview back a couple of hours," Ronnie instructed.

"Why?" Tess asked, her voice wary.

"Because you and I are having lunch. I'll meet you at Vincent's in thirty minutes."

"What's going on, Ronnie?" Tess demanded suspiciously.

"That's what I intend to find out."

And before Tess could argue, Ronnie hung up the

phone. After making a quick stop in her office for her car keys and purse and to advise her assistant where she'd be, Ronnie headed out of the station, intent on getting some answers.

"All right, Ronnie," Tess said once the two of them had been seated at a table and placed their orders. "What are we doing here?"

Ronnie reached for the basket of crackers on the table. "Well, since all I had for breakfast was coffee and a bagel, I'm hoping we're about to have lunch because I'm starved."

Tess eyed her skeptically. "You and I both know that you don't 'do' lunch without a reason, Veronica Hill. And if you think that by feeding me you'll be able to convince me to pull another weekend shift as news anchor, I'll save you the trouble. The answer is no."

"My, my, you are a suspicious one," Ronnie said as she began to butter a cracker. She glanced up, looked across the table at her from behind the tortoiseshell-framed glasses. "As it so happens, the weekend news shifts are covered."

"All right. I'll bite. What are we doing here then?"

"I'm your producer. Can't I ask you to lunch once in a while?"

"You can, but you don't. Not without a reason," Tess told her.

Ronnie sighed. "Sometimes I think you know me a little too well."

"It works both ways. That's why we make a good team. So why don't you tell me just what it is you want."

"I want to know what's bothering you."

"Nothing's bothering me," she replied. Yet even as she

made the statement, Tess knew it wasn't true. She'd been bothered a lot lately. First by the anonymous phone call claiming Jody Burns's death hadn't been a suicide. And now by the response from the Mississippi prison system after she'd made some inquiries about his death. According to the medical examiner and the review board's reports, Jody Burns had been greatly depressed the week prior to his death—which in itself seemed odd since he was up for parole. But, following an investigation, his death had been ruled a suicide due to strangulation by hanging in his cell.

The waitress arrived and served Tess her minestrone soup and Ronnie her green salad. Once she was gone, Ronnie said, "Then explain to me why you look like you haven't had a decent night's sleep in a week?"

"Gee, thanks, Ronnie. I think you look nice, too."

"Oh, don't get all pissy on me," Ronnie told her as she dragged the strip of lettuce through the side of creamy Italian dressing. She paused, glanced up and met Tess's gaze. "On your worst day, you look better than most of us do after a week at a health spa. Now quit pretending you're insulted and tell me what's wrong."

"I told you, nothing is wrong."

The waitress who'd taken their orders stopped at the table again and topped off their ice water. She eyed Tess curiously from beneath lashes thick with blue mascara. "Excuse me, but aren't you that news lady? The one from Channel Seven who does those investigative reports?"

"No, that's her sister," Ronnie offered before Tess could respond.

"Oh," the waitress replied, her expression falling. "I guess that explains the resemblance."

Tess bit the inside of her cheek at the fib. She didn't kid herself. Unlike some of the reporters on the show, she never for a moment believed herself to be a celebrity simply because she appeared on television to report on a story. And although it didn't happen with great frequency, she was occasionally recognized.

"People confuse them all the time," Ronnie told the girl. "But Tammy here is actually Tess Abbott's older sister."

"Well, now that you mention it, I can see that you look older than the lady on the news. But your sister's good. I liked her report on the plastic surgery stuff."

"Thank you. I'll tell her," Tess managed to say.

"You do that. Your orders should be up in a minute. Can I get you anything else?" she asked over the din of voices.

"No, thanks. I'm fine," Tess said.

"Me, too," Ronnie echoed.

"That wasn't very nice," Tess admonished once the waitress had moved on to the next table.

Ronnie shrugged. "If you'd told her the truth, we'd have had half the people in this place craning their necks and stopping by the table to chat with you."

"I'd think that would make you happy. You're the one always looking for ways to pump up the station's ratings. The truth is, I'm surprised you didn't get her to swear she'd tell everyone to tune in to the show tonight."

"I considered it," Ronnie advised her. "But if I had, we wouldn't have been able to finish our little chat. Now, are you going to tell me why you've got circles under your eyes that look like they belong to a raccoon? Or am I going to have to torture you to get the truth?"

She'd probably do it, too, Tess thought. Despite her

small stature, the feisty redhead in the chic navy suit had the heart and soul of an army drill sergeant. One of the first things she'd learned about the producer was that the woman didn't know the meaning of the word no. Still, she wasn't at all sure she wanted to share with Ronnie, or anyone, the reason behind her sleepless nights. Instead, she said, "If I'm looking tired, it's probably because you've been working me too hard."

Ronnie waved aside her comment. "You're an investigative reporter. You're supposed to work hard. It's in your contract."

"Funny, I don't recall seeing that particular clause."

"Oh it's there all right, buried in the fine print."

Tess lifted her eyebrow skeptically as she added more sugar to her tea.

"Trust me, the boys in black make sure it's standard in everyone's contract," Ronnie explained, referring to the top brass at Channel Seven News.

She could almost believe it, Tess thought. She had covered as many stories during the past few months as she had for the entire previous year. The primary reason was that they'd been short staffed after losing a veteran reporter to a news station on the West Coast, and another reporter had been placed on doctor-ordered bed rest for the remainder of her pregnancy. As a result, Tess had been forced to pull double and sometimes triple duty working as the station's investigative reporter, society reporter and occasionally filling in as news anchor.

"Just be glad you're not a producer. Producers have to sign the thing in blood," Ronnie claimed before taking another bite of her salad.

"In that case, I'll stick to reporting."

"Smart girl. It's probably what I should have done. If

I had, I wouldn't be sitting here trying to find out why my top reporter looks like hell and has been moping all week."

Ignoring the accusation, Tess said, "You love working in that pressure cooker and you know it."

Ronnie curved her lips into a smile. "True. But if I'd known it was going to take over my life so completely, I would've at least held out for more money. A word to the wise, kiddo. If Stefanovich ever shows up at your desk singing your praises and dangling a fancy title at you, run. Otherwise, he'll reel you in like a fish. And before you know it, you'll be working eighteen-hour days and making the same money you did as a reporter."

"I'll be sure to remember that." The truth was, she hadn't really minded the extra workload during the past few months. Work had kept her too busy to think much about Jody Burns's death or the ending of her year-long romance with Jonathan Parker. But now with David in the news-anchor spot and Angela due back Monday from her maternity leave, her days weren't nearly so busy, Tess admitted. Neither were her evenings now that Jonathan was out of the picture. As a result she no longer dashed out of the station to attend some event, or dragged herself home late at night to crawl into bed and collapse. No, now she lay awake at night and thought. And the one thing she couldn't stop thinking about was that phone call she'd received and the woman's claim that Jody Burns's death had been murder. Mostly, she hadn't been able to stop thinking about the woman's claim that someone other than Jody Burns had killed her mother.

"Earth to Tess."

Tess yanked her attention back to Ronnie. "Sorry. Did you say something?"

"You're really starting to worry me, kiddo. That's the second time you've zoned out on me since we got here."

Tess set her soupspoon aside and sighed. "I'm sorry. I guess I'm just tired. I haven't been sleeping well lately."

"That's obvious," Ronnie reminded her. "This trouble sleeping wouldn't have anything to do with Johnny, would it?"

"No," Tess replied, not bothering to remind Ronnie, again, how much Jonathan detested being called Johnny. She'd long suspected that Ronnie only called him that because she disliked the man and wanted to irritate him. "As I told you at the time, we ended our relationship amicably. He and I are still friends."

"Uh-huh." Ronnie reached for her glass of tea and took a sip. "So he didn't come by the station yesterday to try to get you to change your mind about marrying him?"

"No. He didn't. If you must know, he came by to pick up the key he'd given me to his apartment."

"Any second thoughts about turning down his proposal?"

"None," Tess assured her. "You were right. Jonathan and I were all wrong for each other. I just can't believe it took me so long to see it."

She patted Tess's hand. "Don't be too hard on yourself. We all make mistakes—especially when it comes to men."

"Easy for you to say. I dated the man for nearly a year and not until I was faced with the prospect of marrying him did I realize that he and I would never work. You, on the other hand, knew it almost from the start."

Ronnie smiled—the smile of a woman who had

lived nearly fifty years and was wiser for it. "That's because I wasn't emotionally invested in the relationship. You were. And if there's one thing I've learned in life, it's that when it comes to the male species, women don't always see things clearly—especially if our emotions are involved."

But she should have seen it, Tess thought. Yet, despite the fact that she enjoyed Jonathan's company and being with him was easy, there had been no real passion between them. It wasn't until he'd surprised her with an engagement ring for her birthday that she'd been forced to face the truth. She didn't love him. At least not in the way you should love someone you married. "That still doesn't make it right. It was unfair of me to lead him on the way I did."

"Come on, Tess. Johnny's a big boy. I don't recall you holding a gun to the man's head and forcing him to go out with you."

"I know. But it was still embarrassing for him. He'd told his family and friends, even my grandparents, that he was giving me the ring. They were all expecting an engagement announcement, not a breakup."

"So he was embarrassed," Ronnie conceded. "From what I saw of him yesterday, he didn't appear to be suffering from a broken heart."

It was true, Tess admitted. Her refusal had appeared to bruise Jonathan's ego far more than his heart.

"He'll get over it," Ronnie assured her.

Tess had no doubt that he would. Jonathan knew what he wanted—a dutiful wife whose dreams and desires mirrored his own—which was to see himself in the White House someday. But that woman wasn't her. It could never be her because she had her own dreams, her own desires, and she had no intention of abandoning them. Nor did she want to be with a man who would expect her to do so. "Still, I can't help wishing I hadn't let things reach that point."

"Did it ever occur to you that maybe the reason you let things reach that point was because you knew it's what the senator wanted?"

"It wasn't my grandfather's mistake. It was mine." Although the senator had introduced her to Jonathan and hadn't hidden the fact that he'd welcome the up-and-coming attorney as a grandson-in-law, he hadn't forced her to go out with the man. "As you pointed out, no one held a gun to his head and forced him to go out with me."

"So I take it the senator isn't giving you grief for breaking up with golden boy?"

"He's not happy about it, but he's accepted it," Tess replied. And she hoped that was true. Her grandfather had been furious with her over her decision to end things with Jonathan. If there was one thing she'd learned in the years since she'd come to D.C. as a four-year-old to live with him and her grandmother, it was that her grandfather did not like it when things didn't go according to his plan—be it on Capitol Hill or in his family. Her turning down Jonathan's proposal was not part of his plan. But marrying the man was not part of her own plan.

"So no more schemes by the senator to throw you and Johnny together?"

"I made it clear to my grandfather that I'm not going to change my mind," Tess informed her. The final straw had occurred ten days ago when she'd arrived for her weekly dinner with her grandparents and had been advised that Jonathan would be joining them. Her grandmother had been clearly distressed by the senator's announcement, but Tess had been furious with him for, once again, trying to run her life. As a result, she had left the restaurant, leaving him to explain her absence to Jonathan.

"I can imagine how that went over. I got the impression at that charity dinner last month that the senator had earmarked Johnny boy as his future grandson-in-law."

"He may have, but it wasn't his decision to make. It was mine, which is what I told him." The day after the scene in the restaurant, she'd threatened to sever all contact with her grandfather if he continued to interfere in her personal life.

Ronnie arched one perfectly groomed eyebrow. "And what was the senator's response to that?"

"Let's just say, he wasn't thrilled with my decision." The truth was, she and her grandfather had barely spoken since that night. "And I'd really like to drop the subject."

"Sure," Ronnie told her as she slathered butter on another cracker. She paused, looked up at Tess. "So if it's not the senator or Johnny causing you to lose your beauty sleep, what or who is?"

"Ronnie," Tess said, making no attempt to hide her exasperation.

"Two chicken specials," the waitress declared and Tess was grateful for the interruption. After the young woman removed the salad plate, she placed the plate of grilled chicken with a rice pilaf in front of Ronnie. She paused at the sight of Tess's soup, which had barely been touched. "Something wrong with the soup?"

"No. It's fine, but I've had enough. You can take it," Tess told her.

She added the soup plate and cup to her tray and promptly served Tess her own plate of chicken. "You ladies let me know if you need anything else," the woman declared and hustled off in the direction of the kitchen.

"This looks good," Tess said as she picked up her fork.

"If that's your subtle way of ignoring my question, you should know me well enough by now to realize that I'm not going to stop hounding you until you tell me what's wrong." When she said nothing, Ronnie asked, "Is it work, Tess? I know sticking you with Kip on that last assignment wasn't fair, but I didn't have a choice. The jerk's uncle wields a lot of power around here."

"It doesn't have anything to do with work. It's personal."

Ronnie paused, and a concerned look came into her hazel eyes. "All right, Tess. I'll back off. But as your friend, I have to tell you that I'm worried about you. I've never seen you this stressed out before—not even when all that crap was going on about your father's suicide. Just so you know, if you need to talk, I'm here."

"Thanks, Ronnie. I appreciate it." Yet Tess wasn't at all sure she wanted to share with anyone the thoughts that had been running through her head since she'd received that phone call. But mostly, she wasn't sure whether she wanted to voice aloud what had been really troubling her—the idea that perhaps someone other than Jody Burns might have been responsible for her mother's murder.

Chapter Two

"I'm so glad you called," Elizabeth Abbott said that Saturday morning when she greeted Tess at the front door of the elder Abbotts' town house. "I do hate it so when you and your grandfather are at odds."

"I know, Grams," Tess said as she returned her hug. She drew back a fraction. "And I'm sorry that you're the one who always gets caught in the cross fire."

Her grandmother reached up and brushed the hair back from Tess's face. "Don't worry about me, dear. I'm a lot stronger than you think."

"I've never doubted your strength," Tess told her and she meant it. Her grandmother was a strong woman in her own way, having handled the loss of her only child, battled breast cancer and remained married to a strong-willed man like Senator Theodore Abbott for more than fifty years. "But sometimes I don't understand how you can put up with Grandfather when he gets in one of his moods."

"By one of his moods, I take you mean his being out of sorts because things haven't gone as he planned?" her grandmother asked, a twinkle in her blue eyes as the two of them headed toward the breakfast room.

"Yes," Tess replied. In truth, out of sorts was a mild description. Her grandfather was dictatorial and often nasty when he failed to get his way. She took a seat at the glass-and-rattan table where colorful place mats had been laid out with coffee cups and sterling.

"It's called marriage, dear. When you marry some-one you take them—warts and all." She poured Tess a cup of coffee. "He's a good man, Tess. He's done some remarkable things in his life. And he only wants what's best for you."

"I know, Grams. But that doesn't give him the right to try to manipulate me and decide who I should marry."

Her grandmother took a seat at the table next to her. "He just doesn't want you to make a mistake."

"You mean the way my mother did?" Tess asked. "Maybe marrying Jody Burns was a mistake in Grand-father's eyes. But it was her choice. Not his. And whomever I marry, it's going to be my choice, not grandfather's."

"You're so stubborn and righteous. Even more so than your mother was." Her grandmother sighed. "Sometimes, I wonder if things would have turned out differently if you and your mother had taken after me more instead of your grandfather."

With the morning light spilling in from the window across her grandmother's face, Tess noted the lines bracketing her eyes. The tasteful short coif of hair that had once been blond had given way to a lovely silver. Despite her seventy-plus years, Elizabeth Abbott's skin remained smooth, her face lovely. "You're stubborn in your own quiet way, Grams."

"Yes, I suppose I am," she conceded. She reached over and patted Tess's hand. "So, are you going to tell me why you needed to talk to your grandfather and me?"

Tess was tempted to tell her grandmother, to confide in her all the questions that had been running through her head since receiving that phone call and the decision she'd finally reached. "I think maybe it'll be better if I talk to the two of you together. When will Grandfather be home?"

"He had an early golf game with Senator Wilke. I expect him home any minute now."

Any minute turned out to be nearly an hour later. And when her grandfather entered the breakfast room, the entire house seemed more alive. "Tess, I wasn't expecting to see you here," her grandfather said gruffly, and Tess knew from his tone that he was still miffed at her over walking out on him at dinner more than a week ago.

"Tess called after you left this morning and asked if she could come by, Theo," her grandmother explained as she poured her husband a cup of coffee before resuming her own seat.

A big man with a head of thick silver hair and skin darkened by hours spent golfing, her grandfather remained a formidable man even at the age of seventy-five. Ignoring the coffee, he popped a stick of the cinnamon-flavored gum that he favored inside his mouth. A onetime smoker, Theodore Abbott had kicked the habit some twenty-seven years ago, but he had taken to chewing gum. Since then, he was never without a packet of gum stuffed inside one of his pockets.

Taking the silver foil from the gum, he proceeded to tie it into a knot. It was a ritual that she had watched her grandfather perform thousands of times. After a moment, he said, "If you've come to apologize for your rude behavior last week at dinner, you should know that I'm still quite upset with you, young lady. Your grandmother and I brought you up to behave better. You also owe Jonathan an apology."

"Jonathan and I have already spoken, Grandfather."

He pitched the knotted wrapper beside his coffee cup and sat back in his chair. "I'm pleased to hear that," he said, sounding somewhat mollified.

"Don't be, because I haven't changed my mind about marrying him and I didn't come here to apologize for walking out on your little setup at the restaurant to get us back together."

He scowled. "Then why are you here?" he demanded.

"To let you know that I'm planning to ask the station for some time off."

"Why, I think that's an excellent idea, Tess," her grandmother said, cutting the tension that permeated the air. "I was just telling your grandfather that you've been working too hard. It'll do you good to take a little vacation."

"Your grandmother's right. Perhaps a few weeks' rest will improve your disposition."

"I won't be taking a vacation. But I will be traveling to Mississippi. I've been in touch with the prison where Jody Burns died. I'm not sure his death was a suicide. I intend to look into it and his murder trial."

Her grandfather slapped his hand down on the table, rattling the coffee cups and silver. "You will do no such thing. I forbid it!"

"I wasn't asking for your permission, Grandfather." Tess stood. "I just wanted to let you both know where I'll be so you don't worry about me."

"You expect us not to worry when it's obvious that you've lost your mind?" her grandfather fired back.

"Calm down, Theo," her grandmother soothed. "Remember what the doctor said about your blood pressure."

"To hell with my blood pressure," he shouted. His face turned bright red. "I would think you'd be glad that the man was dead. Need I remind you that he killed your mother? That you were the one who found him over her bloody body holding the weapon in his hand?"

Tess heard her grandmother's gasp, saw the horror register on the older woman's face. Tess looked back at her furious grandfather. "I was four years old. A child," she reminded him. She had never seen Jody Burns following his conviction, and had long ago written him off as her father. But since that phone call, claiming his death hadn't been a suicide and that someone else had been responsible for her mother's murder, she had been plagued with questions. More importantly, she had begun to question her own memories of what had happened that night. "What if I was wrong about what I saw?"

"You weren't wrong. He killed her," her grandfather insisted.

"That's what I intend to find out."

And despite her grandfather's angry protests and her grandmother's dismay, Tess was determined to do just that.

"Okay, Tess, I need you to give me that sign-off again," the sound engineer told her in the news studio the next day as she completed the edits on the piece she'd done on a local playwright.

"Reporting on 'What's New in Entertainment This Week' for Channel Seven News, this is Tess Abbott."

"That should do it," the engineer advised her.

"Looks good. The guys upstairs are gonna like this one," the cameraman told her.

"Let's hope you're right, Bobby," she replied with a smile. She couldn't help noticing Ronnie watching her, that worried look in her eyes again. It was a look she'd seen several times since their talk over lunch last week. She could only hope that telling Ronnie about her plans would go smoothly.

And there was no time like the present, Tess decided as she unclipped the microphone from her jacket. Dodging the booms of the cameras and lights, she sidestepped the trail of cables that snaked across the small studio where they'd been taping. She started over toward Ronnie, who was tossing out directions to the assignment editor, production assistant and technician.

Without even taking a breath, she turned her attention to the news anchor. "David, we're going to lead with the story on the three-alarm fire downtown and move the president's speech to second," Ronnie instructed him while she continued to scribble notes that she handed off to her assistant. "We should be able to run Tess's piece on the playwright near the end of the news hour, right after the weather."

"Got it," the news anchor replied. "I've reworked the copy some on the lead-in story, punched it up a bit."

"Let me take a look," Ronnie said and took the script from him.

Tess stood back and waited for Ronnie to finish. But in typical Ronnie Hill fashion she multitasked, flicking a glance up at her even as she scanned the script changes. "This looks fine. Go with it," she said as she handed him back the script.

When the anchor left, Tess moved closer. "When you've got a few minutes, Ronnie, I'd like to speak with you."

If she was surprised by the request, Ronnie gave no indication. "Now's good for me. Why don't we go to my office."

Tess followed the other woman down the hall to the place where Ronnie spent the majority of her time. The room was a reflection of Ronnie—neat but lived in, and a testament to how busy she was. The mahogany desk was covered with stacks of papers, videotapes, folders and two phones. One wall was filled with framed awards and certificates interspersed with photographs—Ronnie with D.C.'s governor, Ronnie with a Hollywood celebrity, Ronnie receiving an award from the station's president, Ronnie with the White House press secretary. Another wall was dominated by three television sets and another with an eclectic mix of watercolors that included a Monet copy and an abstract by a local artist. Still another wall featured a huge write-on calendar that was filled with information. Beside it was a graph charting the station's ratings. A ficus tree added a splash of green in one corner and a potted marigold-colored mum brightened a corner table.

Evidently Ronnie read something in Tess's expression because she paused at her desk and buzzed through on the intercom. "Patsy, I'd like you to hold my calls for the next thirty minutes."

"Sure thing, Ronnie," the assistant replied.

"Why don't we sit over there," Ronnie suggested, indicating the sitting area where a small navy couch and two covered chairs had been positioned around a coffee table that sported a hardcover picture book of Washington monuments, an art book and issues of the *New York Times*, the *Washington Post* and *USA Today*.

Tess chose one of the overstuffed chairs. Clasping her hands together, she wondered exactly where to begin. She opted to just be direct, "Ronnie, I—"

"Wait," Ronnie said, holding up her hand. "If you're here to bitch at me for sticking you with Kip on that school-bus story next week, let me tell you right now that it wasn't my idea. The word came down from Stefanovich himself. According to him, we're not giving his nephew enough camera time. Of course, I couldn't tell him the little prick is an idiot and doesn't know one end of the microphone from the other."

Tess almost laughed at Ronnie's frustration with the station manager's nephew whom they had been asked to hire during the summer. An aspiring television reporter with a communications degree, Kip Edwards was pleasant enough and eager to be a part of the news team. Unfortunately, the man was a total klutz who could—and had—wiped out hours of work by just walking across a room. Whenever he was assigned to a story, the engineers safeguarded their equipment and the reporters their persons. Kip also came up short in the personality department—a fact that was apparent whenever he was on camera. As a result, no one was eager to work with him, and Ronnie was stuck with the unpleasant task of using him.

"Anyway, Stefanovich asked for a copy of the assignments and decided Kip should do the piece with you. I'm sorry, kiddo. My hands are tied. I'm afraid you're stuck with him on this one."

"I understand. But that's not what I wanted to talk

to you about. I need some time off. There's something personal that I need to take care of."

Ronnie seemed to relax a bit. She sat back on the couch, some of the stiffness leaving her shoulders. "Well, I don't see where that should be any problem. David seems to be working out fine, and now that Angela's back from her baby break, I can probably clear you for a few days at the end of next week."

"I'm afraid I'm going to need more than a few days. Actually, a lot more."

Ronnie narrowed her eyes. "How much more?"

"I've got a month of vacation time and sick leave due. I'd like to take it."

"A month!" Ronnie whipped off her tortoiseshell glasses, pitched them to the table. "You've got to be kidding! You can't honestly expect me to approve a month's vacation for you. Not even the anchors get that much time off all at once."

"I wouldn't ask if it wasn't important."

"No. Absolutely not." Ronnie stood up and began pacing about the room. "It's out of the question. You're my best reporter. I can't have you taking off for a month."

"It's not impossible," Tess argued. "You said yourself that David's on board now and Angela's back from maternity leave. So you're fully staffed again."

"We won't be fully staffed if you're out."

"You've also got Kip," Tess pointed out.

Ronnie glared at her and sat down again. "You're not helping your case here, kiddo." She shook her head. "No. There's no way I can spare you for a month. A week maybe, but not a month."

"Then I quit."

"You can't quit. You have a contract."

"My contract's up for renewal at the end of next month. I'll ask the GM to release me early," Tess told her, hating that it had come to this. She liked her job, liked Ronnie and the people she worked with, but she had to find out the truth. And to do that she was going to need time to go back to Mississippi. She stood. "I'm sorry, Ronnie."

"Oh, stop with the dramatics and sit down." Once Tess had done so, Ronnie said, "Now tell me what in the hell is going on and why you're threatening to quit on me."

"I don't want to quit," Tess told her. "But there's something I have to do, something personal, and I need the time off to do it."

"That's it? That's all the explanation you're going to give me?"

"I told you. It's personal."

Ronnie leveled a "give me a break" look at her.

Tess sighed. "It has to do with my mother, about when she died. And about my father's suicide," Tess said finally.

"So that's what's been bothering you," Ronnie said, and Tess suspected the remark was more to Ronnie herself. "Which I suppose is understandable. I mean, it hasn't been all that long since that stuff happened with your father. I'm sure that whole suicide thing brought up some bad memories for you."

"Yes."

"But, kiddo, instead of taking off you should be keeping busy, and trying to put all that stuff out of your mind."

"I can't," Tess told her.

Ronnie narrowed her eyes. "Wait a minute," she said. "Have those dirtbags from the tabloids been hounding you again? Because if they have—"

"No. You know how this business is, everyone's moved on to the next scandal and forgotten all about me and my family."

"I would hope so," Ronnie told her. "You poor kid. All that mess, then breaking up with Johnny and me loading you down with work. No wonder you've been having trouble sleeping. It's a miracle that you haven't been having nightmares."

But there had been no nightmares. At least not in a very long time. That hadn't always been the case. For months after her mother had been murdered, she did wake up screaming, unable to get the image of her father kneeling over her mother's body, blood on his hands and shirt, the bloody bookend in his hand, out of her mind. But with time, the nightmares had grown fewer, the memories less sharp. Thanks in large measure to the psychologists her grandparents had insisted she see when she first came to live with them in D.C. Also, it had helped that she'd been so close to her grandmother, a bond that had only strengthened when she had feared she might lose the older woman to cancer. Thank heavens Grams had beaten the disease. But in those months and the years that followed they had clung to each other.

"Do you want to talk about it?"

Then they talked about it. Tess began by telling Ronnie about the phone call she'd received claiming that Jody Burns's death hadn't been a suicide. She told her about her own inquiries at the prison, about the questions that had been running through her mind since then. Questions that she found she could no longer ignore.

"I don't know, Tess. It all sounds pretty far-fetched to me, you getting a call out of the blue like that. I'd be willing to bet that woman was a reporter working for one of those supermarket rags. She probably told you that garbage hoping to get a story out of you," Ronnie reasoned.

"I thought so, too, at first. But the more I've thought about it, the more convinced I am that she was on the level. I can tell you for certain that her accent was real."

"A lot of people can fake a Southern accent," Ronnie pointed out.

Tess shook her head. "My grandparents are from Mississippi and I've met enough people from there over the years to recognize a Mississippi drawl when I hear one. Hers was genuine."

"That still doesn't mean she was legit. You and I both know it wouldn't be the first time a tabloid has used an out-of-state stringer to pull a fast one in order to nail a story."

"I know. But my gut tells me she was telling the truth." Tess recalled the fear she'd heard in the woman's voice when she'd mentioned calling the police. "She wasn't acting, Ronnie. She was genuinely afraid."

"Of what? You said the report from the prison ruled your father's death a suicide."

"I know what it said. But after talking to that official at the prison and reading the report, I don't know, something just doesn't feel right."

"Is that the reporter in you talking, or the child who's lost her father?"

"Probably a little of both," Tess admitted. "All I know is that if the woman was telling the truth and Jody Burns was murdered, then I have to ask myself why. And why try to make it look like a suicide?"

"You're making some pretty big leaps on the basis of one anonymous phone call, don't you think?"

"Maybe. But what if she was telling the truth? What if he didn't hang himself in that cell? What if someone else did it for him? Think about it, Ronnie. He was coming up for parole in a few weeks and he stood a good chance of being released. So why, after all these years, would he decide to kill himself? Why now, when he was so close to gaining his freedom? It just doesn't make any sense."

"Neither does murder," Ronnie pointed out. "Yet people keep on committing it."

"There's also the woman's claim that Jody Burns wasn't the one who murdered my mother," Tess reminded her.

"Tess, I'm sorry. But you seem to be forgetting one very important fact."

"What?"

Ronnie stared into her eyes. "*You* were the one who told the police that he killed your mother."

What Ronnie said was true. And her accounts of finding her father over her mother's dead body had been recounted in the press again when the report of her father's suicide had hit the airwaves. "I was four years old at the time," Tess defended. She dragged a hand through her hair. "I was a child. A child who woke up because I heard loud voices and a woman's scream, then stumbled out of bed and found my father kneeling over her body. But I never saw him actually hit her with the bookend. I just assumed that he did it because he was the only one there," Tess argued. "Suppose I was wrong? What if he didn't kill her? What if he came in and found her dead, just the way he claimed?"

"I don't know, Tess."

Tess read the pity in Ronnie's face. "You think I'm

wrong, don't you? That this is all some Freudian thing that's going on inside my head where I'm having to deal with my mother's murder again because my father is dead now."

"You know me better than that. I don't buy into all that psychobabble stuff. So don't go putting words in my mouth."

It was true. When she had done a story on how up-bringing factored into the problems of today's young adults, Ronnie had been the first to scoff at the notion of blaming the parents for everything that went wrong in a person's life. "Then what do you think?"

"Exactly what I said. That you shouldn't jump to any conclusions based on a single phone conversation with a stranger." Ronnie sighed. "Look. You said yourself you had no contact with the man, not even a letter or a phone call from him for over twenty-five years. How could you possibly know what his state of mind was— whether he was suicidal or not?"

"You're right. I don't know. And that's why I want to go to Mississippi, so I can find out the truth."

"As your friend, I'm telling you I think your going there is a mistake.

"But, as your producer, I say if you need to, take a few days off, go see the people at the prison and satisfy yourself that your father's death was a suicide. Then put it behind you and come back to work."

"It's not just the people at the prison I want to see. That's why I need more time off." She wasn't sure how much more she would be able to learn from the prison staff. "I want to talk to the people who were involved in my father's case—the prosecutor, the witnesses who testified against him at his trial and the attorney who handled his defense. If my father did find some evidence that could prove he was innocent the way the woman claimed, the chances are he contacted his attorney."

"Tess, I don't know what you hope to accomplish, but I can tell you right now no judge is going to reopen a twenty-five-year-old murder case based on an anonymous phone call."

Ronnie was right. The claims made in an anonymous phone call and her own gut feelings weren't evidence. "I'm an investigative reporter, remember? I know how to look through things, dig up information. I can find the truth."

"And suppose what you find out is that your father really did kill your mother and that he really did commit suicide? Will you be able to accept that?"

"I'm not looking for redemption for my father or myself, Ronnie. I just need to know if I've spent the better part of my life hating and blaming the wrong person for my mother's death."

"And if you did?"

"Then I want to see the person who was responsible pay for stealing both of my parents from me." She met Ronnie's gaze. "Will you help me? Will you give me the time off?"

"I can't approve a month's leave for you," Ronnie told her. "But I may be able to explain your absence if you're on special assignment. Of course, that means you're going to have to come up with something damn good when you get back or it's going to be both of our butts on the line."

"I don't want to get you in trouble," Tess told her, touched by the woman's gesture.

Ronnie waved the comment aside. "I've been in trouble before."

"Suppose I actually make my investigation the special assignment?" Tess offered as an idea began to form in her mind. "What if I do a piece on prisons and suicides, one man's road down that path?"

"It's a good idea, but you could do that right here. Just pick a prison close to home. No trips to Mississippi. No extended time away from the station."

"What if I were to give them a story with a personal angle? What if I give them Jody Burns's story?"

"I'll admit that story would be an easier sell because of who you are, and who your grandfather is. There's been a lot of viewer interest since the senator's press conference following the man's suicide and his push for tougher penalties on criminals. It could certainly be a ratings winner for the station. But what about you, kiddo? Do you want to open yourself up to that?"

"No. But it would be an easy way for me to explain my interest in my mother's murder and the trial. And it might even open a few doors."

"What about the senator? What will he say?"

"I've already told him."

"And?"

"Let's just say I wouldn't be surprised to find out he's having a new will drawn up as we speak."

"That bad, huh?"

"Worse," Tess admitted, recalling how furious her grandfather had been when she'd left yesterday. To have his granddaughter turn the cameras on the man responsible for killing his only child and possibly even garnering sympathy for Jody Burns infuriated her grandfather even more. "I wouldn't put it past him to try to stop me by going to the board of directors," Tess admitted. She didn't doubt for a moment her grandfather would seek out the station's board members to prevent her from working on the story. "That's why I'll need the station to hold firm on me doing the report. Do you think Stefanovich will go along with that?"

"Are you kidding? If he thinks it would mean a jump in ratings, he'd defy the pope."

"So it's okay? I can have the time off?"

"Let's get a few specials in the can and then you're officially away on special assignment."

Tess jumped up, hugged her friend. "Thanks, Ronnie. I won't let you down."

"Don't worry about letting me down, kiddo. Just take care of business and get your rear end back to D.C."

"I will," Tess promised and started for the door.

"Tess?"

She paused, glanced back at Ronnie, noted the worry was back in her hazel eyes. "Yes?"

"Be careful."

"You got that column finished yet, Reed?"

Spencer Reed glanced up from his computer screen at his desk at the *Clarion-Ledger* in Jackson, Mississippi, and stared at the scowling face of his editor, Hank Weston. "If you and everyone else would quit yammering at me, I'd have it finished by now."

"I must have been out of my mind to have agreed to let you do a special series in addition to your regular column," Hank complained.

"You agreed because you knew a series on 'The Road to the Governor's Mansion' would be a ratings winner for the newspaper."

"Yeah, but I forgot how damn close you always cut your deadlines. It's a wonder the pressmen don't have bleeding ulcers like me."

"They don't get paid enough bucks to get ulcers," Spencer pointed out as he continued typing.

"I don't get paid enough to have ulcers either," Hank said. "But thanks to you, I've got 'em."

"You're a born worrywart, Hank. You know that?"

"Can you blame me?" the editor countered. "Do you realize that if you don't turn that thing in within the hour we're going to have an empty spot in the newspaper?"

"Hank, have I ever missed a deadline?"

"No," Hank admitted. "But you've come damn close."

"But I've never missed one. And I'm not going to miss this one either. Not unless you keep standing there and bellyaching at me. Now, shut the door and let me work."

"I should have listened to my mother and become a doctor," Hank muttered as he turned away, yanking the door closed behind him.

Once the door closed, Spencer went back to work. As a freelancer for the newspaper, he didn't keep regular office hours and more often than not he just e-mailed in his biweekly column, "The Political Beat," which was now being circulated in forty-three newspapers across the country. But the *Clarion-Ledger* remained his home base. So he tried to show his face around the place every week or so. Doing so this afternoon had proven to be a mistake he decided as the phone at his desk rang. Spencer snatched up the receiver. "Spencer Reed," he barked out.

"You disappoint me, Mr. Reed. I had expected some mention of Everett Caine's misdeeds to be in your last column." The voice was soft with a marked Southern accent.

Spencer sat back in his chair and focused his attention on the anonymous female caller who had contacted him before, claiming to have information about shady dealings by gubernatorial candidate and current lieutenant governor Everett Caine. "Since you won't tell me who you are, I can't very well report your claims as fact and open myself and the newspaper up to a libel suit."

"Did you check out the information I gave you? About that murder case Caine worked on as an A.D.A. in Grady, Mississippi?"

"I checked it out. The Burns murder trial was twenty-five years ago. He prosecuted the man responsible for killing Senator Abbott's daughter. The case made him a real hero and launched his political career."

"I'm aware of the facts, Mr. Reed," she told him.

"Then you'll also know there was nothing in any of the accounts that I read that even remotely suggested that the trial was fixed."

"It was," the woman insisted. "If you'd bothered to talk to the people involved, you would know that."

"Were you involved? Is that how you know?" Spencer asked her.

"I know because I know Everett Caine. He went to great lengths to make sure the evidence suited his needs."

"How do you know?" he pressed her.

"Because leopards don't change their spots. He was a liar and a cheat back then. And he's still a liar and a cheat."

"Hey, I agree with you," Spencer admitted. "Unfortunately, I haven't been able to prove it. For my own personal reasons I'd like nothing better than to see Caine lose the election next month. But my hands are

tied unless you can give me something concrete to go
on. Can you?"

There was a pause. "I can't. But there is someone
who might be able to help you."

"Who?"

"Tess Abbott. She's the daughter of Jody Burns."

"I know who she is," he said, remembering that after
the first call from the mystery woman, he had dug up
what he could find on the old murder case. Tess Abbott,
née Tess Burns, had been a child at the time of her
mother's death and it had been the girl's testimony that
had helped to convict her father. Her grandparents, Senator Theodore Abbott, and his wife, had become her
guardians following the trial. From what he had been
able to find out, Tess Abbott was now a TV investigative
reporter in D.C. "What makes you think she can help?"

"It's my understanding that she's here in Mississippi asking questions about her father's suicide and her
mother's murder. Talk to her, Mr. Reed. She knows
who really killed Melanie Burns."

"How could she know? She was only a kid—"

But suddenly the line went dead.

Frustrated, Spencer slammed down the receiver and
glanced at the clock, turning his attention back to his
column. Fifteen minutes later he'd finished the piece,
e-mailed it to his boss and printed himself a hard copy.
He then picked up the phone and dialed a number in
Grady.

"Hello," a sultry Southern female voice answered.

"Mary Lee, darling, it's Spencer Reed. How's the
most beautiful girl in Grady doing these days?"

"Why, I'm just fine, sugar," she told him, and he
chuckled because he could easily imagine the little sex-
pot preening.

"Glad to hear that. You still dating that quarterback at Ole Miss?"

"Donny graduated two years ago. He's an accountant at his daddy's CPA firm now," she told him.

"And he still hasn't married you yet?" he teased.

"Oh, he's asked. I just haven't accepted yet."

"Poor fellow. You ought to put him out of his misery, Mary Lee."

"Maybe I will," she told him.

"Listen, darling, you still working at that bed-and-breakfast, aren't you?"

"Three days a week," she told him.

"So if anyone new were to show up in Grady, you'd pretty much know it. Wouldn't you?"

"Sugar, things in this town are so boring that a visit from the FedEx man is big news."

"I guess that means there aren't any strangers in town then?"

"Other than a few tourists and some folks who are in for Miss Opal's ninetieth birthday, no one worth mentioning. Who is it you're interested in?"

"A woman by the name of Abbott. Tess Abbott."

"Never heard of her," Mary Lee informed him.

"Do me a favor then. If she shows up, give me a call, will you?"

"You got it, sugar."

Chapter Three

Tess continued driving along the Mississippi interstate in the fog toward Grady. Lord, but she was tired, she thought. That last week at work had been a killer. She'd not only had her normal workload, but she'd taped a slew of segments to be aired during her absence. The only good thing about being so busy was that she hadn't had time to dwell on the fact that her grandfather was no longer speaking to her, and that her grandmother was seriously distressed. The strain had been there on her grandmother's face when Tess had left the town house the previous Saturday, and she'd heard it again in her voice when she'd called her from the D.C. airport yesterday morning.

She groaned as she thought of yesterday. Things had gone downhill beginning with that call. Then her flight from D.C. to New Orleans had been delayed because of equipment problems. After being forced to take a later flight to the Big Easy, she'd also had to reschedule her flight from New Orleans to Jackson, Mississippi, only to find that the car she had originally reserved was no longer available. As a result she'd had to settle for a Ford Mustang when what she had wanted was a larger, more comfortable car.

Then, because of her late arrival, she ended up spending the night at a hotel in Jackson and driving out to the state prison that morning. She'd spent the better part of the day wading through the red tape at the prison in her efforts to get information about Jody Burns. Granted, she hadn't exactly been up front with the prison personnel about who she was, or why she wanted the information. But she'd stuck as closely to the truth as she could, explaining that she was doing a story about prison suicides and that she wanted to follow the history of Jody Burns and his journey from citizen to criminal, his life behind bars and how it led to his own suicide. But other than a few facts, figures and standard statements, she'd come away with very little. Her attempts to contact both the former prosecutor, Everett Caine, and her father's defense attorney, Beau Clayton, had also proved futile. She'd even wondered if the roadblocks she'd encountered were courtesy of her grandfather, then decided that she might be just a little bit paranoid. As an investigative reporter she knew that she seldom got what she wanted on the first try.

If she were superstitious and believed in omens, she'd be on her way back to the airport now instead of traveling on the interstate after nine o'clock on a Saturday evening feeling exhausted and hungry. She couldn't help wondering, yet again, if her decision to come to Mississippi and dig up the past had been a mistake.

At the sound of her cell phone ringing, Tess reached for her bag and retrieved the instrument. "Hello."

"Hi, kiddo. How's Mississippi?"

"Hi, Ronnie," Tess said, pleased to hear the sound of her producer's voice. "At the moment I'm on the interstate heading to Grady, so Mississippi consists of a stretch of concrete and glimpses of pine trees. How are things up there?"

"They've been better."

Tess tensed. "Something wrong?"

"Nothing I can't handle. But I thought you should know the senator gave me an earful this afternoon. He is one unhappy man, and my guess is he's going to put a call in to Stefanovich."

"I'm sorry, Ronnie."

"Like I said, it's nothing I can't handle. How's it going on your end?"

"Not exactly the way I'd hoped. I hit a brick wall at the prison and I haven't had any luck reaching the prosecutor or defense attorney yet. But you know me, the more obstacles I hit, the harder I go at it."

"That's the mark of a good reporter."

"Or at least a stubborn one," Tess replied. "Either way, I'm not giving up yet. I'm going to Grady now to do some digging there, and then I'll try the prison and lawyers again."

"You sure it's worth all this effort?"

"What do you mean?" she asked.

"I mean, once I got past the senator's angry bark and him ordering me to call you off this assignment, I listened to all his reasons for not wanting you to go nosing around in the past. And the truth is, a lot of it made sense. Are you sure you're doing the right thing?"

"No." Which was the truth. She wasn't sure. And

more than once during the past week remembering how much she'd upset not only her grandfather, but her grandmother, she had wondered the same thing. "But whether it's the right thing to do or not, it's something I have to do, Ronnie. I need to find out the truth and whether Jody Burns really did kill my mother."

"Then what? Will knowing be enough?"

"I don't know. But it's a start."

"All right, kiddo. But if someone else was responsible and they made your father's death look like a suicide, they aren't going to like you nosing around. So you watch your back."

"Don't worry, I will," she promised.

"You'd better. I gotta run. Make sure you stay in touch, kiddo."

"I will. 'Night, Ronnie."

After she ended the call, Tess felt more alone than ever. Despite what she'd told Ronnie, she couldn't help wondering if she had made a mistake by coming to Mississippi. While she wanted the truth, and was prepared to deal with whatever she did discover, she hadn't given a lot of thought to how her investigation would affect her grandparents—in particular her grandmother. The last thing she wanted to do was hurt either of them. Yet, didn't they deserve to know the truth, too? she asked herself.

Deciding she was too tired and hungry to think straight, Tess stared at the exit signs. What should have been a three-hour drive from Jackson to Grady had turned into four-plus hours because she had left in the middle of rush-hour traffic. And based on the exit number, she still had a good half hour to go before she reached the exit to the Magnolia Guesthouse.

So when she spotted the sign indicating gas and restrooms at the next exit, Tess flicked on her turn signal. She'd stop, refuel and grab something to eat, she told herself as she took the dark winding off-ramp from the interstate that turned into a blacktopped country road. She stopped at the end of the exit, looked both ways and noted the light to her left had turned red. She had just pressed on the accelerator when a beat-up old pickup ran the light. Tess gasped as she slammed her foot on the brake. The pickup sped by, narrowly missing her car.

"So much for Southern manners," she muttered before starting on her way. Five minutes later when she pulled the Mustang up to the gas pumps at the Quick Stop, Tess thought she spied the old pickup parked in front of the store. She considered going over and giving the owner a piece of her mind. And doing so, she reasoned, was not the way to start off her stay in Grady.

Lester De Roach saw the little red Ford Mustang pull up to the gas pump as he shut off his old truck at Bobby Ed's Quick Stop. Some rich bitch using her daddy's car, he figured, and chuckled to himself because he'd probably scared the hell out of her back there at the interstate.

Served her right, he thought. She probably didn't know the first thing about what it was like to have to work for a living. Unlike himself who had been working his whole damn life. Climbing out of the truck, he ignored the Mustang and its driver and headed inside the convenience store to grab a six-pack of beer.

"How ya doing, Mr. Lester?" the kid behind the counter called out.

Lester ignored him and went straight to the cooler at the back of the store. He eyed the six-pack of beer in the cooler, and debated whether or not to spend the extra buck and buy his brewskies cold. He wiped the back of his oil-stained hand across his mouth, barely noticing the dry, cracked skin that never lost the scent of car grease, or the stiffness of the whiskers on a chin that hadn't seen a razor in days. He'd spent the past seven hours locked up in J.W.'s garage working on a busted engine for that penny-pinching slavedriver. He hadn't finished it yet. But he was close. And hell, he deserved a cold drink for all his hard work, not warm-as-piss beer. But he also needed to eat, Lester reminded himself. That's the only way he'd been able to get that skinflint J.W. to give him an advance on his pay—by telling him if he didn't eat, he wouldn't be able to work.

He was a damn fine mechanic—the best one in Grady. Hell, he was probably the best damn mechanic in the whole State of Mississippi. He'd just run into some hard times. Wasn't his fault that bitch Loretta he'd been married to had robbed him blind and bankrupted his mechanic shop, then run out on him. And it wasn't his fault that he'd banged himself up in that car wreck and had taken to drink and drugs to ease the pain. He'd kicked the drugs and the drink, but not before he'd gotten the bad rap of being a drunk.

Well, he weren't no damn drunk. He was a top-rate mechanic and he deserved to be working for himself, not for the likes of a prick like J.W. Hell, J.W. wouldn't even own the garage if it weren't for his shyster of an old man who had been robbing folks in these parts for years by jacking up the rates on work at that old service station of his. Maybe if his own old man hadn't cut out on him, his sister and momma like he'd done, he'd have known better than to trust that bitch Loretta with the books. Well, he'd know better next time. Sooner or later, his luck was going to turn. He was due a break and he'd catch one. And when he did, he was going to get his old shop back and then he'd tell J.W. what he could do with his job because he'd be working for himself again. Yes, that's just what he was going to do, Lester assured himself. Just as soon as he got on his feet again, he was going to show them. He would show them all.

But right now. Right now, he needed a drink.

"You finding everything okay back there, Mr. Lester?" the Smith boy called out from the front of the store.

"Yeah," he snarled in response. Lucky little bastard, he thought, glancing in the direction of Bobby Ed and Mabel Smith's snot-nosed grandkid. The punk had it made. He got to work weekends at his grandparents' convenience store and gas station. According to Mabel, the boy was smart as a whip and would be graduating from Ole Mississippi come springtime, then going on to law school. In the meantime, he didn't need to worry about working for dickheads like J.W. just to pay his rent or buy himself a couple of beers.

Just didn't seem fair, Lester decided. It seemed that pricks like J.W. and the Smith boy got all the breaks while hardworking decent folks like him had to bust their asses. But then, it was easy to get breaks when you had money. Both J.W.'s old man and the Smith boy's family had plenty. While he had never had a pot to piss in—except for that one time, back when he and Jody Burns had been friends.

At the thought of Jody, his old friend in prison all those years, and hearing about how he'd hanged himself, Lester's legs went weak.

"Why are you doing this to me, Les?" Jody's words echoed in his head. "Please, tell them the truth!"

Bells sounded at the front door of the store, signaling another customer had entered the Quick Stop. Lester tried to shake off the memory, unsure of where it had come from in the first place.

Don't think about Jody. What's done is done.

Lester swiped his hand down his face, tried to make that image of Jody swinging from a rope in the jail cell go away. No point in thinking about Jody now, he told himself. It was too late to change the past. Yanking open the cooler door, he grabbed the six-pack of cold beer. His stomach grumbled, reminding him he hadn't had any food that day. So he snatched a bag of chips from the rack beside the cooler and then began making his way up the aisle.

Damn, but he needed a drink. That's all that was wrong with him.

"Will that be cash or charge, ma'am?" the Smith kid asked the tall brunette woman at the counter.

"Credit card," she said and handed over the piece of plastic.

Impatient for a drink and still shaken by the memories of Jody, Lester wrestled one of the beers free from the plastic loops that held them together. He popped the lid, and the hiss had the Smith kid looking his way. Ignoring the disapproving look the boy shot at him, he drained half the can in one swallow. The cold brew hit his empty belly like an icy fist and he sighed with pleasure. While he waited for the chick to finish so he could check out, he took another swig. He could feel the beginning of a buzz. Already he was feeling better. Except for the two beers he'd had when he went home for lunch, he hadn't had a thing in his belly all day. By the time he got home and finished off the six-pack, he wouldn't be thinking about the likes of Jody Burns or anyone else that night.

"Here's your receipt, ma'am."

"Thank you," she said and stuffed the receipt and credit card into her purse. "Could you tell me how to get to the Magnolia Guesthouse from here?" she asked the Smith boy.

"Sure thing, ma'am. When you pull out of the parking lot, go down the road to the first light," the kid explained, gesturing toward the highway. "That road'll put you back on the main drag. Once you get on it, go down past three lights and then take the first street on your left. You'll be on Magnolia Lane then. The Magnolia Guesthouse is the big white house. You can't miss it. Enjoy your visit."

"Thanks," she said and turned around.

And as she did so Lester dropped the half-empty can of beer and chips, spilling the liquid on his grease-stained work clothes before it fell to the tile floor with a thud. The rest of the six-pack hit the floor with a crash, breaking free of the plastic loops and rolling in several directions.

"Mr. Lester, you okay?"

Lester's hands began to shake. Instantly sober, he felt something damp and cold on the front of his pants, and wasn't sure if it was the beer or if he'd pissed himself. Either way, he didn't care.

"Sir, are you all right?" Tess asked him.

Unable to move, Lester felt the blood drain from his head as he stared at her face.

"Mr. Lester?" The Smith boy came from around the counter.

"Sir, are you ill?" Tess asked and started to step toward him.

"Stay back. Stay away from me," Lester warned as he shrank back and stared at the face of a dead woman.

"Mr. Lester, what in the devil has gotten into you?" The fresh-faced young man who'd waited on her had come out from behind the counter. Although the boy was only of average height, he was built like a football player and had placed himself between the disheveled-looking guy and her.

Tess didn't feel in any real danger and didn't know what to make of the man's outburst. She'd watched him exit the beat-up pickup truck that nearly hit her when she'd exited the interstate. When she'd spotted him at the back of the store eyeing the beer in the cooler she decided not to bother confronting him. Last year she had done a feature for the news station on alcoholism and the senior citizen. So she recognized the signs. The unsteady hands, the restlessness, the total focus on that next drink. She knew from her interviews that the urge for a drink was a daily battle, one that never went away. Judging by the man's demeanor, she assumed that he had been struck by that urge tonight. And given his appearance, she'd concluded that he'd either just come off a drinking binge or was about to start one.

Seeing him up close now only reaffirmed her suspicions. The stench of beer and perspiration on him was strong. He was dressed in a set of standard garage-issue workman's clothes that she suspected had once been navy, but were now faded with wear, axle grease and sweat. The beer he'd spilled left a new set of stains to compete with the engine grime on his clothes. His black work boots were scuffed and dull, stained with what she assumed was engine oil. The man's hair was mostly gray and looked as if it hadn't been shampooed or combed in days. His face was thin, his lips chapped, his skin pasty. Surprisingly, his teeth were white. Several days' growth of salt-and-pepper whiskers covered a weak chin line and a jaw that had gone soft. But it was the man's bloodshot brown eyes that surprised her most. She'd expected to see despair, hopelessness, maybe even regret. Instead, what she saw was fear.

"I mean it. I don't know why you come back, but you stay away from me," the man yelled at her. "Stay away," he shouted again, staggering backward as though terrified, until he crashed into a display of two-liter sodas. The plastic bottles went tumbling to the ground.

"Look out," the clerk warned and grabbed the man by the arm to stop him from falling to the floor.

One of the two-liter bottles came barreling toward her like a bowling pin hit by a ball and Tess jumped, dropping her purse and keys in the process.

"Are you all right, ma'am?" the boy asked, glancing back in her direction.

"I'm fine," Tess assured him as she stooped down and retrieved her purse and keys. She still didn't know what to make of the man's reaction to her. Was it possible that he thought she was her mother? From old family pictures Tess knew that she resembled her mother. She had the same almond-shaped gray eyes, the same strong cheekbones and pointed jaw. But she had her father's straight dark hair, not her mother's honey-blond curls. And her lips were fuller, her nose a shade longer. Still she supposed it was possible that the man had mistaken her for her mother.

"You okay now, Mr. Lester?" the clerk asked, having turned his attention back to the older man he was holding upright.

But Lester didn't respond. He simply continued to stare at her face through dark, terror-filled eyes.

"Mr. Lester?" the boy repeated. "Are you all right?"

Finally, he jerked his gaze back to the young man. "Yeah. Yeah, I'm okay. Let go of me," he said, shrugging off the boy's hold.

"You don't look okay to me," the young man insisted. "You want me to call Doc Howell for you?"

"I said I'm okay, you little twerp," Lester spat out. He looked around as though only now realizing the mess he had made. "I didn't mean to knock over the sodas."

"Don't worry about it," the clerk told him. "Maybe you should just go on home now."

"I need to get my beer first," Lester told him and, stooping down, he began gathering up the fallen beer cans.

"Maybe you should just forget about that beer," the boy said.

Lester glared up at the young man from his position on the floor, where he had three cans of beer gathered against his chest. "I ain't leaving here without my beer."

The young man hesitated. He looked over at Tess for a second as though he was unsure whether or not to challenge Lester. Tess shook her head, not wanting the younger man to get into a situation with someone who didn't seem stable.

"I tell you what," the boy said as he picked up the bag of chips. "I need to clean up that beer that spilled and pick up those drink bottles before somebody comes in here and slips and hurts themselves. So why don't you just take your beer and chips and go on home now. You can pay for them the next time you come in the store."

"Suit yourself." Lester grabbed the bag of chips from him, hugged them to his chest with the beer, then scrambled toward the exit. When he reached the door, he paused and looked over at her once more, holding her gaze for long seconds.

And there it was again, Tess thought. The terror. The man was terrified of her.

Then he shoved through the door, sending the overhead bells clanging in the silence as he disappeared outside into the night.

"I'm sorry, ma'am. I don't know what got into old Lester tonight. He drinks some, but he's usually harmless. That's the first time I ever saw him get all crazy like that. I guess he'd had one too many for him to go off on you like that."

"Don't worry about it. There was no harm done," Tess assured him. She picked up the plastic bottle that had fallen closest to her. Walking over, she handed it to the young man who was restacking the soda display.

"Thanks," he said.

"Just out of curiosity, who is he?"

"His name's Lester De Roach. He works off and on as a mechanic at a garage in town. According to my grandpa, Lester really knows his way around a car's engine when he isn't drinking." The young man, who had continued to restructure the display of bottles, paused and scratched his head, ruffling the thick brown hair. "Funny thing is, I didn't think he was drunk when he came in here. I mean, he looked like he was hungover, but not drunk. Otherwise, I would have sent him on his way and not let him get anywhere near the beer case."

Sure, he had smelled of beer, but when he'd looked at her, his eyes had been as clear as glass—not dulled by the effects of alcohol. No, for some reason, she had spooked him. And the only thing she could think of was that he had thought she was her mother—Melanie Burns. She could understand his being shocked, even a little frightened at the prospect of seeing someone he thought was dead. But terrified? It didn't make sense. "He seemed more scared than drunk to me," she told him.

"He did, didn't he?"

"Either way, I'm not sure he should be behind the wheel of a vehicle. You might want to alert the local police that his driving might be impaired. I would hate to see him cause an accident." Like the one she'd almost had with him, she added silently.

"It's sheriff in these parts, ma'am," he corrected. "And I'll give him a call. Sorry again about him carrying on like that."

"As I said, no harm done."

"Thanks for being so understanding," he said. "I wouldn't want you to have a poor impression of Grady because of Mr. Lester. Most of the folks here are really nice, friendly people."

"I'm sure they are."

The bells on the front door sounded and in came a pretty blonde wearing tight-fitting jeans and a sweatshirt with Ole Miss emblazoned across the front. She sashayed over toward them. "Hi there, Bobby. Ma'am," she said with a nod of her head to acknowledge Tess. "Gee, what happened in here?"

"We had a little accident," Bobby informed her. "Don't forget your candy bar, ma'am."

Tess scooped the chocolate bar off the counter and dropped it in her bag. "Then she started for the store's exit, leaving the two young people alone.

"Enjoy your visit in Grady," Bobby called out to her retreating back.

"Need some help cleaning up?" the girl offered, but Tess didn't hear Bobby's reply as she pushed open the door and headed out into the parking lot. Outside, the air had turned a bit cooler, and Tess hugged her arms to herself, glad that she'd worn the heavy sweater. Quickly she made her way over to the gas pumps where she'd left the rental car. After unlocking the door with the keyless remote, she slid behind the wheel and immediately relocked the doors. She started up the engine, then took a moment to reset the mileage gauge and fasten her seat belt before putting the Mustang into gear.

Recalling the directions the clerk had given her, Tess drove to the edge of the parking lot. When she reached the road, the hairs on the back of her neck prickled. Pausing, she glanced back in the rearview mirror at the parking lot. She saw no one. But as she pulled out onto the main road, she continued to look in her rearview mirror, unable to shake the feeling that someone was watching her.

Chapter Four

Lester stood in the dark behind the Quick Stop where he'd parked his truck and watched the little red Mustang drive away. Once she was gone, he debated about what to do. Still shaken, he decided he needed to make a phone call.

But not there at the Quick Stop, he reasoned. Too many eyes and ears in that place. Damn cell phones he thought, as he opened the door to his truck. Everybody and his brother had one of the blasted things these days. Everybody but him. Hell, he didn't even have a regular phone anymore—not since the greedy phone company had disconnected the thing when he hadn't paid the bill. He needed a pay phone. Trouble was, there weren't nearly as many places to find one these days. Then he remembered the one in that old vacant shopping strip a few miles from his place. Hopping in his truck, Lester headed toward home.

Twenty minutes later he dropped a quarter into the

coin slot and punched in the number he had committed to memory—a number he had been warned never to call unless it was an emergency. Seeing a dead woman come back to life was an emergency in his books.

As the phone started to ring, he drained the last of the beer in the can, then wiped his mouth with the back of his hand. He dropped the empty can to the ground and crushed the aluminum beneath his work boot. But the beer did little to ease the fear that had knotted like a fist in his stomach since he'd seen the woman in the Quick Stop.

A cool blast of wind whipped through the concrete strip of deserted shops with broken windows and sagging roofs, but Lester barely felt it. He jumped as the sign in front of a burned-out dance studio squeaked from a rusty chain. Growing more on edge by the minute, he gazed over to his truck just to be sure he was still alone. "Come on, come on. Answer the phone," he demanded as he listened to the phone continue to ring.

Finally, it was picked up. "Hello?"

"Jesus! I thought you'd never answer."

"Who is this?"

Lester gritted his teeth. "It's Lester. Lester De Roach," he spat out, irritated that he'd had to identify himself to the man. Considering what he'd done for him, he'd think the SOB wouldn't forget his voice so easily. But then, he was always the one who'd come up with the short end of the deal—even all those years ago.

"Didn't I tell you never to call me," the man said, his voice cool, angry.

"You said I wasn't to call unless it was an emergency. Well, it's a fucking emergency, okay?"

"Hang on a minute," he ordered, and while Lester waited he heard a door shut. Then he came back on the line. "All right. What's the emergency?"

"Melanie Burns. She's alive."

The man swore. "Listen to me, you drunken fool. Melanie Burns is dead and has been for twenty-five years."

"And I'm telling you I seen her with my own eyes. She's come back—just like old lady Burns said she would. She's come back to make us pay for what we did."

He swore again. "You stupid piece of shit!" he said furiously. "You did not see Melanie Burns. She's dead. Understand?"

"But—"

"No buts. Go home and sleep it off and don't call me again."

"I'm telling you, I'm not drunk," he insisted, despite the beers sloshing through his system. "Melanie Burns is here. In Grady. I saw her not thirty minutes ago with my own two eyes at Bobby Ed's Quick Stop. She was paying for gas. If you don't believe me, fine. But you better remember, I'm not the only one who lied about what happened that night."

After a pause, in a somewhat calmer voice, he said, "All right. Start from the beginning and tell me exactly what happened."

Lester told him. "...then after she paid for the gas and got directions, she turned around. That's when I saw her face. It was her, I'm telling you. It was Melanie Burns."

"How much have you had to drink tonight, De Roach?"

"I told you I'm not drunk."

"How much?" he demanded.

"A few beers," he lied. "But I'm nowhere near being drunk. I know what I saw. I saw Melanie Burns."

"Do you hear yourself, De Roach? Do you have any idea how crazy you sound? You're telling me you saw a woman who's been dead for twenty-five years."

"Don't you think I know how the fuck it sounds?" Lester fired back, feeling scared and confused, but needing the man to believe him. "But I'm telling you, it was her."

"What you saw was a woman who reminded you of Melanie."

"It was *her* I tell you," Lester insisted. "I looked right into her eyes. They were Melanie's eyes. There's no way I'd ever forget those eyes." Hell, he'd seen them in his nightmares for more years than he wanted to remember.

He paused again. "All right. Tell me what this woman you saw looked like."

"I told you. She looked like Melanie."

He released a breath. "Describe her to me, you moron."

"She was tall, a little on the skinny side. Her hair was darker than it used to be and shorter, but everything else was the same. One thing I'm sure about, she had those same spooky gray eyes." He bit back a shudder. "You remember those eyes of hers."

"Yeah, I remember them." After a moment, he said, "She must be Burns's kid."

"Melanie's kid?" Lester repeated.

"Yeah. Don't you remember, you moron? Melanie and Jody Burns had a kid, a little girl. She was sleeping in the next room. And when she woke up, she found Jody Burns standing over his wife's body. It was her testimony that helped put her old man away."

"Melanie's daughter," Lester repeated more to himself than the other man. Relieved that the woman hadn't been Melanie after all, he slumped against the cold wall. "Christ almighty, I thought for sure it was Melanie. That she was one of those reincarnations and she'd come back to make us pay just like old woman Burns said she would."

The other man swore again. "How many times do I have to tell you there's no such thing as ghosts. Only drunks with shit-for-brains believe in all that voodoo crap."

Lester didn't argue. But he knew what he knew. He'd heard the stories about Jody Burns's mother, how she'd lived for a time in New Orleans in the French Quarter. Sin City, his own momma used to call the place because the people there were wicked. They even messed with black magic and stuff.

"De Roach, did you hear me?" he snapped.

"What?" Lester asked, pulling his attention back.

"I asked if you said anything to her."

"No. I never said nothing to her," he said. No reason to admit that he'd told her to stay away from him, he decided. After all, it wasn't like they'd had a real conversation or anything. "I just got my stuff and got out of there as fast as I could. Then I called you."

"Okay. Good. That's good. It's best if she didn't notice you. She didn't, did she?"

"No," he answered quickly. "Like I said, she was paying for gas and getting directions from the kid behind the register."

"Directions to where?" he demanded.

"I don't know. I wasn't paying no attention."

"Try to remember, De Roach," he insisted.

Lester thought for a moment, tried to recall what the kid had been saying to her. "She wanted to know how to get to one of those guesthouses."

"*Which* guesthouse?"

"I don't know. One with a name like a flower or a tree or something like that."

"The Magnolia Guesthouse?"

"Yeah. That's it. That's the place. The Magnolia Guesthouse," Lester told him.

"All right. And you're sure she didn't say anything else or ask questions about anyone?"

"I already told you what happened. She paid for her gas, got directions and left. And then I got out of there as fast as I could," Lester repeated. He jammed his fist into his jacket pocket and his fingers brushed against a slip of paper—a gas receipt. He must have picked it up from the floor at the Quick Stop when he'd had to crawl around and pick up the beers he'd dropped. If he were to tell the guy now that the bitch had dropped it when her purse had fallen, it would only piss him off. He wouldn't understand how scared he'd been and that he'd grabbed the thing in fear.

"All right. Then I don't think we have anything to worry about."

"How can you be sure?" Lester asked, not wanting to admit that he was still afraid. "I mean, if she is Burns's kid, then she's come back here for a reason. Maybe she knows what we did and she's here for revenge and—"

"Would you stop saying that shit?"

"But if she knows—"

"She doesn't know. Nobody does." He all but spit out the words. "You got it?"

"Yeah. I got it," Lester muttered grudgingly. Still, he had to ask, "So we aren't going to do anything? Just sit around and wait?"

"*I'm* going to do some checking around, confirm she

is the Burns kid and then find out why she's here. And while I'm doing that, *you* are going to go home, lay off the booze and keep your damn mouth shut. Understand?"

Lester muttered his favorite four-letter word.

"What was that?"

"Nothing," Lester grumbled.

"So, do you understand me?" he repeated.

"Yeah, yeah, I understand you." But he sure as hell didn't appreciate being given orders by the likes of him. Just who in hell did he think he was? If it wasn't for him, the son of a bitch wouldn't be where he was. The bastard owed him. They all did. None of them had had the balls to pull off the gig. They had needed him then, he remembered. They still did. And he'd show them, too.

"Then go home and keep your mouth shut. And, De Roach?"

"Yeah?"

"Don't call me anymore."

"But suppose she finds out that we were there that night?" Lester fired back, the panic building again.

"She won't."

"But what if she does? I'm not going to sit around and do nothing if she comes after me."

"She's not going to come after you."

"How do you know?" Lester asked.

"Because I'll take care of her. In the meantime you need to keep your mouth shut. And don't call me again."

Then the line went dead.

Lester stood there listening to the dial tone. "Self-righteous prick. I'll show you. I'll show all of you," he yelled into the receiver before he slammed it down onto the phone hook so hard that it fell off. Not bothering to pick up the receiver that dangled from the aluminum cording like a doll's arm, Lester stormed away. He stuffed his curled fists into the pockets of his jacket and headed for his truck.

He climbed inside the dirty old pickup, too angry to notice the torn seats, the empty beer cans on the floorboards, the overloaded ashtray or the stench of cigarettes and fast food. He grabbed one of the two remaining beers, popped the top and chugged it down to calm his nerves. When he finished, he threw the can on the floor and then reached for the last one. He opened it, drained half the can, then leaned his head back against the seat. Closing his eyes, he sighed as he felt the buzz start up again.

When he opened his eyes again, he took another swig of beer. Then he pulled the crumpled gas receipt from his pocket and smoothed it out. For a moment, he remembered looking into those spooky gray eyes again and his hand trembled. "Not a ghost," he reminded himself, shaking off the attack of nerves.

He hit the interior light switch of the truck, but nothing happened. Then he remembered the thing had been out for months. Lester angled the piece of paper near the dashboard so that the overhead light from the parking lot fell on it. Squinting his eyes, he could barely make out the name stamped on the receipt because the inked copy was so faint. "T. Abbott," he read the name aloud. At least that's what it looked like to him.

"Abbott," he repeated as he sat back in his seat and took another swallow of beer to steady his nerves. Why did that name sound familiar? he wondered. But the buzz in his head was getting louder and his limbs were feeling looser. He'd remember later he promised himself, and started up the truck's engine.

Maybe he'd go by his sister Doreen's tomorrow. Her kid had a computer. Could find out all kinds of stuff on a computer these days. With a name and credit card number, he could probably even find the bitch's bra size. Laughing out loud at his own joke, Lester pulled the pickup truck out of the parking lot and onto the road.

Yep, that's what he'd do. He'd go to Doreen's and tell her he was hunting for a job out of state. Yeah, she'd buy that. She was always after him to clean up his act and get a good job.

And once he found out who the woman was, he'd call that asshole and rub his arrogant nose in the information. He'd show him. He'd show them all. Lester De Roach wasn't no fool. He was smart. Just as smart as the rest of them. And just like the last time, he'd be the one who saved all their asses. Only this time they were going to have to pay him for his help.

He put the beer can to his lips and drained what was left in it. Wishing he'd thought to grab an extra six-pack from the Quick Stop since the kid had let him go without paying, he debated going back now, but decided against it. No point in pushing his luck. The kid might ask him to pay for what he'd already drunk. So he continued on and headed for the battered unpaved road that led to his own place.

When he reached it, the tires on the truck hit the deep ruts in the road, jostling him. As something furry dashed across the road to the other side, Lester swerved hard, hit another rut in the road and ran the truck into a tree. "Damn rabbits and coons." He'd have to get his rifle and go hunting soon or the varmints were going to take over the place.

Putting the truck in Reverse, he sent the tires spinning as he hit the gas pedal, then he jerked the gearshift into forward. In need of another beer, he hit the gas pedal harder and sped toward home. As he did so, he kept thinking about Melanie Burns and those spooky ghost-gray eyes.

Seated at his desk, he hung up the phone and skimmed down the Mississippi government's Web site, clicking on the bio for Senator Theodore Abbott. Skipping over his political accomplishments, he went straight to the personal data. And there it was, the name Tess Abbott, listed as the granddaughter he and Mrs. Abbott had raised, now working as a TV investigative reporter in Washington, D.C.

After jotting down the station's name, he exited the site and typed in Washington, D.C., then the station's name. When the Web site popped up, he scrolled over to the news-staff listing and clicked on the icon marked Tess Abbott. He stared at the smiling female whose image filled the screen.

Damned if De Roach hadn't been right, he thought. The girl did have Melanie Burns's eyes. Picking up one of the prepaid cell phones he kept for just this type of occasion, he dialed a private number, which was answered on the second ring.

"Yes?"

"We may have ourselves a little problem."

"What kind of problem?"

"Another loose end," he explained. "One that talks too much and could be damaging to you."

"You assured me that Jody Burns was the only loose end we had to worry about—that when he killed himself this would be over."

"I thought it would be, but something else has come

up. It's nothing I can't handle as long as no one starts spilling their guts. I can take care of it for you."

"How much will it cost me this time?"

"The same as last time."

The other man swore. "All right. Take care of it."

"Since it's so close to home, I'm going to bring in an associate to handle it." While he hated giving up any of the money and could easily handle the situation himself, he opted to play it safe. That idiot De Roach may have called him from someplace where the number could be traced back to him, and this was no time to take chances. "But don't worry, it won't cost you any more."

"You can afford it with what I'm paying you."

It was true, he admitted to himself with a smile. The association the two of them had formed all those years ago had afforded him a good life—a life he had no intention of giving up just because De Roach was a loose-lipped drunk.

"Whatever you do, just make sure that you keep my name out of it."

When the line went dead, he sat back in his chair. Unlocking his desk drawer, he retrieved the small black book he kept hidden in a secret compartment. He dialed another number, safe in the knowledge that the call was routed through an intricate untraceable network system across the country.

"Father Peter."

The man smiled at the irony. "Father, I have a donation for the church. I'd like you to say a mass for a sick friend."

"And what is the name of your sick friend, my son?"

"Lester De Roach." He'd long admired the creativity of the man who made the contracting of a hit sound like a donation to a religious group.

"And did you have a particular mass that you want me to remember him in?" he asked.

"Tomorrow if possible. Or just as soon as you can."

"Consider it done. I'll remember him in my morning prayers," he promised.

"Thank you, Father Peter. I'll put the donation in the mail to you in the morning."

"It's my pleasure to be of service, my son. God be with you."

He hung up the phone and smiled again. This time tomorrow Lester De Roach would be with God or, more likely, with his counterpart in hell.

Tess braked when she approached the first red light. As she waited for the light to change to green, she opened the candy bar and bit off a chunk. The calorie-laden chocolate was just what she needed to give her the energy to make the rest of the trip.

When the signal flashed green, Tess continued through the next two lights, traveling along rolling hills and quiet streets. The sliver of a moon and the stars that she'd noted before stopping for gas seemed to have ducked behind a blanket of clouds, making the night sky even darker. Unlike the big city, there were no neon signs flashing every few yards, and only an occasional lamppost on a street corner provided light.

Finally, she saw the sign that read Magnolia Lane and flicked on her turn signal. And the moment she turned onto the lane, Tess knew she'd made the right decision in choosing the quaint-sounding guesthouse over the two hotels in town. As she drove down the road toward the main house, she felt as though she'd stepped back in time. There at the end of the road, resting atop a bluff and surrounded by trees, was a picture-perfect

Victorian house. Painted all in white, curved brackets framed the inviting front porch. As she drew the car to a stop, Tess noted the cane rockers, also painted white, that dotted the porch. She could easily imagine herself sitting there in the summertime, sipping glasses of lemonade to beat the heat.

She shut off the engine. For several moments, she sat there, staring at the house and taking in the details. Open shutters surrounded the multipaned French-style windows, giving the house an added charm and a sense of protection. She knew a little about architecture, and she recognized the columns that braced the roof of the porch were a Queen Anne design. Exiting the car, Tess continued to admire the house. She noted that the mill-work on the base of the columns featured a cloverleaf theme that had also been adapted for the rafter tails and the post brackets. The white-on-white scheme pulled it all together, giving the building a sense of unity. At the bottom of the porch, white and yellow chrysanthemums had been planted along the border of a white wooden skirt that echoed the same detailing on the house. Five wooden steps led up to the porch, where white flower boxes placed on either side of each window were filled with more lush, yellow chrysanthemums.

Suddenly eager to go inside and see the rest of the place, Tess popped the lock on the trunk of the car and hurried to the rear to gather her bags. With her suitcase and computer travel case in tow, she headed up the stairs and into the guesthouse. It was like walking into someone's home—someone's beautiful antebellum home, Tess amended. The floors were made of polished oak. An heirloom rug filled the center of the floor. On it rested an antique table with a cut-glass vase filled with fresh white roses.

"Good evening, ma'am. Welcome to Magnolia Guesthouse," a lovely blond woman with a sugary accent greeted her from behind the counter. "May I help you?"

With those blue eyes, skin like milk and pretty smile, all the girl needed was a hoopskirt, Tess thought, and she would have been convinced that she had been transported back to the nineteenth century. Shoving aside her foolish thoughts, Tess walked over to the registration desk. "Hello. I'm Tess Abbott," she said as she set down her bags. Up close, she realized the girl was a little older than she'd thought at first glance, probably in her mid-twenties. Yet she'd ma'amed her as if she was pushing forty instead of someone who had just turned twenty-nine. "I believe you have a reservation for me."

"Did you say Abbott?"

"Yes, I did," Tess informed her and thought she'd caught a flicker of recognition on the other woman's face. But it was gone so quickly, Tess was sure she'd been mistaken.

"Just give me a sec," the woman said as she punched data into a computer system.

Definitely not the nineteenth century, Tess thought, smiling to herself.

While the girl worked at the computer, Tess used the opportunity to scan the rest of the room. She noted the small silk pillows in rich jewel tones with needlepoint appliqués propped along the back of a settee. A lush green ficus tree sat in one corner. Another table with more roses sat near a window. Her gaze gravitated to the far wall, dominated by a traditional fireplace. A fire burned invitingly in the grate, reminding Tess of the damp chill in the air when she'd gotten out of the car. Her eyes lifted to the painting above the mantel. It was the portrait of a beautiful redheaded woman sitting in a garden that looked very much like the one that she'd seen outside.

"Oh, here you are, Ms. Abbott. It looks like we were expecting you yesterday," she said in that same slow, sweet voice.

"Yes, I had hoped to arrive yesterday evening. Unfortunately, I was delayed. I did call and leave a message that I'd be arriving a day later than planned."

"Yes. So you did. It looks like you spoke with Ms. Maggie. She's the owner of Magnolia Guesthouse. She's left a note in the system for me to call her when you arrive." The girl picked up the phone. "If you'll just give me a sec, I'll let Ms. Maggie know that you're here."

A few moments later, a striking pixie of a woman with a friendly smile came bustling down the hallway. "Ms. Abbot," she called out and extended her hand. "I'm Maggie O'Donnell. Welcome to Magnolia Guesthouse."

"Thank you," Tess told her.

"I realize it's late and you must be tired, so I won't keep you. But I wanted to talk to you about your accommodations."

The woman was right. She was tired, and after the day she'd had and the incident at the convenience store, she didn't need anything else to go wrong. "Ms. O'Donnell, please don't tell me there's a problem with my reservation."

"The name's Maggie," she corrected. "And there's no problem at all. It's just that you requested one of the cottages and since you were arriving so late and wouldn't have a chance to view them this evening, I wanted to suggest that you spend tonight here in the main house. Then tomorrow when it's light and a bit warmer, I'll give you a tour of the grounds and show you the cottages. That way you can decide which one you'd like to stay in for the remainder of your visit. Does that sound acceptable to you?"

Tess paused. She'd thought being in a cottage, away from the main house, would afford her more privacy while she investigated. She'd also hoped that she might even do some Internet research tonight on Lester De Roach.

"Of course, if you'd prefer, I can go ahead and put you in one of the cottages tonight."

"No. You're right. I would like to look over the cottages tomorrow. So the main house will be fine for tonight. Thank you for suggesting it."

Maggie smiled at her. And Tess couldn't help herself. The woman's energy and friendliness were contagious. "Excellent. Then I'll leave Mary Lee to get you registered and show you up to your room. Tomorrow morning, you just let me know when you're ready and I'll give you that tour I promised."

"Thank you," Tess told her, and after giving the girl behind the counter instructions, Maggie disappeared back down the hall.

"Ms. Maggie's right. You'll like staying here in the main house. Truth is, I think the rooms here are prettier than the cottages," Mary Lee said in a whisper, as though she was sharing privileged information. She punched more information into the computer. "Here we go. Now, do you want to put the charges on a credit card or will you be writing a check?"

"Credit card, please." Tess retrieved her Visa card from her purse and handed it to the girl.

The young woman zipped the piece of plastic

through the machine, then handed it back to Tess, along with a receipt. "If you'll just sign right here."

Tess signed the receipt and the girl gave her a copy, which she stuffed into her purse.

"You'll be in the Lady Charlotte Suite tonight," she explained, handing Tess an old-fashioned door key, the kind that up until now, she'd only seen in old movies. "It's right up the stairs and the last door at the end of the hall. If you'll just give me a sec, I'll help you with your bags."

"That's okay, I can handle them," Tess told her as she hooked her computer bag to the front of her suitcase. "But thanks anyway."

"Sure thing. Oh, by the way, we serve a country breakfast beginning at seven-thirty in the dining room. You don't want to miss it."

"That sounds good. Is it possible for me to get a wake-up call for six-thirty?"

"Of course. And if you need anything in the meantime, just ring down to the front desk. I'll be here all night."

"Thank you, Mary Lee," Tess said, and once again she thought she'd detected something in the way the girl looked at her. An eagerness, almost as if she was bursting with a secret, Tess mused. Dismissing the notion to an overactive imagination brought on by fatigue, Tess headed toward the stairs, eager to set up her laptop and get to work. With any luck, she might just be able to find out who Lester De Roach was and whether or not he'd had any ties to either of her parents.

Chapter Five

"I don't like this any more than you do, pal," Spencer told the twelve-pound black-and-white cat he'd named George that sat meowing beside him on the couch in his apartment in Jackson. "But if you want me to keep you in cat food, I've got to finish this column. So stop with all the racket so I can think."

Apparently insulted, George jumped off the couch and headed for the kitchen. Not that he blamed the cat, Spencer admitted. With the governor's election less than a month away, he'd had his fill of campaign rhetoric, too. He'd also had a bellyful of Everett Caine. Damn, but he didn't want to see that man get in the governor's mansion. But Caine had covered his tracks well. Except for a few questionable appointments and the steering of some legal work to his cronies' law firms, he hadn't been able to find anything to derail Caine's bid for the governorship, and to prove, once and for all, what a lying snake in the grass he was.

When his cell phone rang, Spencer ignored it. Instead he went back to staring at the computer screen on his laptop. Deadlines were a bitch, he thought as he looked at the half-finished column. He needed to finish the damn thing and turn it in before Hank had another hissy fit. Not to mention that the other newspapers that carried his column would be none too happy with him if he didn't deliver the goods for which they were paying him.

Rubbing his face, he pretended not to notice that his face felt as if it belonged to a grizzly bear. He reread what he'd written.

WHAT ARE FRIENDS WORTH?

By Spencer Reed
Associated Press

Or perhaps the question gubernatorial candidate Everett Caine has been asking his friends and business associates is how much is friendship with the man who wants to be the state's next governor worth to them? Quite a lot it seems if Saturday evening's fund-raiser at the Ritz-Carlton in Oxford, Mississippi, is any indication. It was there that Lieutenant Governor Caine collected another $1,000,000 for his campaign war chest from two hundred of his closest friends at a $5,000-a-plate black-tie dinner. Let's hope that for that price steak and lobster were on the menu. What shouldn't be a surprise to anyone is to learn that three individuals, who each purchased tables of ten at the fund-raiser, have had their names mentioned as part of Caine's management team if he should win the governor's race next month.

While Everett Caine and his supporters are quick to point out the candidate's record of good government, and purport him to be the man to wipe out the good-old-boy network that has long been the bane of Southern politics, this reporter has to disagree. Based on his own track record as a district attorney and lieutenant governor, Everett Caine has surrounded himself with friends who have helped him get into office. Payback? It sure seems like it to me.

Lieutenant Governor Caine claims to be the candidate who will keep his promises, a man who pays his debts. A $1,000,000 dinner is no small favor and we can only wonder how this debt will be paid, and how much it will cost the State of Mississippi and its citizens if Caine wins the governorship....

Spencer sat back in his chair, considered what he'd written and wished he could make the people see Everett Caine for what he was—a lying, self-serving politician who used people and tossed them aside. People like Jenny.

That familiar ache in his chest started again at the thought of sweet, innocent Jenny. Jenny Wyatt—the girl who had been his friend and practically a kid sister to him, but who had died before she'd even had a chance to live. Dead before her twenty-second birthday because she'd gotten mixed up with the likes of Everett Caine.

His cell phone rang again and this time Spencer snatched it up instead of letting it go to voice mail. "Yeah," he snapped.

"Now, sugar, is that any way to answer the phone?"

Spencer paused, glanced at the caller ID feature, noted the number was the Magnolia Guesthouse in Grady. He smiled. "Well, now, Mary Lee, if I'd known it was you calling, darling, I would have been a lot nicer."

"I bet," she said with a sniff. "I haven't seen you in ages, Spence."

Spencer didn't have to see Mary Lee to know that the sexy little blonde was pouting. The woman was flat-out gorgeous and she was used to men tripping over themselves whenever she batted those baby-blue eyes of hers at them. He had neither the desire nor the in-clination to be one of those men. "Darling, I've been working. I thought I told you that when we talked the other day."

"But I miss you," Mary Lee cooed.

Spencer laughed. "From what my momma tells me, Shane Russell's been giving old Donny a real run for his money. You didn't mention that when I called you."

"I didn't see any reason to mention it," she informed him. "Besides, I was happy to hear from you—even if you did only call me for a favor."

"Darling, you know I like hearing that sweet voice of yours."

"Then prove it and come pay me a visit."

Not about to go that route, he said, "And just when would you manage to see me if I did come down? From what my momma tells me, you're being wined and dined by those two fine gentlemen seven nights a week."

"Your momma's exaggerating," she said.

"You mean Shane hasn't been sending you flowers from my momma's shop every day for two weeks now?"

"Well…"

"My momma said she's having to get roses from Jackson because she's gone through all her local suppliers filling Shane's orders to you."

Mary Lee giggled. "It is kinda sweet, isn't it? Shane is such a nice boy."

Spencer winced. "Darling, no male over the age of twelve likes being referred to as a boy and sending a woman flowers every day isn't sweet. It's serious. The man's obviously in love with you."

Mary Lee sighed. "I suppose he is."

"Let's not forget poor old Donny either. From what I remember, that fella's got it bad for you, too. Darling, you need to put those two men out of their misery and marry one of them."

"I just might do that," she informed him. "That is unless a certain newspaperman gives me a reason not to."

"Mary Lee," he began, a warning note in his voice because he didn't like the direction of the conversation.

"Come on, Spence, haven't you ever wondered what it would be like if you and I got together?"

"Sure I have, darling. I'm a man, aren't I?" He laughed. "But you know as well as I do that it would never work. Aside from the fact that I'm too old for you—"

"You're only ten years older than me," she protested.

Ignoring her, he repeated, "Aside from the fact that I'm too old for you, the two of us as a couple would never work. We're too much alike. We both like getting our own way too much. You'd want to be out partying and I'd want to chase down a story. We'd end up breaking each other's hearts and ruining a good friendship. You wouldn't want to see that happen, now, would you?"

"No," she conceded. "I suppose you're right. We probably wouldn't work."

"We wouldn't. But if I thought we had even a snowball's chance in hell, I'd be first in line knocking on your door," he said, stretching the fib to ease her bruised ego.

"Well, I guess I'll just have to satisfy myself with us being friends."

"That's my girl. And as much as I love talking to you, darling, I've got a deadline staring me in the face. So I need to get back to work."

"Wait," Mary Lee said. "For a minute there I almost forgot why I called you. Remember you asked me to let you know if a woman named Abbott showed up here in Grady?"

Spencer went still. He'd called Mary Lee after he'd received that last call from the mystery woman, chiding him for not attacking Caine outright in his column. When she'd claimed that Tess Abbott was in Mississippi asking questions about her father's suicide and the long-ago murder case handled by Caine, he hadn't put much faith in it. He'd come to the conclusion that the woman was probably one of Caine's jilted lovers, but that she wasn't going to provide him with anything he could use. Even if she had, given the records of the nation's top politicians, he doubted that documentation of an affair would derail the man's campaign anyway. He certainly hadn't put any stock into her claims about the Abbott woman. Still, on the off chance that the lady knew what she was talking about, he'd called Mary Lee. When Mary Lee had told him that no one named Abbott was in Grady, he had written it off as another lead that went nowhere. He certainly hadn't expected anything to come of it.

"Spence, you go to sleep on me, sugar?"

"Sorry, Mary Lee. Yeah, I remember asking you about her. You said no one by that name had been in Grady."

"Well, she hadn't. But she's here now. And she's staying right here at Magnolia Guesthouse. She checked in not ten minutes ago."

"What did she look like?" Spencer asked, wanting to be sure it was the right Tess Abbott, the one whose picture he'd found at the TV news Web site in D.C.

"Tall, dark-haired, late twenties. Nice eyes. Kind of pretty, I guess, if you like your women on the skinny side. She seemed nice enough, but very serious. She didn't talk much. Not even to Miss Maggie, and Miss Maggie's so nice, I swear even a mute would talk to her."

Spencer didn't bother commenting on Maggie O'Donnell. It wasn't her he was interested in. "And she registered as Tess Abbott?"

"Sure did. I ran the credit card myself."

So, Jody Burns's daughter really was in Grady—which meant the mystery caller had known what she was talking about after all. Maybe she was also right in claiming that Tess Abbott would be able to provide him with the information he needed to take down Everett Caine.

"Don't I even get a thank-you for spying for you?"

"Thanks, Mary Lee. You're a real sweetheart," Spencer told her.

"So who is this Tess Abbott anyway? She an old girlfriend or something?"

Spencer laughed and imagined Mary Lee's baby blues turning a shade of green. "Hardly, darling. I've never even met the woman. She's just a means to an end, a connection to a story that I'm working on."

"Well, I'm glad to hear that. But then I don't know why I'm surprised, I mean, she's really not your type. Seemed a little cool, if you ask me."

Spencer didn't comment. From the photo he'd seen of Tess Abbott on her station's Web site, she'd struck him as cool and sophisticated. He knew the type, had come across them often enough in his thirty-four years—rich, cool beauties who might not mind playing footsies with a journalist, but when it came to getting serious they'd look for somebody at daddy's stock brokerage firm. Or in Tess Abbott's case, probably an up-and-coming attorney at some D.C. law firm. Not that it mattered to him one way or another. Like he'd told Mary Lee, Tess Abbott was nothing to him but a means to an end.

"But then as my momma's always telling me, I shouldn't go making judgment on a person just because of the way he or she looks, should I?"

"If you did, I'd hate to see what you'd think of me," Spencer teased.

Mary Lee laughed. "You don't want to know what I thought about you the first time I saw you."

"You're right, I don't," Spencer told her. "I owe you one, darling. Next time I'm in Grady, dinner—on me."

"And just when is that going to be, Spencer Reed?"

"Soon. Real soon," he promised.

"Well, be forewarned. I fully intend to collect on that dinner."

"I'll remember that, darling," he said, and after thanking her again he ended the call.

Leaning back in his chair, Spencer cupped his hands behind his head and thought about Tess Abbott's arrival in Grady. He'd reviewed what he could find about her father's murder trial after the mystery woman's last call. He'd been surprised to discover that the man's four-year-old daughter had been allowed to testify against him. Given her age and relationship to the defendant, he would have thought any judge in his right mind would have rejected her as a witness. But then Jody Burns's dead wife hadn't been just anyone's daughter. She'd been the daughter of a U.S. senator, and the little girl in question had been his one and only grandchild. Spencer had come to the conclusion that it had been with Senator Abbott's approval that the four-year-old had been put on the witness stand. He couldn't help but wonder if that had been the senator's idea or Caine's. Either way, the decision sucked. And if the mystery caller was to be believed, Caine had rigged the trial.

If he had rigged it, the guilty verdict had paid off in spades for Caine, Spencer thought. With the notoriety of the trial, Caine had quickly moved up the legal ranks from assistant D.A. to D.A., and then he'd made a successful run for lieutenant governor. Now he was only a few weeks away from the election that could make him the state's next governor.

Unless he found a way to stop him. And right now the only way it seemed he might be able to do that would be to prove that the mystery caller had been right—that Caine had somehow rigged that long-ago trial resulting in a man's conviction and eventually, his suicide.

The television screen across the room flashed with an image of Caine on the late-night news. Spencer reached for the remote and hit the sound button.

"With the governor's election less than a month away, both candidates have been busy on the campaign trail," the news reporter stated. "Lieutenant Governor

Caine made an appearance in Oxford, Mississippi, today at his alma mater, Ole Miss, where he was met by thunderous applause."

"Ladies and gentlemen, fellow Rebels," the smiling Caine began, referring to the team's athletic mascot and evoking cheers from the crowd.

"Enjoy it while you can, Caine, because they're not going to be cheering you much longer," Spencer muttered. "Soon, real soon, the people of Mississippi are going to know you for the coldhearted, conniving bastard that you really are."

Because somehow, someway, he intended to expose the real Everett Caine—the man who had used an innocent girl, then tossed her aside like garbage and caused her to take her own life. And while she didn't know it yet, Tess Abbott was going to help him bring the man down.

When George came strolling back into the room and jumped up beside him, Spencer stroked the cat behind the ears and listened to him purr. Then he went back to the article. After fine-tuning it, he sent it off then set the laptop aside. He reached for the cat, stroked his silky fur. "Looks like I'm going to have to take a trip to visit the folks, fella. How'd you like to spend a few days with Miss Rosie next door?"

As if in answer, George purred even louder.

Spencer laughed at the cat's reaction to the mention of the elderly widow who kept an eye on his apartment and George whenever he was away. "I thought so. The woman spoils you rotten. Just don't get used to eating fresh tuna and chicken while I'm gone. Because when I come home, it's back to the canned stuff. Understand?"

George gave him an indignant look out of his green

eyes, then he flicked his tail and hopped off his lap to the floor. Without missing a beat, the cat walked over to the door and waited.

Tess exited the bathroom of the suite of rooms she'd been given and yawned. She shook her head, still surprised to discover a Jacuzzi tub and modern bathroom attached to a room that looked as if it had been designed during the Civil War. Heavens, but the room was beautiful, she thought as she flicked off the bathroom light. She padded on bare feet across the plush carpet to the antique four-poster bed. Running her fingers along one of the ornately carved posts, she stared up at the canopy that spanned the entire length of the bed. It had been done in the same rich blue satin fabric that had been used in both the bedspread and the drapes on the windows. The color scheme had been carried through on the pillows, too.

Glancing around the room, she took in all the little touches—the vase of fresh flowers, the oil paintings, the crystal candlesticks, the old-fashioned miniature frames with black-and-white photos, the intricate design of the fireplace screen. She looked at the fireplace, where logs had been placed in the grate, just waiting for someone to strike a match to the kindling wood. There was something so old world and Southern and inviting about the place.

Tired, but eager to explore a bit more, Tess moved across the room to the window. Kneeling on the chair beneath it, she unlatched the window and pushed open the shutters. The sheers billowed in the breeze. After propping her elbows on the windowsill, Tess lifted her face to the sky. The air was cool and damp against her skin. A strong wind coming from the north blew her hair across her face and Tess brushed the tangles from her eyes. Chilled, she shivered lightly, but continued to let the wind and the night wash over her.

And she listened to the sounds of the night: an owl hooting for its mate, frogs croaking near a pond, a dog barking in the distance. Somewhere, someone played a mournful tune on a harmonica that made her think of another time, another night when the air had been cool and damp like this one. The night her mother had been murdered.

Uncomfortable with the turn of her thoughts, Tess opened her eyes and gazed up at the starless sky. The moon had managed to escape the cloud cover, providing a sliver of light in a sky that was now an inky black. There were no high-rise buildings, no garish neon signs, no billboards here. But there were lots and lots of trees and cottages scattered across the landscape. Below her, Tess could make out some sort of garden with a bench beneath a tree. And there was a pebble path that led away from the house. She promised herself that in the morning she would follow that path and see where it led.

As she knelt at the window, the scents and sounds continued to wash over her, evoking old memories. Memories that she'd spent most of her life trying to forget. Memories that she knew she would have to face again if she was going to find the answers she sought— find out who was really responsible for killing her mother. Reminding herself that it was the reason she was here, Tess closed the window and turned back to the room.

Still chilled and feeling a little achy, Tess wondered if she was coming down with a bug. Deciding not to take a chance on getting sick, she returned to the bathroom where she retrieved two aspirin from her toiletry bag and washed them down with a glass of water.

When she exited the bathroom again, she spied the case with her laptop, resting beside the night table. It was late, but she could still do some research tonight. And she wanted to see if she could find out anything about Lester De Roach, she reminded herself as she recalled the strange incident at the convenience store earlier.

But she felt so tired, she admitted and yawned again. Giving in to fatigue, she walked over to the bed and climbed in. After switching off the lamp, she crawled beneath the duvet and closed her eyes. Tomorrow she would see what she could find out about De Roach, see if there was any connection between him and her mother, she promised herself while she snuggled into the pillows and waited for sleep to claim her.

As she drifted off to sleep, Tess's thoughts were filled with her mother. Tossing and turning, Tess dreamed…

Tess dreamed that she heard voices—her mother's voice. Only it wasn't her nice, inside voice. It was her angry voice. And she was crying. Just like she had been crying that morning when she had argued with Daddy first about Mommy wanting to get a job and then about them going to Jackson to see Grandma Elizabeth and spending the night at a hotel. Daddy hadn't wanted her mommy to work. And he hadn't wanted them to go to Jackson. He had yelled and said that Grandma Elizabeth was not to pay for their hotel. That he would pay for it.

But they hadn't stayed at the hotel after all. Because of her. She'd gotten sick. So she and Mommy had come home. So why was Daddy still mad? And why was Mommy crying? Tess heard a crash and her mommy screamed. Scared, she hid under the covers and cried. She cried and cried for a really long time. And then she slept.

When she heard her daddy yell again, Tess opened her eyes. She didn't feel good. Her throat hurt. And she felt hot and thirsty, too hot and thirsty to keep hiding. "Mommy," she cried. "Mommy."

But Mommy didn't come. Mommy always came when she was sick.

Still sobbing, Tess climbed out of bed and opened the door. She ran down the hall from her bedroom. "Mommy, my throat hurts," she sobbed as she turned the corner and came into the living room.

Tess stopped and stared at her Daddy kneeling on the floor over her mommy, holding the statue from the bookshelf in his hands. "Is Mommy sleeping?" she asked.

But her daddy didn't answer. He never even looked at her. He dropped the statue and reached for her mother. So Tess moved closer. She touched her daddy's shoulder. Then she saw it—blood. Lots and lots of blood. On her mommy's head, on the floor, on the statue, on her daddy.

"Tess," her Daddy cried out. "Get out of here, baby. Go back to your room, baby. Go now," he shouted, turning away so that she couldn't see her mother.

"What's wrong with Mommy? Why won't she get up?"

"She's hurt. Now go to your room."

"I want my mommy," she cried.

"Tess, please—"

And then she heard the sirens. The phone began to ring. Fists banged on the door. And the phone kept ringing and ringing…

* * *

Startled by the ringing phone, Tess sat up in bed and looked around the unfamiliar room. Then she spied the phone on the night table. She grabbed the receiver. "Hello."

"Good morning, Ms. Abbott. This is your six-thirty wake-up call."

"Thank you," Tess said.

After hanging up the phone, she fell back against the pillows. And once again she questioned her decision to come back to Grady. What if her grandfather had been right? That she should allow the past to remain buried.

She also recalled Ronnie's question. Would she be able to handle whatever it was that she discovered?

She didn't know, Tess admitted. But what she did know was that she owed it to her mother, if not to herself, to find out what really happened that night twenty-five years ago.

Chapter Six

Tess sat at a table in the back corner of the Grady Public Library. The library itself was small. The two-story brick building was composed of no more than a dozen rooms, but those rooms were filled with an array of books. Everything from Shakespeare to the classics to the latest Sandra Brown thriller and everything in between. But while the library had lots to offer in the way of books, the selection of past newspapers and periodicals left much to be desired—particularly the ones dating from twenty-five years ago. So far, she'd only found a handful of articles that provided details about the murder trial.

Unfortunately, she'd had little luck with the newspaper search since the library was in the process of microfilming its back issues to free up storage space. It was a wise move, one she was surprised that they were only now getting around to implementing. It was simply her misfortune that the segment of newspapers that were being microfilmed at present were the ones in which she was interested.

Still, she hadn't completely struck out thanks to the old, now defunct, town weekly. From it, she had been able to get a bird's-eye glimpse of the defense attorney who'd been appointed to handle her father's case—one Mr. Beau Clayton. Research done when she was still in D.C. revealed that he'd long ago left the public defender's office and was now in private practice in another county between Grady and Jackson. What she hadn't known, and had only discovered while at the library, was that Mr. Beau Clayton had been a green attorney, not long out of law school, with nothing more than a few petty theft cases under his belt when he had been handed her father's murder case to defend. She couldn't help wondering now just how good a defense he had been able to provide Jody Burns.

Adjusting her glasses, Tess typed in the next call number she'd copied from the periodicals/reserve desk that logged the location of all stored periodicals and newspapers at the library. And as had been the case with most of the call numbers she'd entered, she received the now familiar message: "Microfilm reel—Not Currently Received." Sighing, Tess typed in the next one on her list.

"Wanda told me you were hiding in here again today," a soft female voice remarked in that melodic tone to which Tess was quickly becoming accustomed. "Or did she mean you were still hiding in here because you haven't bothered to leave?"

Tess looked up at Anne Marie Gillroy and smiled. "Hi, Anne Marie," she said to the head librarian whom she had met for the first time when she'd visited the library on Monday. The lady hadn't exactly fit Tess's image of what a small-town librarian should look like. In addition to being under thirty, the brown-eyed brunette had the well-toned body of a dancer and a complexion the cosmetics firms would have paid a fortune to be able to duplicate. She also had a wardrobe much more fashionable than Tess would have expected, given the woman lived in a town of less than eighteen thousand people that didn't boast designer boutiques on every corner. Today Anne Marie wore a rich burgundy pantsuit with a silver and leather belt that accentuated her curves. She'd draped a scarf in striking jewel tones across one shoulder and had anchored it with a silver clip. A pair of smart ankle boots completed the outfit. The added touches took the outfit from simply pretty to chic. "Believe it or not, I actually did go back to the guesthouse last night to sleep."

"Are you sure? Because I could have sworn I left you in that very same position yesterday evening." She leaned closer as though to study Tess's face. "In fact, I think you were even wearing the same frown."

Tess chuckled. Removing her glasses, she stretched. "I feel like I've been here all night. But the truth is, I've only been at it a couple of hours," she said. "I was hoping I might have better luck today."

"And did you?" Anne Marie asked.

"Not really," Tess admitted as she glanced at the small cache of notes she'd made. "It seems just about everything I've tried to access for viewing is out being microfilmed. And the few things I have found are pretty much a repeat of info I already have."

"Sorry," Anne Marie said with an apologetic smile. "But getting all those old newspaper issues on storage film was something I've been itching to do since I took over this job. It took me eight months to get the council to approve it in the budget because they thought Miss Tilly's old system worked just fine," she explained, referring to the retired librarian whose position Anne Marie had been hired to fill. "Once they gave me the go-ahead, I decided I'd better move quickly before they changed their minds."

"I understand," Tess replied. And she did. Although Anne Marie Gillroy held a degree in library science from a major university in Texas, to many of the townspeople she was still little Anne Marie who had grown up in Grady. But apparently Anne Marie was winning them over slowly but surely. She couldn't help but admire the woman's dedication and determination to bring the town's library into the twenty-first century. From what Tess could see, she was well on her way to accomplishing that goal. It was just unfortunate for Tess that the timing for the revamping of the library's records storage system proved a hindrance to her own research. Deciding it was time to hit another source, she said, "Since I don't seem to be getting too far here, I think I'm going to try the newspaper office."

"That's probably a good idea."

Tess stood and began gathering her notes and stuffing them into her bag. She had hoped to gain most of the information she was looking for from the library because it afforded her anonymity. Anne Marie hadn't questioned her need to view old documents and had readily accepted her explanation that she was doing research for a potential project. The newspaper was always her second choice, as they asked more questions. Probably came from being in the business of reporting the news. She'd also learned that the print media and the visual media didn't always get along well, as they were often vying for the same stories. On more than one occasion she'd clashed with a newspaper reporter in D.C. because he'd been denied access at the scene of a breaking story while she had been granted it for the simple reason that she was more recognizable because of her airtime. It wasn't fair, but it was the way it was. Tess snapped her bag closed and stood. Extending her hand, she said, "Thanks again for all your help, Anne Marie."

"My pleasure. Hopefully, you'll be able to find whatever else you need at the *Grady Gazette.* Be sure to ask for Bill Reed. He's the owner and editor."

"I'll do that."

"But if by some chance, you strike out at the *Gazette,* you can always come back to see me in a few months. I promise, the library will have all the back issues available for you to study before the year is out," Anne Marie told her.

"I'll remember that," Tess replied. But as she left the library and made her way over to the newspaper office, Tess hoped she wouldn't need to come back. She also hoped that Bill Reed and his newspaper would be able to provide her with the information she needed, the answers to those questions that had brought her to Grady in the first place.

Looking up from the reception desk of the *Grady Gazette,* Spencer Reed spied the woman the moment she exited the snazzy little red Mustang. There was something to be said for those old-fashioned glass front offices, he mused as he watched Tess Abbott cross the street and make her way over to the newspaper office. While Carole, the receptionist, responded to an incoming call, Spencer lounged against the wall next to her desk and studied the lady as she approached.

He had seen a few clips on the D.C. news station and had checked her out on the station's Web site before he'd come home to Grady. So he'd known she was attractive with that thick dark hair, smooth skin and light eyes. But he hadn't realized she had such great legs, he admitted as he swept his gaze down the length of her. Mary Lee had been right about one thing though, he decided as she opened the door and entered the newspaper offices. Tess Abbott had a way-too-serious look about her.

"Morning," he said, offering her a friendly grin.

"Good morning," she replied without even the hint of a smile.

"Can I help you?" Spencer asked.

"I was looking for Mr. Reed."

"You've found him," he told her and flashed her another grin. Stepping away from the wall, he extended his hand. "And you are?"

"Tess Abbot," she replied and shook his hand firmly. But there was no mistaking the wariness in those gray eyes of hers. "You're Bill Reed?"

"No, he's not," Carole replied as she hung up the phone. "Quit fooling around, Spence," she said, shooting him a reproachful look.

"Hey, she asked for Mr. Reed. My name's Reed," he pointed out to Carole before turning his attention back to Tess Abbott. He hoped she'd be amused, but judging from the set of her mouth, she wasn't. "I'm Spencer Reed. Bill Reed is my father."

"I see." Shifting her gaze from him to Carole, she said, "I was hoping I might be able to speak with Mr. Bill Reed. I understand he's the owner of the newspaper."

"Owner, editor, publisher, you name it. My pop does it all," Spencer told her. He parked himself on the edge of the reception desk. "He'd probably print and deliver the papers, too, if my mother didn't insist he come home once in a while."

Still not even a flicker of amusement at his remark.

"I'm afraid Bill's stepped out for a bit," Carole told her. "Was he expecting you, Miss…"

"Abbott," she repeated. "Tess Abbott. And no, he wasn't expecting me. That is, I don't have an appointment. Do I need to make one?"

"No, not at all," Carole assured her. "We don't stand on ceremony around here."

"Then perhaps if you could tell me when you expect him and I'll come back."

"You can come back if you want to, but you're welcome to just wait if you'd like. I don't imagine Bill's going to be gone long. He just ran over to his wife's flower shop for a bit. She had a leaky pipe that needed fixing," Carole informed her.

"I see."

But it was clear from her perplexed expression that she didn't. "My pop holds plumbers with the same regard that he does a bank robber. He thinks they both commit robbery. So he avoids calling one if at all possible," Spencer explained.

"Ah, now I understand," she said, her lips curving slightly and softening her expression.

"So did you want to wait for Bill?" Carole asked.

"If you're sure it won't be any trouble."

"No trouble," Carole assured her.

"Or perhaps you might be able to—"

"Excuse me a second," Carole said, holding up her hand as the phone started to ring. "The *Grady Gazette*."

"Maybe I can help you," Spencer offered.

She trained those gray eyes on him, giving him a dubious look. "Does your father employ you here at the newspaper, Mr. Reed?"

"It's Spence," he corrected. "And I do some work here occasionally." He figured it wasn't really a lie. His father did carry his column and ran some of his articles. When she hesitated, he tried to get her to relax by saying, "I practically grew up in this place. So I know my way around it pretty well. You sure I can't help you?"

"Maybe you can. I wanted to talk to your father about viewing some old issues of his newspaper. I went to the library first, but they're in the process of copying the papers onto microfilm, so they aren't available. Anne Marie…Ms. Gillroy," she amended. "She suggested I speak with your father. She thought he might still have copies of some of the older editions and allow me to see them."

"Are you kidding? My pop keeps everything. The man still has my and my sister's report cards from grade school."

"And from what I heard yours weren't all that great," Carole chimed in as she hung up the phone.

Ignoring her, Spencer asked, "So how old are we talking about? A week? A month?"

"Twenty-five years."

Spencer whistled. "You weren't kidding when you said old."

"I'm doing some research for a project I'm working on," she explained.

When the phone started to ring again, Spencer said, "Carole, Ms. Abbott and I will be in Pop's office." And before she could protest, he ushered Tess down the hall and into his father's office.

"Oh my," she said as she stepped into the room. "This is…"

"Antiquated? A fire hazard?" Spencer offered, trying to see the room through her eyes with its scarred wooden desk piled high with papers and pasteups. The walls covered with framed articles and photos. The old-fashioned lamp. The credenza jam-packed with family photos and books.

"Actually I was going to say that except for the computer monitor, this room looks like something out of a Norman Rockwell painting. It looks like an old-time newspaper office. Sort of like the one in that old Clark Gable/Doris Day movie from the fifties, the one with the newspaper editor and the teacher."

"Teacher's Pet."

"Yes. That's it," she said. "This looks a lot like the newspaper editor's office in that movie."

"That's because my pop is an old-time newspaperman, probably a lot like that Clark Gable character. He started out working here as a newspaper delivery boy and worked his way up to pressman, reporter and then editor. He bought the paper about a dozen years ago and became the publisher, but he's still the same guy. When it's time to roll the presses, more often than not you can find him out back up to his elbows in pasteups and printer's ink."

"Sounds nice," she said, her expression wistful.

He'd always thought so. And that Tess Abbott could appreciate his father and not just see him as a dinosaur who refused to keep abreast of the times touched something inside him.

"So do you think your father has copies of those old editions?"

"I'm pretty sure he does. When he bought the newspaper, I convinced him to convert a lot of the older stuff to discs because he needed the space. So whatever he doesn't have in actual hard copy, he's got stored on a disc. I think I can see a few inches of free space left over there," he said, pointing to the chair-and-sofa grouping that his mother had insisted his father put in the office for those nights when he worked late. "Why don't we sit down over there and you can tell me exactly what it is you need."

Tess told him. She explained that she was an investigative reporter for a television station, working on a spec piece about suicides in Southern prisons, and that she had decided to follow the conviction and death of a man who had recently committed suicide at a Jackson, Mississippi, prison, a man who had once lived in Grady.

"Why choose a Mississippi prison?"

"Because you can't get much more Southern than Mississippi," she told him.

The lady didn't lie worth a damn, he thought as he watched her cross her legs. But damn she had killer legs, the kind a guy like him had fantasies of finding wrapped around him.

She wrote the dates in question on a slip of paper and handed it to him. "I'm hoping to be able to look through the newspapers for that three-month span or so in search of anything that might have been written about the murder and trial."

"Do you mind if I ask why you chose this particular man?"

But before she could answer, the door opened and in walked his father. At six-two, two hundred twenty pounds, William "Big Bill" Reed was built like a lumberjack. And although he was well into his sixties and his hair was more silver than black now, he still moved like a man half his age. "Spencer, what's this Carole tells me about a pretty female coming to see me and then you hustling her off to my office?"

"Hi, Pop." Spencer stood. He strode over to the door and gave his father a bear hug. "It's good to see you."

"You, too, son," his father said, but the man was already looking past him and over to where Tess sat. "Now, who is this young lady you're hiding in here?"

Tess stood. She walked toward them, her hand extended toward his father, a smile on her face. "Hello, Mr. Reed. My name is Tess—"

"Burns," his father finished, an astonished look on his face as he caught both of Tess's hands in his two larger ones.

Surprise flitted across her face for a second. Just as quickly, she recovered. "Actually, it's Abbott, sir. My grandparents had it legally changed after they became my guardians."

"Yes, yes. Of course, they would have. I should have realized that."

"Forgive me, Mr. Reed," she began, her forehead wrinkling as she looked at him. "But you've caught me off guard. How is it that you know who I am? Or rather, who I was?"

Big Bill Reed didn't miss the cool note in the lady's voice, nor the wary look that came into her gray eyes. He also didn't miss the way his son was watching the woman. "That's because you and I have met before."

"We have?" she replied, losing some of the stiffness.

He nodded. "Although I suspect you were a little too young to remember. The last time I saw you, you were about three feet high and had ribbons in your hair. But even then you looked like your momma."

Those big gray eyes of hers looked even larger in her small face. "You knew my mother?"

Given the fact that the girl was on the skinny side, unlike his Ellen, he didn't trust her not to faint. "Maybe you better sit down again," he suggested.

He had to give Spence credit. That boy of his had a great poker face. He'd have to suggest a trip to the casinos on the Gulf Coast sometime. Because not for a minute did he believe that Spencer hadn't made the connection between her and the senator. The boy wrote about politics for a living. He lived, ate and breathed the stuff. He also had a real hair up his butt when it came to the lieutenant governor, and had been like that ever since Jenny had died while working for the man. Caine's friendship with the Mississippi senator was no secret. So if she had told him her name was Abbott, there was a strong possibility he had known who she was. Why hadn't he told her so?

"Do you want some water or something to drink?" Spencer asked her.

"No, I'm fine. Thank you." She looked at him again. "Did you really know my mother, Mr. Reed?"

"Yes, I did," Bill told her. "I met her shortly after she and your daddy moved here. You were about three then, I guess. Anyway, your daddy had just gotten a job at the lumber mill in the next county and they'd rented a place on the outskirts of Grady. You and your momma came into town to buy groceries and she stopped in here to buy a paper. She said she was hoping to find a job."

"One of the things I remember about those last few weeks before she died was that she and my father were arguing about her going to work," Tess said, and Bill suspected she was speaking more to herself than to them.

"Apparently your daddy wanted her to stay home with you. But times being what they were, money was tight," he offered. What he didn't tell her was what he'd heard. That it was her grandfather who had made things so tough on the young couple. Jody Burns had only been at the lumber mill six months when he'd lost his job. Rumor had it that the senator had had the young man fired. "I didn't know your daddy well. But I ran into your momma every now and then. She was a nice lady. She loved you a great deal."

"Thank you," she murmured as she lowered her gaze to her clasped hands.

"I knew the senator and your grandmother took you back to Washington with them. And I often wondered what became of you," he told her honestly because it was true. The image of that little girl with the sad gray eyes being led from the courthouse had stayed with him for a long time.

"As you can see, I grew up," she told him. "I'm an investigative reporter now for a television station in Washington, D.C."

But she still had those same sad eyes, Bill thought as he looked at the woman she had become. As a newsman, even one whose primary news focus centered around his hometown and state, he was aware that her grandfather was a powerful man in the senate. "Grady's a long way from the nation's capital," he pointed out.

"I'm working on a story about suicides in prison, following one man's trial, his conviction and eventually his suicide," she said.

"Do you have a particular case in mind?" Bill asked her.

"The Jody Burns case."

"It seems to me that would be a tough story to do since the subject is your own father," Spencer pointed out.

She tipped up her chin defiantly. A spark of temper flashed in her eyes, Bill noted as he watched the interplay between the woman and his son. "I'm a professional, Mr. Reed—"

"Spence," he corrected.

"As I was saying, I'm a professional, Mr. Reed. Investigative reporting is what I do. I'm used to keeping my personal feelings out of the equation in order to get the job done."

"Even when the story hits so close to home?" Spencer countered.

"It's because the story *does* hit so close to home that my boss agreed that I should do it. That's why I'm here, Mr. Reed," she said, turning her attention away from his son and back to him. "I'm researching my mother's murder and Jody Burns's arrest and trial. I'm hoping you can help me."

"I will if I can. What is it you need?" Bill asked.

"Access to your old newspapers. I'd like to see whatever coverage there might have been on my mother's murder and on the Burns case."

Bill couldn't help noticing that she referred to the man as Jody Burns, not as her father. "Well, Ms. Abbott," he began.

"Please, Mr. Reed. It's Tess."

"All right, Tess," Bill amended with a smile. "That shouldn't be a problem. I've got copies of all the editions on microfilm. But be prepared. There's a lot there to go through. Grady's not a big town, and it was even smaller back then. Your mother's murder, tragic as it was, was big news. The people here are good people.

But given who your grandfather is and the way your mother died, well, it was like a juicy Hollywood movie to the folks around here. It's all they talked about and it's all they wanted to read about, too."

"In other words it was a media circus," Tess offered.

"Yes. For months leading up to the trial, there was something written almost daily about the case. A lot of it was filler, mind you. Interviews with neighbors, people who worked with your father at the mill, patrons he'd waited on at the bar. And during the trial itself, there was a daily account of what was happening in the courtroom—most of it written by me since I was assigned to cover the trial. A lot of the testimony given was unpleasant."

"I understand," she assured him. "I've already read some of the accounts that were published by the town weekly when I was researching at the library."

"The *Gazette* gave a fuller account," he explained. "And while there aren't any pictures because the judge wouldn't allow cameras in the courtroom, there are some artist renderings from the trial. There's even one of you on the witness stand," he told her. He wanted the woman to understand what she'd be facing.

"As I told your son, I'm used to having to separate my emotions from my job."

Personally, he wasn't sure she'd be able to, Bill thought. But it wasn't his decision to make. He slapped his hands on his legs. "All right then. I'll give you full access to all of the newspapers."

"Thank you," she murmured. "I really appreciate it."

"No problem," Bill said.

"I have a question," Spencer told her.

"Yes?"

"Just what is it that you hope to find?" Spencer asked.

"As I said, the story I'm doing is about one man's road from husband to murderer to his life in prison and his suicide. In order to explain what led to his suicide, I need to know what led him to prison in the first place."

"He was convicted of murdering your mother," Spencer pointed out.

"I'm aware of that. What I want to know is what led to the murder, how the trial was handled and what led to his being convicted for the crime when he maintained all along that he was innocent."

"Do you think he was guilty?" Spencer asked her.

"I don't know. But if Jody Burns didn't kill my mother, I want to know who did."

Chapter Seven

"How well do you know Bill Reed?" Tess asked Maggie that evening as the two of them sat in the kitchen of her cottage and shared a glass of wine. In the few days since she'd been there, she and the other woman had become fast friends. She'd been so at ease with her, she'd confided her real purpose in coming to Grady. She also knew that, regardless of the outcome of her trip to Grady, when she returned to D.C. her friendship with Maggie was something she intended to maintain.

"He's a real pussycat," Maggie told her. "Why?"

"I went to see him today about accessing some of his old newspapers. I told him I was working on a story about prison suicides and following the Jody Burns case."

"Did you tell him about your connection to Jody Burns?"

"I didn't have to. He knew who I was. He was the reporter who covered the trial for the newspaper."

"I'm not surprised," Maggie told her before dragging a chip through the bowl of salsa. "Bill's pretty sharp. He's married to Ellen Reed, the florist who supplies the flowers for Magnolia Guesthouse. They're a terrific couple."

"But do you trust him?"

Maggie gave her an odd look. "Yes, I do. He and Ellen are good people. I take it from these questions, you didn't tell him the real reason you're looking at those newspapers?"

Tess shook her head. "I started to, but decided against it."

"How come?" Maggie asked.

"I'm not sure really. But it's probably because I wasn't really comfortable with his son."

"Spencer was there?"

"Yes," Tess told her.

"I saw Ellen on Sunday. She didn't mention he was visiting."

Tess frowned. "He doesn't live here?"

"He lives in Jackson where the *Clarion-Ledger* is based. That's where he started his column. Although I understand from Ellen his column is being carried in so many newspapers now that he probably doesn't need to stay there if he doesn't want to."

"He's a journalist," Tess said more to herself than to Maggie. No wonder the man's name had seemed familiar. And no wonder he'd asked her so many questions.

"Sure. It's something you and he have in common."

Only, the rat hadn't mentioned it to her. She tried to think if she'd said anything about her grandfather, but didn't recall doing so.

"Is that a problem, Tess?"

"No." At least it wasn't an immediate problem. "What do you know about him?"

"Spencer?"

Tess nodded.

Maggie sat back, took a sip of her wine. "Let's see. Besides the fact that he's handsome, he's single, around thirty-four and well-respected by the people in Grady. He's also lusted after by quite a number of the women."

Tess rolled her eyes. "You know what I mean, Maggie. Can he be trusted? The man writes a political column. My grandfather is a senator. The last thing I need is for him to put something in his column about me being at odds with my grandfather over coming here."

"Oh, Tess, I don't think Spencer would do that. From what I know of him, he's a pretty straight shooter. I've only read his column a few times. But from what I have read, he seems pretty fair. The only politician that I know the man doesn't like is the lieutenant governor, Everett Caine."

"Why doesn't he like him?"

"I asked Ellen once. All she said was that Spencer had a friend who died and that he blamed Caine for it."

Tess sighed. "Caine is the attorney who prosecuted Jody Burns. He and my grandfather are close friends."

"Ouch," Maggie said.

"I guess that's one more reason for me to steer clear of Spencer Reed."

"Do you really think you're going to be able to keep what you're doing a secret for long?"

"Probably not," Tess admitted. Because if Bill Reed had recognized her, and she already thought that fellow De Roach had mistaken her for her mother, it wouldn't be long before someone else who remembered the murder trial would put two and two together.

"Then why not try being straight with Bill and Spencer about what you're doing? I know Bill will go out of his way to help you."

"And his son?"

"If Spencer is anything like his father, and I suspect he is, my guess is he'll do the same. It seems to me that it would make things a lot easier to find out what you want if you let someone help you."

"I work well by myself," Tess defended.

Maggie reached over and touched her hand. "If there's one thing I've learned since Mack died and I moved here, it's that life's too short to go it alone. I've found most of the people in Grady are nice, hardworking and honest. They'll be your friends if you let them. Try being up front with the Reed men. They just might surprise you."

Tess decided to take Maggie's advice. The next morning when she went back over to the *Grady Gazette,* she explained her primary reason for coming to Grady, beginning with the anonymous phone call and her own inquiries into Jody Burns's supposed suicide.

Looking from one man to the other, she tried to gauge their reactions to her statement. She'd already noted that neither of the Reed men gave much away when it came to what they were thinking or feeling. But she was good at reading people, what they said—and what they didn't say.

"So this mystery woman who called you, did you believe her—that your father didn't kill your mother? That the same person who killed her engineered your father's death and made it look like a suicide?" Bill Reed asked her.

"I'm not sure what to believe," Tess confessed. "That's why I'm here. I thought I might find the answers somewhere in the coverage and case files. At least that's where I'm starting."

"It's a smart move. That's where I'd start," Spencer told her.

"Yes, I'm sure you would. I understand that you're a journalist. I didn't realize yesterday when you told me that you occasionally did some work here at the newspaper that you were referring to your column 'The Political Beat.'" At least he had the grace to look uncomfortable, she thought.

"It never came up," Spencer told her as he met her gaze.

"And I don't suppose it crossed your mind to mention it to me when you found out I was Senator Abbott's granddaughter."

"It did, but since our discussion wasn't about your grandfather or politics, I decided that there wasn't any point in mentioning it."

"And now?" she asked.

"I don't see how that's changed. According to you, you're interested in your mother's murder and your father's trial. So why don't you tell me what else you've done?"

She took him at his word. "I'm hoping to speak to his defense attorney and witnesses, the arresting officer and the prosecutor. I've already left messages for both attorneys."

"You do realize the prosecutor was Everett Caine," Spencer stated.

"Yes, I know. And I'm aware that he's running for

governor, which is one of the reasons I suspect I haven't been able to reach him." She waited to see if he'd mention his animosity toward Caine, but other than a hardness in his voice when he'd said the man's name, there was no change in his demeanor.

"This woman who called you, do you have any idea who she was?" Bill asked, drawing her attention back to the subject at hand.

"No, I don't."

He sat back against the couch, rested his hands on his thighs. While Bill Reed was by no means an open book, there was an honesty about him that made her feel comfortable after only minutes in his company. It was one of the reasons she'd opted to tell him the truth.

His son, Spencer, was another matter. Physically, he was a younger version of his father. Tall, probably a good six inches taller than her own five-foot-eight frame, and built like an athlete. His hair was dark, but his eyes were blue whereas his father's were brown. Ronnie would have labeled him a hunk. And she could understand Maggie's remark about the women in town lusting after him. The man was good looking, had a sexy smile and gave the appearance of being easygoing. Yet, there was a dangerous edge about him. Or maybe it was just her own awareness of him as a man. She hadn't expected to experience that tug of attraction. But then, something told her neither had he. Lots of layers to Spencer Reed, she thought. And her every instinct screamed out for her to be careful around him.

Shaking off the unsettling feelings and her thoughts about Spencer Reed, Tess turned her attention back to his father. "Bill, you met Jody Burns and you covered his trial. What do you think? Was the woman telling the truth? Do you think that someone other than Jody Burns killed my mother?"

Long seconds ticked by during which he rubbed his jaw as though unsure how to answer her. Finally, he said, "I honestly don't know. What I can tell you is that I sat through the trial, listened to the testimony given by both sides. And my gut feeling, when I walked out of that courtroom, was that your daddy was telling the truth. I don't think he killed your momma."

It wasn't the answer she had expected. She had anticipated he would remain noncommittal, or even declare that the evidence pointed toward Burns's guilt. She hadn't expected his belief in her father's innocence. "But what about the jurors—those twelve men and women—they heard the same testimony that you did. They convicted him."

"I know. But I always believed that they were wrong in their verdict."

"But how is that possible?" Tess asked, still stunned by Bill Reed's remark.

"As I tried to explain, times were different back then. The evidence against your daddy, well, it was mostly circumstantial. It probably wouldn't hold up in a court of law today."

"But if that's true, then why did they convict him?"

"In my opinion and that's all this is, my own personal opinion," he stressed. He leaned forward, met her gaze. "I think all the media frenzy about the murder had the jury and most people in this town thirsting for blood. They saw a beautiful young woman dead and a sad-eyed little girl left without a mother and they wanted someone to pay. The prosecutor painted a pretty unflattering picture of your daddy as a jealous loser, a man who couldn't hold down a job and who went into a murderous rage when he heard his wife was leaving him."

"But she wasn't leaving him. We were just going to spend the weekend at the hotel with my grandmother for her birthday. We came home early because I got sick. I told them that," Tess pointed out.

"I know you did. But the jury thought your momma really did plan to leave your daddy, and that she hadn't told you. So when you testified about them arguing that morning and how you woke up and found him holding the bloody bookend…" He paused, sighed. "Well, it was pretty damning testimony."

"But I was telling the truth."

"I know you were. So did that jury. And I think that's why they convicted him. They believed you. So they thought he did it."

"But you didn't," Tess pointed out.

"No, I didn't."

It was suddenly important to her to understand why this man who hadn't really known her father could be so sure of his innocence while she…she had always believed him guilty. "But what about the witnesses? His girlfriend? The woman confessed that they were having an affair."

"That was heresay on her part. Besides, I didn't believe her," Bill told her. "The woman had worked with your daddy at the lumber mill before he was fired. She admitted that she'd had a crush on him for a long time. But none of the woman's friends or co-workers had ever seen them together. And according to your daddy, he didn't return her feelings."

"Well, what about the owner of the bar—he said they left the bar together that night and drove away in Jody Burns's car," she insisted, remembering the account she'd read, remembering the things her grandfather had told her.

"Your daddy said that she came into the bar that night and hung around until his shift was over. She claimed she'd had too much to drink and she couldn't drive herself home. Your daddy said he felt sorry for her and gave her a ride. After he dropped her off, he went to your house. And that's when he found your momma."

Tess swallowed, considered everything Bill Reed had said. What if he was right? What if it had been her testimony that was responsible for her father's conviction?

"I've upset you. I'm sorry," Bill said.

"No. I mean, yes, I am upset, but it's not your fault. It's mine," she admitted. "I've spent my whole life believing he was guilty and hating him for taking my mother away from me, for destroying our family. I never really let myself consider that he might have been innocent."

"If that's true, then what are you doing here?" Bill asked her. "Why dig up the past now? Since your daddy's dead, it's too late to help him. So why put yourself through this?"

She'd asked herself that same question a number of times since making the decision to come to Grady. And only now did she realize that she hadn't come back here to prove her father's innocence or guilt, or even to find her mother's killer. She'd come back for herself. Tess looked up, met Bill Reed's eyes. "Because I need to know if I was justified in hating him all these years."

"And if it turns out that you weren't? That someone else was responsible?" Spencer asked. "What happens then?"

"Then I find out who was responsible for stealing my family from me." And when she found that person, she intended to make them pay.

"You're sure you want to do this?" Bill asked her.

"Yes."

"Then I guess we better get going," Bill told her and stood. "I've set you up in another office with one of the microfilm readers. I just need to get my storage logs and then you can get to work."

Tess rose. "Thank you, Bill."

"Don't thank me yet. You haven't seen all the stuff you've got to go through," he said. "I'm afraid you're going to be here for quite some time."

"Speaking of time, two sets of eyes searching through all those newspapers would be a lot faster. Why don't you let me help you?" Spencer offered.

While she wouldn't mind the help, Tess wasn't sure she wanted to be cooped up for days with Spencer Reed. "Not that I want to look a gift horse in the mouth, but why would you want to help me?"

"You mean other than the fact that I get to spend time with a very attractive woman?"

Tess didn't even acknowledge the lame come-on. She merely gave him a withering look. "If that's the best reason you can offer, I'll pass."

"All right. It's because I smell a story."

Tess's hand curled into a fist at her side. "I told you, I don't want my grandfather's name dragged into this."

"It's not your grandfather I'm interested in. It's Everett Caine. Your father's trial was the launching pad for his political career. If he made any mistakes in that trial, I want to know it."

"Why? So you can destroy him?"

"Yes," he said boldly.

"But why?"

"Because I despise the man," he stated.

"Why?"

"It's personal."

"So is what I'm doing. And I don't want to see it played out as grist for the political gossip mill in your column."

"You won't. The only one I'm interested in is Caine."

She considered him for a moment. On the few occasions that she'd met Everett Caine, she'd liked him. True, she'd found him a little full of himself, but then a lot of politicians were like that—including her grandfather. That didn't mean she wanted to see him hurt by what she was doing. "If I accept your offer, you give me your word that you won't print anything about Caine that isn't true."

"I'm a journalist, Tess. Not a liar."

"And you'll keep my grandfather's name out of this?"

"I told you, it's Caine I'm interested in. Not your grandfather."

"In that case, I'd appreciate the help," she said, then turned to Bill. "With the exception of Maggie O'Donnell, the two of you are the only ones in Grady who know about my connection to Jody Burns. They think I'm just writing a story on him and suicides in prisons. I'd like to keep it that way."

"The only person I've told about you is my wife, Ellen, and she won't say anything. Neither will Spence or I. But I'm not sure you're going to be able to keep who you are under wraps," Bill told her. "Anyone living here who remembers the trial is going to recognize your resemblance to your mother just like I did."

Tess remembered her encounter with Lester De Roach on the night she arrived. "Actually, I think someone has already recognized me. Or rather, they mistook me for my mother."

"Who?"

"A man at the convenience store where I stopped for gas and directions on the night I arrived."

"Do you know who he was?" Bill asked.

"The store clerk said his name was De Roach. Lester De Roach." A strange look crossed Bill Reed's face. "What is it? What's wrong?"

"Tess, Lester De Roach is the 'friend' of your father's who testified against him. He claimed to have overheard your parents fighting on the day your momma was killed. He's also the one who called the police to the house the night she was murdered."

Sheriff Andy Trudeaux looked down at the remains of Lester De Roach. His body laid sprawled, faceup, brown eyes open wide and staring up at the sunny October sky. His face was bloated and the stench was strong enough to kill a mule. It was hard to tell how much of that smell was due to decomposition and how much was due to Lester himself. Of course, the two days of high temperatures after that cold spell probably hadn't helped either. But there was no question what killed him—the hole in his chest. From the massive amount of damage to the skin and soft tissue around the hole, his guess was a shotgun blast. Probably from a 20-gauge or maybe a 410.

"Sheriff, I've got some shell casings over here," his deputy, T-Boy, called out.

"Be sure to bag them," he reminded the deputy, and went back to examining the area around the body. The wooded area located about three miles from the dilapidated shack that Lester had called home for the past few years was situated on a track of marshy land out-side Grady that had remained undeveloped. As a result, it often drew hunters—both greenhorns and old-timers—hoping to bag a squirrel or shine for rabbits. It had been two old-timers who'd been checking out hunting spots in preparation for the season opening next month who had come across the body and called it in.

"Jesus! That smell. How long you think he's been out here?" T-Boy asked as he came over and joined the sheriff.

Andy looked at the spiders that had come to feed on the body, noted the blisters on the skin and swelling from bodily gases. "Three days at least," Andy told him.

"Poor bastard."

"Yeah," Andy said. "Let's see those shell casings you found."

T-Boy handed him the Ziploc bag. "Twenty gauge."

Andy examined the shells, noted the standard-issue green wrapping and brass ends, the type of shell every owner of a 20-gauge shotgun used for hunting. And un-like the markings left by a rifle or handgun, there would be no way to track the shells to the shotgun they came from because there would be no rifling.

"Looks like a hunting accident," T-Boy claimed. "Since no one reported it, I'm guessing it was kids out here shining for rabbits or hunting squirrels. They got old Lester by mistake."

It was a reasonable assumption, Andy decided, and probably the right one. Yet he looked at the dead body and his first thought was murder until proven other-wise. Old habits die hard, he told himself. In the eight months since he'd decided he'd had his fill of fighting crime as a cop in New York City and returned home to Grady to take the sheriff's position, he hadn't come across any dead bodies. Nor had he been faced with scenes of bullet-riddled bodies of kids who weren't even old enough to drink who'd been dumped in some alley after a drug deal had gone bad. Since he'd been back in Grady, there had been no bodies beaten and tossed in Dumpsters like trash, and no horrific scenes like the one after the World Trade Center attacks.

"You could be right," Andy said. He didn't bother pointing out that hunting season hadn't opened yet because he knew there were any number of hunters who didn't abide by the gaming rules. They'd grown up on the land, done things one way their entire lives and found it hard to obey someone else's rules. "But I wonder what he was doing out here, this far from his place."

"Maybe he saw the hunters and came after them, tried to run them off."

"On foot?" Andy countered. "He's a good three miles from his place and I don't see Lester as the type to run through these woods. He would've taken his truck."

"Maybe his truck wasn't running. Or maybe he was drunk," T-Boy offered. "You know how Lester was, Sheriff. The man was hardly ever sober."

"Yeah, I know," Andy conceded. He'd locked the man up twice for being drunk in public since he'd been sheriff. But still Andy couldn't help wondering what Lester had been doing out here.

"Somebody's going to have to tell his sister, Doreen."

"I'll tell her," Andy said with a grimace. Advising a person that a member of their family was dead was one of those jobs that never got easier. "In the meantime, you better radio in and have the coroner's office send a truck out here."

"Will do."

"And, T-Boy. Why don't you bring me that camera I've got in the glove box so I can take some pictures of the scene."

"Sure thing, Sheriff."

While his deputy climbed back up to the road to the squad car, Andy continued to study the area around the body for a clue as to what Lester had been doing there and who might have shot him. Andy trudged through the soft mud and grass. If there were any footprints or tire tracks, last night's rain had washed them away. He scanned the site for signs of Lester's shotgun or the handgun he knew Lester carried in his truck.

If Lester had been chasing kids or hunters, he'd have taken a weapon with him, Andy reasoned, remembering it had only been a month ago that he'd had complaints about Lester brandishing a shotgun at some schoolkids who'd been trespassing near his place. But Andy saw no sign of the shotgun. Holding a handkerchief over his mouth and nose with one hand, Andy leaned closer to the body to check the pocket of Lester's jacket for a handgun. One pocket was empty. He checked the other. He didn't find a gun. But he did find some loose change, four singles and a charge card receipt.

"The coroner's on the way," T-Boy said as he made his way down the slope. "Here's the camera."

Andy stood and walked over to where his deputy waited. "You got another evidence bag?"

"Sure," T-Boy responded and pulled one from his pocket. "Whatcha got?"

"Contents of Lester's pockets." He dumped the dollar bills and change into the bag. Then he smoothed out the crumpled credit card slip.

"What's that?" his deputy asked.

"A receipt for gas," he said and read the name on it aloud, "T. Abbott." He turned it over, saw what looked like a license-plate number written on it.

"Wonder who T. Abbott is and what Lester was doing with their gas receipt?"

"I don't know," Andy told him as he dropped the credit card slip into the evidence bag with the money and sealed it. "But I intend to find out."

Chapter Eight

Once he'd delivered the news to Doreen about her brother's death, Andy had gone to work on identifying the owner of the credit card receipt he'd found in Lester's pocket. It hadn't taken him long to trace it and discover that 'T. Abbott' was one Tess Abbott of Washington, D.C. A run on the license-plate number written on the back of the receipt through the DMV showed the vehicle was registered to a car-rental agency out of Jackson, Mississippi. The car-rental firm, in turn, had reported leasing the car with that tag number a week earlier to the same Tess Abbott. For a local address, the lady had listed the Magnolia Guesthouse in Grady. A call to the establishment run by Maggie O'Donnell confirmed that Ms. Abbott was indeed a guest.

Turning his truck onto the lane leading to the main house, Andy wondered if he'd see Maggie. Their paths hadn't crossed since he'd bailed on the brunch at his mother's two weeks earlier. At thirty-four he considered himself well past the age where he would tolerate his mother's matchmaking. So he'd practically bolted once he'd realized the purpose of the brunch was to throw him and Maggie together again. It hadn't improved his disposition to realize that Maggie seemed to find his annoyance at the situation very amusing. As a result, he'd been just shy of rude in his exit, not even bothering to apologize to his mother or to Maggie.

Pulling his truck to a stop, he shifted to Park and exited the vehicle, then headed for the main house. He marched inside and went straight to the reception desk. Not seeing anyone, he hit the service bell.

A head of reddish-blond hair popped out from behind the door. "Why, Sheriff Trudeaux," Maggie O'Donnell said, the twinkle in her voice matching the one in her green eyes. She started toward him and his eyes followed the sway of her hips. Unlike a lot of women these days who were skin and bones, Maggie had curves he noted, not for the first time. "What a surprise to see you here," she said with a smile, and Andy felt his gut tighten.

"'Afternoon, Maggie," he said, tipping his head in acknowledgment. He gripped the hat in his hand a little tighter at the sight of her. Her hair was all tumbled and her cheeks were pink as though she'd been rushing around or had just climbed out of bed. A looker was how his grandfather had described her. The old guy had been right, Andy admitted. Maggie O'Donnell was a looker. And apparently she was smart. From what he'd heard, the pretty Yankee widow had swept into Grady three years ago and purchased the old Jefferson Plantation. According to his mother and grandfather, Maggie had sunk a fortune into refurbishing the run-down estate and had turned it into a revenue-producing inn for tourists. In the eight months since he'd been back, their paths had crossed a number of times thanks to his well-meaning and none-too-subtle mother. Both his mother and grandfather looked at her and saw wife potential. But he wasn't interested in a wife and somehow he didn't think Maggie O'Donnell would just settle for an affair.

"Don't tell me your mother's plot to throw us together worked this time. I was so sure you'd figure a way to wiggle out of this one, too."

"I beg your pardon?"

She gave him a sassy smile. "You do know that she's planning on us getting married, don't you?"

Andy frowned, recalled now the message his mother had left for him on his voice mail, asking him to be a dear and pick up some books that Maggie had ordered from her shop and drop them off to her on his way home. After finding Lester De Roach's body, he'd been too busy to call her back and nix her latest ploy to put him in Maggie's path. But the amusement in Maggie's eyes and the fact that she knew he'd been sidestepping those attempts to throw them together irritated him. "I'm not interested in a wife."

"Well then, I guess it's a good thing I haven't bought a wedding gown, isn't it?" she said, that glint in her eyes again.

Andy scowled. "If you know what she's doing, why don't you just tell her you're not interested in me?"

"Because I adore Susan and she'd be crushed if I told her I wasn't interested in her baby boy." She laughed when he bared his teeth at her reference to him as someone's baby boy. "Besides, I *am* interested. Or at least a little curious. Aren't you?"

"You know what they say about curiosity. It killed the cat."

"Why, Sheriff, haven't you heard?" she asked, leaning closer and dropping her voice to a whisper. "We cats have nine lives. Besides, doesn't the rest of that rhyme say something about satisfaction bringing the cat back?"

Suddenly Andy recalled the Tennessee Williams play, *Cat on a Hot Tin Roof* and Maggie the cat, the character played by Elizabeth Taylor in the classic movie. Maggie O'Donnell could easily have played the part, he thought. She was beautiful, sensual and bursting with life. And getting involved with her would be like playing with fire, he reminded himself.

"You know what I think?" she said.

"No. But I suppose you're going to tell me."

Ignoring his rudeness, she forged ahead. "I think that if you really want Susan to stop playing matchmaker, you should take me out a time or two. Nothing special—maybe lunch or dinner or a movie, something that could be considered a real date. Then if there's no chemistry between us, we can both tell her that we tried, but it simply wasn't meant to be."

"And what happens if there is chemistry?"

She smiled at him again and Andy's insides tightened as he contemplated that mouth. "Then I guess we see where it leads."

Where he wanted it to lead was to sex—hot, mindblowing sex in his bed, with her wrapped around him and no messy emotions involved. But before he could say as much, the front door opened. Shifting his attention to the entrance, he watched as Mary Lee Hollister waltzed in. Watching her twitch her hips in the tight little black suit, Andy wondered how on earth she managed to walk in the high heels as she made her way over toward the desk.

"'Evening, Sheriff. Ms. Maggie. Sorry I'm late," she said as she moved behind the desk and tucked her purse away. "But I was on the phone with T.-Boy's sister. She told me about old Lester De Roach."

"What about him?" Maggie asked.

"Why, didn't the sheriff tell you? He's dead. A hunting accident. Somebody shot him right square in the chest and killed the poor man. The sheriff and T-Boy found him out in the marsh."

Maggie paled. She touched his arm. "Is it true, Andy?"

It was the first time she'd ever called him by his name and he liked it, he realized. He was also keenly aware of her hand on his arm. As though she sensed his tension, she dropped her hand. "Yes. We found him earlier today."

"I'm sorry," she told him. "How awful for his sister. And for you."

That she would recognize it would be difficult for him as well stirred something inside Andy. He didn't want to be moved by this woman. He didn't want to be drawn to her and resented the fact that he was. And because he resented it, his voice was sharper than he'd intended when he said, "I need to see Tess Abbott."

Maggie blinked. "Tess?"

"Yes. I understand she's a guest here."

"Oh, she's not staying in the main house anymore. She's in Dogwood Cottage," Mary Lee told him. "Although why a body would want to be over there all by themselves instead of here in the main house is beyond me."

"Mary Lee," Maggie said, a warning note in her voice.

"Sorry," Mary Lee said sheepishly. "You want me to show you where the cottage is, Sheriff?"

"I'll show the sheriff," Maggie informed her.

"Yes, ma'am," Mary Lee replied, and Andy suspected the girl didn't have a clue that her boss was none too pleased with her for revealing that bit of information so easily.

"Is Tess expecting you?" Maggie asked him.

"No."

"Then perhaps I should call first to be sure she's in the cottage."

"I'd just as soon you didn't," he said. And because he didn't trust her not to do what she wanted anyway, he took her by the arm and motioned toward the door. Once they were outside, he said, "If you want to just tell me which cottage it is, I'm sure I can find it on my own."

"Tess is a guest here. And she's also my friend. So I'll show you."

"Suit yourself. My truck is over there," he said, indicating the dark green and black vehicle marked with the town's emblem.

"I don't suppose you're going to tell me what this is about, are you?" she asked when he opened the passenger door for her.

"It's official business, Maggie."

"Dogwood Cottage is on the other end of the property," she said as she buckled herself into the seat.

They made the drive in silence, the only words spoken were Maggie's instructions on where to turn. When he pulled his truck up in front of the quaint-looking cottage surrounded by bare dogwood trees, he noted the red Mustang parked out front. He slid his gaze to the license plate and ran the number mentally against the one he had found on the credit card slip. They matched.

With Maggie beside him, he knocked at the door and waited. Within moments a tall, dark-haired woman with the most arresting gray eyes opened the door. She looked at him, did a quick glance at the badge he wore, then shifted her gaze to Maggie.

"Ms. Abbott? Tess Abbott?"

She turned her attention back to him. "Yes. I'm Tess Abbott. What's going on, Maggie?"

"I'm not sure," Maggie began.

"I'm Sheriff Andrew Trudeaux," he told her, cutting off further questions. He pulled out his identification from his pocket and showed it to her. "I'd like to ask you some questions. May I come in?"

"Questions about what?" she countered.

"About Lester De Roach."

Maggie gasped beside him and Andy shot her a look.

"Why would you want to ask me about him?"

"Then you know him," Andy said.

"Not really. The night I arrived in Grady there was a man in the convenience store where I stopped for gas and directions who appeared to have been drinking. The clerk said his name was Lester De Roach."

"And that's the only contact you had with him?"

"Yes," she told him, but for a fraction of a second Andy could have sworn she'd held something back. "What's this all about, Sheriff? Why all the questions?"

"Lester De Roach's body was found out in the marsh a few hours ago with a shotgun blast to his chest."

"Oh, my God," she murmured.

"Come on, Tess," Maggie said, taking charge. She led the taller woman into the cottage and over to the couch. "Andy, why in the world are you asking Tess questions about Lester?"

"Because a credit card receipt belonging to Ms. Abbott was found in his pocket. And the license number on her rental car was written on the back of it." He handed her the clear plastic bag containing the credit card receipt and watched her examine it.

"This is the receipt for the gas that you bought at the convenience store. It is yours, isn't it?"

"Yes, it is."

"Any idea how it ended up in Lester's pocket?" he asked.

"No, I don't."

"You're sure?" he asked, because he couldn't shake the feeling that she wasn't leveling with him.

She frowned as though trying to recall. "Wait. It must have been when he dropped the six-pack of beer he was holding. He was behind me in the checkout line," she explained. "When the beer cans scattered, I jumped to dodge one of the cans and my purse fell. I guess the receipt fell out of my purse then and he picked it up."

It sounded logical, Andy thought. Yet, something didn't feel right. "I suppose he could have. But I wonder why. And why write your license-plate number on the back?"

"I don't know, Sheriff. Maybe he was working with one of those credit card theft rings and was going to use it."

"Could be," Andy said. "But Lester wasn't exactly the brightest bulb in the pack. Somehow I doubt that he had the smarts to pull off something that sophisticated. Petty larceny was more his style."

"I really wouldn't know," she told him and stood. "But if you don't have any more questions, I've got some work to do."

Andy followed her lead and stood. "So you're not here vacationing?"

"Tess is a television reporter," Maggie offered.

"Grady, Mississippi, is a long way from Washington, D.C." At her questioning look, he explained, "When I traced the credit card receipt, it gave me your address as D.C."

"I see," she replied.

"So are you working on some kind of story about Grady?"

"Actually, I'm working on a special-interest feature about prison suicides. I'm following one man's life from the time of his trial for murder to his conviction and eventually his suicide in prison."

"We don't get a lot of murders in Grady," he pointed out.

"It's an old case."

"Which one? I might remember it."

She hesitated, then said, "It's the trial of Jody Burns. He was convicted of killing his wife twenty-five years ago."

"It doesn't ring a bell. But then I was only a boy at that time," he admitted.

"If there's nothing else, Sheriff, I really do have to get to work."

He tipped his head. "I appreciate your time, Ms. Abbott. You ready, Maggie? I'll drop you off back at the main house on my way out."

"That's all right. I'm going to stay and visit with Tess for a while. I'll get someone to pick me up later," she informed him.

"Suit yourself," he told her before directing his attention to Tess again. "Just to be on the safe side, Ms. Abbott, if I were you, I'd notify my credit card company in case you're right and Lester was planning some kind of credit card scam."

"I'll do that."

The two women walked him to the door. As he reached it, he paused and turned back to Tess. "One more thing, Ms. Abbott."

"Yes, Sheriff?"

"That night in the convenience store, did you happen to see anyone else in the store?"

"Only the clerk behind the counter. Just before I left, there were some schoolgirls who came in. Why?" she asked.

"The coroner thinks Lester was shot between the time he left the convenience store and dawn. So you were probably the last person to see him alive—except for the person who shot him."

"But I thought you said it was a hunting accident," the Abbott woman pointed out.

"I said it *looked* like a hunting accident," he clarified. "I haven't made an official ruling yet."

"Surely you don't think anyone shot him deliberately," Maggie said, her shock at the suggestion evident.

"I'm not ruling out anything yet. Thanks again for your time, Ms. Abbott. Maggie." After tipping his head, he left.

But as Andy climbed into his truck, he couldn't shake the feeling that Tess hadn't been leveling with him. He hadn't survived as a cop in New York City without learning to follow his gut instincts. And right now his gut was telling him that Tess Abbott was hiding something.

Whatever that something was, he intended to find it out.

Tess shut the door behind the sheriff, then leaned her head against it. *Dead. Lester De Roach* was dead. After learning from Bill Reed that Lester had been one of the witnesses who'd testified against Jody Burns, she had scoured the papers for mention of his name. She'd located several articles containing statements he'd given to the sheriff's office and the prosecutor. He'd claimed to be a close friend of her father's and that he knew of Jody Burns's affair and his arguments with his wife. He'd also recounted hearing a loud argument between her parents the morning of her mother's murder when De Roach had claimed to come by to work on her father's car. The final blow had been his testimony that he'd been on his way home when he'd seen the lights on in their house and had planned to stop and ask his friend Jody about the car, when he'd heard her mother scream. He'd rushed to the door, seen her father standing over her mother's body and then he'd raced away to call the police.

Tess recalled now seeing an artist's rendering of him sitting in the courtroom on the witness stand, testifying at her father's trial. She had planned to speak with him, to ask him questions about that night. But now, now she would never get that chance. That realization bothered her. So did the fact that he'd taken her credit card receipt.

But why? Had he been waiting outside the store and watched her leave? He must have, she decided. How else would he have known which of the four cars parked in the store lot belonged to her?

"Tess, are you all right?"

Tess shook off her silent questions, remembering that Maggie was still there. "Yes, I'm okay. Just a little shaken, I guess."

"You poor thing. It makes me shudder just thinking about that man being found dead like that and to have your credit card receipt on him… Well, I can't even imagine how upset you must be. That's so…so creepy."

It was creepy. It was also worrisome. "Did you know him? Lester De Roach, the man who was killed?"

"Oh, I knew who he was. Most of the people around here did. Not the most pleasant man, as I'm sure you saw. But to die in a hunting accident like that, well, it's such a tragedy."

"I got the feeling your sheriff isn't so sure it was an accident," Tess pointed out.

"He's not *my* sheriff," Maggie insisted, her cheeks all flushed.

Maggie's response surprised her. In the short time she'd known her, Maggie O'Donnell had not struck her as a woman who flustered easily. Tess wondered if she'd missed something because she'd been so unsettled by the sheriff's news.

"Sorry. I just get so mad when I think of the way that man came in here, grilling you like you were a…a suspect or something. I just can't imagine what Andy Trudeaux was thinking."

"He was just doing his job."

"Well, I for one think his technique could use some improving."

Tess smiled at Maggie's defense of her. While she could claim a number of friends back home in Washington, the truth was that with the exception of her producer, Ronnie, she hadn't allowed herself to get too close to anyone. The shrinks would probably say it stemmed from her losing her mother so young and the near miss they'd had with her grandmother because of the woman's cancer. And as much as she adored her grandmother and loved her grandfather, she didn't necessarily think of them as friends. Aware of her grandmother's health, she'd limited her confidences with the older woman because she hadn't wanted to upset her in any way. As for her grandfather, he wasn't a man easy to be close to. Oh, he loved her. She never doubted that. But things had to be on his terms. He was not someone with whom she would share confidences.

Maggie, on the other hand, was a different story. She'd taken an instant liking to Maggie the night she'd arrived and the two of them had spent several enjoyable evenings chatting. She'd learned how Maggie had married her soul mate, the man with whom she'd planned to grow old. When her husband suffered a fatal heart attack at thirty-one all the years of planning and saving for the future had proved worthless. Thanks to wise investments in the then rapidly rising dot-com market, her husband's death had left Maggie a wealthy woman, but with no one to share her life. So rather than put her dreams on hold any longer, she set out to fulfill her dreams of running a bed-and-breakfast—preferably someplace warm. As a wealthy widow she realized she could do as she pleased, so she had packed her bags, collected the insurance money and headed south where she'd spent the better part of two years renovating and refurbishing what was now the Magnolia Guesthouse.

"Now, why don't you come sit down and let me fix you something special to drink."

"Thanks, Maggie. But really, I'm okay. And I really do have some work to do." She also needed to return her grandfather's calls. So far, she'd been able to put off another confrontation with him by letting the cell phone go to voice mail. But she was going to have to return his calls soon—preferably in private and not when she was at the newspaper offices, or while Maggie was around.

"I tell you what. Why don't you tell me how your research is going while I fix us both a mint julep."

"What ever happened to a cup of tea?" Tess asked.

Maggie wrinkled her nose. "Tea is boring. I think we need something a little more exciting after what Andy just put you through."

"It wasn't that bad."

"Don't defend him," Maggie insisted.

"Whatever you say." Deciding the sheriff was a touchy subject for her friend, she said, "I thought mint juleps were supposed to be a summer drink."

"So we'll pretend a little. After all, we've had a few warm days. Besides, you're going to love it. Now, no more protests, come sit and talk to me while I play bartender."

Tess sat and watched as Maggie went to work. The cottage had been surprisingly well stocked with goods, she thought. And her own trip to the store had given her all the essentials she needed. So she wasn't surprised to see that Maggie knew where everything was since the other woman had obviously put a lot of time and planning into the cottage's amenities.

Maggie opened the cupboards, pulled out bourbon, sugar, mint leaves and ice. She lined the bottom of two glasses with half an inch of sugar, damped it with water, then went about crushing the ice by wrapping it in a dish towel and pummeling it with a wooden mallet. Fascinated, Tess watched her slip two sprigs of fresh mint against the inside of each glass, then she crammed the ice in right to the brim, packing it in with her hand.

"The key is the crushed ice and good bourbon whiskey, the older the better," Maggie explained as she up-ended the bottle of bourbon and filled each glass to the rim. Finally, she put a pinch of grated nutmeg atop each drink and shoved in a short straw. "Here you go," she said, handing Tess a glass.

Tess took a sip and gasped as the taste of bourbon, sugar and mint exploded in her mouth. "I can see why you like this. It's delicious," Tess told her and took another sip.

Maggie took a sip of her own and closed her eyes dreamily for a second. "Mint julep sounded like such a Southern thing, I had to try one my first summer here and I've been hooked on them ever since. Now, why don't we go sit a spell. You can tell me how your investigation's going and how you're getting along with Bill and Spencer Reed. And we can both put all that mess about Lester De Roach's accident out of our minds."

So Tess told Maggie about her conversation with both Reed men and her mixed feelings about working with Spencer Reed. She also told her about Bill Reed's revelation about Lester De Roach and the other man's role at the trial.

"I'm sorry, Tess. That's got to be disappointing, knowing you won't be able to ask Lester any questions now."

"It is," she confessed. "But I'm still hoping I'll be able to track down this Virginia Lee who claimed she was Jody Burns's girlfriend and talk to her. She apparently left the lumber mill after the trial. Spence is trying to locate her now. Mr. Reed said the sheriff from back then is retired, but he's going to try to arrange for me to talk to him. I'm supposed to see the attorney who handled the defense next week and I'm still waiting to hear back from Everett Caine. His staff keeps telling me he's on the campaign trail."

"What about your grandfather? Surely he could help."

"My grandfather was against me doing this. If anything, he'll bring whatever pressure he can to get Caine not to talk to me."

"But why?" Maggie asked.

"My grandfather hated my father. He had plans for my mother to finish college, make her debut and marry someone prominent. Instead she quit college her freshman year because she was pregnant with me and eloped with my father—a boy with no social standing."

"Wow, talk about sounding like Romeo and Juliet."

"Pretty close," Tess said. "My grandfather even tried to have their marriage annulled. But my grandmother convinced him that since my mother was pregnant with me, there would be an even bigger scandal if there was an annulment. But that didn't stop the senator from blaming my father for ruining his daughter's life."

"How awful."

"I imagine it was for my parents. But to be fair to my grandfather, he really did love my mother. She was his only child. He wanted a better life for her," she said, searching for a way to explain. Yet as she said the words, Tess realized how her grandfather had set his mind on her following the path he'd once outlined for her mother. And while she hadn't eloped with someone he hadn't approved of, she had disappointed him all the same when she had turned down Jonathan's proposal.

"I take it your father didn't fit the bill."

"Not even close. His mother was a waitress in Louisiana and he never knew his father. He got a football scholarship to college and that's where he met my mother. When she got pregnant with me, he quit school to take a job and support his family." What she didn't tell Maggie was about all the different jobs her father had had. While she couldn't remember a lot, she did remember always having to move because her father had another new job. "Anyway, after my mother was murdered and my father went to jail, I went to live with my grandparents in Washington."

"You never saw or heard from your father again?"

Tess shook her head. "My grandfather wouldn't allow it when I was younger. Later when I was an adult, I blamed Jody Burns for taking my mother from me. I believed he'd killed her."

"Until you got that phone call," Maggie said.

"That and after I contacted the prison about his suicide. The more I thought about it, the less sense it made for him to kill himself after all of this time, when he would have been a free man in only a matter of weeks. Now after reading some of the newspaper accounts and talking to Bill Reed, I'm beginning to think he might have been innocent just like he claimed. And if he was, that means that someone framed him."

"But who? And why?"

"That's what I need to find out. Unfortunately, now with Lester De Roach dead, there's one less person who was there that night that I can ask about what happened."

"And you don't have any idea who the woman was that called you at the TV station?" Maggie asked.

"None. But I think I'm going to make another trip to the prison, try to talk to the warden in person and see if I can find out anything else."

Maggie shuddered. "I can't imagine what it must feel like to be in a place like that."

"I can think of places I'd rather be. But someone there must know something that can help. I just have to find out who."

Chapter Nine

"Quit sulking," Spencer told Tess as he drove along the interstate, heading for the Mississippi prison where her father had spent the last twenty-five years of his life.

"I'm not sulking. I just don't understand why you insisted on coming with me. I don't need a chaperon or a bodyguard. I *have* been inside a prison before, you know."

"I'm sure you have. But I'm not coming to play chaperon or bodyguard. I'm coming to help you get some answers."

"In case you've forgotten, Reed. I'm an investigative reporter. I know how to get answers."

"I know you do," Spencer told her and bit back a grin. She'd pitched a fit when he'd shown up that morning, insisting on accompanying her to the prison. But after learning about Lester's death and finding out Tess's credit card receipt was on him, he had gotten a bad feeling about the whole thing. His conversation with Andy hadn't done anything to alleviate that bad feeling either. "But getting those answers may not be as easy as you think."

"Would you stop treating me like I'm some kind of…of cream puff? I know how to conduct an interview and find out what I need."

"There's no chance I'd mistake you for a cream puff. But you're not dealing with a bunch of politically correct socialites down here. These people are die-hard, Confederate flag–waving Southerners who will see you as a Yankee not to be trusted. They're not going to tell you squat beyond the official statements. Which is what I'm guessing you got when you showed up before."

She didn't deny his claim—which was an admission as far as he was concerned. "And I suppose you think you can do better?" she challenged.

"Sure," he said confidently. "In case you haven't noticed, I'm a homegrown boy. Unlike you, I can be trusted. They'll talk to me."

"I'm from Washington, D.C., the nation's capital—not some foreign country."

Spencer chuckled and slid a glance in her direction. "Darling," he said, deliberately exaggerating the Southern drawl, "if you live anywhere north of the Mason-Dixon Line, you may as well be from a foreign country, because to us you're a Yankee. We Southerners haven't forgotten the Civil War."

She looked at him as though he'd lost his mind. "That's the most ridiculous thing I've ever heard."

"That may be. But it's the way things are down here," he told her, which was the truth. His father once explained the attitude to him as being the result of the South being a conquered nation. It was something a true son or daughter of the South never forgot. "Besides, you're a TV reporter, a celebrity, not a bona fide news journalist like me."

"Speaking of being a news journalist, isn't there a governor's race you should be covering instead of getting in my hair?"

"That's the beauty of freelancing. I'm not tied to a desk and I've already sent in my next column." Of course, he still needed to see to the next installment on "The Road to the Governor's Mansion" series, but he'd work on it tonight. Besides, the truth was, the more time he spent with the woman, the more she intrigued him.

"Don't you need to at least attend a few of the debates and speeches if you're going to report on them? After all, the election is next month."

Her mention of the governor's race reminded him that if he hoped to derail Caine he was going to have to do it soon, because he was running out of time. It was the other reason he'd accompanied her today. He was pretty sure that Tess Abbott would be the one to lead him to the information he needed. He just wished he'd found a way to tell her that her mystery caller had contacted him, too. The problem was, she was so gun-shy around him he worried that she might totally cut off communication with him if he told her now. It was a risk he couldn't take. At least not yet. "The truth is, it's not much of a race," he conceded. "If the election were held tomorrow, Caine would be a shoo-in."

"What did he do to you to make you hate him so much?"

"Not to me," Spencer told her. "To someone I cared about. A sweet, innocent girl who was little more than a kid," he said, describing Jenny, the girl who'd been like a sister to him, the one he was supposed to look out for and had failed. "She was a law-school student who signed on as a volunteer at the Capitol, and she worked with Caine in the lieutenant governor's office. She was young and impressionable. And he took advantage of her naïveté, her trust. He used her and when he was finished, he kicked her aside like she was a piece of garbage. Like she didn't matter." He gripped the steering wheel tighter as he remembered Jenny's call to him that night a little more than a year ago, how heartbroken she was, how ashamed she was when Caine had snuffed out her romantic dream about the two of them.

"What happened to her?"

"She killed herself," he said grimly, unable to forget arriving at Jenny's place that night and finding her in the garage dead. "Caine may not have been the one who locked Jenny in the garage with the engine running, but he as good as turned the key when he had an affair with her. She got pregnant, and instead of leaving his wife like he'd promised, he told Jenny to get an abortion and had her removed from his staff."

Tess gasped. "Then how is it possible he's running for governor? If the voters knew what he did—"

"They don't know because I could never prove it. It was my word against his."

"But a DNA test—"

"There was no DNA test. Jenny's parents had a hard enough time dealing with her death. Grady's a small town, Tess. They didn't want to add to their own pain by stirring up a scandal. In their eyes, revealing Jenny's pregnancy, and then accusing a married politician of being responsible, would have only made things worse. So they refused to have a DNA test done and then they had Jenny's body cremated."

"I'm sorry," Tess told him and touched his arm.

"Not as sorry as Caine's going to be. If we're able to prove Caine sent an innocent man to prison and now that man's dead, it may be enough to put an end to his political career."

"Reed, it's not that I'm siding with Caine. I'm not. The truth is, I don't know much about him other than the fact he convicted Jody Burns and, in doing so, he earned my grandfather's respect. But even if Jody Burns was innocent, Caine was only doing his job as prosecutor. It was the jury who returned the guilty verdict."

Spencer hesitated, then decided to tell her what he suspected. "But suppose Caine manipulated the evidence? What if he railroaded your father for the crime for his own political aspirations?"

"What evidence?" she asked.

"Remember one of the newspaper accounts said that your father claimed there was a car speeding away from the house when he arrived?"

"Yes."

"Suppose he was telling the truth? Suppose there was someone at the house, but Caine made sure no one ever found out about that mystery car or driver?"

"But what would be his motive?" Tess countered. "If someone else was responsible, convicting them would have been just as effective. He would still have jump-started his political career."

"Not if the person responsible was connected to Caine," Spencer told her.

"But who?"

"For starters, Lester De Roach." Spencer flipped on his turn signal and took the exit for the prison. "I found out that De Roach used to be a snitch for the sheriff of Grady back then. When he was working as a prosecutor Caine had used him as a witness in at least a half-dozen cases involving a car theft ring. So Lester wasn't just some random witness who happened to come forward with damaging information about his so-called pal, Jody Burns." Spencer stopped at the red light and looked at Tess. "Caine knew De Roach, and he knew the man had a questionable background. But that was never mentioned at the trial."

Tess stared at him and he could see, in those pale gray eyes of hers, that she was digesting the information, assessing it. "But you said yourself Grady is a small town. Would that have been so odd for them to know each other?"

"Not by itself. But Lester had always had to hustle from one job to the next. He never had two dimes to rub together. Yet the month after your father's conviction he suddenly had money to buy a body shop for himself. A loan from a friend. Guess who that friend was?"

"Everett Caine," she said in disbelief.

"No. But close enough. It was Caine's wife's cousin. My pop says Lester eventually lost the place, but I'm willing to bet that so-called loan was never repaid. Yet six months later, A.D.A. Everett Caine beat his then boss in a landslide victory to became the new D.A. of Grady. A key part of his platform was his successful conviction of your father for murder."

"That's still a long way from proving he was involved in any coverup at the trial," she pointed out. "I mean, why would he risk it? What would have been his motive?"

"His political career for starters. He's an ambitious man and from everything I've learned about him, he's power hungry. Winning that trial was a way to put him in the spotlight and help him move up the political ladder. From what I've read about the trial, it was no secret that the senator hated his son-in-law and wanted him out of his daughter's life. So, convicting Jody Burns of your mother's murder also gained Caine a powerful political ally." The light turned green and he turned off onto the long expanse of road leading to the prison.

"It all sounds pretty bizarre."

"I know it does and I'm the first to admit that it seems like a stretch, but I know I'm right about that connection between Caine and De Roach—the loan for the business."

"It could just be a coincidence."

"We both know there is no such thing as a coincidence. Caine was involved. I know he was."

"Maybe you want to believe he was involved because of your friend."

He thought about it. "I'll admit I do want to see him brought down because of what he did to Jenny. But I also believe I'm right about this. I think he manipulated that trial and had your father convicted for his own benefit."

"If you're right and Caine is as cunning as you claim, it won't be easy proving it because he'll have covered his tracks," Tess said.

"Yeah, but the problem with a guy like Caine is that he's so arrogant, he won't think anyone can touch him. But he'll have made a mistake somewhere." Like leaving that credit card receipt in Lester's pocket. As he approached the entrance to the prison and the guard's gate, he said, "If the woman who called you was right and your father was onto something that would prove his innocence, chances are someone here at the prison will know about it."

"That's what I thought the first time I came here, but I got nowhere."

"So you try again. This time see if you can get the warden to let you talk to some of the guards or other prisoners. Ask them about your father's state of mind before the suicide."

"Aren't you going to come with me to see the warden?"

Spencer flashed her a grin. "Nope. I have a few friends who work for the prison. I think I'll nose around and see what I can find out." He pulled the car up to the guard gate.

"IDs, vehicle registration and the purpose of your visit," the guard said, barely looking up from his clipboard at them.

"How you doing, Pete? Spencer Reed with the *Clarion-Ledger*. Remember me?"

The guard glanced up and his rotund face split into a grin. "Sure I remember you, Mr. Reed. How ya doin'?"

"Just fine, Pete. Just fine. This is my friend Ms. Abbott," he said, indicating Tess with a nod of his head. "She has an appointment to see the warden and I thought I'd tag along for the ride."

"I'll still need your driver's licenses or some form of ID."

"Sure." Spencer handed over his press credentials and Tess did the same.

"From Washington, D.C., hmm?" the guard remarked. "We don't get many people from them northern TV stations down here. Seems to me most of you folks stay closer to home."

Tess glanced his way. "Actually, Mississippi is home for me. It's where I was born."

Pete seemed to warm up immediately. "Should have

known a pretty little thing like you had to be from the South. Here you go, ma'am, Mr. Reed," he said, handing them back their identification. He recorded the information from the vehicle registration then handed it back to Spencer. Then Pete slid a visitor's pass onto the dashboard, but remained hunkered down, one arm on the driver's-side door. "Sure did like that story you did last year on the prison, Mr. Reed. My missus, she got a real kick out of that picture you ran of me here at the gate. The whole family acted like I was some kind of celebrity 'cause I was in the newspaper."

"That's because you were a celebrity, Pete," he told the guard. "You and the other officers here do a hell of a job. Without you they couldn't run this place."

"Just doing my job. But that's mighty nice of you to say so. You folks can go on through to the main building. You'll need to sign in at the registration desk."

"Will do. Thanks again, Pete," Spencer said and headed for the main building of the prison. "Once we get inside, I'm going to excuse myself while you talk to the warden."

"And what are you going to be doing?"

"Seeing if I can find out what really happened to your father."

Not only had she not spoken to any of the prison guards who'd been on duty the night that Jody Burns had killed himself, she hadn't even spoken to the warden yet, Tess fumed. After filling out the necessary paperwork and being checked for concealed weapons, she'd been ushered into an office and told someone would be with her shortly. That had been thirty minutes ago.

Resisting the urge to glance at her watch again, Tess

stood and walked across the floor, her heels clicking on the tiled surface as she made her way over to the window. She stared outdoors and noted that the sun in the October skyline had dipped behind the clouds, adding to the air of gloom that permeated the Mississippi prison. As she looked past the administration buildings, she could see the outline of the housing units that held the 5,700 inmates who resided at the penitentiary. She thought of the men locked behind those walls, wondered what their lives must be like. What had Jody Burns's life been like living in such a dreary place?

Tess sighed as thoughts of the man she'd once called daddy surfaced. Even after twenty-five years, she remembered him clearly. A big man, tanned from hours of working in the hot Mississippi sun, with a shock of black hair, blue eyes and an infectious smile. But he hadn't been smiling those last few times she'd seen him—kneeling over her mother's body with her blood on his hands, being hauled away in handcuffs, being led from the courtroom to prison.

"Ms. Abbott?"

Tess turned at the sound of her name and stared at the man coming toward her. A quick assessment of the young man told her he wasn't Warden Graystone even before he extended his hand to her.

"Russ Hayden," he said, giving her what she suspected was supposed to be a friendly smile. "I'm Warden Graystone's assistant. I believe we spoke on the phone when you called a couple of weeks ago about inmate Jody Burns's suicide. Again, my condolences on your loss."

"Thank you," Tess murmured.

"I understand you had some more questions," he remarked with just a hint of the South in his voice. Tess wondered, as she had during their phone conversation, how long he had had to work to temper the strong twang so prevalent in the speech of most Mississippians—including that of her grandparents.

"That's right. I do."

"Please have a seat then," he instructed, motioning to one of the chairs positioned around the table. "Now, if you'll tell me what it is you want to know, I'll see if I can help you."

Deciding to cut to the chase, Tess said, "Forgive me, Mr. Hayden, but I was under the impression that I would be speaking with Warden Graystone. I made an appointment to see him."

"I know, and the warden asked me to offer you his apologies. He's been unavoidably detained and won't be able to see you today after all. He asked that I see if perhaps I can be of any assistance."

"I see," Tess said, not at all pleased.

"Of course, if you'd prefer to speak to the warden, I can reschedule the appointment for you. I believe he has another opening in two weeks."

She'd worked enough investigative stories to smell a roadblock when she ran into one and she smelled one now. "No. Perhaps you can help me after all."

"I'll do my best," he assured her and sat back in his seat. "Now, what can I help you with?"

"I wondered if it would be possible for me to speak with the guard who was assigned to the section where my father was held before he died."

"That's an odd request. May I ask why?"

"I'm having difficulty understanding why my father would have committed suicide when he was up for parole. I thought if I spoke to someone who had contact with him on a regular basis I might get an idea about his frame of mind."

"I see," he said and paused. "The assignment schedules vary and I'm not sure who was assigned to that area," Hayden told her. "But I'll see what I can do."

"I'd appreciate it. And one other thing, Mr. Hayden," she said when he started to get up.

"Yes?"

"I'd also like to know if I could get a list of any visitors my father had."

He sank back down in his seat. "Assuming that I can get approval to provide you with that information, you must realize that that's a lot of visitor logs to go through, Ms. Abbott. After all, your father was an inmate here for over twenty-five years."

"I can fully appreciate the enormity of the task and I wouldn't dream of asking you to go to all that trouble. What I was hoping is that I could see his visitors' list for the past year."

"As I said, I'll have to get approval to release that information to you. It may take a few days. Perhaps if you'll leave me a number where I can reach you," he suggested.

"Actually, I was hoping I would be able to get that information today. If you'll tell me who I need to speak with about getting the approval, I'll ask my grandfather, Senator Abbott, to speak with the proper party and save you the trouble."

The friendly smile and dimple in Hayden's cheek disappeared. He regarded her through narrowed eyes. "That won't be necessary. Was there anything else that you wanted?"

"I'd like to have whatever personal effects my father may have left."

"Very well," he said, standing. "If you'll excuse me for a few moments, I'll see what I can do."

Russell Hayden was able to do more than she'd expected. When he returned to the room, he handed her a list of names of her father's visitors during the past year. Scanning the list, Tess realized that during the last six months of his life, he'd been visited three times by a Sister Amelia and once by his former defense counsel. Both of them had visited him the week before he died. "I recognize the attorney's name, but do you know who this Sister Amelia is?"

"From what I gather, she was a teacher at a school your father attended as a boy. She was transferred to a convent nearby and came to pray with him."

"And the guard? Will I be able to speak with him?"

"I'm afraid not. At least not today. He's out on vacation for the next two weeks."

"I see. And I don't suppose there's any chance you could give me his home phone number or address, is there?"

"It's against policy," he told her. "I'm sure you understand."

"Of course." She did understand. She was fairly sure she was hitting that roadblock again.

A knock came at the door and a woman came in and handed Hayden a box. "Thank you," he told the woman, who nodded and exited the room. He handed the box to Tess. "These are your father's personal effects."

"Thank you," she said as she took the box and held it on her lap.

"Now, if you'll excuse me, I'm afraid I have another meeting." He stood and extended his hand. "It was a pleasure meeting you, Ms. Abbott."

Tess shook his hand. "Thank you for your time."

Walking out of the office, Tess was directed back to

the reception area where she had checked in upon entering the prison. When she didn't see Spencer, she chose a far corner seat and sat down. She hesitated a moment. Then she opened the box containing her father's effects. Inside was a man's old black suit—the suit she recalled her father had worn in the courtroom. There was a Bible, a packet of letters, a harmonica and a wallet. Tess picked up the harmonica and felt a pang as she remembered seeing her father play it. She put it aside and picked up the wallet. It was worn, the leather cracked. Inside there was no cash, but there was an old driver's license and his social security card. She dug through the folds and withdrew a picture that was faded and tattered around the edges as though it had been handled often. It was a shot of her and her mother. Tears welled in Tess's eyes as she looked at the smiling faces of her mother and herself as a child, wearing the matching dresses that her mother had made for them.

"Ready to go?"

Tess jerked her gaze upward and realized Spencer was standing in front of her. She'd been so deep in thought she hadn't even heard him approach. "Yes. I'm ready," she told him and dropped the photo and wallet back into the box, then put the lid on it.

"Are you all right?"

"Yes," she said with a swipe at the corner of her eyes with her fingers.

"Then let's get out of here."

As Spencer and Tess's vehicle exited the prison gates and headed toward the interstate, a man sitting in a silver truck watched them leave. He considered himself a broker, the person people came to when they needed to get a job done, or if they needed help sealing a deal. He was good at both, he admitted. And over the years he had pocketed a tidy sum for his skills. Unfortunately, bad luck at the gaming tables had taken a huge chunk out of that tidy sum. Fortunately, he had a shot now at refilling those coffers. Only this time, he was going to raise his price. With that thought in mind, he dialed a number on his cell phone.

"Yes."

"Good afternoon, sir. I'm calling to report on that stock you asked me to keep an eye on, the one you were thinking about investing in. It looks like you were right. There's been a lot of interest in it lately and I wouldn't be surprised to see the level of trading activity increase soon. You may want to consider buying those shares now."

"No," he said. "Not yet. Why don't you watch it for another day or so. If it continues to do well, then I'll have you purchase some shares for me."

"Are you sure? The price has already gone up to a hundred dollars a share," he said, letting his buyer know that, unlike the hit on De Roach, which he'd farmed out for a mere twenty grand, this hit was going to cost him an even hundred grand.

"That's a pretty big jump in price. Maybe I need to find myself another broker—one who can find me some shares at a more reasonable price."

"That's your prerogative, of course. But considering the profit potential for this particular stock, I don't recommend it. You might just find no one wants to sell you their shares or, if they do, there may be strings attached. At least with me as your broker, you know you don't have to worry about any middleman fees."

"Your point's well taken," he said, an edge in his voice. "Just keep an eye on the stock and if it looks like the trading is getting brisk, buy me the shares. Understand?"

"I understand."

When the phone line went dead, the man in the truck smiled. After starting his engine, he pulled his vehicle out onto the road and headed toward the interstate in the direction of Grady.

Chapter Ten

Spencer took the interstate exchange that would take them back to Grady. As he did so, he glanced across the seat of the car to Tess. Just as she had for most of the three-hour drive, she stared out the passenger window in silence. "Abbott, did something else happen back there at the prison that you haven't told me about?"

She looked over at him as though confused. "No. Just what I told you already."

"Then what's wrong?" he asked.

"I was just wondering if my grandfather was the reason I was being stonewalled again. I did imply that I could have him make a phone call and get clearance to give me that visitors' log, but I'm not sure the warden's assistant bought it."

"He must have. He gave you a copy of the log," Spencer pointed out.

"Yes. But other than finding out that his attorney and

a former teacher came to visit him, we didn't get any new leads. I had really hoped to talk to the guard, but since both he and the warden were conveniently unavailable, I have a sneaking suspicion my grandfather made a phone call. He's furious with me for coming here and digging up the past."

"I can't say that I blame him," Spencer remarked, unable to ignore the fact that if De Roach's death hadn't been an accident, as Andy thought, then Tess could be putting herself in danger.

She gave him a searing look. "I was hoping I'd find the name of the woman who called me in that log," she reminded him.

"Maybe it was the nun who called you."

"I doubt it."

"Why?" he asked, although he knew it was no stretch to assume that Tess's mystery caller and the woman who'd phoned him were one and the same. Like Tess, he couldn't reconcile the image of a nun with the woman who'd bitterly declared Caine a liar and a cheat.

"Because a nun is someone holy and fearless, someone who will do the right thing no matter what the consequences. The woman I spoke with was afraid. She said she couldn't risk going to the police and she wouldn't give me her name. Does that sound like a nun to you?"

"No. But then I'm not Catholic and all I know about nuns is that they wear ugly getups, orthopedic-looking shoes and pray a lot."

She chuckled. "Not a very flattering description, Reed."

"Hey, I call them like I see them," Spencer said and realized it was the first time he'd heard Tess laugh. He liked the sound of it and he liked her, more than he thought he would. Probably more than he should, he reasoned, given the fact that his exposure of Everett Caine could very well impact both her and her grandfather. While he'd picked up on the sometimes combative nature of her relationship with her grandfather, he hadn't missed the fact that she loved the old man a great deal. And if he brought Caine down as he planned to do, his supporters were going to feel the heat and the spotlight. Senator Theodore Abbott was a key supporter. "Anyway, if Sister Amelia isn't the one who called you, she might know who did."

"Maybe. Assuming we can locate her." She sighed. "Did you find out anything?"

"My contact said your father spent a lot of time in the prison library during the past six months going through law books. Maybe he was on to something and really was planning to get his case reopened."

"If he was, his lawyer should know," she said. "I'm supposed to drive over to River Falls day after tomorrow to see Beau Clayton. He was my father's defense attorney and since he came to see him not long before he died, he might know what Jody was planning. Maybe he'll be able to tell us who Sister Amelia is and how we can reach her."

"I have to go to Jackson tomorrow to cover the gubernatorial debate. While I'm there, I'll check with a few of my contacts and see if they can help me track her down."

"You think she's in Jackson?"

"It seems likely since it's the nearest city to the prison and she came to visit him several times," he explained. Even though the prison facility was built outside the city limits for isolation purposes, it was within a thirty-minute drive of the capital. "Mississippi isn't a big Catholic state. So there aren't a lot of Catholic churches in Mississippi. There are even fewer convents. I'm guessing that there's not more than one or two in Jackson. Pete, the guard at the gate," he clarified. "He said there's a group of nuns from a little church in Jackson who come out regularly to pray with the prisoners. I'm going to check there first."

"Hayden said that Sister Amelia was a teacher, that she had taught my father as a boy," Tess told him. "So she'd have to be pretty old now. She might be retired. I'll see if I can find out if there's a motherhouse for retired nuns in Mississippi." She ran her fingertips along the edge of the box on her lap—the box that contained her father's effects.

"Anything of interest in the box?" he asked, because other than telling him it was her father's effects, she had said little about what was in it.

"Not really. An old suit, his harmonica and a wallet, some letters."

"Who were the letters from?"

"I didn't really look that closely," she said and opened the box. She picked up the bundle of letters and thumbed through them. "It looks like some legal correspondence from an attorney, a couple of cards and letters from people I don't know and…what's this?"

Spencer slid a glance in her direction. She pulled out a small packet of papers tied with a piece of string that had been stuffed inside the coat pocket. "What is it?"

"Letters," she said and began digging through the envelopes. "They're addressed to me and marked Return to Sender. There are a good ten or twelve of them. And there are at least another dozen with just my name written across the front and the year."

"You didn't know he tried to contact you?"

"No. Yes." She whooshed out a breath. "I knew he tried to call me in the beginning, but my grandfather refused the calls. He said I shouldn't speak to him, that it would be unhealthy for me. And...and that it would be a slap in the face to him and my grandmother. He said I owed it to my mother's memory not to allow him in my life." She looked down at the bundle of letters in her hands. "I never knew he'd written to me."

"Your grandparents probably thought they were doing what was best for you," Spencer offered.

"I'm sure you're right. It's just... I thought he had forgotten me or wanted to forget me because of my mother. Maybe I should have tried to contact him."

Spencer couldn't help but react to the sadness in her voice. In the dim light of the car, she looked lost and alone. Her unhappiness tugged at him. He reached across the seat, caught her hand and squeezed her fingers. "Don't start second-guessing yourself. If you do, you'll drive yourself crazy. I should know. I've done it often enough and, in the end, it won't change what's already happened."

"You're talking about your friend Jenny."

He nodded and put both hands back on the wheel. "I saw her a few days before she died. She was glowing. I'd never seen her so happy. I teased her about it, asked if she'd fallen in love and she confessed that she had. Jenny was like a kid sister to me, so I was glad for her. But I knew how sheltered she'd been, growing up, and I'd always sort of looked out for her, I guess. Anyway, I told her I wanted to meet this guy and check him out since I was sort of like her big brother."

"What did she say?"

"She said I already knew him, that he was someone

important. Right away I figured it was someone she'd met working at the Capitol. But she wouldn't tell me his name. Finally she admitted that she couldn't tell me—at least not yet—because he was married. I was furious with her," he recounted and squeezed the steering wheel tighter. He tried to remember Jenny's face that night, the hurt in her eyes at his anger. "I demanded that she break things off with him. But she refused. She said that they loved each other and they were going to make a life together, and if I couldn't accept that, then she didn't want me in her life anymore. I was so mad at her, I said fine and walked out.

"A couple of days later, I came back from covering a political rally out of town. I'd run the battery down on my cell phone, so when Jenny couldn't reach me, she left a string of messages on my answering machine at home. She begged me to pick up the phone, to call her, to please forgive her. She said I'd been right, that the man didn't love her after all and that he didn't want the baby she was carrying. He wanted her to get rid of it."

"She hadn't told you she was pregnant?" Tess asked.

"No. But I should have suspected it. Like I said, that last time I'd seen her she was bursting with happiness and had this look in her eyes, like she had a wonderful secret. Looking back I realize she must have just found out she was pregnant and hadn't told him yet. The last message Jenny left on the machine was to tell me goodbye and that she loved me. She said she hoped someday that I would forgive her and that I would help her parents to understand, but she simply didn't want to live anymore. I raced over to her apartment, but when I got there, she was already dead. Later I was able to piece together that the guy she was involved with was Caine."

"I'm sorry," she said.

He rubbed his face and tried to shake off the memories. "I beat myself up a lot over not being there for Jenny. I kept telling myself that if I hadn't been so wrapped up in my own life and career, I would have realized sooner that Jenny was involved with someone and questioned it. And then I'd tell myself what if I had charged the cell phone the night before and had gotten Jenny's call? What if I had thought to check the machine at home for messages? But I finally came to the conclusion that I couldn't go back and do it over. We don't always get second chances to get things right. I wasn't there to save Jenny. And you can't go back and change things for your father. What you can do is what you're doing—searching for the truth. If your father was innocent, then find the proof and clear his name. Let that give you peace."

"What about you? How do you find peace with Jenny's death?"

"I don't expect peace," he told her. And he probably didn't deserve it either because he had failed to do what he had sworn to do—look out for Jenny. "But I'll settle for a good story and seeing Caine lose the election."

"You want revenge."

"Call it what you want."

"That's what it is when you want to cause someone ill out of spite and not for a greater good," she pointed out to him. "Is that what Jenny would have wanted you to do?"

"Jenny's dead thanks to him. And why are you defending the man when there's a good possibility that he sent your father to prison for a crime he didn't commit?" Spencer demanded.

"I'm not defending him. And if he's guilty, I want

him to pay for that crime because he was wrong, not because I'm blinded by the need for revenge. And no matter how much I appreciate your help, I won't allow you to use me to get back at Caine."

"I'm not using you any more than you're using me. You're looking for answers about your mother's murder and your father's trial. I'm looking for a story that will expose Caine for the man he really is."

"You want more than a story. You want to destroy him."

Spencer hadn't liked her comments, particularly because they hit very close to the truth. "I'd be lying if I said I didn't want Caine to go down because of Jenny. I do, and I've never tried to hide that fact from you. But I also want to help you, Tess."

"Why?"

"Because it's the right thing to do. No kid should have to grow up without her family."

"I had my grandparents," she reminded him.

"It's not the same. If Caine took your father from you, he needs to account for that." He paused, and added, "And maybe if I expose him, it'll stop other girls like Jenny from ending up like she did."

"Careful, Reed, your noble streak is showing," she said and gave him a half smile.

"That's me. Noble Spencer Reed. And all this noble talk is making me hungry," he said as they approached the outskirts of Grady. "What do you say we stop in town and get something to eat?"

"I don't know. I was planning to go back to the cottage and start sorting through these letters. I also need to call my grandparents."

"Both the letters and your grandparents will be there after you eat."

"But—"

"No but. You need to eat and so do I. How does a big, juicy burger and fries sound to you?" he asked as he turned off onto Main Street.

"Actually, it sounds pretty good."

"And I know where they serve the best burgers this side of the Mississippi River." He pulled his SUV into the packed parking lot of the Dixie Belle Diner. He swung into a spot as a pickup truck left. Shutting off the engine, he exited the vehicle and went around to open the passenger door for Tess.

"Thanks," she murmured and he led her to the restaurant's entrance.

The place was packed. The jukebox was wailing and the bar was doing a bang-up business, Spencer noted as he stepped inside. He sniffed, caught the strong scent of good home cooking.

"It looks pretty busy," Tess remarked. "Do you think we'll be able to get a table?"

"Sure. I know the manager," he said.

"Why am I not surprised?"

He laughed. "Come on," he said, ushering her over to the woman whose back was to them, but who was as round as she was tall. He wrapped his arms around her ample girth and whispered, "Hi, beautiful."

She swung around and his aunt Sarah's eyes lit up. "Spencer James Reed," she said and hugged him to her apron-covered bosom that smelled like onion rings, grease and fries. "Your momma told me you were in town and I was wondering if you were going to come see me. Oh and who is this pretty girl you have with you?" she asked upon noticing Tess.

"Aunt Sarah, this is Tess Abbott. Tess, my aunt, Sarah Reed."

"How do you do, Mrs. Reed?" Tess replied politely, extending her hand.

His aunt looked at her hand a moment, finally shook it and then said, "My goodness, child. You're certainly tall enough, but there's no meat on those bones of yours." She looked over at him. "You're not feeding her enough."

"That's why I'm here. You think you can squeeze us in for dinner?"

"Of course I can." She scanned the busy rooms, then her face brightened. "Come, come, let me see what we can do to fatten your girl up for you," she said and began herding them to the rear of the restaurant.

"Thanks, Aunt Sarah," Spencer told her after she'd seated them in a booth.

"I'll send you over some hush puppies to munch on," she said.

"Hush puppies?" Tess repeated as she looked across the booth at him.

"Sort of a cornmeal batter with onions, jalapeños and spices that's shaped into a ball and deep-fried. They're delicious," he assured her.

"Ginger," his aunt called over to the blond waitress coming out of the kitchen. "Bring my nephew and his girl over here some hush puppies."

"Your aunt's quite a character," Tess told him after they had been left alone. "Do you have a big family?"

"Sometimes I think it's too big," he joked.

"What?"

He leaned closer in order to hear her over the din of the restaurant where the voices had risen to compete with the jukebox and the clanking of glasses and dinnerware. "I said sometimes I think it's too big. There are only three of us kids, but both of my parents come from big families, so I have an army of aunts, uncles and cousins. What about you?"

"Just my grandparents. Both of my parents were only children. I don't remember my father's mother well. I was told she died the year after he went to prison."

"Then I guess you don't know the joys of fighting for the bathroom and no hot water in the mornings," he teased. But Spencer couldn't help but feel sad for her. He'd always taken his own family for granted and though they drove him crazy at times, he wouldn't trade them for anything.

The waitress arrived and plopped down the dish of hush puppies on the center of the table. "Here you go, folks. Tonight's special is chicken-fried steak," she began and started to serve Tess a glass of water, when suddenly the glass slipped from the woman's hand.

Tess grabbed the overturned glass, righting it while Spencer reached for a stack of napkins. Quickly he piled them atop the spill to stop it from spreading. "Did it get you?" he asked Tess.

"No, I'm fine."

"I'm sorry," the waitress mumbled. "I'm so sorry."

"It's all right. Really. It's no big deal," Spencer told the waitress who had paled and whose hands were still unsteady.

"He's right. It's okay," Tess assured her.

"But I think we're going to need some more hush puppies since these got a little soggy," Spencer pointed out.

"Yes, sir. I'll bring them right out."

Maggie O'Donnell sat in the bar of the Dixie Belle Diner and tried to remember the last time she'd been stood up on a date. Her freshman year in high school for the winter formal, she recalled. That was when Mack had broken his leg during football practice and had been taken to the emergency room at the hospital. Since he had finally shown up in a cast and on pain medication, she wasn't really sure that counted. And if that didn't count, then Sheriff Andy Trudeaux would have the distinct honor of being the first man to have ever stood her up.

You're an idiot, Maggie. That's what you are. Why on earth did you even suggest the man meet you for dinner when you ran into him this morning?

Because she'd been lonely, Maggie admitted. A part of her had died along with Mack in that hospital room four years ago. During those first six months after he was gone, she'd had a hard time even facing each morning without him. She'd prayed and prayed for direction on what to do with the rest of her life. When she'd received that magazine in the mail and it had fallen open to the advertisement about the auction of a Southern estate, she'd taken it as a sign from Mack and the Almighty that she needed to move on with her life. Of course, she'd horrified her family and friends when she'd packed herself up and headed for Mississippi. But she'd never regretted the decision. It had been love at first sight for her when she'd seen the property with its rolling hills, bluffs and thickets of trees. Even in its rundown state the main house had stolen her heart. She knew at once it was where she belonged. So she'd bought it and spent two years restoring it and turning it into one of the premier guesthouses in Mississippi.

Yet even as busy as she was, she hadn't been able to fill the hole the loss of Mack had left in her heart. Oh, she had dated. After all, she was fairly attractive, she acknowledged, and the fact that she was also wealthy didn't hurt. Men asked her out and well-meaning friends were always introducing her to eligible men. But no matter how handsome or nice any of them had been, not a one of them had made her heart beat faster, or made her stomach get all jiggly.

Until she had met Sheriff Andy Trudeaux.

For the first time in the four years since Mack had died, she had actually felt a stirring of desire for a man. And every feminine bone in her body told her that Andy had felt something, too. Unfortunately, the man seemed bound and determined to outright ignore that spark between them and to outright ignore her. So she'd taken the bull by the horns and asked him out. It was probably because she'd caught him off guard that he'd accepted, she realized. Only now, he had evidently thought better of the idea and decided not to come.

"You want another soda while you wait, Maggie?" Harry the bartender asked.

She checked her watch again, noted Andy was thirty minutes late and decided to cut her losses. "I don't think so, Harry. It looks like my date is a no-show." She opened her bag, withdrew a five-dollar bill and slid it over the counter.

"Put it on my tab, Harry" a deep voice with a touch of the South sounded from directly behind her. He touched her shoulder and whispered in her ear, "Sorry I'm late."

Maggie's pulse jumped as she caught the whiff of his cologne—something that smelled like pine trees in a forest. When she turned on the stool and looked up into his deep green eyes, her stomach somersaulted. "I thought you'd chickened out. I was about to give up on you."

He arched one dark eyebrow. "You obviously don't know Southern men very well. I would never stand up a lady. I had to handle an incident—sheriff's business—on the other side of town and it took longer than I expected." He lifted his hand and motioned to the bartender. "What are you drinking?" he asked her.

"Plain soda."

"You want another one or something stronger?"

Maggie hesitated. "Mint julep."

He smiled. "I see my mother's introduced you to what she considers the proper spirits for a Southern lady."

Maggie laughed. "I didn't realize that's what it was. But you're right. Susan was the one who introduced me to them."

"A mint julep for the lady, Harry. And a beer for me."

"Coming right up, Sheriff," the jolly-faced man said and set off to the other end of the bar to prepare their orders.

Andy slid onto the stool next to hers, his long legs brushing against her knees in the process. "What made you accept my dinner invitation?" she asked.

"You mean besides the fact that I knew it would make my mother ecstatic?"

"Yes, besides that," she said, smiling.

"Because you were right. I am interested."

He made the admission with such utter self-disgust that Maggie couldn't help herself. She laughed aloud.

"Go ahead and laugh. But my mother's probably making up the guest list for the wedding as we speak."

Maggie leaned closer, patted his arm. "Don't worry, Andy. As much as I adore your mother and would do just about anything to make her happy—even marry you—I promise I won't start picking out china until you're ready."

"One mint julep and one beer," Harry said as he presented the drinks. "If you folks need anything else, just give me a holler. Miss Sarah says she should have a table for you in about ten minutes."

"Thanks, Harry," he said. Keeping his eyes on her, he took a swig of his beer. When he set the bottle down again, he told her, "I meant what I said the other day. I'm not looking for a wife."

"Well shoot, I guess I better cancel that subscription I just ordered to *Bride's Magazine*."

She hadn't thought the man could look any more somber, but he did. "I'm serious, Maggie. I'm not looking for a relationship."

Maggie sighed and set her drink aside. Leaning forward a fraction, she said, "I know you're not, Andy. And the truth is, I'm not looking for a husband. I already had one. He was the love of my life and when he died, a part of me died with him. I remind myself every day how lucky I was to have the years that we had and I don't delude myself thinking that I'll find that again."

"Then why'd you ask me to dinner?"

"Because I thought it might be nice to enjoy an evening out with an attractive man, someone near my own age, and you were selected."

"I didn't realize I was on the menu."

"Susan put you on the menu. She loves you and she loves me and she wants us both to be happy. And for her generation being happy means being part of a couple. That's why she keeps pushing us together," she explained.

"I don't need to be married to be happy."

"Neither do I. But where's the harm in having someone to share a meal with, some conversation once in a while?"

"I don't see where there is any. Unless you count my mother's disappointment when we tell her we're not getting married."

"I told you, we'll just tell her there's no chemistry. She'll understand."

"We both know there's chemistry, Maggie. The question is, what are we going to do about it?"

Maggie was saved from answering when Sarah Reed called out, "Sheriff, Maggie. Your table's ready."

The table was crammed into a small corner next to a window that looked out onto the parking lot. A simple red-and-white-checked cloth covered the two-top instead of fine linen. A plastic rose shoved into a colored glass adorned the table instead of fresh flowers. The napkins were made of paper and the music was a lonesome tune on a jukebox—not a live orchestra. Yet, it was one of the most romantic evenings she'd ever had, Maggie thought as she took another taste of the Mississippi mud pie she'd ordered for dessert.

"You planning to eat that whole thing?" Andy asked her.

"I'm thinking about it. Why? Did you want some?"

He made a face. "I'm not a chocolate fan."

"Well, there you go," she said with a sigh. "I guess there's no chance for us now. I could never marry a man who didn't like chocolate."

He laughed and the curve of his mouth changed his entire face. He went from handsome and brooding to downright gorgeous and lovable. "Then I guess that puts me out of the running."

"You folks need anything else?" the waitress asked as she appeared at the table with the check.

"I think we're fine," Andy said.

"I'll take that," Maggie said, reaching for the check.

Andy scooped it away. "My treat," he said and plunked down several bills before handing it back to the waitress. "Keep the change."

"But I invited you," she told him.

"You're in the South, Maggie O'Donnell. No self-respecting Southern gentleman allows a lady to pay for the meal. Besides, I enjoyed myself."

She laughed. "You sound surprised."

"I guess I am. I wasn't sure I would," he answered honestly. He stood, walked around the table and held out her chair. "I'd like to see you again."

Her heart skipped a couple of beats at the statement. But she kept her voice light as she said, "You know where I live and my phone number's in the book."

As they left the table, Maggie nodded to various acquaintances and tried to maneuver through the busy restaurant. When she felt Andy stiffen beside her, she stopped, glanced up at him. His face had gone hard again and she noted the direction of his gaze. It was Tess, she realized, and Bill Reed's son, Spencer. "Is something wrong?"

"I just saw your friend, the Abbott woman. I left several messages for her today and she hasn't returned my calls. I had some questions I needed to ask her."

"She's been out all day," Maggie told him, her protective instincts kicking in. Even at a distance, she could see her friend looked drained. She'd known Tess was supposed to visit the prison where her father had served his time, and Maggie had a sneaking suspicion that Andy's questions would only add to her friend's strain. "I'm sure she'll get back to you tomorrow." She hooked her arm through his. "Would you mind walking me to my car?"

Andy didn't argue. He led her outside where the night had turned chilly and a breeze was blowing from the north. "The little white convertible over there," she said, pointing to her car. He walked her to the car and after unlocking the door, she turned to him and said, "Thank you for tonight. I really enjoyed myself."

"Me, too," he told her.

And before she changed her mind, she pressed a quick kiss to his lips. But when she started to withdraw, he pulled her back and gave her a real kiss. He slid his hands into her hair, angled her head for better access and kissed her. His tongue skimmed her lips, danced along her tongue. She could taste the wine he'd had at dinner, the apple from the slice of pie he'd had for dessert. She could taste the hunger, carefully held in check.

She heard the wind whistling through the trees. She heard a car door slam somewhere. She heard his soft groan as he eased his body away from hers. Then he lifted his head. And it took Maggie a moment to focus again.

After he'd opened her door and she'd slid inside, he leaned in and said, "Good night, Maggie."

And as Maggie drove from the parking lot, she touched her fingers to her lips, still warm with the taste of Andy Trudeaux, and smiled. She couldn't help wondering if he realized that he was already in over his head.

Chapter Eleven

"You were right about the burgers," Tess told Spencer as he walked her to the door of her cottage that evening. "Thank you."

"Anytime," he told her. He shifted the box containing her father's things under one arm and held his hand out for her key. She gave it to him and he unlocked the door.

She went in ahead of him and flipped a switch just inside the door, sending a soft glow from the lamps spilling into the living room. "You can put the box over there on the coffee table," she said, indicating the square wooden piece around which two small sofas had been grouped.

He set the box down and then placed the key in her outstretched palm. He did a quick glance around the room. "This is nice, cozy. But it's kind of isolated."

"That's why I chose it. I wanted some space and my privacy."

He walked over to the windows where pretty, lace curtains added to the coziness of the room. He checked the locks on each of the windows then asked, "Is there a guard on the grounds?"

"Reed, I'm a big girl. I'm used to being alone, and right now I'm beat. So I'd like to call it a night," she told him.

For a moment, she thought he was going to argue with her, but instead he simply said, "All right. Just make sure you lock the door behind me and put on the safety chain."

"I will," she promised as she led him to the door. "And, Reed?"

He turned back, looked at her. "Yeah?"

"Thanks for going with me today. Being in that place…" She had kept imagining her father living there, dying there, writing to her from his cell. "It was a lot more difficult than I thought it would be, more difficult than when I went the last time."

"He was your father, Tess. No matter what he did or didn't do, or whatever else has happened since, he was a part of you. Being in the place where you know he died—that would have been hard for anyone."

"I know. It's just that it's been so many years since I thought of Jody Burns as my father, so I…" She paused, searching for a way to explain. "I didn't expect to feel anything. I expected to just go there, talk to the warden, find out what I could and analyze the data so that I could solve the puzzle."

"And instead you discovered you had a father who apparently never stopped loving you."

She nodded. "All those years. He wrote to me all those years."

He cupped her cheek with his palm and she looked

up at him, met the warmth in those clear blue eyes. "You were still his little girl."

"But I hated him for so long."

"And now?"

"Now I don't know what I should feel."

"Forget about what you should feel. What do you feel?"

"Sad. For him. For me. And angry." She felt angry toward her grandfather for returning those letters, year after year. Angry with him for not telling her about their existence. And she felt angry with herself. For closing her heart and mind to the fact that she had a father. A father who had loved her, who had written her a letter each year on her birthday for twenty-five years, letters he knew she would probably never read.

"It's okay to feel those things and anything else you want to feel. I'd be worried if you didn't feel anything. Believe me, it's the trying not to feel that's a problem, because when the emotions finally do come through— and they will—the explosion is even worse."

"Experience talking again?" she asked, recalling all the anguish she'd heard in his voice, read in his face when he'd told her about Jenny.

He nodded. He looked beyond her over to where she realized he'd placed the box on the table. "You sure you're going to be okay here by yourself?"

For a moment she considered asking him to stay because she wasn't sure she wanted to face the box of letters alone. Just as quickly she dismissed the notion. As she'd told him, she was a big girl, a competent investigative reporter. She'd promised herself that she'd research the murder like any other story and those letters might hold clues to the puzzle. "I'm sure."

"Then I'll say good-night."

She'd expected a peck on the cheek, maybe even a swift buss on the lips from one colleague to another who just happened to be of the opposite sex. She'd been given those friendly kisses dozens of times from friends and co-workers alike. What she hadn't expected was for Spencer to kiss her the way a man kisses a woman.

But that's what he did. He gave her a real kiss, one in which he cupped her head in his hands and brought them together, body to body, mouth to mouth. She also hadn't expected that flash of heat, that stab of need when his tongue slid between her lips and sought her out.

She could feel his arousal pressed hard and heavy against her. Desire pooled in her belly like liquid heat. She felt a throbbing in her blood and she slipped her arms around his neck, speared her fingers through all that thick dark hair and took the kiss even deeper.

It was Spencer who broke the kiss. He eased his head up a fraction, looked at her through eyes that had turned the color of midnight. "What in the hell just happened?"

"I'm not sure," she said, stunned by her response to him. She took a step back. "It was probably the alcohol," she offered.

"We each had a beer," he reminded her.

"Well, it shouldn't have happened. I don't even like you," she said in frustration, because the last thing she needed was to complicate things by getting involved with the likes of Spencer Reed.

"You're not exactly my type either."

"Good. Then let's just forget what happened."

"I don't think so."

She eyed him warily. "Why not?"

"Because I don't want to forget it," he told her. He eased closer, slid a lock of her hair behind her ear, and the feel of his fingers on her skin sent a shiver through her that had nothing to do with the chill in the night air. "The truth is, I'd been wanting to do that for some time now. And I wouldn't mind doing it again."

She caught his hand, met his eyes. "I *would* mind. Back off, Reed. I've got enough on my plate to deal with right now. A relationship with you is a complication I don't want or need."

He hesitated a moment, then dropped his hand. "You're right. The timing sucks. So I'll back off. For now."

"Reed—"

He kissed her forehead. "I'll see you tomorrow. Try to get some rest."

And then he was gone.

Tess closed the door behind him, then leaned her head against it. Before things got any more complicated than they already were, she had to find the answers she came for and then go home.

Home.

That meant Washington. The news station. Her grandparents. She'd been gone little more than two weeks, but already it seemed as though they belonged to another lifetime. Or perhaps it was she who didn't belong, Tess thought. Feeling exhausted, she bolted the door and turned off the lights and started for the bedroom. She paused by the coffee table and stared at the box marked Burns, Jody, with a number stamped on the side, along with the date of his death. Removing the lid from the box, she retrieved the bundle of letters bound by a knotted string. She sat down on the couch and stared at the letters…all addressed to her.

Tess was still sitting there staring at the letters in her lap when her cell phone began to ring. She reached for her purse on the end of the table and fished out the phone. She stared at the caller ID, recognized her grandfather's private number at the senate. Although she'd spoken with her grandmother several times, she hadn't spoken to her grandfather since the night she'd told him she was coming to Mississippi. The message she'd left on his voice mail just before she'd left D.C. telling him she was sorry he didn't approve of what she was doing and hoping he would understand someday, remained unanswered. Knowing him as she did, she doubted he was calling her now because he'd had a change of heart. Taking a deep breath, she answered, "Hello."

"You want to tell me just what in the hell you think you're doing calling the lieutenant governor's office and demanding to see him?"

"It's nice to hear from you, too, Grandfather."

"Don't use that tone with me, young lady," he said, lowering his voice to that deep Southern rumble that had often frightened her as a child because she'd known it was his angry tone. Just the sound of his voice evoked his image—a big man, well over six feet and two hundred pounds, silver hair combed straight back from a broad forehead and dark gray eyes in a face that stayed tanned year-round. "You know I won't tolerate a fresh mouth or disrespect—particularly not from my own flesh and blood."

"I meant no disrespect, Grandfather."

"Then what do you call what you're doing? It's a total lack of respect for me and your grandmother, as well as to the memory of your mother."

"I'm sorry you feel that way. But believe it or not,

my presence here has nothing to do with you or grandmother. It has to do with me. If you'd bothered to listen to me the last time we spoke, I tried to explain to
you that I needed answers about what really happened
to my mother, and about my father's death."

"You already know what happened to your mother.
That worthless scum she married killed her, and his
conscience finally got the best of him and he killed
himself."

"I'm not so sure that is what happened, and that's
what I intend to find out."

"Is that why you've been browbeating the staff at the
Mississippi State Penitentiary for information about
Burns?"

Tess's jaw tightened. "Maybe you're the one who
needs to do the explaining, Grandfather. Like how you
knew I was there."

"I don't have to explain myself to you."

"Actually, you do. And I think you also need to explain why I was never told that my father had written
to me, and why his letters were returned?"

"That you should even have to ask me why tells me
that you're obviously not yourself. I knew that spat
you and Jonathan had upset you, I just never realized
how much. Perhaps if I called him—"

"Stop it, Grandfather! This has nothing to do with
Jonathan. This is about you keeping something important from me. Those letters were to me. Me," she told
him. "You had no right—"

"I had every right! You were in my care and I swore
on your mother's grave that I would see Jody Burns
burn in hell for what he did to her. I may have been too
late to save Melanie, but I wasn't going to let him ruin
your life the way he did hers. Why do you think I had

your name changed to Abbott? I wanted every trace of him erased from your life and, by God, I did it."

"Actually, you didn't. My name may be Abbott, but half of me is still Jody Burns. And nothing you do will ever change that."

"You obviously don't care about my feelings, but maybe you do care about your grandmother. Do you have any idea how hard this is on her, having you dig up all this stuff from the past? You know she's not as strong as she used to be—not since the cancer."

"Don't," Tess said, dropping her voice in warning. She closed her eyes a moment and struggled to hang on to her temper. "Don't you dare try to use Grams to manipulate me. I've spoken to her more than a half-dozen times since I left home. She may not particularly like what I'm doing, but she understands why I'm doing it, and the only thing that is upsetting to her is your anger with me."

"There's obviously no reasoning with you, Tess. So I won't waste any more of my time."

And without so much as a goodbye, he hung up the phone.

Spencer sat outside the cottage in his car and rested his head against the steering wheel, waiting for the chilly night air to bring his temperature down.

Jesus. Talk about getting knocked on your ass. One little kiss and he'd been like a randy teenager—hot, hard and tied up in knots!

Hell, he'd known there were sparks between them. It had been pretty difficult to ignore. He was a red-blooded male and she was an attractive female. That equation usually added up to lust. Lust he could handle. But no way had he expected the explosion of passion generated by that kiss. And no way had he expected the flood of emotion.

It was the sadness in her eyes, knowing she was hurting and feeling guilt over those letters, that made him wait outside the cottage now. Not until he saw the lights go off did he start his engine. Getting involved with Tess Abbott was a complication he hadn't counted on, he admitted as he navigated the dark roadway. The lady was smart, strong-willed and as stubborn as a mule.

Every journalistic instinct told him he was close to finding what he needed to bring down Caine, and that Tess Abbott would be able to provide the key. He was close, so close he could almost taste it. The problem was, he hadn't counted on Tess's feelings. Nor had he counted on his own.

You're walking a fine line, Reed.

But it was too late to turn back now, he admitted. While he'd tried telling himself that they were using each other, working as a team, he hadn't been able to fully justify that in his own mind. He couldn't help wishing he'd told her straight out that he'd gotten calls from the mystery woman, too.

And if you had, she would have shut you out.

It was true. She'd been as wary as a long-tailed cat in a roomful of rocking chairs, and if he had said a word about the calls he'd gotten she would never have let him get this close. Second-guessing himself now wouldn't help, he reasoned, because there was no way he could back off now. He would just have to hope that he'd be able to make her understand when he finally did tell her everything.

Since he always stayed with his parents when he was in town, he took the exit to Grady. A short time later, he turned onto the tree-lined street that led to the house he'd grown up in. He parked in front of the two-story ranch and made his way up the walkway to the front door. Using his key, he let himself inside, locked the door and turned off the outside lights. He started for the stairs that led upstairs to the bedrooms, avoiding the floorboard that creaked so as not to awaken his parents. But as he reach the bottom of the stairs, he noted the light on down the hall in his father's study and headed in that direction.

He tapped lightly on the door and opened it. "Pop?"

His father swiveled the old leather chair around and looked up at him over the rim of the glasses perched on his nose. "Hey, son. You just getting in?"

"Yes. What are you still doing up?" he asked as he came into the room.

Big Bill Reed removed his glasses, rubbed his eyes. "Just going through some old files from my reporting days."

Spencer sat down in one of the chairs in front of his father's desk. He couldn't help remembering all the times he'd sat in that same chair as a kid and a teenager while his father had sat on the other side of the desk and dispensed advice, outlined punishments and offered him an ear when he'd needed one. It had been something he'd taken for granted, he realized. "Find anything interesting?"

"Actually, I did. I came across some of the notes I made during the Jody Burns trial. Mostly just observations, things I jotted down before writing my story. I even found a couple of tapes I'd made during the trial."

"Tapes?" Spencer repeated.

"Yeah. I never trusted myself to get statements verbatim, so I usually carried a pocket recorder with me when I did a story. I taped some parts of the testimony in the murder trial to use for my reports. Most of the time, I erased the tapes and used them over again. But for some reason, I stuck these two in an envelope with my notes and filed them away."

Spencer thought of the anonymous caller. Whoever she was, she was someone who knew about the trial. He wondered if maybe he'd be able to recognize her voice again if it were on the tape. "Would you mind if I listened to them?"

"No. As a matter of fact I was going to see if Tess wanted to take a look at any of my notes—see if they might help her."

"I'm sure she'd appreciate that. I can give them to her, if you'd like."

His father handed him the envelope and the file, then sat back in his chair. He rested his elbows on the arms of the chair and steepled his fingers together. "You and she have been spending a lot of time together."

"I'm helping her research her father's murder trail, remember?"

"Is that what you two were doing out at dinner tonight? Research?"

"Aunt Sarah," he said.

His father nodded. "Called to let your mother and me know you were in the restaurant with a pretty girl tonight. Said you two looked real cozy and she wanted to know if it was serious."

"It was just dinner, Pop. We went to the prison today. They gave Tess her father's personal effects," he explained, still recalling the stricken look on Tess's face when she'd found those letters in the box. "It was kind of rough on her and I wanted to take her mind off things for a while." Although he worried about her now that she was alone for the night.

His father picked up his pipe. "If that's the only reason you took her out tonight, then I haven't done a very good job of raising you. In case you haven't noticed, Tess Abbott is a beautiful woman."

"I've noticed. But just because I'm attracted to her doesn't mean I can afford to lose focus on what I have to do."

"You mean, using her to help you bring down Everett Caine because of what happened to Jenny."

"I'm not using her," Spencer retorted. "I'm helping her find out what role Caine played in her father's conviction. And yes, I'm hoping that by doing so I'll find something that I can use against Caine."

"And you think that's fair to Tess?"

"I haven't made my motives any secret, Pop. She knows about Jenny and she knows why I want to get Caine."

"And she's okay with that?" he asked.

"She just wants to find out the truth. And I have to tell you that from the stuff I've read so far," Spencer told him, "personally I don't think the man did it. I think someone else killed Melanie Burns and I think Everett Caine knew it."

"You don't think you're letting your personal feelings about Caine cloud your judgment?"

"No, I don't. One of the first things you taught me when I started reporting was to examine the facts and listen to my gut. Well, the facts don't add up and my gut keeps telling me they don't add up because Caine had a hand in them. Somehow I'm going to prove it. For Jenny's sake—and for Tess's."

His father looked at him for a long moment. He set

the pipe aside and leaned forward. "Everett Caine's a smart and ambitious man with a lot of friends, Spencer. He won't sit back and do nothing while you try to destroy him. Especially not now when he's so close to winning the governor's race. You need to be careful, son. For your sake, and for Tess's."

"I will," he promised as he stood up. He picked up the file folder and the envelope containing the tapes that he'd rested on the edge of the desk. "Can I borrow that old tape player of yours?"

"Sure." His father reached down to the corner of a shelving unit and retrieved the dusty, black recording device. He handed it to Spencer.

"Thanks, Pop. I'll see you in the morning," he said and exited the study. He took the stairs two at a time, eager to get to his room so he could listen to the tapes from the trial and see if he recognized the voice of any of the witnesses as belonging to the mystery caller.

But nearly two hours later when he shut off the recorder in the middle of Virginia Lee's testimony about her relationship with Jody Burns, Spencer was no closer to identifying his mystery caller than he had been when he'd started. Tomorrow he would have Tess listen to the tape and see what she thought. After turning off the lamp, he collapsed onto the bed. And his last thought before drifting off to sleep was of Tess. The feel of her in his arms. The taste of her on his lips.

Tess tossed and turned in bed, too restless to sleep. In the two hours since Spencer had left and she'd talked to her grandfather, she'd roamed the tiny cottage. At first, she'd been too disturbed by her conversation with her grandfather to sleep. And as she paced the room, trying to settle down, her gaze kept returning to the box on the coffee table. Finally, she'd retrieved the bundle of letters from her father and sat down on the couch. She simply sat there for the longest time, just holding them. A part of her wanted to read them. A part of her feared doing so.

When exhaustion began to set in, she'd taken the packet of letters with her into the bedroom and placed them on the bureau. She wasn't ready to read them yet, she acknowledged as she prepared for bed. She was afraid to open the door that had been closed for so many years.

But now more than an hour later as she lay awake in bed, her eyes once again strayed to the white wicker chest and the stack of letters atop it. Sitting up, Tess turned on the bedside lamp. She flung back the mountain of covers and padded across the room in her bare feet. She stood for a long moment, staring at the letters. Then she snatched up the bundle and crawled back into bed. She looked down at the plain white envelopes, the faded blue ink that spelled out Tess Burns. She untied the string and opened the first letter.

My Darling Tess—

Happy birthday, sweet girl! It's hard to believe you're five years old today and that I'm not with you to celebrate. But I'm sure your grams and grandfather bought you a cake. I worried that they wouldn't know that pink is your favorite color and I hope that you told them. That's how I imagine you today. In a room filled with balloons and presents, standing on top of a chair in front of a cake with pink icing and pink candles, blowing them out.

I know you can't read this letter, but I've asked your grandparents to read it to you so that you

*don't think I've forgotten you. I haven't, Tess. I
worry whether or not you will be able to understand everything that has happened and why I'm
not with you. I know I frightened you that night
when your mother died, and you thought I was
the one who had hurt her. It wasn't me, Tess. I
swear to God it wasn't me. I loved her so much
and would sooner have died myself than hurt her.
In fact, I wanted to die because she was gone and,
in my grief, I didn't fight as hard as I should
have. I didn't fight for you. Forgive me, Tess.
Please forgive me.*

*I'm going to fight now. I'm going to try to get
a new trial and gain my freedom. But until I do,
I know you'll be in good hands with your grams
and grandfather. Until then, know that Daddy
loves you, Tess. I haven't forgotten you. I'll never
forget you or stop loving you.*

I love and miss you, Tess.
Daddy

Tess folded the letter and slipped it back inside the
envelope. She placed it on top of the stack and stared
at two dozen envelopes all written in that same neat
script. She didn't want to read any more of the letters. It hurt too much, she admitted. But she needed
to read them, she told herself. She owed him at least
that much.

She picked up the next letter and the next, continuing
to read, her heart aching more with each one she read.
Her cheeks now damp with tears, she opened another one.

Happy Birthday, Tess—

Today you're sweet sixteen. Sixteen! You're almost a woman now. Your mother was only a few years older than you are now when I first saw her walking across the campus. She was so beautiful and had the prettiest smile. I fell in love with her right then and there.

When you were born I was so glad that you looked like her, that you had her eyes and her smile. I know that you're beautiful because you were beautiful even when you were just an infant and most babies aren't really pretty at all. But you were. You were always beautiful, Tess. Still, I wonder what you look like now. Do you look even more like your mother now than you did at four? I have the picture of the two of you, the one where you wore the matching Christmas dresses. I look at it every day and it makes me feel closer to both of you.

What I wouldn't give to be able to see you, Tess. Sometimes at night I dream that these past twelve years are just a nightmare. That your mother is still alive, that we're still living in Grady in that little blue house, that you're a happy teenager and I'm a proud father eyeing the young man who's coming to call on you. Then I wake up and the nightmare is real. Your mother is dead. I'm in a jail cell, and you, you don't even know who I am.

The guards here at the prison think I'm crazy because I keep writing to you and my letters keeping coming back. But I write anyway. I'm hoping that once you're an adult and the decision of whether or not to have any contact with me is

*yours and not the senator's, you will want me to
write to you. So I'm keeping the letters for you,
Tess, and hoping that someday you will read them
and know how very much I continue to love you.*
    I love and miss you.
    Daddy

Tess folded the letter and slid it back inside the envelope, then she retied the bundle. After placing the packet on the nightstand, she turned off the lamp and laid down in the bed. Then she buried her face in the pillow and wept.

Chapter Twelve

Spencer studied Tess's face as she entered the offices of the *Grady Gazette* the next morning. She'd been crying, he realized, noting the puffiness around her eyes that her makeup hadn't been able to quite cover. It made him wish, not for the first time, that he had insisted on staying with her the previous night. Not because he wanted to be with her in a sexual way, although he did want that, too, he admitted. But because he might have been able to comfort her, hold her while she cried.

He poured a cup of coffee, added sugar and cream, then walked over to the reception area where she was talking to his father. "'Morning," he said and handed her the cup of coffee. "Two sugars and a touch of cream, just the way you like it."

She eyed him warily. "Thanks," she murmured, taking the cup from him.

Ignoring the questioning look his father gave him,

he said, "Mind if I steal Tess for a few minutes, Pop? I'm going to need to leave soon and there's some stuff I want to go over with her."

"Not at all, son." He turned his focus back to Tess. "But before I forget, my wife, Ellen, wants me to invite you to dinner on Friday night."

"I…yes, of course," she said. "Can I bring anything?"

"Nope. Just yourself. It won't be anything fancy, but the food will be good."

"I'll look forward to it then," she told him.

Spencer walked with her down the hall to the office where she'd been working. "I wondered when my mom was going to get around to having you over for the family inspection."

She stopped in front of the door and looked up at him out of curious gray eyes. "The inspection?"

Spencer smiled. "Uh-huh. Thanks to my aunt Sarah, my mother got wind of our date last night and—"

"It wasn't a date."

"—and since I'm her favorite and only son, she wants to take a closer look at the lady I'm involved with."

"We are not involved."

He planted a swift kiss on her lips. "Sure we are," he said, determined to distract her and take her mind off yesterday's visit to the prison. "After you," he said and urged her into the office, then closed the door behind them.

Tess dumped her bag on a chair and placed her coffee cup on top of the conference table. She immediately turned to face him and he was pleased to see some color in her cheeks again. "Listen, Reed," she began. "I think we need to get something straight about last night."

"What about it?" he asked, crowding her.

"I wasn't myself. I was tired and emotional. And while I'll admit I did enjoy the kiss, I don't want you to get the wrong idea."

"Tess, darling, I'm not sure if you'd call the ideas I've been having about us wrong, but I can tell you they're a bit on the wicked side."

She blinked, looked at him as though he'd lost his mind.

"But as much as I'd like to tell you about them, I think we're going to have to put that on hold—at least for the time being. I have to leave for Jackson in an hour to cover the gubernatorial debate and I wanted you to listen to some tape recordings from your father's trial to see if you recognize the woman's voice on them."

"What tapes? Where are they? How did you get them?" She fired off the questions and completely dropped the subject of their relationship and the kiss.

Spencer breathed a little easier, relieved to see that the haunted look that had been in her eyes when she'd arrived had been replaced once again with the fiery determination of the woman who had waltzed into the *Gazette*'s offices in search of information less than two weeks ago. "These tapes," he said, indicating the two cassettes in his palm. "And I got them from my father, along with some of his handwritten notes from the trial. He had them in a file at home. Apparently he taped portions of the testimony because he didn't trust his reporter's shorthand to get it down correctly."

"Have you listened to them?"

"Yes." He wished now more than ever he had told her about the mysterious calls. But to do so now would destroy any trust he'd developed with her. He needed that trust to carry through on his plan. He also didn't want to ruin what was happening between them. Later, he promised himself. When all of this was over, when she had the answers she needed about her father and he had brought down Caine, he would explain everything to her and make her understand.

"Whose testimony is it?"

"Virginia Lee's," he said, naming the woman who claimed she was having an affair with Tess's father.

"You think she might have been the one who called me at the TV station?"

"I think it's a possibility since she claimed to be a friend of your father's. If it is her, then we would at least know who we were looking for," he explained. Although he'd listened to both tapes twice himself and hadn't thought Virginia Lee was the woman who'd called him, he wasn't a hundred percent sure. It made him wish he was one of those people who had an ear for voices. "Why don't you sit over there at the end of the table. I've already got the tape player set up."

Tess took the seat. She laced her fingers together and sat perfectly still while he slipped the tape into the machine. For several seconds the only sound in the room was the whirring noise of the tape rewinding in the old black recorder designed for the small cassettes. Finally the humming sound ceased and the tape clicked.

"This is the one where your father's attorney, Beau Clayton, is cross-examining her." He had deliberately chosen to play that tape for her because it at least refuted some of the allegations that were made under Caine's examination of the woman. "The sound quality isn't that great and some of the stuff she says…well, the picture she paints isn't a pretty one."

"I understand. Play the tape."

Spencer played the tape and together they listened as the woman acknowledged that her name was Virginia Lee, that she was employed at the Southern Lumber Mill and that it was there that she met Jody Burns with whom she began an affair that continued even after his employment at the mill ended. According to her the affair was still going strong at the time of his wife's murder.

"Miss Lee," the defense attorney began, his drawl thick but his enunciation clear. "You expect this court to believe that Jody Burns, a man whom his friends and neighbors knew as a devoted husband and father, was cheating on his wife and planning to leave her for you?"

"Like I said, it wasn't something that we planned on. It just happened. We were victims of love."

"A victim of love. Tell me, Miss Lee. Is that how you saw yourself when you deliberately pursued my client even though you knew he was married and he'd told you repeatedly that he was not interested?"

"It wasn't like that," Virginia sobbed, her sniffles loud and crackling on the tape.

"Then tell us what it was like, Miss Lee? If you were having an affair with my client and he was planning to leave his wife for you as you claimed, then how do you explain that no one ever saw you together as a couple?"

"People saw us. They saw us at the lumber mill, and at the bar where he worked."

"No, Miss Lee. They saw you talking to him in the break room at the mill and they saw you come

*and sit at the bar where he was working. But no
one saw him coming to see you."*

"We was being discreet," she defended.

*"So discreet that the two of you were never
alone together? The truth is, it wasn't discreet,
was it, Miss Lee? The entire affair is a figment of
your imagination. It is nonexistent, isn't it?"*

"Objection," Caine shouted.

*"That's why he never went to your home,"
Clayton continued.*

*"He couldn't come to my home because I lived
with my grandma. That's why we went to a hotel."*

*"But you just can't remember the name of the
hotel, and the prosecutor couldn't produce any
witnesses or receipts that showed my client was
ever in a hotel with you."*

*"Objection. Your Honor, the defense counsel
is making statements, not asking a question," the
prosecutor called out.*

Spencer hit the stop button, not wanting her to hear
the rest of it.

"Why did you stop it?"

"You've heard enough," Spencer told her.

"That's for me to decide. Play the tape, Reed. I want
to hear what else she has to say."

Spencer hit the play button and the testimony resumed.

*"I'll rephrase the question," Clayton coun-
tered. "Miss Lee, isn't the reason you can't remember the hotel name, and no one can identify
you as being in a hotel with my client, because
the two of you never had an affair? Isn't it a fact
that you never had sex with him at all?"*

"Yes, we did," she sobbed. "We did."

The judge's gavel pounded, objections rang out.

Yet, Virginia Lee went on, "We did it in my car and in his truck when no one was around to see us. He loved me. Jody loved me and he wanted to marry me. And he said if he had to, he'd kill that bitch he was married to so that he would be free and we could be together."

Spencer shut off the tape and waited.

"It's not her."

"Are you sure? Virginia Lee is twenty-five years older than she was on that tape, and the quality on the recording isn't that good," he pointed out.

"I know. But the woman I spoke with…her voice was more…more refined. I'm sure that's not her."

"Okay," he said and hit the rewind button on the cassette player. "It was worth a shot."

"Yes, it was," she told him. "What's on the other tape?"

"More of the same—testimony from Virginia Lee. Since she's not the caller, there's really no point in listening to it."

"I appreciate what you're doing, Reed. But it's not necessary."

"What is it you think I'm doing?" he asked.

"Trying to protect my feelings. I'm a big girl. I can take care of myself."

"I know that, but—"

"There is no but. I never expected this to be easy, but I am determined to see it through."

"I understand that, but why listen to that garbage if you don't have to? What purpose does it serve?"

"Because it gives me some insight into what my father went through. I started reading his letters last night," she said, her voice so soft it was almost a whisper.

At that moment the tape clicked as it reached the end of the rewind and the silence in the room was deafening. Spencer removed the tape and replaced it in the cassette case. He said nothing, waiting for her to continue.

"And I know all that stuff the woman said about her and my father being in love was a lie. She lied in that courtroom and they sent him to prison because of it. But none of it was true. He wasn't having an affair with her and he didn't kill my mother. He loved her. And he loved me." She looked up at him. "He wrote to me every year on my birthday. He never gave up hope that one day I might contact him. But I never did. I gave up on him and now he's dead."

"You can't blame yourself for that." Spencer knelt down beside her and stroked her hair. "If you blame anyone, Tess, blame your grandparents. They were the ones who returned the letters without telling you."

"That was my grandfather's doing and he knows how I feel about what he did. But not all the blame is his. No one stopped me from contacting my father once I was an adult. I was the one who chose not to. And now it's too late."

Spencer knew there was little use in pointing out that her mind had been poisoned against her father from the time she was a small child. But she didn't see it that way right now.

"I need to find the woman who called me and get her to tell me what she knows about my father's death and my mother's murder. And I need to locate Virginia Lee—and find out why she lied at the trial."

"We'll find them," he promised.

"Why are you doing this? Why are you helping me?" she asked him again. "You have no way of knowing this will lead to anything about Caine."

"It will, and when it does I'll not only have a great story...but vengeance for Jenny." He paused and added, "And I told you. I want to help you. I care about you, Tess."

"Spencer..."

He could already sense her withdrawing. So he stood. "I've got a friend who is going to help me check the convents between here and Jackson to see if we can locate Sister Amelia."

"When I see my father's attorney, I'll ask him if he knows how to reach her. Since he went to see my father around the same time, there's a chance he ran into her."

"In the meantime, I'd better get out of here if I hope to make it to Jackson in time to cover the debate. My father's notes from the trial are in that folder," he said, indicating the manila file next to the tape recorder. "I looked through a couple of pages last night, but nothing jumped out at me. I've already checked out the address Virginia Lee gave at the time of the trial but no one there has ever heard of her. My guess is she's either married and changed her name or she took off after all the publicity from the trial."

"What about her grandmother? Didn't she say on the tape that she lived with her?"

"I didn't find any listing for her either. But you may want to see what you can find."

Tess glanced at her watch, then stood. "I'll see what I can come up with when I get back."

"You going somewhere?"

"To get my hair done at Sugar Lou's Beauty Shop. I have an appointment with Sugar Lou herself in twenty minutes."

Spencer checked out the thick dark hair that fell in a sleek bob just above her shoulders. "Your hair looks fine to me."

"Thank you," she said with a smile. "But I'm really going for information. According to Maggie, if you want to find out the scoop on anyone or anything, Sugar Lou's is the place to go. Apparently news breaks there long before it ever makes it to the TV stations or the newspapers. With a little luck, I might be able to get a lead on Virginia Lee."

Sugar Lou's was typical of the small Southern beauty shop with its old-fashioned hair dryers, teasing combs and supersized cans of hair spray. Stacks of fashion magazines surrounded the pink Naughahyde chairs attached to the dryers. The mirrored stations were cluttered with clips, bobby pins and styling gels. The walls boasted posters of models with upswept dos and big hair. The manicurist, a petite blonde wearing a cotton-candy pink smock chattered away while she painted the nails of a Lucille Ball look-alike. And the shop's namesake, Sugar Lou Adams, fit right into the setting. A big woman who could have been anywhere from forty to sixty. Her fluffy blond hair was a cloud of soft curls that surrounded a round face with bright pink lips and inch-long eyelashes. But her quick smile made Tess feel immediately welcome. And just as Maggie had promised, the woman was a wealth of information.

"Oh, I remember that trial, all right," Sugar Lou said as she shampooed and rinsed Tess's hair. "I'd just opened my shop back then and it's all anyone was talking about. Such a sad thing about the Burns woman being killed like that. Apparently the woman's little girl saw the whole thing. And to think it was all on account of that fellow Burns not being able to keep his pants zipped. But what he ever saw in that home wrecker, I'll never know."

As Sugar Lou shut off the water and Tess sat upright, she squirmed a little in the seat, uncomfortable because Sugar Lou didn't realize that she was that little girl. "Her name was Virginia Lee, and she claimed to be having an affair with Burns," Tess offered as Sugar Lou wrapped her hair in a towel and led her to the styling station. "Do you know what happened to her?"

"Oh, she got her comeuppance, that's what happened. Ending up marrying a fellow up in Vicksburg who ran around on her. I heard he ran off last year with a hostess who worked on one of those riverboat casinos. Left her flat broke and with a stack of bills."

"Is she still living in Vicksburg?" Tess asked, trying not to convey her excitement at the news.

"Gracious, no. She came back here with her tail tucked between her legs about six months ago and took a job waiting tables at the Dixie Belle," Sugar Lou informed her as she removed the towel and began combing Tess's wet hair.

"She works at the Dixie Belle?" Tess repeated, unable to believe it.

"Sure. Only she don't go by Virginia Lee anymore. She changed her name when she got married and didn't bother changing it back after her divorce. Nowadays she goes by the name of Weakes. Ginger Weakes."

Ginger Weakes.

Suddenly Tess remembered the waitress at the restaurant last night. Spencer's aunt had called her Ginger.

"So what did you have in mind?" Sugar Lou asked. "You've got good hair. I could fix it in an updo with some pretty curls for you."

"Maybe another time. Today I think I'll just have a blow-dry and style."

"All right," Sugar Lou told her and sighed. She proceeded to style Tess's hair. Twenty minutes later when she'd turned off the blow-dryer and finished off the style with spray, she handed Tess the hand mirror to check out the results.

"It looks wonderful. Thank you," Tess told her.

"Shoot, honey, it doesn't look all that different than when you came in. You coulda done that style all by yourself and saved the fifteen dollars."

"Trust me, Sugar, it was worth every penny." And after slipping a twenty on the station's counter, Tess left the salon and headed to the Dixie Belle for lunch.

Lunchtime at the Dixie Belle was every bit as busy as the dinner hour had been the previous evening, Tess realized as she entered the restaurant and saw the packed tables. While she waited for the hostess to finish with the group in front of her, she scanned the crowded room in hopes of spying the waitress from last night. But it was Sarah Reed who spied her first.

"Ah, Tess, I'm so glad you've come back again. I'll take care of her, Tina," Sarah told the hostess. "Where is that nephew of mine?" she asked, looking past Tess toward the doorway.

"He's not with me," she said, still amazed at the speed with which Spencer's family had apparently decided to classify them as a couple. "It'll be just me. I was hoping to get some lunch, but it looks like you're pretty busy."

She waved away the comment, saying, "Not too busy for my Spencer's girl. Besides, we need to fatten you up a bit. Let me see where I can put you."

Focused on talking to Ginger, she didn't even bother trying to correct Sarah about her relationship with Spencer. Instead she asked, "Would it be at all possible for me to be seated at one of Ginger's tables? She was the waitress we had last night."

"She did a good job for you then?"

"Yes," Tess told her.

"I'm glad to hear it. Things have not been easy for that one," she said while she scanned the busy establishment. "Ah, there is a table just emptying in her section now. If you'll give me a second to get it cleaned, I'll have Tina seat you."

A few minutes later, Tina led Tess to the table. "Ginger will be with you in a minute," she said, handing Tess a menu. "Today's lunch specials are inside."

"Thanks," Tess murmured. Once the hostess had left, Tess unfolded her napkin, smoothed it on her lap and glanced around for Ginger. She spotted her waiting on a corner table across the aisle.

This time Tess studied the woman more closely. In her late fifties now, Ginger looked every one of her years, Tess thought. Now that she knew she was Virginia Lee, Tess could see a vague resemblance to the woman in the old newspaper photo that identified her as she'd exited the courtroom. Gray roots were showing in the bleached-blond hair that had been teased high and combed into a French twist and pinned with rhinestone bobby pins. The tomato-red lipstick and thick black eyeliner were too harsh for her aging skin, Tess thought. The Virginia Lee in the newspaper photograph had worn a short, tight skirt and snug top that emphasized her figure and full bustline. As Ginger Weakes, she wore her black uniform skirt and blouse equally snug, only now she was carrying at least another thirty pounds of weight.

"Be back with your drinks in a second, hon," she told the men at the table, her voice chipper and her smile friendly. She tucked her pencil behind her ear and looked over in Tess's direction. Her smile faded immediately. Her steps slowed a bit as she approached Tess's table.

"Hi, Ginger. I don't know if you remember me. I was in last night for dinner," Tess began.

"I remember." She whipped out her pad and retrieved her pencil. "Did you want something to drink?"

The question was not the least bit friendly and anyone within earshot would have probably classified it as rude. But Tess did her best to sound pleasant and said, "Iced tea, please."

"You ready to order or do you need some more time?"

"I haven't looked at the menu yet. What do you—"

"I'll go get your tea while you look over the menu."

And before Tess could say another word, Ginger was racing in the direction of the kitchen. But before she reached it, a big man seated at the bar called her over. The two exchanged words and an unhappy-looking Ginger continued toward the kitchen.

While she was gone Tess scanned the menu, but kept her eyes on the doors to the kitchen and waited for Ginger to emerge. She did, and not saying anything further to the man, she went to the end of the bar and filled glasses with tea and soda. She then returned to the table of men and after serving their drinks, she made her way back over to Tess.

She placed the iced tea in front of Tess. Then she took the order pad from her pocket. "You decided yet?"

"I'll have the club sandwich," Tess said, not the least bit hungry but knowing she needed to order something.

She jotted it down, never once meeting Tess's gaze. "It'll be out in a few minutes."

"Ginger, wait," Tess said and the other woman paused.

"You changed your mind?"

"You know who I am, don't you? You recognized me last night," she said, deciding it was the only thing that could explain the other woman's attitude toward her.

"I know that you're the girlfriend of Miss Sarah's nephew, and that you're some kind of reporter like him."

"I'm Jody Burns's daughter," she said, trying to keep her voice soft. "I'd like to talk to you. It's important."

"I can't imagine why you'd want to talk to me."

"Because you used to be Virginia Lee."

The other woman's knuckles went white as she held the pencil tightly. She darted a glance toward the bar. "I ain't got nothing to say to you."

"But—"

"I told you, I ain't got nothing to say to you," she repeated. "Now, I need to go turn in this order and take care of my other tables or I'm gonna lose my job."

Tess let the woman go. Deciding not to press her further, she watched her work, noted her talking to the big man at the bar again. While he seemed familiar, Tess wasn't sure why.

"You don't enjoy your lunch?" Sarah Reed asked as she stopped by the table later to check on Tess.

"It's delicious," Tess told her and took another bite of the sandwich.

"I'll send you over some of my apple cobbler."

"That's very kind of you, Mrs. Reed, but I've got more than I can eat here."

"Nonsense," Sarah told her. "A strong wind would blow you away. You eat the cobbler. If you like it, I'll teach you to make it. It's one of Spencer's favorites."

Tess bit back a groan. She realized she'd be wasting her breath to try to dissuade the lady. She couldn't help wondering if it was like this for all big families or if this was something unique to small southern towns.

After paying her bill, Tess sought out Sarah before she left. "I just wanted to thank you again. You were right about the cobbler. It was wonderful."

She beamed. "I'll give you the recipe."

"Thank you." Tess paused and said, "Mrs. Reed, there was a man sitting at the bar area earlier who seemed familiar to me, but I couldn't place him. He left already, but I wondered if you might be able to tell me who he was."

"What did he look like?"

"He was an older man, maybe around sixty or so. About six feet tall, stocky build with salt-and-pepper hair that looked like it was getting thin. Ruddy complexion. He was wearing alligator boots and a belt with a big silver horseshoe buckle."

"That was Lucky Gates."

"Lucky?" Tess repeated.

Sarah laughed. "That's the nickname Larry Gates gave himself years ago after he hit it big at the craps tables in Vegas. Imagine making a fortune rolling dice. He came back here with his winnings and opened up a car dealership. It's the biggest one in Grady."

"I guess he must have just reminded me of someone

else," Tess told her, and after thanking her again, she left. As she did so, she made a point of noting the restaurant's hours. Since it was open at six o'clock in the morning for breakfast, served lunch until two o'clock in the afternoon and then began serving dinner at five o'clock in the evening, Tess guessed that Ginger had worked a breakfast and lunch shift. Even though the place was busy, she doubted that Sarah Reed would ask her employees to work double shifts and pull overtime. That gave her an hour to kill, Tess reasoned, before Ginger would leave the Dixie Belle and head for home. After a call to information from her cell phone revealed no listing for either a Virginia or Ginger Weakes, Tess opted to wait and follow the other woman.

For the next hour, Tess busied herself on Main Street. She window-shopped and even purchased an interesting ceramic plaque with a mint julep recipe on it from a kitchen store's sidewalk sale as a gift for Maggie. All the while, she made sure that she kept the entrance to the Dixie Belle in her view.

Finally at a quarter of three, Ginger exited the restaurant. The moment she came outdoors, she lit up a cigarette. Taking a deep drag she scanned the street. Tess ducked into the alcove of a pastry shop and pretended to be considering the confections on display. But out of the corner of her eye, she watched Ginger as she smoked. She watched and she waited.

There were a half-dozen vehicles left in the parking lot next to the restaurant. So when Ginger tossed down the cigarette and crushed it with the toe of her black sneakers, Tess waited to see which car was hers. She went to the dented blue Toyota against the far wall. Tess headed down the street to where she'd moved her car earlier. Sliding behind the wheel, she slipped on her sunglasses and waited for the Toyota to pull out of the lot. Then she started her engine and followed Ginger.

Chapter Thirteen

For the next thirty-five minutes, Tess followed the Toyota. Traffic picked up as school let out and Tess found herself inching along behind school buses and mothers transporting their children home from school. When she got caught behind a yellow school bus at a red light, Tess thought she'd lost Ginger. Then she spied the Toyota waiting to turn at the next corner.

Once outside the city limits the traffic grew lighter and Tess stayed back several car lengths, hoping Ginger wouldn't spot her. The area grew more shabby, and the quality of the road deteriorated the farther they traveled from Grady. Tess was just beginning to wonder if perhaps Ginger had seen her and was leading her on a wild-goose chase, when the Toyota turned left onto a bumpy dirt road aptly named Lonesome Road. A battered sign on a crooked metal post that read Dead End had been splattered with green paint and stood like a drunken soldier amidst a scattering of pine trees that ap-

peared to have suffered through a few storms. At the far
end of the road, she could see the murky waters of a
bayou.

With the cloud cover above, the dark bayou stretching out ahead and the trees growing thicker on either
side of the road, Tess got an eerie feeling in the pit of
her stomach. Suddenly, all kinds of crazy thoughts
started racing through her head. She was in a strange
and remote place. No one knew where she was. And
the woman she had been following had not only been
hostile toward her, she had deliberately sent an innocent man to prison. Who knew what she would be capable of if confronted? For all she knew, the woman
might have a gun. She could be shot and thrown in the
bayou and no one would ever be the wiser.

For the space of a heartbeat Tess considered turning
around and simply confronting Ginger the next day at
the restaurant. But what if the woman never went back
to the restaurant? Suppose, to avoid a confrontation
with her, she decided to take off for parts unknown?
Tess thought of her father, remembered reading his letters. She couldn't risk letting her get away. Not without finding out why Ginger had lied at her father's trial.

Tess continued for what had to be the longest quarter of a mile she'd ever traveled, dodging potholes the
size of craters in the dirt road. When she hit a particularly large hole in the road that sent dust and gravel flying, Tess saw stars as the jolt sent her bouncing in her
seat and her head nearly snapped from her neck. Lord,
she thought as she slowed the car to a crawl, she was
going to feel that one tomorrow.

Finally she reached the clearing where Ginger's tail-
lights had disappeared, and Tess turned off to follow
her. She arrived at a small stretch of land that looked

as if it might have been someone's fishing camp at one time. In stark contrast to Maggie's place where the rolling hills and landscaped grounds were ripe with fall flowers and foliage, the ground here was flat and barren—just dirt, broken tree branches and pieces of rock. Here and there a stray thicket of grass had managed to survive, adding a spot of color to the slice of land that led to the shanty. Made of weathered pine that had turned dark, the place looked ready to fall over. Several steps leading up to the porch appeared loose and broken and only one storm shutter remained on the windows and it dangled haphazardly on the rusted hinge. Two of the windowpanes were cracked and another one had been broken. As a result, what appeared to be a gray sheet that had been tacked up as a curtain in front of the window battled to keep the wind and stench from the bayou out. To the left of the shack was a ramshackle pier at the edge of the water where, to Tess's surprise, a sleek black speedboat was anchored.

Tess drove her car up closer to the house and parked behind Ginger's Toyota. As she exited her vehicle, a strong gust of wind blew across the dirt and brought with it the smell of rotting garbage spilling from the trash can at the side of the house. Glad she had worn boots with a sturdy heel, Tess made her way to the steps of the house. She could hear a radio blaring oldies somewhere inside the house and raised voices—a man's and a woman's. Tess hesitated a moment, then knocked on the door.

The radio continued playing, the disc jockey announcing the station's call sign and telling listeners to stay tuned for this week's top-ten country tunes. But then the voices stopped. Tess knocked again, this time harder.

The door opened and Ginger scowled at her. "What are you doing here?"

"All I want to do is talk, Ginger."

"And I already told you that I ain't got nothing to say to you. You wasted your time coming out here."

When she started to shove the door closed, Tess stuck her foot between the door and the jamb. "I'm not leaving until you tell me why you lied at my father's trial."

"Who says I lied?" Ginger countered, hitching her head up a notch.

"I do," Tess informed.

"Why? You think just because your momma was fancy-looking and talked nice that Jody wasn't sweet on me. Well, you're wrong. Back then I was every bit as pretty as Melanie was and Jody loved me. He and I was having an affair and that's what I told them in court."

"You were lying then and you're lying now," Tess told her. She braced her arm against the door to keep the heavier woman from trying to crush her foot with the door. "And your lies and Lester De Roach's lies helped to send my father to prison. What I don't know is if you did it on your own or if De Roach put you up to it, or if it was someone else."

"Your daddy went to prison because he killed your momma," Ginger insisted.

"No, he didn't," Tess countered and noted the way the woman's eyes kept darting to her right. "And thanks to you, people thought he did. But he found out who really did kill my mother and he was going to prove it. That's why he was killed. To stop him from exposing the truth and exposing you as a liar."

"He committed suicide. I read it in the papers."

"The papers got it wrong. But I intend to fix that and when I do, I'm going to come after you, too, Ginger.

I'm going to see to it that you're charged with perjury and as an accessory to murder unless you tell me what you know. Was De Roach the one who got you to lie?"

"I don't know anything. I swear I don't," she said, her eyes wild and darting to something, or someone, behind the door. The woman was afraid.

"Then tell me why you lied."

"Please go," she said, her voice now desperate. "I don't need any more trouble. I'm sorry about your daddy. But I can't help you."

"All right," Tess said. She retrieved a business card from her jacket pocket and handed it to Ginger. "Here's my card with my cell-phone number on it or you can reach me at the Magnolia Guesthouse. If you change your mind, call me. I meant what I said about filing charges."

Tess descended the stairs and got inside her car. As she drove away, she kept looking through her rearview mirror because she couldn't shake the feeling that a pair of eyes watched her leave. And she didn't think those eyes were Ginger's.

"Sheriff, I got Doc calling in for you," Hazel informed Andy over the dispatch radio the next morning as he sat in his truck at the red light. He had just left the scene of another fender bender and the rain continued to pour.

"Go ahead and put him through to my cell phone," Andy instructed.

"Will do," Hazel, his dispatcher, telephone operator and administrator all rolled into one, replied. "Hang on, Doc, I'm patching you through."

When the phone rang, Andy hit the hands-free switch, not wanting to add his own vehicle to the casu-

alties on the wet roadways. "'Morning, Doc," he answered, referring to Dr. Tom Thomas who served as the
county's coroner. "You got something for me?"

"'Morning, Andy. Sure do. I finished the autopsy on
Lester De Roach's body. It looks like you were right,
it was the shotgun blast that killed him. Although he'd
probably have been dead within a year because his
liver was a mess. I won't bore you with everything else
that was wrong with him. The tox screen came back
negative for drugs, but his alcohol level was three times
the legal limit."

Striving for patience, which Andy had been told
often enough was not one of his strengths, he listened
for several more seconds. Finally, he prompted, "Doc,
the shotgun blast? What can you tell me about it?"

"Well, now mind you, I don't have myself one of
them fancy crime labs with all those machines like
them coroners you were used to working with in New
York City have," he began, drawing out the words *New
York City* as though it was the name of a foreign country. "So I can't go running all those tests for trajectory
and other nonsense. But what I can tell you from examining the body is that there was stippling at the entry
wound, which means he was shot at close range."

"Which also means the shooter was close, not fir-
ing from a distance the way he or she would in a hunting accident," Andy said.

"That's right. Even at night, for the bullet to make
that kind of mark, the shooter would have had to have
been close enough to see Lester's face. He'd have
known, before he ever pulled the trigger, that he had a
man in his gun sight and not an animal."

Which confirmed his first impression upon viewing
the crime scene, Andy recalled. Lester's death was not

an accident. It was murder. "What about a time of death? Were you able to pinpoint when he was killed?"

"Like I said, I don't have those fancy machines like they have up North, but my best guess is he was killed sometime between ten o'clock and twelve midnight on Sunday."

"Not exactly hunting hours," Andy said more to himself than to Doc.

"Nope. I'm classifying his death as a homicide in my report. But I'm sure that comes as no surprise to you. That's why you were asking me all them questions when they brought the body in because you thought somebody killed him, didn't you?"

"Yes, Doc. I did," Andy admitted.

"You always were a smart boy, Andy. And you're turning out to be a fine sheriff."

"Thanks, Doc. I appreciate that." And he meant it. He appreciated the fact that a man who'd known him since he was in short pants could see past the kid he'd been to the man he had become.

"I'll send you a copy of my report."

"Appreciate it, Doc."

"And, Andy?"

"Yes?"

"I'll be the first to tell you that Lester De Roach was a real SOB. He was an ornery drunk, and he probably cheated half the people in this town out of money on repair work he did on their cars at one time or another. Including me. And if the man had to choose between telling the truth or telling a lie, he'd choose to lie every time."

"Doc, I know the man had enemies," Andy told him.

"He had a lot of them," Doc conceded. "But no matter what Lester did, he was still one of God's creations.

Nobody deserved to die like he did. You find his killer, son. And you make sure they account for what they did."

"I will, Doc," he promised.

And it was a promise he intended to keep, Andy vowed silently as he ended the call. To do so meant questioning Maggie's new best friend, Tess Abbott. As yet, the lady hadn't bothered to return his calls and he'd been told repeatedly when he'd called the guesthouse that she was out. So, if he wanted any answers about the information that came up on his personal inquiry on her, he had no choice but to track her down.

Andy finally found Tess Abbott shortly after ten o'clock that morning at the *Grady Gazette*. He took one look at Spencer's face, noted the protective stance in his friend's body language, and decided his instincts about Spencer's interest in the lady had been correct. He supposed he could understand the attraction. The woman was pretty—if you liked them tall, lean and with haunting gray eyes. Lately it seemed his taste ran to petite, curvy redheads with sassy smiles.

And realizing he had been thinking about Maggie O'Donnell again—something he had been doing much too often of late—Andy frowned and turned to the business at hand. "I'm sorry for the intrusion, Ms. Abbott. Spence," he said with a nod of his head.

"Hey, Andy," Spence told him. "We're kind of busy at the moment," Spence began.

"So am I," Andy said, cutting him off. "But I need to speak with Ms. Abbott and since I haven't been able to reach her at the guesthouse, and she hasn't seen fit to return my calls, I didn't have any choice but to come here." He looked at the woman in question. "We can speak here, Ms. Abbott, or I can have you come to my office. It's your choice."

"Now wait a minute, Trudeaux—"

"I can speak for myself," she said, staying Spencer with her hand.

And there was no mistaking the steel in her voice, Andy thought. He'd heard it often enough in his own mother's voice when he was growing up—just before she clipped him one for mouthing off.

"My apologies, Sheriff Trudeaux, for not getting back to you. I was out of town the first time you called and returned very late in the evening. I didn't receive your message until yesterday morning. I should have called you first thing, but I got tied up with something else and it wasn't until late last night that I realized you'd called again."

Andy nodded, acknowledging both her apology and her explanation as he sized her up. This lady was no meek female in need of a man to protect her. Independent was the description that came to mind. Although given Spencer's expression, he doubted his friend realized that yet. Or perhaps the protective instincts were inbred, he reasoned. Because if the tables were turned, and it was Maggie being questioned, he would feel the same way.

Dammit. There was Maggie again, creeping into his thoughts when she neither belonged nor was wanted there.

"Sheriff?"

He yanked his attention back to the matter at hand. "Ma'am?"

"I asked what it was you needed to speak with me about."

"Lester De Roach. He was the man on whose body I found your credit card receipt."

"I remember and I've already notified my credit card company about the incident. Is that what this is about?"

"It's not. I'm here because his death has been ruled a homicide and I need to ask you some questions."

She sat down, lifted her hand to her throat. "A homicide? I thought you said he was killed in a hunting accident."

"I said it *looked* like a hunting accident. But based on the physical evidence, it's been ruled a homicide. He was murdered."

"What does that have to do with Tess?" Spencer demanded.

"Reed," she said, a warning note both in her voice and in the glance she gave him. She turned her gaze back to him. "You said you had some questions for me, Sheriff."

"I wondered why when I reported finding your credit card receipt on De Roach's body you didn't think to mention your connection to him."

"Because I don't have a connection to him."

"Maybe not directly. But I'd say the fact that he was a witness for the prosecution at your father's murder trial counts as a connection. Where were you Saturday evening between ten o'clock and midnight, Ms. Abbott?"

"You think I killed him?"

"I think the fact that his testimony helped send your father to prison would classify as motive."

"For your information I didn't even know he had been a witness at the trial at the time he was murdered. It wasn't until Bill Reed told me later that I realized there was any connection."

He had to give the lady points. She didn't rattle easily. "You never answered the question. Where were you Saturday evening, Ms. Abbott?"

"I was in my cottage at the Magnolia Guesthouse. And before you ask, the answer is no. No one can verify that I was in the cottage, because I was alone."

He jotted down the information she gave him on a pad and stuck it and the pen back in his jacket pocket. "And you had absolutely no idea who Lester was that night when you saw him at the convenience store?"

"None whatsoever." She paused. "As I told you the night you questioned me about the credit card receipt, he appeared to be acting strange and I thought he was drunk. I'll admit, I did wonder if he had mistaken me for my mother because he seemed, well…almost frightened when he saw me."

"And you didn't think that was worth mentioning?"

"Sheriff, I had no idea who he was or whether or not I was right. So there was no reason for me to mention it," she informed him coolly.

"And was there a reason you didn't mention that this story that you're researching was your mother's murder?"

"I didn't think it was relevant."

"You apparently thought it and Lester De Roach were both relevant yesterday afternoon when you went out to Ginger Weakes's place and threatened her."

"What?" Spencer said, his shock apparent. "You said you went to the restaurant to talk to her after you found out she was Virginia Lee."

"And I did, but she wouldn't talk to me. So I followed her after she left the restaurant to try to get her to tell me why she lied at my father's trial," she told him.

"Dammit, Tess!"

She ignored Spencer's outburst and turned her defiant gaze on Andy. "But I didn't threaten her."

"According to her you did. She also claims you were trespassing and tried to force your way into her home."

Tess's mouth flattened. "I stuck my foot in her door. And trust me, from the looks of that place, all it would take is a good strong wind to blow the thing down."

He knew she was telling the truth because he had seen the place. It was nothing more than an abandoned shack that, had he been back in New York, he'd have had shut down as uninhabitable. "Either way, she phoned my office to make a complaint against you."

"So, are you here to arrest me?" she asked and, judging by the way she said it, she wasn't the least bit frightened at the prospect.

"The hell he will! And don't tell me you can speak for yourself," Spencer told her when she started to open her mouth. He stood, leaned over and stuck his face right in Andy's own. "You even think about arresting her, Trudeaux, and badge or no badge, I'll whip your ass the way I did in junior high."

"As I recall, it was *your* ass that got whipped. But anytime you want a rematch, buddy, you let me know." And before Spencer could say anything more, he turned back to the Abbott woman. "But as it happens, I'm not here to arrest you, Ms. Abbott. I told Ginger Weakes or Virginia Lee or whatever name she goes by these days that she would have to come in and sign out a formal complaint against you. So far she hasn't done that. But in the meantime, I recommend you stay away from her."

"I appreciate the advice, Sheriff, but I intend to find out why she and Lester De Roach lied at my father's trial, and whether either of them had anything to do with his murder."

Andy's eyes narrowed. "I understood your father committed suicide in prison."

"I have reason to believe he may have been killed and it was made to look like a suicide," she informed him.

"Why?" Andy asked.

"Because I think he may have been about to expose the person who really murdered my mother and he was killed to keep him quiet. That's why I'm here."

"You knew this?" Andy asked his friend.

Spencer nodded. "I'm helping Tess."

"You have no business playing detective. Either of you. If what you say is true, let the authorities handle it," he told them. "The prison can do an investigation, find out what happened."

"They've already closed the file and labeled my father's death a suicide," Tess told him. "That's why I'm going over the original murder case. If I can find my mother's murderer, then chances are I'll find out who was behind my father's murder, too."

"I've already turned up a couple of leads," Spencer told him. "We're hoping one of them will lead us to the killer."

Andy braced his hands on the table where the two of them sat side by side. He leaned forward, stared first at Spencer, then at Tess. "I want both of you to listen to me and listen good. I don't care what kind of super reporters either of you are or how many leads you've uncovered. This is not a game. That bullet blast in Lester De Roach's chest was real. It was made by a real gun, by a real killer, a killer who looked him square in the eye and pulled the trigger."

"Sheriff—"

"I've been a lawman a long time, Ms. Abbott," he

said, cutting off her protest. "I've learned to follow my gut. And my gut tells me that Lester's death has something to do with you showing up here and asking questions," he stated honestly. "So my advice to you and to my friend here is back off and let me and the prison authorities do our jobs."

"I appreciate your advice, Sheriff," she said, apparently not the least bit intimidated by him or what he'd said. "But I have no intention of backing off—not until I get to the truth."

Spencer waited until the door closed behind Andy, then shoved away from the table and began to pace. He had a knot the size of Texas in his stomach as he thought about Tess following Ginger home. He knew where the place was, an isolated stretch of land out on Lonesome Road that had an eerie history shrouded in mystery and death. Imagining Tess out there, all alone, confronting Ginger—a woman who had a good forty pounds on her—did nothing to ease that knot. He stopped in front of the table where she sat silently watching him. He was beginning to know her, he realized, because from the tilt of her chin, he knew that she was hopping mad and just waiting for him to argue with her.

She was going to get her wish, he decided. "Despite his less than charming manner, Andy's good at his job. He racked up a whole slew of commendations as a homicide cop in New York before he came back home to Grady and took the sheriff's job. So the man knows what he's talking about. If he thinks Lester's death is connected to you looking into your father's murder trial, then chances are he's right," Spencer began. He didn't bother adding that he agreed with Andy.

"Maybe he is right, or maybe he just gets his kicks trying to scare people so they'll do what he says. Either way, I meant what I said. I'm not backing off of this, Reed. Not until I find out the truth," she told him. She stood and began stuffing files and papers into her bag.

"Dammit, Tess!" He marched over to her, yanked the files from her hands and pitched them to the table. He pulled her close, so close he could smell the roses and springwater scent she wore, could see the darkening awareness in those gray eyes. "I don't expect you to quit. What I do expect is for you to be more careful. Going after Ginger like that was just plain stupid. You could have been hurt. Or worse."

She looked at him as though he'd just grown two heads. "Reed, I was careful. And I was never in any danger."

"You don't know that. You should never have gone out there by yourself. Lonesome Bayou isn't a safe place." He released her, took a step back. "Hell, it's a wonder Ginger isn't afraid to live there."

"Granted, the place is a dump and probably even a health hazard. But I hardly think that makes it dangerous."

"It's a bad place, an evil place. Some even say that it's haunted," he told her. "People have been known to disappear from there and never be seen or heard from again."

"Whoa, Reed. You need to explain that. Who disappeared? And when?"

Spencer released a breath and told her the stories surrounding Lonesome Bayou that had been circulating since he was a boy. "The first person to disappear was the man who built the place. He was a big timberland owner who used trees from his farms to have the house and dock constructed for him as a weekend place. The story goes that he came up every weekend like clockwork for more than a year. Then one weekend he came up like he usually did. People in town saw him arrive and he told them he was going out to his place to catch himself some fish for a dinner party he and his wife were having that next week. But he never came home, and by Monday evening his wife started to get worried. So she had the sheriff go check out the place to make sure he was all right. His truck was still there. There was food on the table like he'd just sat down to eat and the radio was playing. But there was no sign of him. No one ever saw or heard from him again."

"It's an interesting story. But a lot of people disappear and turn up twenty years later living under a new name and with a new wife and family," she offered.

"So far, he hasn't turned up. Later, after the place changed owners, a female who was a guest at a weekend party there turned up missing, too. And the last owners, a family from Arkansas, lost a child there."

"What happened?"

"It's said that this couple used to come and spend long weekends fishing and exploring the bayou with their three kids. One night the couple's youngest, a little girl about four, snuck outside while the rest of the family was sleeping. Apparently she was playing near the bayou and she either fell in or was dragged in. All I know is that the next morning they found blood on the dock and one of her shoes, but no body. They think one of the gators must have gotten her."

Tess shuddered.

"It's said that sometimes late at night you can hear thrashing in the waters and a little girl's cries for help."

Tess rubbed her hands up and down her arms. "Well, I can certainly understand why people would think the bayou's haunted. But I don't believe in ghosts and apparently Ginger doesn't either since she's living there."

"The fact that she's living there at all should tell you the woman either isn't playing with a full deck or she's desperate."

"My guess is she's desperate. I saw her car and she's waiting tables at your aunt's restaurant. She doesn't strike me as a person who has a lot. And I think she has some other kind of troubles. Despite her tough talk when I confronted her, I think she was scared."

"Scared? Why do you say that?" he asked, because although he'd only encountered Ginger a handful of times at the restaurant, she had struck him as more brazen than scared.

"She had someone at the house with her—or at least I think she did. I never saw anyone, but she kept glancing away as though someone was behind the door with her and whoever he was, she was afraid of him."

"Him? I thought you said you didn't see anyone."

"I didn't. But I did a story once on domestic violence and interviewed a lot of battered wives and girlfriends. The one thing they all had in common was that they would get a look in their eyes—like a trapped animal bracing for an attack. Ginger had that same look."

"Maybe it's because you threatened her," he offered.

She shook her head. "My so-called threats of legal action didn't faze her. No, whoever was with her was the one who frightened her, not me. Besides, I saw a boat parked by the dock, a fancy-looking one with lots of gadgets on it. And unless Ginger has been raking in some huge tips, I doubt it's something she could have afforded."

"What did it look like?"

"Like I said, it was fancy, black with silver trim, with two raised seats on either end of the boat. Why?"

"No reason," Spencer told her, but he didn't like the sound of someone with an expensive boat whom Ginger was afraid of being on the other side of that door while Tess was there. "But if Ginger's having problems with some guy who's abusing her, that's one more reason you need to stay away from her."

"Spencer, I need to find out why she lied at the trial. If she lied and Lester lied, they must have done it for a reason. I need to find out what it was and who put them up to it." She paused, her expression softening as she looked at him. "I know you think Everett Caine was somehow involved, but I'm sorry. I don't see it. While he may have profited from the trial outcome, I just don't see him putting his career on the line to ensure it. It would have to be someone who had something more to gain by my mother's death and my father's conviction." She shook her head. "For the life of me, I can't figure out who that would be. My parents had no assets. Even the house they were living in was rented."

Spencer hesitated, wondering if he should even mention one of the suspicions that had been nagging at him. "They did have one asset."

"What?" she asked.

"You. From what you've told me, and from what I've read about your grandfather's testimony at the trial, he hated your father and would have done anything to get you and your mother away from him."

For a moment she looked as though she didn't understand. Then her mouth tightened. Her eyes went cold. "What are you implying, Reed? That my grandfather had his own daughter killed?"

Spencer swore. "No, of course not."

"Then what are you suggesting?"

"I'm suggesting that from what I know of him, the senator is a man who gets things done. With your mother dead, your father would have gotten custody of you. He and your grandmother would have had to fight him for custody and chances were that they would have lost. So if he wanted to make sure that that didn't happen he would have to make sure that your father was convicted of murder."

"He wouldn't," she said, but her expression crumbled a little. "That would be tampering with a witness. He wouldn't do that. No matter how much he hated my father, my grandfather would never have broken the law. He wouldn't."

"Not even if he thought by doing so he would save you?" He went to her, held her close. "I'm sorry, Tess. But you're too smart a woman for it not to have crossed your mind."

After a moment, she stepped back from him. She sat down in the chair, stared at her hands for a moment. When she lifted her eyes to his, there was pain there and he hated that he had helped put it there. "I've been trying to tell myself as I've been going through all these documents that my grandfather wasn't involved in the trial in any way. That he was simply a grieving father, out for vindication for the death of his child."

"But?" Spencer prompted.

"But he hated Jody Burns, continued to hate him all these years and even when he found out that he was dead, the hate didn't end. He never forgave him for eloping with my mother and taking her away from him and from the life he'd planned for her."

"Was his hate strong enough that he would have

gotten Ginger and Lester to lie at the trial to make sure your father was convicted?"

She took a deep breath, released it. "Yes," she admitted. "But if he did bribe them to lie, he'll never admit it to me. That's one of the reasons I wanted to talk to Ginger, to get her to tell me the truth."

"Maybe I could try to talk to her," Spencer offered.

She shook her head. "I need to hear it for myself. Besides, even if my grandfather was responsible for the lies at the trial, I still don't know who killed my mother. And if that woman who called me was telling the truth, the same person killed my father, too."

"Which brings us back to your mystery caller," he said and wished once again he had been honest with her at the outset and told her that the mystery caller had contacted him as well. He couldn't help thinking about that old adage about tangled webs and deceiving.

"We have to find her," Tess said. "Maybe Mr. Clayton will have an idea of who she is. I'm supposed to see him this afternoon. What about you? Did you have any luck locating Sister Amelia?"

"I checked with the convents when I was in Jackson yesterday and they have no nun by that name there. I've got a friend in the prison communications department who's trying to see if they have any security video that we can look at. Maybe if we have a face to go with the name, we'll have better luck. In the meantime, I remembered what Pete the guard at the security gate said about the nun saying she taught your father in school in New Orleans. Do you have any idea what school that was? Or what church he attended?"

She shook her head. "If he ever mentioned it, I guess I was too young to remember."

"That's okay. It was a long shot. I'm going to start

calling the convents in the New Orleans area, see if any of them have a Sister Amelia living there or knows of a nun by that name who used to live there and taught in one of the schools. It's a big Catholic town, so I may be a while. I've got a list of convents, religious orders and churches over there in my brief-case," he said, indicating the worn black bag next to the chair.

She glanced at her watch and stood. "I'd offer to help, but Beau Clayton's secretary said he would be in court all morning and that he could see me sometime after lunch. He wasn't very encouraging when I spoke with him earlier. But I'm going to drive over to see him anyway. And I want to give myself some extra time since the weather's so bad."

"Maybe I should go with you," Spencer offered.

She zipped her bag closed and reached for her jacket. "I appreciate the offer, but I'd rather you stay here and try to find Sister Amelia. I'm afraid I'm run-ning out of time. My leave from the station will be over in another week. My producer called me this morning. She's getting heat for me being gone so long. So I need to find answers soon and get back to D.C. or I won't have a job to go back to."

For the first time Spencer thought about Tess leav-ing and he realized he didn't like the idea. "You ever consider moving back to Mississippi? I know people at the TV stations in Jackson who'd probably jump at a chance to hire you."

She wrinkled her forehead in that way she did when she was trying to work through a problem. "Are you suggesting I leave my job and move down here?"

The offer had been out of his mouth before he'd re-alized he'd said it. But now that he had, he liked the idea. "Yes, I am." He moved in, caged her by the table, then reached for the collar of her coat and used it to bring her close. "In case you haven't noticed, Ms. Abbott, I like having you around. In fact, I think I could get used to having you around a lot more."

"I'm not ready for this, Spencer. I barely know you."

"Then why don't we fix that?" he suggested and lowered his mouth to hers. He kissed her softly, slowly. He wasn't trying to seduce her. Although kissing her was a seduction in itself—a seduction for him because he wanted her physically. But he wanted more than just the physical. He wanted all the messy emotions and tangles that went with it. So he lifted his head.

Her eyes were closed, her mouth wet and parted and he considered kissing her again. But then her lashes fluttered and her eyes opened. And within seconds the glazed look turned to panic. "I need to go," she said.

He dropped his arms and watched her grab her bag and race out the door. And once she was gone, Spencer walked over to the phone and dialed Andy Trudeaux's cell number.

"Trudeaux," he answered.

"Andy, it's Spencer. We need to talk."

"I was wondering when you'd call. I've pulled the old case file. Rusty kept some pretty decent records back then and he was a firm believer in taking photographs of the crime scene. So you'll have some visuals to go with the report. What is it you hope to find?"

"That the murderer made a mistake."

Chapter Fourteen

Tess sat in the lobby of the old Denton County courthouse and waited for Beau Clayton to exit the courtroom. Although the city of Denton was located only fifty miles from Grady, it had taken her nearly two hours to get there—only to be told that Mr. Clayton's trial was running late. He could meet her at the courthouse or try to reschedule. It was her call. She'd opted to meet at the courthouse. Tess glanced at her watch and realized she'd now been waiting for over ninety minutes.

Restless, she stood and began to pace the floor, the heels of her shoes clicking on the tiled surface. While the courtrooms were in session, the rest of the courthouse was practically deserted, save for the security officers at the doors with their scanning equipment. It seemed that since 9/11 even small courthouses like this one were now subject to sophisticated machinery and searches.

Not that many people were interested in braving the courthouse in this weather, she thought. Beyond the doors she could see that the rain continued to come down relentlessly. According to the weather reports on her drive over, the record rainfall was proving to be a hazard not just for travelers but for all the people who resided in the state. With the riverbanks already cresting and more rain forecasted throughout the remainder of the afternoon and night, there was a serious danger of flooding. She thought of Maggie's place and hoped that everything was all right over there. And, she thought of Spencer.

Sighing, Tess walked to the far end of the lobby and looked out at the steady rain. The man was definitely beginning to occupy her thoughts with much too much frequency. She didn't know what to make of him or the fact that he kept throwing her off balance—the way he had that morning with the remark about her moving back to Mississippi. He made her feel things, things she wasn't sure she wanted to feel. And it bothered her that he seemed to know her—to anticipate her reactions, to understand what she was feeling. Not even Jonathan, whom she'd considered marrying, had ever understood her. Yet Spencer did.

Then there was the sexual attraction. As much as she might want to deny it, it was there and seemed to be growing stronger by the day. She wished she could chalk it up to stress and the emotional shocks with which she'd been hit lately. But the simple truth was, she was attracted to Spencer Reed. That he was determined to make them both face that attraction head-on and deal with it didn't help matters.

She knew Spencer had an agenda—exposing Everett Caine to avenge his friend Jenny—and he'd made no bones about the fact that he was helping her in order to attain that goal. It could be a career-making story for him and, more importantly, he would have the vengeance that was so important to him.

She frowned. It seemed she had a knack for picking men who saw her as a means to their own ends. In Jonathan's case it had been to advance his political career. He may have loved her, but deep down inside she'd known his love was self-serving, and it was why she had refused to marry him. She hadn't wanted to become a carbon copy of her grandmother—the perfect political wife, the proper hostess, a quiet supportive woman in the background who showed up on her husband's arm at charitable events, public outings and at election time. As much as she loved her grandmother, she didn't want to be like her. The realization saddened her and it made her think of her mother. For the first time in a long time, she wondered what her mother would have thought of her choices in life. What would she have thought of Jonathan? Of Spencer?

Walking back down the corridor, she sat on the wooden bench outside the courtroom. In many ways the two men were very much alike, she thought. Both were confident, dedicated to their own causes and didn't understand the word *quit*. But whereas Jonathan's motives were self-serving, Spencer's were not. For Spencer it wasn't about the news story. It was about justice. Justice for a friend who could no longer fight for herself. There was something about the nobility of his actions that she found enormously appealing. And his need for justice was also something she could readily identify with since it was justice that she wanted for her mother and her father, for the two lives stolen from them and from her. Justice had been what her mystery caller had claimed she wanted as well.

The door to the courtroom opened and Tess stood. Several people filed out and the silent corridor began to fill with soft chatter. Stepping away from the wall, she watched the people exit and kept her eye out for Beau Clayton. Finally, he came through the doorway. He looked very much the same as he had in the newspaper photos she'd seen from her father's trial except that the medium-brown hair had begun to get a touch of gray at the temples and there were a few lines bracketing his eyes and mouth that hadn't been there twenty-five years ago. He wasn't very tall. She estimated he didn't measure more than an inch or two above her own five-foot-eight frame, and in her heels, she guessed they would stand eye to eye. The conservative navy suit and striped tie were standard lawyer issue. So was the briefcase and topcoat draped over his arm. His expression was kind as he shook hands with a middle-aged man and accepted a kiss on the cheek from the woman. Once his clients were gone, he scanned the area and spied her.

Tess walked over to him. "Mr. Clayton, I'm Tess Abbott," she said, offering her hand.

His handshake was firm, his expression genuine as he said, "Ms. Abbott. It's a pleasure to meet you, and my apologies for asking you to come over to the courthouse in this weather. But the docket was backed up and if I'd asked for the hearing to be rescheduled, my clients would have probably had to wait until after Christmas to get a hearing. I didn't want to do that to them," he explained. "They were conned out of their life savings by an unscrupulous developer and have been fighting for more than a year already to get their money back. So I was anxious for their case to be heard."

"It wasn't a problem," she assured him, immediately liking the man.

"You're very understanding," he said. "I have to be back in court in an hour, but what do you say we go grab us some coffee from the machine down the hall and find us a place to sit down and you tell me what I can do to help you?"

Seated in a quiet corner of the courthouse, Tess began by asking, "Would you tell me about your conversation with my father when you visited him that week before he died?"

"Well, as I explained to you on the phone, he wrote and asked me to contact him because he was coming up for parole. He said that he'd obtained new information about his wife's murder that hadn't been presented at the trial. He had questions about what was needed to have the case reopened."

"Did he tell you what this information was?" Tess asked him.

He shook his head. "No. He said once he got out, he would come to me and turn over whatever this new information was and then he'd let me decide whether or not I wanted to represent him. If I agreed, he promised he'd get the money to pay my fee."

"What did you tell him?"

"I was honest with him. I told him that he didn't need me or any attorney to represent him in order to have the case reopened. If he had new information that could clear him, he should bring it to the police and let them handle it."

"What did he say?" Tess asked.

"He told me that he didn't trust the police, but that he trusted me. He said that I was a good lawyer and that if he could have his pick of all the lawyers in the country, I was the one he would choose," Clayton told her. "I reminded him that he was sitting in jail because of me, that I was the one who lost his case. And do you know what he said?"

"What?"

"He told me that I shouldn't blame myself, that not even Perry Mason himself could have won that trial. Can you believe that? The man spent twenty-five years in prison because I was a green rookie in the courtroom who lost a case that was based entirely on circumstantial evidence—a case that a more experienced attorney might have won—and there he was making excuses for me."

Yes, she could believe it. After reading his letters, she could easily imagine her father would put his concern for the attorney above his own concerns, and somehow that knowledge made her feel closer to him. She looked at the attorney, the man whom her father had trusted, the man who had felt compelled to give up half of his day to travel to the prison near Jackson and back because the man he'd represented as a public defender twenty-five years earlier had asked him to contact him. "Mr. Clayton, did you believe my father, that he was innocent?"

"Yes, I did," he replied firmly.

"Why?"

"Several reasons. Mostly the fact that he never struck me as someone capable of murder. Your mother's death nearly destroyed him. And it wasn't an act to gain sympathy from the jury, he was genuinely devastated. For a time I think he didn't want to live. He didn't seem to care whether they convicted him or not, even though I kept telling him the case was circumstantial. Only later, when I convinced him he had to think of you, did he make an effort to save himself."

"So why didn't the jury believe him?" she asked.

"I think part of the blame lies with me. I was a relatively new attorney and this was my first murder case. I wasn't as good then as I am now, I'm afraid," he explained sardonically. "And Everett Caine, he was the assistant D.A., but even back then he was good. He knew how to get just what he wanted out of a witness and I wasn't nearly as good on the cross-examination."

"I heard a tape of some of the testimony from Virginia Lee," she told him. "I think you were better than you give yourself credit for, Mr. Clayton."

He gave her a half smile. "You're kind, just like your father was. But I should have ripped her apart on that stand. The others, too. That so-called friend of your father's, De Roach, and the deputy. Even your grandfather. I shouldn't have let him being a senator intimidate me. But I did. And his testimony hurt your father's case."

"Mine didn't help either," she offered because Clayton hadn't mentioned it.

"You were only a child." He shook his head. "To this day I can't believe your grandparents allowed the prosecutor to put you on the stand like that. I objected, of course, but it didn't do any good. The judge sided against me."

"I suspect that was my grandfather's doing," she admitted, because whether her grandmother had disagreed or not, Grams would have gone along with what the senator wanted. She swallowed, recalling how frightened she had been to walk up to the front of the courtroom, sit in the chair in front of those people and the judge, of being asked questions, of seeing her father.

"I wouldn't be surprised if it was. And you'll pardon me for saying so, but the senator was wrong to have permitted such a thing."

"No pardon is necessary, Mr. Clayton. I shouldn't have had to testify. And I suspect my testimony is the reason they convicted my father. Because I told them he was a killer."

"You can't take all the blame, Ms. Abbott. I told you, Everett Caine was much better at jury selection and courtroom theatrics than I was. But I won't deny that you testifying that you saw your father kneeling over your mother's body holding the bookend that killed her probably helped to convince the jury that he was guilty."

"And my father wouldn't let you cross-examine me, would he? That's why you never asked me any questions, isn't it?"

He nodded. "He didn't want to put you through any more than you'd already been through."

Tess closed her eyes a moment, remembering that horrible day in court and she ached inside for what it must have done to her father. For what it had cost him to spare her from further testimony.

His daughter.

His freedom.

And finally his life.

Emotions slashed through her like a scalpel. Regret. Pain. Guilt. She also couldn't help but think of Spencer's claims about Caine being ruthless. She felt a measure of disdain for the man herself now. Her grandfather's hatred of her father would have made it easy for Caine to convince him to have her testify on the stand, she told herself, because she didn't want to believe that her grandfather would have put her through that experience on his own.

"Ms. Abbott? Are you okay?"

Tess swallowed hard, trying to get past her own anger. "Yes, I'm fine. Mr. Clayton, are you sure you don't have any idea what new information my father had?"

"I wish I did. But he didn't tell me. When I questioned him and asked him where he had gotten this new information, all he would say was that the Lord had sent someone to help him get his life back. At first I thought perhaps he'd had some kind of religious conversion, but the more he talked about this new information he had, the more I was convinced it was some kind of evidence."

"Did you know a nun, a Sister Amelia, who came to see him several times during those last few months before he died? She was there the same week that you were," she told him.

"No. He never mentioned her to me. But maybe this Sister Amelia is the one you should be talking with."

"I intend to—as soon as I can find her," Tess said. "I had hoped you might know who she was."

"I'm sorry, but I don't have any idea who she is."

When he looked at his watch, Tess realized she didn't have much time left, so she asked, "Mr. Clayton, the last time you saw my father, did he seem like a man who was contemplating suicide to you?"

"Absolutely not. He was a man who had a new lease on life. He was talking about starting over and trying to reestablish a relationship with you. When I called the prison to speak with him and make sure he had received the copies of the report and photographs he'd asked me for, I was stunned to find out he had hung himself in his cell."

Tess tensed. "What report and photographs did he ask you to send?"

"The initial arrest report and photographs that were taken at the crime scene," he told her. "I'm sorry. I just assumed when we spoke on the phone and you told me the prison had given you his effects that you had them."

"No. They weren't among the things I was given," she said, her heart beating a little faster. "I didn't realize you had those."

"Technically I'm not supposed to. Since I worked for the public defender's office on his case, the records belong to them. But because this was my first big case and it was a murder, I made copies of everything for my home file and when I left, I just kept them. When your father talked to me about helping him reopen his case, I mentioned that I was glad I'd kept a copy of those files because I wasn't sure the PD's office would be able to find them after all this time."

"When did you send them to him?"

"Let's see. Two days after I saw him, because I had copies made of the photographs first and it took a day to get them back."

And less than a week later her father was dead, the victim of a suicide. "Mr. Clayton, do you think I could get a copy of that report and the photographs? I'd be willing to pay you for the cost of copying them."

"Don't worry about the cost. I'll phone my office and tell my assistant, Dee Dee, to give you the copies."

"Thank you. I appreciate that. I know my father would, too," she said.

After he looked at his watch again, he stood and tossed his coffee cup into the trash bin. "As much as I would like to be able to talk to you more, I'm afraid I'm going to need to go. I have several calls to make—including the one to Dee Dee on your behalf—before I get back in court."

Following his lead, Tess stood and discarded her empty disposable cup. "I understand and I can't tell you how much I appreciate all your help."

He took both of her hands in his and said, "It was my pleasure. I can see why your father was so proud of you."

She tipped her head to the side. "He talked about me to you?"

"Oh yes," he said, a wide smile spreading across his face. "He told me that you were a television reporter working in Washington, D.C., and that you had made something of yourself. Yes, he was very proud of you."

"Thank you for telling me," she said, a lump in her throat.

"I'll make that call to Dee Dee now and by the time you get to the office, she should have the copies ready for you. It'll probably take another day to get the photographs copied though," he told her as he walked her toward the entryway of the courthouse.

On impulse, Tess gave him a peck on the cheek and grinned to herself at her actions. She couldn't help wondering if perhaps the Southern custom of kissing hello and goodbye was beginning to rub off on her. "Thanks again," she said and headed toward the doors.

"Be careful," he called out as she lifted the collar of her coat and dug the umbrella out of her bag, then headed out into the rainstorm.

Seated inside his truck across the street from the attorney's office, the man took another sip of coffee. Of all days for her to decide to make a trip to Denton, he thought. He'd much rather have spent his day sitting in his easy chair at home, or visiting one of the blackjack tables at the casino than navigating in this downpour and watching the Abbott bitch play detective all day.

What in the hell was she doing in there all this time? Was she going to spend another two hours there the way she had at the courthouse?

Growing more irritated and impatient by the second, he kept his eyes pinned on the building and waited for her to exit. Another five minutes ticked by. He looked at the clock in front of the bank, noted that the temperature had now dropped to fifty-two degrees Fahrenheit. Unseasonably cool for October in Mississippi. Who knows, maybe there had been something to old Lester's talk about "signs" after all, he thought, and laughed at himself. Poor bastard, from what the hit man had told him, Lester had never even seen what was coming until it was too late. And if things went according to plan, neither would that Abbott bitch.

He was just about to pour himself another spot of coffee from the thermos, when the Abbott woman came out of the building. She struggled with the umbrella, got the thing open and, tucking a big envelope under her coat, she rushed out into the rain. He waited for her to get in the car and pull out onto the street. When she was a full block ahead of him, he started his truck engine and pulled out to follow her. Once he got to the interstate, he punched in a number on his cell phone.

"Hello, this is Father Peter."

"Hello, Father. It seems that friend of mine I told you I was worried about is going to be in your parish soon. I'm very worried about her driving this late in the evening with the weather so bad. Although she's driving slowly, I'd appreciate it if you'd keep an eye out for her."

"I'll be happy to, my son. What kind of car is she in?"

"A red Ford Mustang," he told him and gave him the

license-plate number as he hung back and kept her tail-lights in his sights. "I'm particularly worried about her navigating that old bridge just outside of Grady."

"Then I'll drive out and wait for her to make sure she gets there safely," he promised.

"I'd appreciate it, Father. As I said, I'm very worried about her."

"Then put your mind at ease, my son. I'll make sure that your friend reaches her destination."

"And I'll be sure to put another donation to the church in the mail to you as a token of my appreciation."

"As always, the church and I are happy to be of service."

He ended the call, knowing that he would collect the hundred grand for handling the hit. And just to be on the safe side, he decided as he took the next turnaround and headed back toward Denton, he would pay a visit to Attorney Clayton's offices. No point in leaving another loose end, he reasoned. Besides, he could always collect for this one later.

"We did have a Sister Amelia Gendusa who lived here," the nun who had identified herself as Sister Catherine responded in answer to his inquiry. "Unfortunately, she's no longer here. She moved to a retirement home about four years ago."

"This Sister Amelia Gendusa, would she be the same Sister Amelia who taught at St. Andrew's School?" Spencer asked. After hours of striking out calling the convents, he did an Internet search on Jody Burns and discovered that, as a young boy, Tess's father had attended a small parochial grade school across the river from New Orleans. A call to that school had led him to a series of other schools in search of the nun, as well as to another convent before he'd eventually been given the current motherhouse where he had been passed on to Sister Catherine.

"Why yes, she did. But heavens, that was a long time ago. Even before she was assigned to Ursuline Academy," she told him, referring to the oldest girls' school in New Orleans that was located in the uptown area. "What did you say your name was again, young man?"

"Spencer Reed," he told her. "Sister Catherine, you're sure she's the same Sister Amelia who taught at St. Andrew's grade school, the one on the Westbank?"

"I'm quite sure. I've been here for more than twenty years myself, so the other sisters who live here are like my family. Since many of us have taught in the same schools at one time or another, we often discuss the schools where we've been assigned to teach," Sister Catherine informed him. "And I distinctly recall Sister Amelia and I discussing her teaching experiences at St. Andrew's because I taught second-graders there myself for a year. Were you one of Amelia's students at St. Andrew's?"

"No, Sister, I wasn't." The truth was, he wasn't even Catholic. "I'm actually trying to locate her for a friend of mine."

"Then your friend was one of her students?"

"No. But my friend's father was," he explained. "Could you possibly give me the name of the retirement home where Sister Amelia is living now? It's very important that I reach her."

"And may I ask what this is about?" the nun asked.

Spencer explained briefly about the nun's visits to Jody Burns, going into as little detail as possible. "So you see it's important that my friend and I speak with

Sister Amelia. If you could possibly see your way to giving me the name of the retirement home, I'd be most appreciative."

"I can give it to you, but I don't see how it can be the Sister Amelia that you're looking for. You see, the Sister Amelia that I knew who taught at St. Andrew's is more than eighty years old and has had Alzheimer's disease for the last six. She was moved to the retirement home because she's no longer capable of caring for herself. So she couldn't have possibly gone to see your friend's father in Mississippi. She doesn't even know her own name anymore."

Spencer's hopes of presenting Tess with the news that he'd located the nun plummeted. "I guess you're right, Sister. It couldn't be the same Sister Amelia."

"I'm sorry, Mr. Reed. What a strange coincidence to have had two Sister Amelias that taught at St. Andrew's though. I do hope you find the one you're looking for."

"Thank you, Sister," he said and ended the call. But he didn't think it was a coincidence. He grabbed his PalmPilot, punched in the data and located the home number for Pete, the security guard at the prison. After leaving a message with Pete's wife that he needed to speak to her husband, he ended the call and waited to hear back from the security guard.

He didn't have to wait long because fifteen minutes later Pete called him from his cell phone while he was taking a break. Quickly, Spencer told him why he was calling.

"Gee, Mr. Reed. It's kind of hard to describe what she looked like. I mean she was a nun—wearing one of them outfits that cover up everything. And to be honest, I can't say I pay that much attention to a woman if she's like, you know, holy."

"I understand, Pete. But you don't get a lot of nuns coming through there, do you?"

"No, just the regulars mostly."

"Well, this Sister Amelia was there only a few times. Can you remember if she was young or old? It's important."

"Let's see now," Pete began. "I'm not sure what you consider young, but this sister she was somewhere in her late fifties I guess."

"You're sure about that? She wasn't like twenty years older?"

"No way. In fact, I remember thinking she wasn't bad-looking for a nun and that she had probably been a looker when she was younger and would have been a downright pretty woman if she hadn't become a nun," he said. "That is, I mean, I know she's a woman and all, but she's, you know, not a real woman. Ah hell," he muttered. "You know what I'm trying to say."

"Yeah, I know, Pete," Spencer said. "Thanks. You were a big help."

"Anytime."

Spencer hung up the phone, stared at the notes he'd made with the description of the two Sister Amelias. Then he drew an arrow that connected the two of them—Jody Burns. He had no doubts that the Sister Amelia at the prison was an impostor, someone who had borrowed the identity of the real Sister Amelia in order to visit Jody Burns at the prison. He drew another line from the woman who had called him and Tess. He was fairly sure Sister Amelia and the mystery caller were one and the same. The problem was, he still didn't know who she really was.

He glanced at his watch, noted it was after four-thirty already. So he put his notes aside and pulled up the next segment of his series that he'd begun working on following the last gubernatorial debate.

Spencer wasn't sure how long he had been working at finishing the piece and tweaking what he'd already written. When he checked his watch again, two hours had flown by. Satisfied with what he'd written, he attached the file and sent it on to Hank at the *Clarion-Ledger* with a memo telling his editor to be sure and note that he could throw away the antacids because he'd made the deadline for the next installment.

He chuckled as he imagined the other man cursing him, yet again, for giving him ulcers in the first place. Once the file was finished transferring, he shut down his laptop and packed it along with his notes on the Burns murder case into his computer bag. Grabbing his jacket and umbrella, he slung the strap for the computer bag over his shoulder and headed over to the sheriff's office to meet up with Andy.

By the time he arrived, Spencer wondered why he'd even bothered with the umbrella. "That rain is a bitch," he told Andy as he dumped the umbrella by the door. He shed his wet jacket.

"Tell me about it. My deputies and I have been running from one fender bender to another all day," Andy informed him. "And according to the weatherman, more rain is on the way."

"Makes me wish I'd bought that boat I was looking at last month," Spencer commented, shaking some of the excess water off himself.

"Hey, man, go shake off somewhere else," Andy ordered as he stepped back from the spray and shielded the cup of coffee he was holding.

"You got any more of that stuff?"

"Help yourself," Andy told him with a nod of his

head toward the coffeepot. "Then come on back to my office and you can take a look at the file."

Nearly two hours later Spencer had gone over the contents of the police file several times. And each time he did, he came up with nothing new. "You were right about Sheriff Toups keeping pretty good files. Hell, he even numbered the crime scene photos," Spencer remarked as he flipped over one of the photographs they'd spread out on the desktop and noted a number written on the bottom left corner.

"Yeah. Rusty can be a bit anal at times," Andy remarked. "But he did a good job as sheriff of this town for a lot of years."

"You get no argument from me on that. I still remember the time he hauled me down here for throwing that cherry bomb down the mail shute at the school one Fourth of July weekend. My pop grounded me for a month."

Andy laughed. "You know Rusty. He believes in toeing the line and paying for the crime."

"Yeah, I know," Spencer said absently as he continued to pick up the photographs one by one and saw numerals written on each.

Three. Eight. Twelve. Eleven.

Silently Spencer read the numbers on the back of each photograph, and out of habit he began placing them in their proper numerical sequence. When he finished, he went back and double-checked to make sure they were in the right order and frowned because one of them was missing. "Where's number six?" he asked Andy.

"What?"

"The number-six photograph. Sheriff Toups numbered each of these. One through twelve, see?" he asked, showing Andy that they were in order.

"All right."

He spread all the photos out on the desk again, but this time with the flip side displayed. "So where is photograph number six?"

Andy stared at the numbered photos and narrowed his eyes. "It must have gotten stuck in the file." He picked up the file folder, shuffled through the contents, then lifted his gaze to Spencer's. "It's not here."

"No, it's not. The question is *why* isn't it here? And if it's not here, then *where* is it?"

Chapter Fifteen

Tess kept a firm grip on the steering wheel of the car as she traveled along the rain-slick roads. She cranked up the defrost button on the dashboard and struggled to see through the windshield. The drive had been exhausting. Probably because what should have been a two-hour drive at best was quickly stretching into three hours because of the weather conditions. Yet despite the horrible weather and the fact that she was tired, she felt good about her meeting with Beau Clayton. She'd liked him, had appreciated his honesty, and hearing him talk about her father had helped to ease some of her guilt. It had also made her feel a connection with her father. Not the father whom she'd associated with hatred because he'd killed her mother. She realized now that that father didn't exist. He'd been a figment of her child's fear and hurt, and yes, she admitted, her grandfather's manipulation. No, the father she thought of now was her real father, the man who had given her piggyback rides and belly tickles and tucked her into bed at night. The same man whom she had banished from her thoughts and her heart for all those years.

I'm sorry, Daddy.

She hoped that he would hear her silent apology. Glancing over at the manila envelope on the seat beside her that was stuffed with the attorney's notes from the trial, she hoped she would be able to make up for what she had done by clearing his name. Perhaps somewhere within those papers she would find something that would lead her to the mysterious Sister Amelia and the new information her father had uncovered before his death.

Finally Tess spied the signs up ahead announcing the road construction on the interstate and she followed the detour signs to the old highway on which she would need to travel for five miles before she would connect up with the interstate again. Once she did, she would only have another fifteen miles to go before she reached Grady.

But she still had the detour to endure, she thought. Although it wasn't a terribly long section to have to navigate, in the downpour it would seem twice as long. As she exited the interstate, she slowed her speed. The old highway was badly worn and the elevation a little lower than the more modern roadway. The lighting was not nearly as good either, she thought. She glanced at the water along the side of the road and swallowed hard. The last weather reports she'd heard had said the riverbeds in the area were cresting. From the way the water was lapping at the banks now, she guessed this one would be flooding over soon.

Thank heavens traffic wasn't too heavy, she thought.

She'd lost the taillights of the last car ahead of her a good fifteen minutes ago when she'd slowed her speed. Only an occasional car passed her coming from the opposite direction, and as far as she could tell, only one car had been behind her for the last five miles. As she neared the bridge up ahead, she was grateful for the slight elevation and the guardrails that spanned the three-mile crossing over the water.

Tess noted the vehicle behind her had been picking up speed and she shook her head, wondering why the driver would risk his life on the wet road in order to reach his destination a few minutes sooner. She hit a bump as she continued climbing toward the top of the bridge and decided she'd better keep her mind on her own driving. Once she reached the very top of the bridge, she glanced in her rearview mirror again and was surprised to see that the pickup truck was still traveling way too fast.

"Idiot," she muttered. Blinded by the glare of the pickup's bright lights, she reached up to adjust her rearview mirror for night driving when the truck suddenly swerved out to the opposite lane and passed her. Silently cursing the crazed driver, Tess quickly put both hands on the wheel.

Then to her shock, the pickup swerved back over into her lane, slamming into the Mustang's front fender and shoving her car sideways. "Oh, my God," she cried out as she realized what was happening.

With the road slick from the rain, the tires on her car began to slide toward the railing of the bridge. For several long seconds, she wrestled with the wheel of the Mustang, trying to keep it steady, trying to avoid crashing into and through the bridge's railing. Clamping her hands around the wheel, she held on, knowing she was going to crash. She braced her arms, stiffened her legs and shoved her heeled boots hard against the floor. She still wasn't prepared for the impact of the crash. The grinding of metal. The shattering of glass. Instinctively, she held her arms up to cover her face and she prayed as the Mustang went flying off the bridge.

Thinking quickly, she hit the button for the car's window, sending the rain and cold air inside the car. And then the scream died in her throat as she watched the lights of her car swipe through the darkness before heading nose down into the river.

Tess died a thousand deaths in those seconds when the car first hit the water. Fighting panic, she fought to free herself from her seat belt as she felt herself being dragged deeper and deeper beneath the surface. Finally the latch gave free and Tess, unable to see, felt for the hole where the window was opened. She found it and swam through.

Frightened, cold and her lungs feeling as though they were ready to burst, she swam for the surface. When her head broke the surface of the water, she gasped and dragged the air into her lungs while an icy rain pelted her face. Treading water, she looked over and up at the bridge where a section of the rail had been ripped away, leaving a gaping hole.

Flashing lights shone at the top of the bridge and then she saw two people looking down, pointing at her and yelling. Relieved to have survived the crash, Tess started swimming toward the bridge. And with each stroke of her arms, each kick of her legs, anger began to burn inside her for the fool driver who had nearly gotten her killed.

"Since Rusty Toups was so organized about his case files, I'd have expected him to have the negatives filed away, too," Spencer told Andy.

"I'll pay him a visit tomorrow and ask him about the missing photo," Andy offered.

"I'd like to go with you."

Spencer could see that Andy wasn't keen on the idea even before he said, "It might be better if I went alone."

"Trudeaux—"

"If you come, Rusty is liable to take any questions about his record keeping as criticism. He won't be as defensive with me because we go way back."

"All right," Spencer agreed.

"But be forewarned, Rusty may still be as sharp as a tack, but we're talking about a photo from a twenty-five-year-old case, Spence. I wouldn't hang your hopes on him remembering what was on it."

"I'd settle for knowing what happened to it."

"Like I said, don't count on anything," Andy told him. The intercom buzzed on Andy's desk. "Yes, Hazel?"

"Sheriff, I just got a call from Captain Morris with the highway patrol. He wanted to let you know about a problem out at the three-mile bridge," she began.

Spencer's thoughts were still on the missing crime scene photo, so he half listened as Hazel relayed to Andy, via the intercom, the news about a nasty accident that had taken out a section of the guardrail and forced a temporary closure of the old road. Although the bridge wasn't located in Grady, it would be Andy's problem because it was close enough to the town to impact traveling.

"Captain Morris says they've got everything under control, but he said you might want to issue a road advisory."

"Go ahead and get one out, Hazel," Andy instructed her. "Did Morris say if we need to send a car over to help direct traffic?"

"Negative, Sheriff. They've got units on the scene, plus the Coast Guard. And they've already fished her out of the river."

Spencer jerked his head up. "Her?"

Andy glanced toward him. "I take it the driver was female."

"Affirmative, Sheriff."

"Do they know who she is?" Andy asked.

"It's that Abbott woman, the one staying at Maggie O'Donnell's place, the one you had me run that personal background check on a couple of days ago."

"Jesus Christ! Is she all right?" Spencer demanded, his heart in his throat.

"Hazel, did Morris say what her condition was?"

"Just a sec," she told him and switched over to the radio. When she came back on, she said, "He says she's a little banged up, but all in one piece."

Spencer loomed over the desk and the intercom. "What hospital are they taking her to?"

"None. She refuses to go."

"Thanks, Hazel. Tell Morris I'm on my way out there."

But Spencer didn't wait to hear whatever instructions Andy gave Hazel because he was already racing out of the office. He didn't bother searching for his umbrella or his coat or his laptop. He hit the exit door at a run, ignoring Andy's shouts for him to wait, ignoring the rain that soaked him, ignoring the blare of horns as he ran across traffic to his car. With his stomach twisting in knots, he cranked up his car and sent the tires squealing as he raced to the accident scene.

Spencer was unsure how many red lights he'd run or how many speeding laws he'd broken in the fifteen minutes it took him to reach the accident scene. The sight of the emergency-response vehicles and Mississippi Highway Patrol cars with their flashing lights lining the road did little to ease his concerns. Portable spotlights illuminated the hole in the bridge rail where a crew struggled to work in the rain to put up a temporary guardrail. Below the rail, the lights from a Coast Guard boat probed the black waters around a flashing buoy, apparently marking the area where Tess's Mustang must have gone down.

Spencer slammed on his brakes, and the SUV screeched to a halt. He scanned the area for Tess and spotted her huddled in the back of an EMT truck with a blanket wrapped around her. He shoved open the door of his vehicle and started over, when he saw a uniformed officer in a rain slicker headed his way. Highway patrol, he realized, recognizing the blue-gray pants with royal-blue striping and red piping. The navy blue campaign hat looked black beneath the onslaught of rain. "Sorry, sir. You'll need to move your car."

"I need to get to Ms. Abbott, the woman in the EMT truck," he told the man as Andy's sheriff's truck pulled in behind him with its lights flashing.

"You her husband?" the patrolman asked.

"No. I'm a...I'm a friend. A close friend," he amended.

"It's okay, Patrolman. Sheriff Andy Trudeaux from Grady," Andy said and flashed the man his badge. "You can let him through."

Not bothering to thank either man, Spencer started across the road to Tess. He had to stop and wait for several vehicles to go by but he never took his eyes off her. Her hair hung down the sides of her face in wet clumps. The smart-looking burgundy pantsuit she'd worn that morning clung to her body. When she shifted her head to answer something the medic asked, he saw a nasty bruise on her cheek and he felt another kick in his gut.

He was halfway across the road, when she looked up. The flash of recognition and relief in her eyes as she saw him eased the viselike grip around his heart some.

Dammit. How had this happened?

He'd known he'd been attracted to her, knew that something had begun to happen between them, that she had begun to matter to him. But the speed and the depth of those feelings shocked him. When he reached her, he wanted to take her into his arms, hold her, to assure himself she was all right. But her face was the color of paste, making the bruise on her cheek stand out even more. So he tried to play it easy. "You okay?" he asked.

"I am, but the car's not. I imagine I'm going to have a hell of a rental bill. What are you doing here?"

"I was in Andy's office when a call came in saying that you'd decided to take your car for a swim. So I thought I'd come on out and see how you did."

Her chuckle turned into a groan.

"Are you all right?"

"Other than feeling like I went ten rounds with a tank, yes. They said I have a concussion, and my face hurts like hell—which is probably how I look," she said, fingering the bruise on her cheek.

"Nah. It's not that bad," he told her as he tipped her chin up to the light. That vise around his heart eased a bit more as her eyes dilated. On the drive out there, he'd worried that the plunge off the bridge might not have been a weather-related accident, but intentional. After all, he'd known that the things they'd unearthed about her father and her grandfather's manipulation hadn't been easy for her. She'd been stressed and eaten up with guilt. Just one of those factors led strong people to do crazy things. Getting a double whammy could be too much. "A little makeup and nobody'll even notice it. But you still should probably let the EMT guys take you to the hospital and check you out."

She eased her head back, ending the contact. "It's just a few bumps and bruises. I don't need a hospital."

"So what happened?"

"Some idiot in a truck sideswiped me," she said, fury in her voice. "Evidently he doesn't know that double yellow lines on a road means no passing, because he tried to pass me. Then the fool either changed his mind or couldn't see because of the rain and he swerved back over into my lane and rammed my car. The impact shoved me through the railing. The worst part about it is the jerk never even stopped to see if I was all right."

Jesus, a hit-and-run.

"Oh, dammit!"

"What?" he asked, alarmed.

"I just realized I had a copy of Clayton's file from my father's trial in the car and now it's ruined."

"So we'll ask him to make you another copy," he offered. "I'm going to go talk to Andy for a minute and then I'll take you home. Okay?"

She nodded.

Grateful the rain had eased up some, he walked over to where Andy was talking to the highway patrol officer who was apparently in charge. After introducing himself, he relayed what Tess had told him about the hit-and-run.

"That's what she said when she gave me her statement. Like I was telling the sheriff here, we've got a couple of sets of skid marks," he began.

The three of them walked about twenty-five yards from where the temporary rail was being mended. Using a flashlight, the highway patrol captain illuminated the black streaks on the concrete. "I figure this one's Ms. Abbott's. You can see where she hit her brakes and was trying to stop," he explained, following the marks with the beam of light. He angled the flashlight to the second set of marks. "These are from the other driver. Looks to me like he fishtailed to a stop right here after he hit her, then the SOB burned a couple yards of rubber when he took off. Probably some damn fool who'd been drinking and didn't want to get ticketed for DWI."

Spencer wasn't all that sure. "Was she able to give you a make and model of the truck that hit her?" he asked.

"She said the rain was coming down so hard she didn't even see him until he was on her tail, blinding her with his headlights. Says it was a big silver job, probably one of them new F150's."

"But there'll probably be a mess of paint scrapings on her car," Andy remarked. "Once they fish the thing out of the river, I'd appreciate it if you'd send some of the chips over to the lab in Jackson. They might be able to find a match in the National Automotive Paint File so we'll have a starting point."

"I'll send 'em, Sheriff. But last I heard, the backlog there was running a good two to three months," the captain replied. "You know how it is, all these new crime shows got people believing we can get DNA and paint analysis at the drop of a hat. When the truth is, the staff and the funds aren't there. My guess is, getting the paint scrapings analyzed is going to be low on the priority scale."

"Captain, I'd appreciate it if you'd keep me—" Spencer paused, shot a glance at Andy "—if you'd keep Sheriff Trudeaux posted," he said as he went through a mental list of possible contacts to get that analysis moved up to priority one.

"He's right, Captain," Andy added. "If you'd keep me posted on any response, I'd be grateful."

"Not a problem."

"Are you finished with Ms. Abbott?" Spencer asked.

"Yes, sir. I was just about to get one of my men to take her home."

"I'll take her," Spencer offered.

"Fine by me," the captain said.

"Thanks for your help, Captain," Andy told him and walked with Spencer in the direction of the EMT truck where Tess sat waiting. "She okay?"

Spencer nodded. Emotions churned through him as he looked at that hole in the bridge rail once more. He released a breath filled with frustration and fury. "She could have been killed."

"I know. She's one brave and smart lady. Not everyone would have had the wits to get themselves out of there the way she did. She's lucky she got out of that car alive."

They stopped, stood in the softly falling rain and waited to cross the road. "I'm not sure she was supposed to," Spencer said. He looked at his friend square in the eye. "I think she was run off that bridge deliberately. You saw the skid marks. Only one set, Tess's. If the guy had hit her by accident, there should have been another set when he hit his brakes to try to stop. There weren't any. He meant to run her off that bridge."

"Why?"

"Maybe because she's been digging into that old murder case and she's getting too close to the truth for somebody's peace of mind."

Andy sighed. "Spence, do you really think Everett Caine is behind this? That the man would risk his political career by trying to kill a senator's granddaughter?"

"If she stood between him and the governor's mansion, yes," Spencer answered. "But Caine wouldn't do his own dirty work. He'd have someone do it for him. Probably the same people who helped him before." He paused. "You saw those reports, Andy. I told you about the things Tess and I have uncovered. Nothing about that trial rings true. The whole case against Jody Burns was a setup."

"You don't have any proof of that."

"Not yet. But I will. I'm not going to sit back and do nothing." He curled his hands into fists at his sides. "I'm going to find the bastard who tried to kill her, and when I do we'll find out if he's half as brave as Tess was."

Andy clamped a firm hand down on his shoulder. "You need to stay out of this. Go take your lady home and let me do my job."

"You do what you have to do, Andy. And so will I," Spencer told him, shrugging off the other man's hand. Leaving a grim-faced Andy, he crossed the road.

When he reached Tess a second time, the bravado and anger had deserted her. A shudder went through her and she wrapped her arms around herself to abate it. He thought of her, fighting and clawing her way out of the car as the water threatened to swallow her whole. Just imagining her terror and what might have happened left him feeling raw. "You ready to go home?"

She looked up at him out of pale gray eyes that were wide and blank. Not waiting for an answer, he gently eased her from the truck. But the moment her feet touched the ground, her knees buckled. Cursing, Spencer caught her and lifted her into his arms.

"I can walk," she told him even as she looped her arms around his neck and rested her head against his chest. Despite his aunt Sarah's complaint that Tess was too thin, she wasn't a lightweight. The shoulder, the hip and soft curve of her breasts were solid against his body as he walked her over to the SUV and eased her inside.

Tess used the drive back to the cottage to regain a measure of composure. She stared straight ahead and clasped her hands together tightly. Every few minutes memories of her car sailing through that rail, the feeling of being airborne and seeing the black water rushing up to meet her flashed through her mind's eye. She shuddered, feared she would be ill.

"Still cold? I can turn up the heat."

"No. I'm okay," she said, her breath shaky, hating this feeling of weakness. She'd never been a simpering female who relied on a man for strength. Yet when she'd looked up and had seen Spencer, relief had flooded through her. He'd looked tall and solid as he'd walked steadily through the rain and emergency vehicles toward her. She'd nearly thrown herself into his arms. The realization that she'd wanted to do so had shaken her almost as much as the crash.

When he pulled his car up in front of her cottage, she was feeling steadier and more in charge of her emotions. She managed to unlatch her seat belt with only a small measure of discomfort. But before she could open the door, Spencer was there, offering her his hand. "I can manage from here," she told him.

"Take my hand, Tess." When she hesitated. "Take my damn hand."

She did so, mostly because she was feeling too exhausted both physically and emotionally to argue with him. He slid his arm around her shoulder and started for the front door. Only then did she realize she didn't have her key. It, along with her purse, her phone and the file had gone down with the car. She stopped.

"What's wrong?"

"I don't have a key. It was on the ring with my car keys," she said, getting angry all over again.

"First thing we need to do is get you out of this rain. Why don't we sit you down over here," he said, indicating one of the chairs on the porch. "And I'll call down to the main house and ask them to bring a key."

"I'm perfectly capable of walking by myself, Reed," she said, hating that she still felt so unsteady.

"I know you are, but you're going to humor me and let me help you anyway."

She was simply humoring him, she told herself as she allowed him to guide her to the chair and out of the rain. Then he went back to his car and she assumed he spoke to either Maggie or someone else at the main house. When he started back over to her, he was carrying the blanket she'd left in the car.

"Maggie should be here in a few minutes with a key. In the meantime, you need to keep warm," he told her and wrapped the blanket around her. He hunkered down in front of her, holding the two ends of the blanket in one fist. Using his free hand, he brushed the hair behind her ear. "You gave me quite a fright tonight, Abbott."

"I gave myself one," she admitted, not wanting to respond to the concern in his eyes, to the spark along her nerves at his touch. To cover her reaction, she lifted her fingers to the bruise on her face.

"You probably should have gone to the hospital and let them x-ray that for you."

"It's just a bruise. If the pain gets worse, I'll ask Maggie to take me to the E.R."

"What do you mean, *if* the pain gets worse? Where does it hurt?"

"My head. Mostly," she admitted, touching the back of her head, where she could feel a knot the size of an egg. "I think I cracked it against the door when the car hit the water."

At the sound of tires tearing down the roadway, he released her and stood. So did she. The car had barely stopped before the door opened and Maggie came flying up the walkway in red high heels, a dashing red suit and without an umbrella to protect her or the clothes. She went right past Spencer as though he wasn't even there. A hard thing to do considering the man wasn't easy to ignore.

Yet Maggie managed to do just that. "Oh my God, Tess. Are you all right?" she demanded. "What happened? Do you know who hit you?"

"She's all right. A truck sideswiped her in a hit-and-run."

"Oh, look at your poor cheek. Does it hurt?" Maggie began.

Spencer clamped a hand on Maggie's shoulder. "The key, Maggie?"

Maggie looked at him, then at her, then lifted her gaze back to Spencer's. She looked like a pixie facing down a giant, Tess thought. And her money was on the pixie.

"She's got a bump on the back of her head, a concussion and that bruise on her face could use some ice on it."

"There should be an ice bag in the back of the bathroom cabinet," Maggie told him. "Somebody's going to need to stay with her, to make sure she's all right."

"I intend to."

Maggie blinked, then got an odd look in her eyes. "Okay," she said and to Tess's chagrin, Maggie placed the key in Spencer's open palm.

"I'm perfectly capable of taking care of myself. And I'd appreciate it if the two of you would stop talking about me like I'm not here," she informed them as she snatched at the key. But Spencer closed it in his fist.

"Take care of her," Maggie told him and zipped back down the walkway to her car without a backward glance.

Spencer moved past her and unlocked the door. He pushed it open and stood back for her to enter. When she simply stood there, he said, "If you're feeling light-headed, I'll be happy to carry you."

Tess hiked up her chin and immediately regretted the movement as pain shot through her head. Saying nothing, she marched into the cottage ahead of him, fully intent on sending him on his way. "Thanks for coming out to check on me and for driving me home," she began when he followed her inside the cottage.

"You're welcome," he told her and navigated his way through the bedroom to the bathroom. He dug in the cabinet, retrieved the ice bag, then turned around and opened the medicine cabinet. He plucked a bottle of Tylenol from the shelf.

"And I appreciate you calling Maggie for a key."

"Glad to do it," he told her.

She followed him into the kitchen where he began opening cupboards. "But I can take things from here, Reed. I'm okay now. Really."

He took out one of the glasses, filled it with water and shook out the pills. "Take these."

Tess gritted her teeth and reminded herself the man was only trying to help. She took the pills, swallowed them and slapped the glass down on the counter. "You need to go, Reed. I told you, I can handle things from here."

"Go change out of those wet things, Abbott. You're beginning to smell."

And before she could light into him for giving her orders, he turned his back on her and began filling the ice pack. She considered arguing with him, but suddenly the thought of battling with Spencer seemed too much. So, deciding that she'd shower, change into something dry that didn't reek of river water and fear, she headed for the bathroom.

When she exited the bedroom fifteen minutes later, Spencer was still in the kitchen and on his cell phone, his back to her. "I appreciate the info, Andy. I'm going to make some calls tomorrow and see if I can speed the process along."

Tess told herself she should make her presence known and send the man on his way. But she hesitated and she listened.

"Like I said, you do what you need to do. And so will I." He hit the off button on the phone and said, "Feeling any better?"

"Yes," she said, embarrassed to have been caught listening to his conversation. "Was that the sheriff?"

"Yes." He picked up the ice pack from the counter

and came over to her. Tipping her chin up, he rested the ice against the bruise on her cheek. "You look better, got a little more color." He made a point of sniffing her. "Smell better, too. No more dead-fish smell."

She gave him a withering look before taking the ice pack from him. She held it to her own face. "What did the sheriff want? Did they find the guy who sideswiped me?"

"No," he said, his expression grim. "He gave me the name of the salvage company that fished your car out of the river."

"Oh, God, the car-rental company. I need to call them, tell them what happened to the car. I've got the card with the phone number in my purse—" She realized once again that she no longer had a purse.

"The salvage company will notify them and the rental company will get in touch with you here. Andy gave them the number at the main house as well as mine."

She wandered into the den, sat down on the couch and curled her feet beneath her. "I'll need to get another car. And another cell phone," she said, thinking aloud about the things she'd lost. What she wouldn't be able to replace immediately were the copies of the files that Beau Clayton had given her from her father's trial.

Spencer followed her over to the couch, shoved a glass at her. "Drink this. It's cognac."

"Where'd you get it?" she asked, setting the ice pack down on the floor.

"Maggie had it in the bar over there," he told her, motioning to the polished mahogany cabinet in the corner.

Tess took a sip, felt the burn of the liquor slide down her throat. But after a moment, the heat of it eased some of the chill that still lingered in her blood as a result of the dive she'd taken into the river.

Spencer stooped down, picked up the ice and rested it against her cheek. She was keenly aware of how close he was, of the scent of rain on his skin, of the darkening of his blue eyes as he looked at her. When he removed the glass from her hands and set it aside with the pack, Tess said nothing. Nor did she say anything when he pressed his mouth to the bruise. Too tired to fight him and herself and the feelings he stirred in her, she made no effort to avoid his mouth when he brushed it across her lips. The kiss was so tender, so caring. She sighed.

Spencer made another gentle pass over her lips with his mouth, then another. But when she expected him to repeat the journey, he lifted his head. "You need to get some rest. I'll be here on the couch if you need me."

"But—"

"I'm staying, Tess."

"Reed, I've told you I'm fine now. You don't need to stay for me."

"I'm not staying for you," he told her. "I'm staying for me."

Chapter Sixteen

Spencer checked on the pan of biscuits in the oven and since they needed a few more minutes before they reached that golden-brown shade, he opted for another cup of coffee. His third, but who was counting. He poured the thick dark brew into one of the dainty cups he'd found in the cupboard.

It had been a hell of a night. He couldn't remember the last time he'd spent the night on a woman's couch—and one that was too short for his six-foot-two-inch frame. But it hadn't been the sleeping accommodations that had interfered with his sleep. It had been the woman asleep in the bed in the next room. Every time she had tossed or turned or made a sound, he'd been up and rushing into the bedroom to check on her. And even when she'd been sleeping peacefully, he found himself checking on her anyway. That plunge she'd taken with her car into the river had been close. Too close for his peace of mind.

Christ! He didn't want her to matter this much to him.

But she did. Lust figured into it. There was no denying that. But it was more than just lust. Somehow, someway, the woman had managed to work herself under his skin, into his head and, it seemed, into his heart. For a time there last night, when he'd been standing over her and watching her sleep, he hadn't been able to stop thinking about how she'd gotten that ugly bruise on her cheek. Of how close she had come to being killed. It had sent a rage through him, a rage rooted in fear and the gut feeling that that sideswipe had been no accident. The fact that Andy hadn't disagreed with him only reinforced his belief that someone wanted Tess dead. And the only reason he could come up with was that they'd been digging into the Melanie Burns murder case.

Sometime around three in the morning while he had lain there awake staring at the ceiling, he'd considered his own hand in things. Granted, he'd wanted to take Caine down for Jenny's sake—and he'd seen Tess as a means to do it. But endangering her hadn't been a part of his plan.

Maybe he could convince her to drop the whole thing and send her packing to D.C. before something worse happened to her. Doing so would keep her out of harm's way and he could continue the investigation on his own. Satisfied with his plan of action, he took his cup of coffee and wandered over to the window. He stared out at what appeared to be the beginning of a beautiful day. After the thirty-six hours of nonstop rain and dark skies, the sun was a welcome sight. The grass and the gardens looked none the worse for wear, he thought, noting the clusters of mums everywhere.

Bursts of gold and orange and cinnamon seemed to be sticking out of every corner and between every bush. Pumpkins had been gathered in a patch near an oak tree. Squirrels scurried beneath the tree, gathering acorns to tuck away for the winter months ahead.

When the buzzer sounded on the oven, Spencer turned around and went over to shut it off. Grabbing a dish towel, he retrieved the pan of buttermilk biscuits and dumped them in a bowl. He piled four of the flaky morsels on a plate for himself and then draped a cloth over the bowl to keep the rest of them fresh and warm for Tess. Digging out the butter and a small jar of grape jelly he'd found in the fridge, he sat down with his breakfast.

He'd just finished polishing off the plate of hot biscuits and was considering having another one when his cell phone rang. "Reed," he answered on the first ring, not wanting the sound to awaken Tess.

"It's Andy."

"Tell me you're going to start my day off right by telling me you've found the guy who ran Tess off the road last night."

"I wish I could," Andy told him and Spencer knew that he meant it. "But I can't. How's she doing this morning?"

Spencer paused, and was about to ask him how he knew that he had spent the night at Tess's. "She's still asleep. I take it Maggie told you I stayed."

"She mentioned it when she phoned last night to make sure I was doing my job and finding the slime who ran her friend off that bridge."

At any other time Spencer would have smiled at the combination of annoyance and fascination in his friend's voice when he spoke of Maggie O'Donnell. Except Tess being run off a bridge and nearly killed didn't make him feel at all like laughing. "So, have you found the slime that ran Tess off that bridge?"

"I'm working on it. I talked to Morris with the highway patrol earlier. He got the paint scrapings off Tess's car. They were silver just like she said. They're on their way now to the forensics guys in Jackson so they can run them through the system to see if we get a match. I've also got a call into someone there that I've worked with before to see if she can help move things along a little quicker."

"Thanks. I appreciate it."

"Don't thank me yet. I'm not sure quicker is going to live up to your definition of the word. In the meantime, I've sent out an alert to all shops within a hundred-mile radius requesting notification on vehicles brought in for bodywork. And I've got word out to all the law-enforcement agencies in the state that we're looking for a silver truck involved in a hit-and-run."

"That all sounds fine. But you and I both know that last night was no accident and we know who was behind it," Spencer told him.

"What I think I know and what I can prove are two different things. When I get confirmation on the paint scrapings or find the truck and can tie it back to someone, you have my word that I'll bring him in. But you have to let me do things the right way. Otherwise, it'll never hold up in the courts."

"Right now I'm not worried about the courts. I'm worried about making sure Tess stays safe."

"Spence—"

"You need proof? I'll get you proof. And I'm going to start by checking out Everett Caine, Sheriff Toups and anyone else involved in that trial and find out if any of them own a silver truck."

"You need to back off, pal. Because friendship or not, you interfere in my investigation and I'll haul your ass in."

"Then you'll need to haul me in because I'm not backing off."

"You dumb son of a—"

Spencer severed the call. After tossing the phone down, he gripped the counter with both hands in an attempt to master his control over the rage that continued to burn inside.

"Why is the sheriff threatening to throw you in jail?"

Spencer stiffened, then turned around to see Tess standing in the doorway. And damn if just looking at her didn't make it hard for him to breathe. She looked a lot better than she had last night when they'd fished her out of the river, he thought. She was dressed in jeans and an ivory-colored turtleneck, and her feet were bare, revealing toenails painted a deep rose shade. She'd pulled her dark hair up on top of her head in some kind of ponytail that had little pieces dangling down the sides of her face. She didn't have on a lick of makeup. But her skin looked soft as silk—except for the bruise on her cheek. While it had already faded some and the ice had taken down the swelling, it was an ugly reminder of how close she'd come to being killed last night. "Good morning," he said. "You hungry? I made some biscuits. Why don't you sit down and I'll serve you a few."

She moved into the room, sat at the table. "You never answered my question. Why does the sheriff want to throw you in jail?"

Spencer served her three biscuits and put another two on the plate for himself. "He and I don't agree on the best way to deal with a problem, and he was trying to convince me to see things his way by threatening me with his badge." He poured her coffee and refilled his own cup.

"Thank you," she said when he handed her the butter. "This problem you're fighting over has something to do with me and my accident last night, doesn't it? That's why he told you to back off."

He didn't want to frighten her. But he didn't want her to be caught unaware again. "I don't think that little swim you took in the river last night was an accident. I think someone deliberately ran you off that bridge."

Tess put her biscuit down. "But who? Why—" Her eyes widened. "You think it has something to do with me investigating my father's trial?"

"Yes. Think about it, Tess. You show up in town and a few days later De Roach turns up dead with your credit card receipt stuffed in his pocket. You track down Virginia Lee and start asking her questions, then a few days later someone tries to run you off a bridge. I don't think that's a coincidence and I don't think last night was an accident. I think you're making someone nervous."

"But why? And who? I never spoke to De Roach. I didn't even know there was any connection between him and the trial until after he was dead. As far as Virginia…Ginger, she wouldn't tell me anything. And so far, I haven't been able to speak with Caine. So who would want to kill me?"

"The person who has the most to lose if you prove that your father's trial was a setup."

"You mean Caine."

"I think if he feels threatened enough, it's a strong possibility."

"I find that hard to believe," she told him.

"Then consider this. How much damage do you think it would do to his bid for governor if it was learned that his star witnesses in his first major murder trial were lying and he'd supported perjury. Not to mention that there are also the witnesses themselves," he added. "While De Roach might be dead, Virginia Lee is still very much alive and you've already threatened to charge her with perjury. Then there's the deputy who claimed your father lied about seeing another car leaving your house when he arrived that night. And then there's also the real killer who, until now, has gotten away with the crime."

She picked up the biscuit and took a bite. Spencer could almost see the wheels turning in her head as she processed everything he had told her. When he saw that hard, determined gleam come into her eyes, he knew that she believed him. "I guess from now on, I'm going to have to be more careful."

It wasn't the answer he had hoped for, but not totally unexpected. "I think you should go back to D.C., Tess, where you'll be safe. I'll stay here and keep digging into the case and let you know what I find out."

"I have no intention of going back to Washington," she informed him. "Not until I find out the truth."

"I'll find out the truth for you. And I'll get Andy to help me do it. As the sheriff, he's got a lot of resources. I'll get him to use them and help me find the answers. But I need you to back off and let me handle it. I need you to trust me."

"This has nothing to do with me trusting you." She threw her napkin down on the table and stood. "It has to do with me making things right. I may not be able to change the past and give my father back the twenty-five years he spent in that prison, but I can clear his name. I owe him that."

"You don't owe him your life," he retorted. "And I don't think he'd want you to risk it just to clear his name."

"Would Jenny want you to risk yours for her?"

Spencer's jaw hardened. "That's different. We're not talking about the same thing. No one tried to send me to a watery grave last night," he snapped.

"Fortunately for me, they didn't succeed. And next time they try, I'll be ready."

Spencer swore. "What is it going to take to convince you to leave this alone?"

"You can't," she told him honestly. "Listen, I appreciate your concern, Reed. Really, I do. And if you want to take a step back from this I'll certainly understand."

His mouth went flat. Heat flared in those blue eyes of his. And he moved in close, so close she could smell the scent of coffee that lingered on his lips. "I'm so far from stepping back, Abbott, it's a wonder you don't feel me every time you take a breath."

Tess's pulse scattered. She read the control he was fighting so valiantly to maintain in the stiffness of his body, in the flexed muscles of the arm that blocked the doorway. He was right. She did feel him. Just as she'd felt his presence during the night when he'd come into her bedroom and smoothed her covers, checked on her, while she had pretended to be asleep.

She felt his fury with her now, and beneath that, the desire that was always simmering near the surface. And if she was going to be honest with herself, she'd have to admit that she felt that desire, too. And that scared her. Because she still remembered how tempted she had been last night to lean into him in the car and draw on his strength, to lose herself in his kisses and forget those agonizing moments when the car had begun to sink in the river and she'd been unable to escape. She was only grateful that he had pulled back when he had because she knew in her heart that she wouldn't have.

"Whether you like it or not, I'm not going to go away."

"I know," she admitted. And the truth was, she wasn't sure she wanted him to. "If you're right and last night was no accident, you could be putting yourself in danger by helping me. I don't want you to get hurt."

Some of the stiffness in his expression softened. "I don't intend to be. And it seems the only way I'm going to be able to make sure you stay safe is if we find out what really happened twenty-five years ago."

"So, where do we go from here? We've got all these pieces of a puzzle but they just don't seem to fit together."

"That's because we still have a couple of pieces missing," he told her. "Maybe it's time we lay out all those pieces and see what we've got."

They sat down, recapped what they already had and filled each other in on what they'd found out the previous day. Tess told him about the files that Clayton had his office turn over to her, the files that she'd lost when her car had plunged into the river. She also told him about her conversation with the attorney and the defense counsel's belief that De Roach had been lying when he'd claimed her father had had a thing going with Virginia Lee for weeks before her mother was killed. He'd also believed that her father had been telling the truth about seeing a dark-colored Cadillac race past him on the road that night, a car which her father was sure must have contained her mother's real killer.

In turn, Spencer told her about his search for Sister Amelia, a woman he was now sure was an impostor. An impostor who had known enough about Jody Burns's background to use the identity of the nun in order to see him at the prison and not arouse suspicions. He also told her about the case files and the photos that Andy had given him access to, as well as the puzzle about the missing crime scene photo. It was the last that caught Tess's attention.

"Maybe if I go to see the sheriff," Tess suggested. "What was his name?"

"Toups. Rusty Toups. And I'm not sure that's a good idea. I know Andy won't think it is. He's already told me as much. He said that he was going to talk to him."

"This isn't the sheriff's call," she pointed out.

"No, it's not. But if anyone has a chance at finding out about the missing photo, it's Andy. I think we should wait and see what he comes up with first."

"I guess you're right," she said, feeling frustrated.

"What's interesting is that you said Clayton told you that your father claimed to have seen a dark Cadillac race by him from the direction of the house that night. You'd think that would be the kind of thing he would have told the deputy that arrived first on the scene that night."

"Yes. I suppose he should have said something. I remember reading in one of the newspaper articles that my father testified to that at his trial."

"I read that, too. But yesterday when I was at the sheriff's office going through the file, I read the arresting deputy's initial report, the one where he took your father's statement. And there was no mention of the Cadillac."

"Maybe he left it out," Tess suggested. "From what Clayton told me, the deputy was a friend of my father's and arresting him for my mother's murder was hard on him. That's why the A.D.A. was called out to the scene—he didn't want to raise any question that might suggest the arrest hadn't been done by the book."

"It's still not the kind of detail a law enforcement officer would leave out of a report, especially if the man was a friend. And from what Andy tells me, Sheriff Toups ran a tight ship. He would have insisted his deputies get all the details."

"You think the deputy left it out intentionally?"

"I don't know. But one of the things that Caine used to poison the jury's minds was that your father conveniently remembered later that he'd seen a Cadillac that night on the road. No one believed him because the deputy said your father never said anything about another car to him when he first arrived on the scene. Of course, everyone believed the deputy since the two were friends. What if he was lying?"

"But why? Like you said, the man was my father's friend. Clayton said he even broke down on the stand because he knew his testimony would hurt, but that he couldn't lie."

"Suppose it was all an act? If it was, it did the trick. Because the jury was convinced the deputy was telling the truth and that your father was lying about seeing another car," Spencer offered.

Tess thought of her father, imagined him sitting in that courtroom listening to the man he thought was his friend betray him with lies. Her anguish for what her father must have felt made her furious with the other man and determined to confront him.

"Anyway, I think it's something worth checking out.

I'm going to swing by Lucky Larry's and pay him a visit."

Tess stilled. "I thought the deputy's name was Lawrence Gates."

"It is. But everyone calls him Lucky Larry because he won a ton of money at a casino and used it to bankroll a car dealership. He's been very successful at it, too."

"That day when I went to see Ginger at the restaurant, she was talking to a man and I got the impression the conversation wasn't a friendly one. In fact, I thought she was afraid of him. When I asked your aunt who the man was, she said his name was Lucky Larry. Surely the man knew who Ginger was. That she was really Virginia Lee."

"It's possible he didn't. My aunt obviously didn't recognize her, and even my father was surprised when he found out Ginger Weakes was actually Virginia Lee."

"I suppose you're right. She does look a lot different now. But from their body language, they didn't strike me as being casual acquaintances." Pressing her case, she continued, "Besides, you're the one who keeps saying there is no such thing as a coincidence."

"You might be on to something. I think I'll pay Gates a little visit."

"Just give me five minutes to change and I'll go with you," she said and started to stand.

Spencer caught her arm, stopping her upward movement. "No."

"But—"

He pressed his finger to her lips. "You're not coming with me. And you're going to keep your distance from Lucky Larry and Ginger."

She pulled her arm free. "You know, Reed, you have a habit of trying to tell me what to do when I'm perfectly capable of deciding for myself."

"No one's telling you what to do. I'm simply trying to point out that you coming with me and confronting the man isn't going to get us anywhere. By now, half this town knows that you're Jody Burns's daughter and that you're digging into your mother's murder case. Anyone who was involved, from Caine right on down to the witnesses who testified against your father, is going to think you're here to stir up trouble for them and they're going to clam up."

"And they won't clam up for you?"

"Not necessarily. You forget, these people know me, besides, I'm not coming at them with an ax to grind. It wasn't my father they helped send to prison," he informed her.

It irritated her no end that what he said made perfect sense. He would probably have more success questioning Gates and everyone else than she would. But it didn't make it any easier to accept.

"More importantly, while I might make them a little nervous with my questions, I don't think any of them will feel threatened enough to try to run my car off a bridge to stop me from nosing around."

His remark was a sobering reminder of how close she'd come to dying last night. It also sent her temper soaring again. She stood and began to pace. "I'm not going to be scared off."

"I never for a second thought you would," Spencer told her.

"I mean it," she insisted. "All these years my mother's killer has gone unpunished. They've had a life, probably a family and a job they enjoyed while my mother didn't even live to see her twenty-fifth birthday. The person who stole those things from her…from me," she amended, "that person deserves to be punished."

"Yes, they do."

"And they need to pay for what they did to my father, too. They took everything from him—his wife, his daughter," she said. "He spent half his life locked up in a cage like an animal for something he didn't do. I owe it to him to clear his name."

He went to her, used his knuckles to nudge her chin upward so that she could see his face. "And you will. But not today, and not until we know who or what it is we're dealing with, and why."

"I thought you were so sure Caine was the one behind this."

"I think Caine had a hand in the outcome of the trial—a big one—for his own selfish reasons. But I also think that we're missing something. I don't know what it is yet, but something. I want to do some more digging around. I haven't given up on the Sister Amelia angle yet. And while Andy is doing what he can through the system to find the car that ran you off the bridge last night, I want to do some of my own—starting with Lucky Larry."

"His owning a car dealership would give him access to all kinds of vehicles, including a silver truck," Tess remarked, following his line of thought.

"Exactly. And I also want to find out if Ginger or anyone else connected to the trial either owns a silver pickup or has access to one."

Trying to reel in her emotions and think like a reporter again, Tess did a mental run-through of resources that might prove helpful. "I don't have any connections that'll give me access to motor-vehicle records," she admitted.

"That's okay. I have a few. What would help is if you could find out who was impersonating Sister Amelia. She might be the person who holds the key to this whole thing."

"Sure," she said. "If you give me your notes, I'll see what else I can find. She paused as another idea struck her. "I wonder if it's possible that Ginger had a relative or a friend impersonate the nun and go to see my father for her. She may have had the same person make that call to me so it couldn't be traced back to her. I'll check it out, see if she has any relatives or close friends that fit the age range."

"In the meantime, I want your promise that you'll stay away from her."

She didn't make the promise because she wasn't sure it was one she could keep. Instead she reminded him, "It'd be kind of hard for me to go anywhere at the moment since I don't have any transportation."

He flashed her that grin, the one that made her heart do an extra blip. "Maybe that's not such a bad thing."

"I intend to rectify that problem just as soon as I can," she informed him. Already, she had begun the mental list of all she had to do. At the top was calling Beau Clayton. Then she'd begin the process of getting her life back by calling her insurance company, the rental-car agency, renting another vehicle, replacing her cell phone. Realizing that Spencer was still standing there watching her, she pushed against his chest and said, "Go."

But she might just as well have tried to move a two-hundred-pound slab of granite, because the chest on which she shoved was rock hard and he didn't budge an inch. When he caught her hand, he pressed it to his heart and she could feel its strong, steady beat. She gazed up at his face. And she caught her breath as she read the intent in his eyes. Slowly, oh so slowly, he eased his hand around her waist, pulling her closer. Chest to chest. Hip to hip. Thigh to thigh. Everywhere her body touched his, she met solid muscle and hard flesh. But his grip was loose and she knew he was allowing her to make the decision. So she did. It was she who lifted her mouth and kissed him.

The hot, sweet taste of him was intoxicating. So much so that she deepened the kiss. When her leg nudged against him, there was no mistaking that he wanted her. But he didn't pounce, didn't press her. He simply allowed her to direct where things went from there. For one crazy moment, she considered ripping off his shirt and giving in to her own desire to make love with him. But at the sound of his cell phone ringing, sanity returned. Tess pulled back, took a breath. "You better answer that."

She read the regret, the frustration in his eyes as he turned away and retrieved his cell phone from the counter. "Reed." He barked out the word. He listened for several moments, then said, "Thanks for letting me know."

When he finished the call and returned to her in the den, one look at the grim set of his mouth and she knew something was wrong. "What is it? What's happened?"

"That was Andy. He just got word that Beau Clayton's office building burned down last night."

Tess gasped, lifted a hand to her throat. "Is he...was anyone hurt?"

"No. But all of his records were destroyed—including your father's case file."

Chapter Seventeen

Spencer pulled his Ford up alongside Andy's cruiser. He'd been told to meet him at the abandoned commercial-truck weigh station on the interstate not far from Grady. As he exited his vehicle, Spencer dodged one of the huge puddles on the wet expanse of concrete courtesy of yesterday's soaking. He started toward Andy who stood by what appeared to be the shell of a silver pickup truck.

"The manager for Lucky Larry's used-car lot reported it missing this morning," Andy told Spencer as he joined him. The tires were missing. So was the radio system. "Dispatch got a call about thirty minutes ago from the highway patrol saying they saw a vehicle matching the description of the one wanted in last night's hit-and-run."

Spencer walked around the truck, stared at the smashed front end. He noted the red paint on the bumper, paint that he was sure would be a match to the red paint of Tess's rental car. Anger coursed through his veins at the thought of the driver of the truck who had tried to kill her.

"My guess is it was dumped here sometime during the night. Vandals probably stripped it and made off with the tires and stereo system. I'm assuming they didn't bother taking the front bumper because it was banged up."

Looking through the smashed window, Spencer noted the ignition switch and said, "Doesn't look like it was hot-wired to me."

"According to the manager at the used-car lot, they keep all the vehicles on the lot locked and the keys are kept inside the office. But they leave a spare key under the mat inside each vehicle."

"What genius came up with that system?"

"Makes you wonder sometimes, doesn't it?" Andy remarked.

"So, in other words, all the thief had to do was pop the door lock and he had the key to start the engine," Spencer remarked.

"You got it." Andy lifted his arm and motioned to the tow truck that had just arrived. "After they bring it in, I'll have it dusted for prints."

"There won't be any. At least not any from the driver," Spencer told him. Of that he was sure.

"That's what I'm figuring, too," he said and the two of them stepped back while the tow-truck driver went to work. After Andy had finished giving the tow operator instructions, he and Spencer began walking back to their respective vehicles. "You told Tess about Clayton's building burning down?"

"Yes. She was concerned, but relieved no one was hurt. He'd given her a copy of his file from her father's trial yesterday, but it went down with her car last night. She'd hoped to get him to make another copy for her."

."But now he can't."

"Right," Spencer said. He could certainly understand Tess's frustration. "I don't suppose anyone knows how the fire started."

"It's under investigation. Last I heard they were looking into the possibility of a faulty wiring system that got shorted out because of the storm."

He stopped in front of Andy's cruiser. "Sounds convenient to me. You buying it?"

"I'm trying to keep an open mind. But, yeah, I think the timing is suspicious. I'll be honest with you, Spence. I'm not sure what's going on here, but I think your girlfriend is making somebody nervous with all her questions. I intend to get to the bottom of it. But until I do, she needs to be careful. And so do you."

"I can take care of myself. It's Tess I'm worried about."

"Maybe the two of you ought to split for a while, go to your place in Jackson."

"Forget it. I've already tried and she won't budge until she gets the answers she came here for." He paused. "Have you had a chance to talk to Rusty Toups yet about the missing photo?"

"I tried to reach him earlier, but he didn't answer. My guess is he's out on the river behind his place fishing. The catfish are usually biting after a big storm like we just had. I'm planning to drive out to his place after I leave here."

"I guess there's no point in my asking if I can tag along."

"No."

"Then I think I'll go pay Lucky Larry a visit and see how good his memory is."

Lucky Larry's memory didn't prove to be much good at all, Spencer admitted as he left the dealership without any answers save one. Lawrence "Lucky Larry" Gates was a liar. The man had been fairly convincing when Spencer had mentioned that he'd heard he'd had a truck stolen. His outrage had even appeared genuine as he'd relayed that he'd been told his truck had been involved in a hit-and-run the previous night. He'd been very concerned about Ms. Abbott's condition and had been relieved that she was all right. Only when Spencer had asked how he'd known it had been Tess Abbott in the other vehicle had he faltered. That's when the nerves had begun to show. He'd claimed to have heard it on the news.

But Spencer knew for a fact that Tess's identity had not been released to any news media. As the granddaughter of a senator, she had specifically requested her name be withheld until she could notify her grandparents herself. So it didn't take much to figure out that Lucky Larry was also lying when he said he hadn't realized that Tess Abbott was actually his old friend Jody Burns's daughter. Nor did he buy the man's profession of sadness and regret for what had happened to his friend.

If nerves had made Gates slip up just now, Spencer reasoned, then maybe he'd slipped up when he'd been a deputy, too. Since Andy was with the former sheriff, Rusty Toups, and Andy would probably give him hell if he showed up asking questions, he decided to go to the next best source—his dad.

After climbing into his black SUV, Spencer started the engine and headed for the *Grady Gazette* with the hopes that his old man would have some answers. He also hoped his pal Andy Trudeaux would have something to show for his chat with the former sheriff.

So far all Andy had to show for the thirty minutes he'd spent with former sheriff Rusty Toups was a string of catfish that he'd need to clean. He tossed his line off Rusty's back door into the river and glanced at the man on his right. Most people who looked at Rusty Toups would see an average man. Average in size at five-ten and a hundred and seventy pounds. Average in looks with his ruddy complexion, fading brown hair, brown eyes and soft jaw. There was nothing extraordinary about Rusty on the surface, but the man himself was anything but ordinary. He'd been a straight shooter, an honest sheriff who had kept law and order and served the citizens of Grady for more than three decades. More importantly to him, Andy admitted, Rusty Toups had been a good man with a kind and giving heart who had taken an abandoned eight-year-old boy and his broken-hearted mother under his wing when Andy's own father had split.

He loved and admired Rusty Toups the way a son loved and admired a father, because that's what Rusty had been to him. For a time when he'd been in his teens, he had even hoped that Rusty and his mother might get married and the three of them would be a real family. But Susan Trudeaux had never seen Rusty in a romantic light. Even though the pair had remained only friends and never fulfilled his fantasy family, Rusty had been like a father to him. It was his admiration and affection for Rusty Toups that had made him want to go into law enforcement.

It had been Rusty he'd turned to for advice when his

fiancée, Caitlin, had wanted them to go to New York, instead of marrying and settling in Grady as they'd planned. She'd been offered a job at a brokerage house, a once-in-a-lifetime dream job. They had their whole lives ahead of them, they could afford a few years for adventures. Only he hadn't wanted adventure. He'd wanted Caitlin and the life they had planned.

"Nothing wrong with getting a little taste of the world, boy. You can always come back here and take over as sheriff so I can retire," Rusty told him. "Go with your woman, son. Let her get all that big-city stuff out of her system now and you go learn how them big-city cops do things. When you're ready to come back, Grady will be here waiting for you."

So he'd followed Rusty's advice. And when his world had fallen apart on 9/11 and Caitlin had been lost in the terrorists' attack on the Twin Towers, he'd stayed on for a long time trying to pick up the pieces, not wanting to let go, not wanting to admit that the dreams that he and Caitlin had once shared had died long before she'd been lost in the explosion. He'd known it that last morning when they'd had an ugly fight before she'd stormed off to work, and he had yelled after her that he wouldn't be there when she got home. Only, she had never come home again. And those cruel things they'd said to one another that morning were the last words they would ever share.

He'd probably still be in New York wallowing in guilt had it not been for Rusty telling him he was needed at home. Rusty was ready to hang up his badge. So he'd come home, leaving the battles of the big city behind, but not the guilt. The guilt and his own failure, it seemed, would be something he carried with him always.

"That's the third time that fish has bumped your line, boy. You waiting for him to haul himself up on the fishing pole for you?"

Andy jerked his attention to the pole dangling in the water. He reeled in the line and grimaced when he found the bait gone. After rebaiting with a shrimp, he cast it out into the river again.

"You going to tell me what's eating at you?"

"What makes you think something's eating at me?"

"'Cause your mind's not on fishing," Rusty said as he reeled in his own line to rebait. "And I've known you since you was the size of a tadpole. You always did get quiet when you had something troubling you." He hooked the shrimp on the metal barb and the thin nylon fishing line made a whirring sound as he sent it sailing out into the middle of the river.

Andy neither acknowledged nor denied his statement. The truth was, he had been troubled ever since he'd gone through that case file on the Melanie Burns murder and found the photo missing.

"Only two things puts a man off his fishing and that's woman trouble or work trouble. I'm figuring it's woman trouble that's bothering you. That pretty little O'Donnell gal got you all hot and bothered, does she?"

"Is that what my mother told you?" he asked, incredulous.

"Nope. All Susan said was that the two of you were keeping company these days. 'Course, she's hoping it's going to lead to wedding bells and grandbabies."

Andy scowled. "Then she's going to be disappointed. Maggie and I have shared a meal or two. That's all. Nothing's going to come of it, as I keep telling her."

"So, you don't find the gal attractive?" Rusty asked while he kept his eyes on the water, dragged his line slowly, luring the fish along and waiting to hook one.

"I didn't say that. Maggie's a pretty woman." Hell, she was more than pretty, she was flat-out beautiful, he admitted as he thought of her with that strange-colored hair that was neither blond nor red, but a little of both, and those big eyes filled with sass.

"Ah, I get it. No chemistry."

"There's chemistry," he said gruffly. There had been so much chemistry that he had lain awake in bed for hours after he'd kissed her good-night in that parking lot.

"Well, I know she's no dummy. Turned that place she bought into a nice little business from what I hear. And from what your momma tells me, and based on the time or two I met her, she seems downright sweet. Or is it all just an act?"

"It's no act. Maggie's smart and funny and…and nice," he said for lack of a better word.

"Then what's your problem, boy?"

"There *is* no problem," he told him, missing another hit on his line and losing his bait again. "I'm just not interested in a relationship with her."

"Then you must be one of the few men in Grady who isn't," Rusty told him.

"What do you mean?" Andy asked as he tugged at his line, which had apparently gotten snagged on something unseen beneath the water.

"I mean, I hear she's had half the men in Grady sniffing after her since she arrived. 'Course, they haven't gotten anywhere. At least not yet. But I figure a pretty, smart and nice woman like that—it's just a matter of time before some fellow comes along who does want a relationship and charms her right out of her stockings."

Irritated by Rusty's proclamation and by the fact that he disliked the thought of some faceless man charming Maggie out of her stockings or anything else, Andy yanked on his line and it snapped. "Dammit," he muttered and reeled in what was left of his fishing line.

"Got a new roll in the box," Rusty told him, indicating the big brown-and-white tackle box that Andy had given him for Father's Day the year he had been twelve. He could still remember the pride on Rusty's face at having been given the gift.

And while he restrung his fishing line, Rusty reeled in another big catfish. For a time they fished in silence, apparently letting the matter of Maggie O'Donnell drop. Then Andy said, "I ruled Lester De Roach's death a homicide."

"So I heard," Rusty said. "I suppose you have your reasons for thinking it wasn't a hunting accident."

"I do, " Andy told him, not going into those reasons.

"You have any idea about who might have killed him or why?"

"A few, but nothing I can prove." The word *yet* remained unspoken, but they both knew it was there. "Rusty, do you remember the Melanie Burns murder? It happened about twenty-five years ago. The woman's husband, Jody Burns, was convicted of killing her and sent to prison."

"I remember," he said, his voice solemn. "I was a young man then, younger than you are now and had only been sheriff a few years. It wasn't a pretty sight, seeing that young woman lying on the floor with her head bashed in. To this day, I can still remember her little girl standing in the doorway watching us with those big sad eyes and asking why her momma wouldn't get up."

"That little girl's all grown up now and she's back in Grady investigating the murder. She goes by the name of Abbott now. And she doesn't think her father was guilty. She's been trying to find evidence to reopen the case and clear his name. Last night someone ran her off the three-mile bridge."

"Jesus! I heard there'd been a hit-and-run last night and a car went off the bridge, but I didn't know it was her. She all right?"

"Yes," Andy told him. "But it was a close call."

"You find the other driver who hit her yet?"

"No, but it looks like we've found the truck. Reported stolen from Lucky Larry's used-car lot and dumped at a weigh station on the interstate. I'm waiting for an analysis from the crime lab on the paint to make it official. In the meantime, I'm having the truck dusted for prints."

"Always by the book, just like I taught you," Rusty said proudly.

"Funny thing about that truck being stolen from Lucky Larry's, don't you think?"

"Funny how?" Rusty asked him.

"That a vehicle from his dealership is used to run Tess Abbott off that bridge, and the fact that he was the first on the scene of her mother's murder. I'd almost forgotten that he used to be one of your deputies."

"He wasn't all that great of a deputy. Did the right thing by getting out and opening his car lot," Rusty said dryly.

"There's a link between him and the murder and, as I'm sure you know, Lester De Roach was a witness at that same murder trial."

"What are you saying, son? You think there's a connection between Lester's death, Gates getting his truck stolen and this Abbott woman getting run off the road last night?"

"You're the one who taught me to look at the whole picture and question coincidences. Lester getting killed right after she shows up in town, and then somebody trying to kill her using a truck from Larry Gates's lot, seem like too many coincidences to me. What do *you* think?"

"I think I did a damn fine job of training you." Rusty reeled in his line, but didn't rebait. Instead, he reached for a beer from his cooler. "Want one?"

"No thanks."

Rusty popped the lid, took a swallow and sat back. "That murder had a profound impact on Grady and the people who lived there back then."

"How do you mean?"

"I mean, it shook them right to their core. Every one of them, from the mayor on down to the trash collector. There wasn't a soul who didn't feel they'd lost something…an innocence, I guess, when that young woman was murdered. Murder just wasn't something that was supposed to happen in a town like Grady. It was a nice place where people raised families and chatted over back fences with their neighbors and left their doors unlocked. They were good, God-fearing people, not murderers. And if somebody was to get killed, it sure wasn't supposed to be a young mother whose daddy was a senator. No, everyone there carried the scars of that murder inside them. It's the only thing they talked about for months."

"I don't remember it."

"That's 'cause you were too young—only about

eight. And we tried to shield it from you kids as best we could," Rusty told him.

Andy reeled his own line in and set the pole aside. He knew from experience that Rusty would get to what it was he had to say, or ask what it was he wanted to know, in his own time. At his own pace. So Andy waited for him to continue, knowing that despite the older man's slow and easy manner, there was nothing slow or easy about Rusty's thought processes.

"When the trial started, it was like one of those Hollywood movie shows. The courtroom was packed, the TV and newspaper people everywhere. And there was Everett Caine—he was the A.D.A. back then—as the star. Damn, but he was good," he said and took another swig from the beer bottle. "The man really put on a show. He had the husband convicted of the murder before they ever set foot inside the courtroom."

"Did you think Burns was guilty?" Andy asked.

Rusty's mouth flattened and he stared out at the sun that was beginning to dip in the sky. "What I thought didn't matter. It's what the jury thought that counted. All the rest of us knew was that a young woman was dead, a little girl had been left without her momma and someone needed to pay for that. The evidence that Caine presented pointed to the husband. So he was the one who paid."

Rusty hadn't answered his question, Andy realized. Not really. And it bothered him that he hadn't. "Even if he wasn't guilty?"

"Like I said. It wasn't my call. It was the jury's."

"I decided to take a look at your old case file on the murder. Even back then you kept very thorough files," he told him.

"It's like I always told you, if something's worth doing, it's worth doing right."

"I know. You've been telling me that since I was a kid. That's why I was surprised to find one of the crime scene photos missing from the case file."

Rusty crushed the empty beer can and pitched it in the trash can, then looked directly into Andy's eyes. "You got something to ask me, son. Just spit it out."

Andy leaned forward, rested his forearms on his knees. "All right. Why is there a photo missing from the file? I know you, Rusty. You could train the academy on how to keep records. There should have been a dozen pictures in that file, but photo number six is missing. So are the negatives. What happened to them?"

"Hell, boy, you're asking me about a picture I took twenty-five years ago. Do you know how many thousands of pictures I took in my thirty years at that office? Maybe I misnumbered them or I put the picture in the wrong file. Considering the circus atmosphere with that particular case, I wouldn't be surprised to learn it's still in the D.A.'s office."

"Yeah, I guess you're right." He stood, dusted off his slacks. "It's getting late. I better be heading back."

Rusty stood. "Why don't you hang around? It'll be dinnertime soon. I'll fry us up a mess of these catfish with some hush puppies the way I used to do."

"I'd like to, but I've got a desk piled sky high with work. The storm that came through yesterday only doubled my workload."

Rusty laughed. "Yeah, I heard you had a mess of fender benders."

"You don't even want to know how many," he said and could feel the beginning of a headache coming on when he thought about all the paperwork he'd be drowning in for the next few weeks. "How about I take a rain check?"

"Sure. But you need to take some of these catfish home."

"I only caught three. You go ahead and keep them," Andy told him.

"I got way too many here for me to eat by myself and my freezer's already full. And you know your momma isn't partial to fish," he said, and Andy felt a little sad that Rusty still was so in love with Susan Trudeaux. "Why don't you hang around a few minutes and I'll clean you up a few of these babies to take home. You can freeze 'em or, if you change your mind about that O'Donnell gal, you could always invite her to dinner at your place."

Andy ignored the comment about Maggie but helped Rusty clean the fish. Twenty minutes later, he thanked Rusty again and hopped off the deck with a cooler loaded with fish fillets and packed in ice. He cut across the yard and headed toward his cruiser.

"Andy," Rusty called after him.

He turned around, stared over at Rusty. "Yeah?"

"You never did say, how come the Abbott woman came back now and starting asking questions about that old murder case? I read where her father killed himself in prison a few months back. So it's not like it's going to help him now. Too late for a new trial."

"Actually, his dying is the reason she came back. She received an anonymous call claiming Burns's death wasn't a suicide and that he had been murdered."

"Murdered?" Rusty repeated.

"That's what the caller said. Supposedly, Jody Burns had found some new evidence that he thought would clear him. He had been in touch with the attorney who'd handled his defense and was looking to get the case re-opened. This caller claimed he was killed to keep him quiet."

"Did this person who called say what this evidence was?"

"No. That's why Tess and Spencer Reed are trying to find her, to see what she knows."

"Do the Abbott girl and Spencer have any idea who she is?"

"No. At least none that have panned out yet. But they have some pretty good leads. I think it's just a matter of time before they find her and when they do, they're hoping it will lead them to the real killer."

Chapter Eighteen

"I really appreciate the ride, Maggie," Tess said as they drove in Maggie's little green Jeep en route to the local car-rental agency in Grady so that Tess could get another vehicle. "I was getting bleary-eyed working at the computer, and I don't think I could have faced another phone call. I never realized how much of my life I carried in my purse."

"Don't we all," Maggie agreed.

In addition to dealing with the car-rental agency and insurance, she'd had to notify her credit card companies, arrange for new checks and a replacement cell phone. Losing her PalmPilot with her schedule and contact data was a major hassle and would take some time to duplicate. Fortunately, Ronnie had been able to provide her with some of the information. Of course, that meant telling Ronnie what had happened and that she still didn't know when she'd be back. Worse was having to notify her grandparents. Since her grandfather hadn't been available, she'd dodged the discussion and lecture, but she'd hated hearing the worry in Grams's voice. She'd been grateful her grandmother hadn't pressed her to come home and had accepted her decision to see this through. Her grandfather would not be nearly as understanding.

But as she'd roamed around in the cottage this morning, she'd grown angry that the incident had stolen some of her sense of security. It had been anger and the trapped sensation of being without a car that had led her to call Maggie. "You really are a lifesaver. I was going stir crazy just knowing that I didn't have a car at my disposal."

Maggie waved the thanks aside. "I was happy to have an excuse to get away from the guesthouse for a little while. As much as I love the place, I hate dealing with the books."

"You could always hire a bookkeeper."

"I have a bookkeeper. An accountant, actually. And the man insists I go over the statements every month. I'd much rather just enjoy my guests," she said and gave Tess a conspiratorial smile.

"Well, this guest is most happy that you do."

They turned off the main street and onto another street that was less traveled and where the businesses were not quite as upscale. "This is a shortcut. It'll save us about fifteen minutes of red lights and stop signs," Maggie explained.

"No problem. They said they'd be there until six," Tess said as she brought her fingers to the area on her cheek where she had the bruise.

"It's hardly noticeable. The makeup covers most of it," Maggie told her. "I can't tell you how horrified I was when I heard what had happened to you."

"You're not the only one. I don't think I've ever been so afraid in my life," she admitted and a shudder went through her. "Spencer and the sheriff think it was deliberate."

"What?" Maggie yanked her gaze to Tess a moment, then back to the road. "But who? And why—because you're digging into your father's trial?"

Tess nodded. She went on to explain everything they had learned thus far, including the impersonation of Sister Amelia at the prison and the missing crime scene photo. She also told her about losing the files given to her by Clayton, and the destruction of the man's office building. "I feel just awful about Mr. Clayton losing everything in his building like that."

"It's not your fault, Tess."

"That's what he said when I called him. But I can't help thinking if I hadn't gone there it wouldn't have happened."

"You had no way of knowing someone would burn the place down."

"I know." And she did know that what Maggie said was true. But it did little to ease her sense of responsibility. "Anyway, I've been stalled trying to get access to the storage records at the D.A.'s office. So I guess my only hope now of ever seeing the case file is Everett Caine—he was the prosecuting attorney. Of course, first I need him to return my calls so I can ask him. But that seems to be impossible right now since he's busy campaigning for governor."

"But didn't I see an endorsement of him by your grandfather? If the two of them are friends, can't you use that personal connection as Senator Abbott's granddaughter?"

Tess frowned. "I think that's the reason I haven't

heard back from him. I think my grandfather has asked him *not* to help me."

"He would do that?"

"Absolutely. Don't get me wrong, my grandfather's a good man and he's doing it because he loves me and thinks it's what's best for me. But he's against what I'm doing. He wants me to forget this whole thing and return to D.C. The truth is, if he had his way I'd come home tomorrow, marry the man he's picked out for me, and never mention the name Jody Burns again."

"I didn't realize you were seeing someone," Maggie remarked.

"I'm not. At least not anymore. I broke it off a while back. Something else that my grandfather was not at all happy about."

"So how do you think he'd feel about you and Spencer Reed?"

"There's nothing going on between me and Spencer. I mean, we've become friends, sort of."

Maggie braked at a stop sign and looked over at her. She arched one perfectly shaped eyebrow. "Really? I got the distinct impression when he informed me he was taking care of you last night that *he* thought something was going on, and whatever it was, it was considerably more than friendship."

"Well, there isn't. Not exactly anyway. I mean, he'd like there to be something more." Realizing that she was protesting and rambling, Tess tried again. "All right, I'll admit that a part of me is tempted, too, but the timing is all wrong. It's complicated," she finally said because she didn't know how to explain that until she resolved her past, she didn't feel she could think about any future.

"Isn't it always?" Maggie countered and sighed.

It was the sigh that drew Tess's attention. "Anything happening with you and the sheriff?"

"Other than a couple of toe-curling kisses, no. The ball is in his court now. It's up to him to make the next move." She paused and gave another wistful sigh. "Or not."

Tess realized the other woman was truly interested in the sheriff. And she supposed she could see it. There was something to be said for the tall, handsome, brooding type—but not for her. "You really like him, don't you?"

"Yes. He's the first man I've met since my husband died that I've felt at all attracted to, and there's chemistry between us. But he's a complex man and doesn't like to let anyone get too close. He's a good sheriff, though. And he'll find out who tried to run you off that road last night. I'm sure of it."

She believed that he would, too. "In the meantime, I'm not going to allow what happened last night to scare me off. I'm going to find out who killed my mother and who framed my father." She didn't add "if it's the last thing I do" because after last night, she was more aware than ever that someone was willing to kill her to stop her from succeeding.

"Is there anything I can do to help?"

"You're doing it. You're taking me to get another rental car," she pointed out. While she didn't think Maggie was in any danger, she also didn't want to draw her in any deeper than she already was.

"Well, if you can think of anything else, you just let me know."

"Thanks, I appreciate it."

Maggie nodded. "The rental agency is in the next block," she said as they pulled up behind a Range Rover which was in line at a red light.

Tess glanced over to her right and noted a faded blue Toyota parked on the corner. A few yards away was the storefront for Lucky Larry's Auto Showroom. On impulse she said, "Maggie, do me a favor and take a right at the light."

"All right. But are you going to tell me why?"

"See that blue Toyota on the corner? It belongs to Ginger and it looks like she's visiting Lucky Larry's." Tess couldn't help wondering why.

"You think this is a good idea, Tess?" she asked as she parked the Jeep across the street. "You said she threatened to take a restraining order out against you, and Andy told you to stay away from her."

"The car lot is a business place open to the public, Maggie. I lost my rental in an accident last night, remember? Maybe I'm in the market to buy a car instead of renting another one." She unhooked her seat belt and when Maggie did the same, she said, "You don't have to come with me."

Maggie made a face at her. "Don't be ridiculous. Of course I'm going with you."

When the two of them walked into the dealership showroom a cherub-faced young man in an olive suit and patterned tie approached them. "Are you ladies in the market for anything special? We just received a new shipment of Cadillacs this week and we have a sweet little Corvette that I can show you."

"Thanks, but we'd like to just look around a bit," Maggie said. "Why don't you give me your card and if we see something we're interested in, I'll have them page you."

"Sure. The name is Marcus. Here you go," he said, handing a card to Maggie and then one to her.

Tess took the card absently while she scanned the

showroom area for a glimpse of Ginger. She didn't see her. What she did see were doors leading out to the back. "I don't see anything in here that grabs me. You have more cars out back, don't you?"

"Yes, ma'am. Right through those doors," he said, motioning down the hall past a series of glass-walled offices and a workstation where two girls seated behind a counter worked at computer terminals. "Why don't I take you on back."

"That's okay," Tess said, not wanting to get the guy into any trouble. "We've got your card, Marcus. If we see anything, we'll call for you."

They made their way down the long hallway to the open doors. They walked outside where the air was decidedly cooler and damper than it had been in the showroom. Massive lights on concrete poles lit up the parking lot so that it looked as if it was the middle of the day instead of only an hour before sunset. A sea of cars in dozens of makes, models and colors stretched out before them.

"Poor guy. He was like a puppy, eager to please," Maggie remarked as she came to stand beside Tess. "I almost feel like I should test-drive something so he won't feel so bad."

Tess looked down at the much shorter Maggie and shook her head. "I bet the kids selling cookies and raffle tickets love you."

Maggie sniffed. "You think I'm a soft touch?"

"Yes. Now come on, see if you can spot Ginger."

Tess began scanning the area where she could see several people, engaged with salesmen, looking at cars. Still she didn't see Ginger. She began walking slowly along the rows of cars, looking carefully for the other woman.

Maggie grabbed her arm. "Over there against that trailer with the pickup trucks on it. Isn't that Ginger?"

It was, Tess realized, recognizing the brassy blond female who appeared to be in a heated argument with the man Tess now recognized from the Dixie Belle as Lucky Larry Gates.

"From the look on Lucky Larry's face I'd say that he's not doing a very good job of selling Ginger on buying any of his cars," Maggie remarked.

"Maybe she's a tougher negotiator than he thought she'd be," Tess said. "Come on, I want to see if I can hear what they're saying."

They managed to move a few feet closer and Tess caught the tail end of Ginger saying, "You've got a lot more to lose than I do."

Gates grabbed her by the arm, his face mottled with fury. "You stupid bitch, don't you threaten me. Or I—"

"Ginger, are you all right?" Tess asked, suddenly fearful for the woman. While she might not like her and even resent her for the role she had played in her father's imprisonment, she couldn't stand back and see her brutalized.

Ginger whipped around. Larry's gaze jerked up and he turned furious eyes on her and Maggie as he released the other woman. It was like watching Jekyll and Hyde, Tess thought as he reined in his temper and pasted a genial smile on his face. "Everything's fine, isn't it, Mrs. Weakes?"

"Everything will be fine once you agree to that trade-in I want on my car," she countered.

From the tightening around Larry Gates's mouth, Tess suspected Ginger had been threatening him. She only wished she knew what she was threatening him with. "As I said, I'll have to check the book value. Your car is an older model and not in the best of shape. I don't think the trade-in value will be that high."

"Check your book, Gates, and I'll be in touch," Ginger said, walking off.

"Can I help you ladies with something?" he asked.

Tess debated talking to him then decided she would have better luck getting answers from Ginger. "Thanks, but we were just browsing."

He straightened his tie and smoothed the line of his silk suit coat. "Let me know if I can be of any assistance. If you'll excuse me," he said and headed for the main building.

"Come on," Tess said. "I want to see if I can catch up with Ginger."

Walking quickly through the showroom and past a smiling but perplexed Marcus, they caught up with Ginger as she reached her Toyota. When she looked up and spied them, she scowled. "There's a law against stalking people," she fired at Tess.

"Who's stalking anyone? We were looking at cars when I saw you. It looked like you and Mr. Gates were arguing."

"Larry Gates is an asshole. And if we was arguing, it's no business of yours."

"Ginger, I know he was in on it with you to frame my father. If you'll help me, if you'll tell me who was behind it and who put you up to it, I'll see to it that you're not charged. Please." She touched the woman's arm as she started to open her car door. "I'll help you if you'll help me. Help me find out who killed my mother and who had my father killed. And I swear, I'll help you."

For a moment, there was something in Ginger's

brown eyes, regret, despair. But then it was gone. "I can't. I've got to look out for me," she said and shook off Tess's hand. "And if you know what's good for you, you'll stop digging where you shouldn't and leave here before you have another accident. Next time, you might not be so lucky."

Tess sucked in a breath and stepped back as Ginger started her car. "She knew," Tess said, more to herself than to Maggie.

"Maybe you should call Andy and tell him."

"No," she said and the two of them started back to Maggie's Jeep. "As you pointed out, he's already told me to stay away from her. And what can I accuse her of? Knowing that someone tried to run me off a bridge? By now, I imagine half the people in Grady know that."

"I don't like it, Tess," Maggie said after they'd strapped on their seat belts. She started the car. "The woman all but threatened you."

"Ginger doesn't frighten me." And she didn't. She didn't believe Ginger was brave or bright enough to have engineered last night's accident. "It's the person pulling her strings that I have to worry about. I must be getting too close. Why else would someone try to kill me and torch Clayton's offices? There must have been something in those files they didn't want me to see."

"But how are you going to find out what it was?" Maggie asked as they turned the corner and headed toward the car-rental agency.

"I guess I'll try Everett Caine again. He's the only one who might still have a complete file on the trial. Since he won't return my phone calls, maybe if I get a list of his upcoming campaign appearances, I can go to wherever he is," she began as the plan started to take shape. "I should be able to use my press credentials to get in and if I can get close enough to talk to him, maybe I can get him to agree to see me." She groaned, ran her fingers through her hair in frustration. "Press credentials that I just realized are now sitting at the bottom of the river."

Maggie pulled her Jeep up in front of the car-rental agency. "Well now, I just might be able to help you out there."

"Maggie, I know you're a marvel and can do just about anything. But I don't think even you can whip up new press credentials for me. I'll need to call Ronnie, my producer at Channel Seven, and see what she can do to expedite getting me a new set."

"I'm not talking about press credentials," she said as she shut off the engine and looked over at her and smiled. "I'm talking about getting you in to see Everett Caine."

"You've lost me. I thought you said you didn't know him."

"I don't. Not personally anyway. But he's going to be here tomorrow night—a campaign stopover and a fund-raiser—to get an infusion of cash for the final two weeks of the governor's race. Anyway, the mayor of Grady is hosting a ritzy little reception for him at the country club tomorrow night. It's private, invitation only, targeting some of the business leaders in the community. And I just happen to have an invitation."

"But I thought you and the mayor didn't get along, that you were even considering running against him in the next election."

"We don't and I am. But I'm also a source of potential campaign funds—too big a source for the mayor to ignore. So he sent me an invitation. Besides, he's probably hoping he can butter me up and offer to put me on some special committee or other to placate my civic-minded interests so I won't run against him. Of course, he's wrong."

"But the invitation's for you, Maggie. I doubt that they'll let me use it in your place," Tess pointed out.

"You don't need to. My invitation reads Maggie O'Donnell and Guest. You can come as my guest."

"Oh, Maggie, I swear I could kiss you," Tess told her, excited by the prospect of finally seeing Caine. "You are no doubt one of the kindest and sweetest people I've ever met in my life."

Maggie rolled her eyes at the compliment. "That's me. Kind and sweet Maggie O'Donnell. Maybe that's why the sheriff didn't call."

"If the man is half as bright as Spencer thinks he is, he'll call," she said, touching a hand to the other woman's arm. "And if he doesn't, he's an idiot."

"You're right. The man is an idiot," Maggie replied with a smile. "But what a sexy idiot he is."

After dropping Tess off, Maggie couldn't stop worrying about her. She hadn't liked that furious gleam in Larry Gates's eyes any more than she'd liked that veiled threat from Ginger. While Tess might be strong, and had miraculously freed herself from that sinking car last night, her friend wasn't indestructible. She turned the Jeep back toward the heart of downtown Grady.

Ten minutes later, Maggie pulled it to a stop in front of the sheriff's office. According to Susan, her son didn't keep banker's hours and spent way too much time at work. Taking a chance that she'd catch him there now and hoping that Tess would forgive her, she walked inside. "Hi, Hazel," she told the woman at the front desk who had a headset on and was dispensing papers to a deputy. "Is the sheriff in?"

"Sure is, Maggie. You can go on back. First door on your right."

"Thanks," she said. Squaring her shoulders, she started toward his office. She'd expected to find the door closed and him with his usual scowl on his face while he was barking out orders or buried in paperwork. What she didn't expect was to find him with an adorable towheaded boy on his lap. Both heads were bent over a drawing and the child was working feverishly with a crayon.

"What do you think, Sheriff? Is it scary enough?"

"Why don't we use some more red around the eyes," he suggested and handed the boy another crayon.

"I can't make it stay in the lines," the boy complained.

"Tell you what, why don't I help you?" Andy suggested and, placing his large hand over the boy's, he guided it across the paper.

His gentleness with the child disarmed her, and for a moment, as she watched them together, Maggie's heart ached. It made her think of the man she'd loved and lost, the man with whom she'd hoped to share children and moments like this. But then the moment was gone, and it wasn't Mack she thought of, but the man sitting before her. As though sensing her gaze, he looked up. His eyes darkened at the sight of her. He swept his gaze down the length of her and Maggie felt his scrutiny like a caress.

"There you go, Dougie. Looks like a pretty scary vampire to me," he said. "Why don't we see what Miss Maggie thinks?"

The boy held up the drawing of a character with fangs and a black cape modeled on the old-time movie monsters. "Does it scare you?"

Maggie walked farther into the room and looked at the drawing closely and shuddered. "It sure does."

"Good," he said with a grin that revealed two missing front teeth. "I'm going to be a Dracula just like this for Halloween."

"If you do, I bet you'll get lots of candy."

"Okay, Dougie, we're ready to go, buddy," the deputy said who entered the room. "Excuse me, ma'am. Thanks for keeping an eye on him for me while I filled out those insurance papers, Sheriff. Hope he didn't give you any trouble."

"He was great," Andy said as he placed the boy on the floor. He handed him his drawing and box of crayons. "You make sure your daddy brings you by to trick-or-treat at the jail, okay?"

"'Kay," he said and gave the sheriff a hug.

"See you tomorrow, Sheriff. Ma'am," the deputy remarked before exiting with his son.

The moment the door closed behind the deputy and his son, Andy's serious face was back. She waited a second, hoping he would give her some indication she was welcome. When he didn't, she asked, "You got a second?"

"Sure." As though he was uneasy, he marched over to the counter where a coffeepot sat beside a mini-fridge. "You want something to drink? A cup of coffee? A soda?"

"Coke, if you've got it."

While he rooted in the icebox for something to drink, she took stock of his office. Big desk filled with papers and files. Lots of framed, official-looking documents on the wall. A photo of him with Rusty Toups, shaking hands. Another shot of a teenage Andy with Rusty Toups holding up a string of fish. A more recent photo of him with a beautiful brunette, their arms wrapped around each other and obviously very much in love. It was that last photo that gave her pause.

"That was Caitlin," he said, coming up behind her, holding two cans of cola.

"She's very beautiful."

"Yes, she was. She's dead now. She died in the 9/11 attacks in New York."

"I'm sorry," she said, not sure what else to say. Susan had told her something of the history. So she knew that Andy had loved the other woman. She turned around, looked at him then, at the serious green eyes, the somberness of his expression. "Truly I am. I know how hard it is to lose someone you love, someone you think you're going to spend the rest of your life with."

He popped the top on the Coke can and handed it to her, then repeated the process on the other can. "We were splitting up," he told her. "The day she was killed…I was already planning to move out."

Which made her dying in the tragedy that much more difficult for him, Maggie realized. A survivor's guilt of sorts. She knew, because she'd felt the same thing after Mack died. Deciding to rechannel his thoughts, she asked, "So, did you have a good time the other night at dinner?"

He narrowed his eyes and she was pleased to see wariness creep back in place of the pain and guilt. "Yes."

"Then why haven't you asked me out again?"

He took a swallow from the red Coca-Cola can. "I was thinking about it."

She walked over toward the desk, could feel his eyes following her rear in the snug black jeans and sweater she'd thrown on to drive Tess into the city. She turned around and was pleased to see male interest in those green eyes. "Still thinking? Or have you made up your mind yet?"

"It's made up. Would you like to have dinner with me?"

"I'd love to. When?" she asked and delighted in the fact that she had him off balance.

"What about tonight?"

Her own balance teetered a bit, so she took a sip of her Coke. "Sure. What time?"

"How about in an hour. My place."

"That sounds wonderful. Can I bring anything?"

"Just yourself. And, Maggie, don't bother changing out of the jeans. I like the way those look on you."

A tingle of pleasure skittered down her spine. "Why, thank you, Sheriff," she said as she set down her can of Coke on his desk blotter.

He placed his own Coke can beside hers. Then he grabbed a sheet of paper. He scribbled a street number and name on the slip of paper. "Here's my address," he told her and handed her the slip of paper.

When she reached for it, he held on to it and her hand. The air was charged between them and Maggie felt as though she couldn't breathe for a moment. And because she was more nervous than she wanted to be, she tried to keep her voice saucy and light as she said, "Well, now that we've got that out of the way, I need to discuss a little business with you."

He narrowed his eyes again and dropped her hand before stepping back. "What kind of business?"

"Sheriff's business. I'm worried about Tess."

Maggie spelled out a quick version of what had transpired and, ignoring his occasional scowl or oath, she explained about Ginger threatening Tess and her own concerns about her friend.

"You're right to be worried," he informed her. "Did it ever occur to either one of you that to go chasing down people you suspect were involved in a crime might be dangerous?"

"We didn't chase anyone down," she said indignantly. "We just sort of…noticed Ginger's car and that she was at Larry Gates's car lot and wondered why. So we decided to check it out."

"And you were told she was looking for a new car. For you and Tess to follow her out and confront her was just plain stupid."

"You know, Sheriff, if you're hoping to score with a woman, calling her stupid is not the way to go about it."

His jaw dropped. "I didn't…I never…"

"Well, then, I guess I should be insulted that the idea of having wild sex with me hasn't crossed your mind," she said, her confidence boosted by his being thrown off balance.

"It has. That is, I mean, I didn't…"

She arched her eyebrow. "Which is it, Andrew? You have been thinking about having wild sex with me? Or you haven't?"

His mouth hardened even as a smile curved her own lips. "No matter how I answer that, I'm going to come off sounding like a jerk."

"In that case, I should probably be going then. I just wanted you to know what happened with Ginger to see if you could maybe…I don't know, assign someone to protect Tess. Or something."

"Or something," he told her.

"Great. I knew I could count on you," she said and gave him a quick kiss on the mouth. "I'll see you at your place in an hour."

"Right."

She paused at the door and looked back at him. "Oh, and just so you know, I never have wild sex on the second date." She smiled at him again. "I usually wait at least until the third date."

Chapter Nineteen

An hour later when Maggie arrived at Andy's place, she still couldn't believe she'd maneuvered the man into asking her out again. Despite her bravado, she wasn't one who engaged in casual sex. In truth, the only man she had ever been with had been her husband and, until brooding Sheriff Andrew Trudeaux had come along, she had never even been tempted to end the celibacy imposed by Mack's death.

"It's open," he called out when she knocked on the door. "Make yourself at home. I'm running a little behind schedule. There's some wine on the bar. Help yourself and I'll be out in a minute."

"Take your time," she answered and used the time to poke around a bit. It looked like a guy's place, she thought. There was nothing remotely fancy about the tweed-fabric couch or the big recliner in an odd shade of brown. The tiled floor was clean. So was the navy, wine and cream-colored area rug, but it clashed terribly with the furniture. She wandered about the room, noted books on the shelves—classics, Westerns, political thrillers and several volumes of poetry. Sports and newsmagazines were stacked neatly on a glass-and-wood coffee table. She spied two football trophies, a photo of a Little League team and several family photos, including more photos of him with Rusty Toups. On the walls were prints of Monet's *Red Boats* and *The River,* a street scene from New Orleans and a child's handprints that had been done in red paint on white paper, then mounted in a bright blue frame. A tough, by-the-book sheriff who read poetry and placed equal value on world-class masterpieces as he did on a child's homemade art was a man she wanted to know better.

She wandered to where she heard the sound of pots rattling and found him in the kitchen. The room was tidy, with ceramic countertops, pine cabinets, a double sink and an island stove. On top of the stove was a huge cast-iron skillet. Ceramic canisters in a spice color were lined up along one counter. Bread box, toaster, mixer were all in a straight line. Pot holders and dish towels were draped on a towel ring near the stove and the sink. An almond-colored refrigerator and dishwasher took up another wall.

And standing in the center of the room next to the stove was Andy. He'd changed from his sheriff's uniform into worn black jeans and a black turtleneck that showed an impressive set of shoulders. A plain white apron had been tied around his waist and looked impossibly endearing on him. His face was a picture of concentration as he added milk to a bowl of eggs and began to beat them. Desire curled in her belly like a fist and she moved into the room.

"Need some help?" she asked.

He jerked his gaze up from the bowl. "No. I'll just be a second. I hope you're hungry."

"Starved," she admitted. Leaning against the doorway, she crossed her arms and studied him. His dark hair was damp around the edges, she noted, as though he'd just stepped from the shower and hadn't bothered to dry it. And seeing him so at home in the kitchen in that silly apron was incredibly appealing.

He set the bowl aside and went to the refrigerator. Shamelessly, Maggie enjoyed the view as he stooped down to retrieve a foil-covered dish, which he placed on the counter next to the bowl. When he looked up, saw her watching him, he asked, "Something wrong?"

"I was just thinking that you actually know your way around the kitchen."

"You sound surprised."

"I am. I wouldn't have pegged you as a man who knows how to cook," she told him. "I'd half expected to arrive and find you'd ordered pizza or picked up something at a deli for dinner."

"That's a pretty narrow and sexist view, don't you think? A man's got to eat. What's wrong with a guy knowing how to cook?"

"Not a thing," she told him with a laugh. "So, what are you cooking?"

"Fresh fried catfish, hush puppies and salad," he said while he went back to beating the egg-and-milk mixture.

"No wonder you're running late. I didn't realize you had to stop and catch dinner."

"Caught them earlier this afternoon out at Rusty's place."

On impulse, she sauntered over to where he was working. "Don't tell me straight-as-an-arrow Sheriff

Andy Trudeaux actually played hooky and went fishing in the middle of the workday."

"Not exactly," he said and she noted that he appeared to be just a little nervous at having her so close. He pulled the foil off the platter of fish and dumped the fillets into the egg-and-milk mixture. "I went to talk to Rusty about the Burns murder case and he was fishing. So I threw in a line while we chatted."

"And you caught all these fish?" she asked, bumping her hip against him as she leaned closer to watch him begin dragging the fillets through the plate of seasoned cornmeal.

"Rusty caught most of them," he told her, his fingers moving deftly to cover the fish strips with the yellow meal. "You want to hand me that plate over there next to the skillet?"

She retrieved the plain white platter and brought it over to him. He began transferring the battered strips of fish onto the plate. "Who taught you to cook?" she asked.

"My mother mostly, and Rusty," he explained. "He taught me how to fry fish and put together a good gumbo."

"You and he are very close, aren't you?" she asked, once more sensing a strength and a depth to him that intrigued her.

"Yeah, we are. He's been like a father to me." He finished battering the fish and wiped his hands on a towel.

"Hang on a second. You've got cornmeal on your face," she told him. Moving closer, she wiped away the smudge from his cheek. And on impulse, she slid her fingers into his hair.

"What are you doing?"

"Sorry, I couldn't resist," she told him. "I think it was the apron. I'm a sucker for a guy in an apron."

His eyes went dark. His gaze went to her mouth and back to her eyes again. "No kidding?"

"No kidding."

He circled her waist with his hands, pulled her against him into the cradle of his thighs and there was no mistaking his reaction to her. "I thought you were hungry," he reminded her.

"I am," Maggie told him.

"Good. Because so am I."

And before she could think of a clever comeback, his mouth swooped down and devoured hers. Anticipation and need hit her lightning quick. She wanted him, was already on her way to falling in love with him. That small part of her brain that told her she was moving too fast, that she needed to give them both more time, dissolved beneath the onslaught of his mouth. She knew all too well how quickly love could be snatched away, how quickly fate could ruin a lifetime of plans. So, without a second thought, she snatched this bit of happiness.

He wanted to swallow her whole, Andy thought as he picked Maggie up and started toward his bedroom. He kicked the door wide. He'd lost his apron somewhere en route to the bedroom. He began toeing off his shoes as he neared the bed.

Her hands were everywhere. Those clever fingers of hers spearing through his hair, racing down his back, squeezing his buttocks. She cupped his rear and drew him into her and he groaned. As he eased her down onto the bed he tried to catch his breath, tried to regroup and to think. But she'd already pulled his shirt from his jeans and dragged the thing over his head and tossed it to the floor. The moment those soft, cool fingers of hers touched his flesh, he was lost.

"Maggie, we—"

She pressed her mouth to his shoulder and he felt what little control he still possessed begin to slip from his grasp.

"Touch me," she whispered.

The last vestiges of reason snapped like a dry twig. He removed the sweater she wore and pitched it aside. She was beautiful, he thought. Her bra was only a piece of black silk that covered the swells of her breast. Her skin was smooth, pale as milk. And he wanted her so badly his fingers trembled as he released the catch of her bra. She gasped as he peeled the bra away and revealed surprisingly full breasts for a woman so small. He filled his palms with her and took her into his mouth.

"Andy," she gasped and arched her back.

He couldn't get enough of her, couldn't get close enough. Her heart thudded beneath his touch and the spike in her pulse as he kissed her neck sent a thrill through his system. The sweet clean scent of her surrounded him, filled him. It scared him how much he wanted her, a desire that bordered on need. It had been building to this, he admitted. From that first kiss in the parking lot. Hell, from the first time she'd sashayed up to him on the street looking all cool and collected with that sassy twinkle in her eyes.

She sank her teeth into his shoulder. Andy groaned. All he could think of was how desperately he needed to touch her, to get rid of the rest of these clothes and be inside her. He eased back just enough to slide his hands between them. "You know, as much as I like you in these jeans, Maggie, I think I'd like you even better out of them," he told her and went to work on the zipper and snap.

She laughed. "I could say the same thing to you, Sheriff."

"We'll get to them in a minute," he told her and he drew the jeans over her hips, down her legs and pitched them to the floor. All that was left was a strip of black lace that made him break out into a sweat. She was small. Almost tiny. But what there was of her was all female curves and smooth skin. He drew his fingertip along the edge of black lace, heard her breath snag. "Not bad, Ms. O'Donnell."

And then it was his breath that snagged as she took her sweet time unbuckling his belt, unsnapping the jeans and slowly, oh so slowly, inching down the zipper. "Not bad, Sheriff. Not bad at all," she told him as she skimmed her fingers along the edge of his briefs.

He tumbled her back to the bed, kissed her mouth, felt her go boneless as he worked his way down her neck, her shoulder, the curve of her breast, the dip of her belly, to the place between her thighs. She was all soft, silky, liquid heat beneath his touch. When he slid back up her body, flesh to flesh, hip to hip, mouth to mouth, she moaned his name.

He slid his hand between them, his fingers beneath the scrap of lace, his fingers inside her, tormenting her, tormenting himself. Her nails dug into his shoulders as he increased the pressure, quickened the tempo. Her breath came in quick pants. Her eyes glazed over. She arched her hips and gasped, "Andy."

When he felt the first shudder tear through her, he captured her sob with his mouth as she exploded beneath him. He brought her up again and again and again, thrilling in her pleasure.

Then she was reaching for him, pulling him free of the briefs and guiding him into that slick, silken heat.

And as he thrust into her, each slow thrust building and stoking that fire, it was he who gasped. When he felt her clutch around him, it was his eyes that rolled back in his head. It was his body that clung to hers and it was he who cried out her name as together they began to spiral from atop the cliff, with no hope of breaking the fall.

Spencer waited in line at the entrance door to the country club's ballroom and watched as some of Grady's most prominent citizens showed their invitations for admission to the reception being hosted by the mayor for Everett Caine. At any other time, he would have welcomed the chance to tangle with Caine. But tonight he was more concerned about Tess than trying to derail the man's bid for governor. He'd been more than a little worried about her since the accident. Finding out from Andy that she'd been foolish enough to confront Ginger Weakes and had been threatened for her efforts had done nothing to ease those concerns. Nor had her refusal to back off from her investigation while he and Andy tried to tie Gates to the hit-and-run on the bridge.

When Tess had informed him that morning that she was attending tonight's reception as Maggie's guest so that she could speak with Caine, he'd known he had to be there. He didn't trust Caine. While he hadn't been able to connect all the dots yet, he'd already been able to tie Caine indirectly to unusual windfalls of two key witnesses in the Jody Burns murder trial. De Roach's loan for his failed mechanic shop via Caine's wife's uncle, and now to Gates. How the then A.D.A. had come to handle Gates's purchase of the car dealership with a big casino win—a casino win that the IRS showed no record of and winnings for which Gates had not paid any taxes. No casino paid out that kind of windfall without notifying the IRS.

Spencer inched a little closer to the front of the line and glanced around for Andy. He didn't think Tess was in any real danger from Caine tonight. But he did want to keep an eye on her. After hearing about the confrontation with Ginger, he didn't trust Tess not to confront the politician. And considering what had happened already, he wanted to be close by and make sure that she stayed safe. Of course, talking his mother out of her invitation to the reception so that he and Andy could attend was going to cost him later. No doubt his mother would have enjoyed the affair and he knew her shop had supplied the flowers for the event. A red, white and blue theme, she'd told him, which had cleaned her out of red and white roses. From what he could see of the decorations beyond the door, they had followed through on the color scheme. Red, white and blue balloons with streamers were everywhere. No doubt to play up Everett Caine's theme of himself as a patriotic American who prided himself on good government and law enforcement. It was a theme he'd begun pitching right after winning the Jody Burns murder conviction.

"This is a private party, Reed. Invitation only. It's not open to the press," the mayor's assistant told him.

"Here's my invitation," Spencer told the toadlike man and handed him the card.

"This says 'S. Reed at Always In Bloom.' This is for your mother," the man told him.

"My mother had a last-minute conflict. Since she'd already RSVP'd her acceptance, she didn't want to disappoint the mayor. After all, he's gone to a lot of trouble and expense to support his friend, Everett Caine. So she sent me in her place. Since it didn't specify which 'S. Reed' on the invitation, we didn't think it would be a problem."

The guy eyed him warily, Spencer noted. He appeared to debate whether to let him through or get clearance from the mayor. Not that he blamed the man. It was no secret to anyone in Grady that he was a strong opponent of Caine's campaign, which his columns routinely reflected.

"Sorry I'm late," Andy said, coming up to join him.

"I'm sorry, Sheriff, but the lieutenant governor has his own security. He won't need your services tonight."

"He's not here to provide his services, Bozo. He's the guest on my invitation," Spencer explained.

"Is there a problem?" Andy asked.

"No, sir. No problem. You can go on through."

Once they had cleared the doorway, Spencer said, "I know I said you didn't have to wear a monkey suit, Trudeaux. But couldn't you have at least worn something besides your uniform?"

"I didn't have time to change. I got a call from Rusty," he said as they approached the bar. Andy's expression grew grim. "He found the missing crime scene photo. Or at least the negative for the roll it was on. I dropped them off and waited for the prints. By the time they were ready, it was too late for me to go home and change and get back here before this thing started."

"Scotch rocks," Spencer told the bartender.

"Got any beer?" Andy asked.

"Sorry, Sheriff. Only wine, hard liquor and sodas for this crowd."

"I'll take a scotch, too," he said.

Once they'd been served their drinks, Spencer asked, "And was there anything in the missing photo?"

"Not that I could see at first glance. It looked like the others as far as I could tell. But I made three sets." He reached inside his jacket and withdrew an envelope. "I thought I'd let you and Tess take a look at them and see if there's something that I missed."

Spencer slipped the envelope inside his own suit coat. "So, did Rusty offer any explanation as to why he had those negatives?"

Andy's expression grew even more solemn. "None that would shed any light on what's been going on."

Spencer had known Andy long enough to realize his friend wasn't going to give him any further explanation. But it worried him that Rusty Toups had the missing negatives and he suspected that Andy was worried, too. Deciding not to press the matter, he brought Andy up to speed on Larry Gates's windfall and its ties back to Caine. As he spoke, Spencer noted the way Andy's gaze kept roaming the room. "Looking for someone, Trudeaux?"

"No. Just keeping my eye out for Tess."

"She's not here yet," Spencer told him. At his friend's questioning look, Spencer explained, "I asked the gal who was greeting people at the front door if Ms. O'Donnell and her guest had arrived yet and she said they hadn't." But Spencer suspected it wasn't Tess his friend had been looking for, but the woman with whom she was supposed to attend.

"There they are now," Andy said and Spencer directed his gaze to the door.

They were a striking duo, Spencer thought. The tiny redhead in the bold red outfit and the tall brunette in the little black cocktail dress with the killer legs. When her gaze scanned the room and met his, Spencer felt that tightening in his chest again. She looked away as Maggie said something to her. And then the pair of them were heading toward the front of the room. Only then did Spencer spot Everett Caine emerging from a group of people with the mayor.

"Ladies and gentlemen," Mayor Dub Wilton called out from the podium. "Thank you for joining me tonight to welcome Grady's own Everett Caine, the next governor of Mississippi."

While the room erupted into applause, Everett Caine made his way to the podium and held out his hand to assist his wife to the dais. Then he shook hands with the mayor and while Mrs. Caine and the mayor stood to the side, Everett Caine moved front and center to the microphone. "Thank you very much, Mayor Wilton," he said, flashing the trademark smile that one reporter had described as ideal for a toothpaste campaign because it was so perfect. "My dear friends and fellow citizens of Grady, it gives me great pleasure to be here tonight…"

As Caine pitched his spiel on all the things he intended to do for the state if he were elected governor, Spencer sized up the man. He was trim and fit and Spencer suspected that it was his wife's family money that kept him in Armani suits and the hundred-dollar haircuts. The tan he'd acquired on the private and pricey golf course was another perk of marriage. His wife, Pamela, was a wealthy heiress, and her money had also funded a major portion of her husband's political campaigns. He ran for lieutenant governor in the last two elections and two years ago when Caine had begun planning to run for the governorship, she had forked over a cool million as a campaign loan to get the ball rolling.

"As your lieutenant governor, I've been proud to assist in bringing to our great state new businesses and revenue…"

Tuning out the speech, Spencer stared at the elegant woman in black who stood at Caine's side and gazed at him admiringly. Spencer shook his head. He couldn't help but wonder why a smart, attractive and wealthy woman like Pamela Caine would stay with the bastard instead of divorcing him for his infidelities. Like one of the nation's former presidents, it was no secret among those in government circles that Caine had an eye for pretty young women. Granted, it was hushed up in most cases and very little was reported in the press. But Pamela Caine would have to have known. Even if she'd turned a blind eye to the others, she wouldn't have been able to do so with Jenny. Not when he himself had been so vocal in his accusations against the man. So why had she overlooked it? Why would the lady stand by a man who'd betrayed her? This was a woman who probably could have run for the governor's seat herself.

"So I ask that you help me to lead our state in this new century by voting for me in November."

The crowd erupted in applause. The mayor returned to the microphone. "And as you all know, this next week of the campaign is crucial because election day is just over a week away. That means if we want to see Everett Caine become our next governor and lead this state into prosperity, we need to get the word out to all of the voters. To do that takes money. And we need your help."

On cue, staff began circulating the room, handing out cream-colored envelopes. Spencer took the card handed to him and removed the donation card inside which requested name, address, pledge amount, and lines for a check number or credit card number, as well as signatures. The opening gambit was for a thousand dollars and escalated in increments up to twenty-five thousand. "I can see why you and I weren't sent invitations," he said to Andy as an aside.

"You can say that again," Andy countered. "What's amazing is that they spend millions of dollars to campaign for a job that doesn't even pay a hundred grand a year. Makes you wonder why they do it."

"I can tell you why Caine does it. Ego." Along with participation in any number of lucrative deals that the man was smart enough to keep within the letter of the law.

"So, my fellow citizens and business leaders of Grady, I ask that each of you be generous," the mayor went on in an impassioned plea worthy of Sunday services. "Pull out your checkbooks and your wallets now and help us put this son of Grady in the governor's mansion where he will lead our state with the same integrity and passion for justice with which he once led our city."

More applause followed and the mayor, Caine and his wife descended the podium. As they began working the crowd, Spencer and Andy began working their way over to Tess and Maggie. When he reached the two women, Spencer said, "Good evening, ladies."

"Reed, what are you doing here?" Tess demanded, evidently deciding there was no point in the pleasantries.

"I have an invitation," he informed her. "You both look lovely tonight."

"Thank you," Maggie demurred. "And you two gentlemen look nice, too."

"Thanks. Although my pal here wasn't able to dig up a coat and tie," Spencer said, trying to lighten things up a bit.

"Well, I think he looks very handsome in his uniform," Maggie informed him, her eyes going to Andy. Spencer could have sworn he saw his friend's face grow flushed.

They inched along in what had become a receiving line of sorts—people waiting to shake hands and exchange pleasantries with the candidate and his wife. "Line's moving," he told Tess and, taking her elbow, he urged her along.

"Reed, I know how you feel about the man. But if you say or do anything to screw this up, and he refuses to see me because of it, I swear, I'll cut your throat."

"I didn't realize you were so bloodthirsty," he teased.

But before she could respond, they had reached the head of the line. "Mrs. Caine, Spencer Reed," he said and shook the woman's hand.

"Hello, Mr. Reed," Pamela said warily. "Have we met?"

"Darling," Caine addressed his wife. "Mr. Reed is the journalist who's been writing those amusing articles about me in the *Clarion-Ledger.* I believe our attorney is reviewing one of them now and considering filing a lawsuit against him and his employer."

"Mr. Caine," Tess said, stepping forward. "I'm Tess Abbott."

"Ms. Abbott," he said smoothly while he continued to hold her hand in both of his for a moment. "Pamela," he continued, addressing his wife. "This lovely young woman is Theo and Elizabeth Abbott's granddaughter."

"How do you do?" Pamela Caine responded warmly as she shook Tess's hand. "The senator and your grandmother are very dear friends of ours. I'm so pleased to get to finally meet you."

"Thank you," Tess murmured. But her attention was already back on Caine. "Mr. Caine, if I could have a word with you, please? It's important."

The mayor stepped in and said, "As you can see, there are a lot of people waiting to see the lieutenant governor. Perhaps you should call his office."

"I have called his office several times and my calls haven't been returned," Tess retorted and Spencer couldn't help but admire the way she stood her ground despite the restless murmurs around her.

"I'm sure you're mistaken, Ms. Abbott," Pamela replied. "My husband prides himself on responding to all of his constituents." She hooked her arm through her husband's. "He is truly a servant of the people."

Caine placed his hand atop his wife's. "It's all right, Pamela. The senator told me what Ms. Abbott wants to speak to me about."

"And I know he asked that you not discuss it with me. But I'm asking that you do," Tess insisted.

"Discuss what?" Pamela asked.

"A murder case that your husband prosecuted when he worked for the D.A.'s office here in Grady. One in which an innocent man was sent to prison for a crime he didn't commit."

"Heaven, it's been ages since he was a prosecutor. I can't imagine the case would be so important that you would think nothing of coming here and disrupting this event for my husband." Pamela declared.

There were a few gasps and then the room went completely still. Even the piano player stopped playing. Before Tess could respond, Spencer said, "Tess, why don't we wait until after Mr. and Mrs. Caine finish receiving their guests?"

"I've already waited twenty-five years," she said, never taking her eyes from Caine. "In response to your comment, Mrs. Caine, the case is very important to me because it's my father's. He was on trial for murder. His name was Jody Burns."

Pamela brought her hand to the diamond necklace that circled her throat. "I remember that case. What a terrible tragedy. But I can assure you, Ms. Abbott, that my husband is a man who believes in justice. I would have thought that you would want justice for your mother's murder, and that's exactly what my husband gave you."

"It's all right, Pamela," he said, patting his wife's hand after her defense of him. "Ms. Abbott, if you'll call my office on Monday morning, I'll see that my aide gives you an appointment. Is that acceptable?"

When she didn't respond, Spencer touched Tess's shoulder. "Tess?" He said her name, but her attention was riveted on Pamela Caine. "Tess, Mr. Caine suggested you call on Monday."

She jerked her gaze away from the man's wife and back to the political candidate. "Thank you, Mr. Caine. I'll do that."

But as Spencer led Tess away, he watched as her gaze shifted once again to Pamela Caine. "Why don't we get out of here," he suggested, noting all the looks being cast their way.

"What?"

Spencer came to a halt and turned around to look at her. "What in the devil is wrong with you? Caine agreed to meet with you, but you act like you don't even care."

"Of course I care. It's just that…" Once more, she looked over to where the lieutenant governor and his wife were greeting people.

"It's just that what? And what's the sudden fascination with Pamela Caine?"

She turned those ghost-gray eyes to him and said, "Reed, I think Pamela Caine is the woman who called me."

Chapter Twenty

"Pamela Caine? Are you sure?" Spencer asked her.

"Her voice, the phrase she used. She said, 'I would have thought that you would want justice,'" Tess explained. "The woman who called me used that exact wording. It's her, Spencer. I know it is."

"Maybe you're right. But it looks like your little speech has made you the center of attention. Why don't I take you back to your place."

Only then did Tess notice the number of glances directed their way, the hands lifted to mouths, the whispers. Unwilling to back down or be embarrassed, she held her head high. "Let them stare. I haven't done anything wrong."

"I know you haven't. But what's the point of sticking around? You got what you wanted. Caine's going to see you. So why not go?"

She did want to leave. And she was enormously

grateful that Spencer was there beside her. "But I came with Maggie."

"I'll talk to Andy. I've got a feeling he won't mind seeing her home. Besides, you and I need to talk. There's something I need to tell you."

Tess didn't like the sound of that. But after the realization that Pamela Caine had been her mystery caller, she was so busy trying to factor the woman's part in the puzzle that she didn't notice how quiet Spencer was on the drive back to the cottage. She was still trying to figure out what the other woman's motivation could be and how to get her to reveal what she knew, when Spencer pulled his SUV up to the cottage.

"This cottage is too far from the main house," Spencer said as he shut off the engine. "Maybe you should think about staying in the main house."

"Maggie already suggested that," Tess informed him as she unbuckled her seat belt. "And I've told her no. I'm not going to let fear of what might have happened make me a prisoner. I won't live that way."

"I don't want anything to happen to you."

At the earnest tone in his voice, Tess glanced over at him. He looked so worried, she couldn't help but be moved. "Nothing's going to happen to me. I promise."

He caught her hand, kissed it. "I intend to hold you to that."

"You do that," she said and exited the vehicle. When she realized he was still sitting there, she said, "Aren't you coming? I thought you wanted to tell me something."

Spencer followed her inside.

Tess dumped her evening bag on the table and kicked off her shoes. "Do you want a drink? Or something to eat?" she asked him.

"No thanks."

"Let me grab some water and chips. I think better when I munch," she advised him, and after she grabbed herself a bottle of water from the fridge and a bag of chips, she joined him in the living room. "If I'm right about Pamela Caine, I need to figure out a way to speak with her alone. Any ideas?"

"Come sit down, Tess."

Suddenly, the adrenaline that had been pumping after discovering that Pamela Caine was her mystery caller waned. So did the urge to dive into the bag of chips. "What is it?" she asked as she joined him on the couch.

"If Pamela Caine is your mystery caller, then she must be the same woman who called me."

"I don't understand," she said, even though she was beginning to think that she did. "When did she call you? And why?"

"The first call came more than a month ago from a woman claiming that I was right about Caine and Jenny, that the two of them were involved and that Jenny wasn't the first. She said I would never be able to prove anything because he'd covered his tracks, but that I should hit him where it really mattered—his career. She said that his business dealings hadn't always been aboveboard and she suggested I check his record when he was a lowly A.D.A. in Grady. She told me to look at the Burns murder trial."

Something inside Tess hardened. "Did you?" she asked.

"Yes. I found out the basics about your father's trial and conviction, about what a victory it was for Caine. But there wasn't anything I could see that pointed to wrongdoing on Caine's part, so I didn't pursue it."

Tess said nothing. She simply sat there, waiting for him to tell her the rest.

"A couple of weeks later she called again. This time she gave me flack for not doing anything with the info she'd given me, and when I explained I couldn't do anything without specifics, she told me Caine had manipulated the evidence to suit his own needs. When I asked her how she knew, then tried to get her to meet with me, she refused. So I told her there was nothing I could do unless she gave me someone who could verify what she'd told me. That's when she told me I should talk to you, that you knew who really killed Melanie Burns." He paused, then continued, "She told me you were in Mississippi, looking into your father's suicide and your mother's murder."

"And that's why you decided to come home for a visit," she said calmly. "So that you could conveniently be at the newspaper office when I showed up there looking for those back issues."

"Yes," he admitted. "I'm sorry, Tess. I should have told you."

"Yes, you should have," she said, feeling angry and hurt and used.

"I wanted to, but you were so defensive when we first met that I was afraid if I told you, you'd shut me out and refuse to let me work with you."

"And you needed to work with me in case I came up with any real dirt on Caine that you could use," she said, making no attempt to mask her bitterness.

"That's what I wanted in the beginning, yes. But that changed as I got to know you. Then I wanted to help you because it was important to you, because you're important to me. By the time I realized I was falling in love with you, I'd let it go too long and I didn't know how to tell you. I was afraid you would think I used you."

"Well, you were right about that. I do think you used me. The worse thing about it is that I convinced myself you were on the level. I allowed myself to trust you, to care about you. God, I feel like such a fool."

"Tess," he said and started to reach for her.

"Don't," she warned him. "Don't touch me." And to make sure that he didn't, she stood and walked over to the window. She looked out into the quiet night where the moon was bright and beautiful in the sky, where a breeze made the branches on the oak trees sway.

"Tess, please," he said, coming up behind her. He touched her shoulders.

She shrugged him off. "Do me a favor, Reed, and just go."

"Not until you let me explain."

"There's nothing to explain. You told me at the outset that you were after Caine, that you wanted to derail his campaign for governor. Since you couldn't do it on your own, you decided to use me to help you do the job." She turned around and faced him. Ignoring the ache in her heart, she said, "Congratulations, Reed. Whether or not I can prove any wrongdoing on Caine's part, the accusations of a senator's granddaughter alone will make for a good story."

"Don't," he told her, an edge in his voice.

"Tell me, Reed. How's your headline going to read?" she asked, driven by anger and feelings of betrayal. She held up her thumbs and forefingers to mimic the large-print type and continued, "How about, *'Senator's granddaughter accuses candidate of withholding evidence to win conviction'?* That should pull the readers in, don't you think?"

Spencer swore. He grabbed her by the arms, dragged her up so close she could see the muscle ticking angrily in his cheek, feel the tension in his body. "This has nothing to do with me getting a story. It never did."

"No, it was for Jenny. Your getting a big story out of it was just what you Southerners call lagniappe. A little something extra."

He swore again. Releasing her, he drew a deep breath. "I'll admit it started out being about Jenny. I wanted to make that bastard pay for what he did to her, and when I got that call telling me Caine had a hand in your father's conviction, I decided to use you as a means to get to him." He drew in a breath, released it, then met her gaze again. "But it stopped being about Jenny the night you were almost killed. You are what matters to me now, Tess. You. I'm in love with you."

Last night, maybe even an hour ago, she would have welcomed the words. She would have believed them because she had begun to fall in love with him. But now, she refused to allow herself to be moved by them or by him. "I think you'd better go, Reed. I wouldn't want you to miss your deadline."

"Tess—"

"If you feel anything at all for me, you'll leave. Now."

"All right. I'll go. For now. But this isn't over." He started toward the door, stopped and came back. "I almost forgot to give you these," he said and tossed a packet from a photo shop on the coffee table. "Rusty Toups came up with the missing negative from the crime scene of your mother's murder. Andy had a set of all the pictures made for you to look at. He didn't see anything different in the missing photo, but he wanted you and I to take a look to be sure." Tess said nothing. Neither did he. He opened the door and left.

Once the door closed softly behind him, she walked over to it and turned the lock. And only then did she allow the tears to fall.

The ringing of her cell phone woke Tess. She jerked her head up and scrambled to orient herself. She was in the cottage at Maggie's bed-and-breakfast, still dressed in the cocktail clothes that she'd worn to the reception at the country club. She glanced at her watch, half past ten. And then she remembered the confrontation with Caine and his wife at the country club, followed by that scene with Spencer, and the ache in her chest started again.

At the persistent ringing of the phone, she shook off the memory. Dropping the pillow she'd been holding, she nearly tripped on the heels she'd kicked off in her race to find the phone. She found it inside her evening bag on the table near the door. She grabbed the phone. "Hello?"

"If I tell you what I know, will you help me?"

Always good with voices, Tess gave herself a moment to register this one. "Ginger?"

There was a pause. "Yes. So, will you help me if I tell you what I know?"

"I'll do whatever I can."

"Then I need you to bring me some money. Five thousand dollars tonight."

"All right. I'll give you the money, but I don't have that kind of cash on me. I can give you a check or get the money for you tomorrow—"

"No. I can't wait until tomorrow. It's not safe for me here no more. I need to leave tonight," she said.

"But, Ginger—"

"I should have known calling you was a waste of time—"

"Wait!" Tess emptied her wallet, rifled through the cash. "I have five hundred and forty dollars in cash that I can give you now and then I can wire you the rest later—wherever you say."

There was a momentary hesitation. "All right. You know where I live. Come by yourself. Don't bring the sheriff or that reporter friend of yours. Be there in an hour and bring me the cash."

Remembering the place where Ginger lived and not wanting to return there, Tess suggested, "Why don't we meet someplace closer."

"No. You meet me at my place where I know you won't have the sheriff or anyone else waiting for me."

"But—"

"It's here. Or not at all."

"All right," Tess agreed. "And if I bring the money, you'll tell me who killed my mother and framed my father?"

"I'll tell you what you want to know."

Then the line went dead.

Tess's first thought was to call Spencer. Just as quickly she dismissed the idea. She considered calling the sheriff, then decided against it. Still, she reasoned as she changed into jeans, a sweater and sneakers, the thought of going back to Lonesome Road alone this late at night sent a shiver down her spine. She was being silly, she told herself as she grabbed her jacket and dumped her wallet and cell phone into her purse. But thoughts of the stories Spencer had told her about the place…about the deaths and disappearances…had her edgy and constantly looking in the rearview mirror as she drove away from the cottage.

She picked up her cell phone several times, tempted to call Spencer anyway. But each time, she resisted.

Don't be an idiot, Tess. No one would go to a place like that and not let someone know they were going.

Deciding to play it safe, she dialed Maggie's private number and felt a measure of relief when her friend answered. "Maggie, it's Tess."

"Tess? Is something wrong?"

"No," Tess said as she exited the grounds of Magnolia Guesthouse and headed in the direction of Ginger's place. "Ginger Weakes called me a few minutes ago. She sounded scared and she wants money to get out of town. She promises to tell me what she knows about my mother's murder and my father's trial if I give it to her."

"Tess, where are you?"

"I'm on my way to meet her. She insisted I meet her at her place on Lonesome Road."

"You shouldn't go out there alone."

"I have to," Tess told her. "I'll be all right. I just wanted someone to know where I was going in case…in case something should go wrong."

"In case something—Tess, where's Spencer?" she demanded and there was no mistaking the alarm in her voice.

"I don't know."

"But I thought he was with you."

"He's not," she told her friend. "And I'd just as soon not talk about him now. Like I said, I just wanted to let someone know where I was going."

"You shouldn't go out there by yourself, Tess. If you don't want Spencer to go with you, let Andy go. He—"

"No. And I don't want you telling either of them. If you don't hear from me by midnight, it means something is wrong and then you can call your sheriff. But not before."

"Tess, please."

"Promise me, Maggie. Promise me that you won't call Andy unless you haven't heard from me by midnight."

"All right. I promise. I won't call Andy."

"Why are you promising not to call me?"

Maggie hung up the phone and turned to the man lying naked in bed beside her. Too concerned about Tess to regret the change in plans, she said, "It's Tess. Andy, I think she's in trouble." Quickly she filled him in on their conversation.

Andy swore. "Somebody ought to lock that woman up," he muttered. And in the space of a heartbeat, the man transformed from the lazy, sexy lover to the serious, somber sheriff. While he barked out instructions for a car to be sent out to Ginger Weakes's place, he pulled on his clothes and strapped on his gun.

"Should I call Spencer and tell him to meet us there?" Maggie asked as she grabbed slacks and a sweater from her closet and began pulling them on.

Andy hung up the phone. "Maggie, there is no 'us.' You're not coming with me."

"Whether I go with you or go on my own, I'm going. Tess is my friend."

Andy walked around the bed to where she sat and was pulling on her socks and shoes. He stooped down, brought himself to her eye level. "I need you to stay here."

"But—"

"Maggie, I don't know what's going on, at least not all of it. But I do know one man is already dead. Someone has tried to kill Tess once and her running off half-cocked tonight to Lonesome Road has disaster written all over it."

"Then that's all the more reason for me to come—"

He silenced her with his mouth. "I don't know where this thing is going between us. I sure as hell didn't plan on this happening," he began.

Maggie's heart squeezed tight at the realization that he was dumping her. But she'd deal with her pain later. Right now she had to get to her friend. "Listen, you can save the 'let's be friends and I'm dumping you' speech for later, Sheriff. Although I should point out that I didn't exactly drag you into my bed kicking and screaming." She tossed back her hair, striving for some dignity. She shoved on her shoes. "Right now, my only concern is getting to Tess before something happens."

"Hang on a second, Red. Who the hell said I'm dumping you?"

She looked up at him. "Well, isn't that where that little speech of yours was headed?"

"Hell no. I'm telling you that I'm nuts about you. You're in my head all the time, under my skin and in my heart." He spat out the last. "And I don't want you going anywhere near Lonesome Road because I don't want you to get hurt."

"Oh," she said and sank to the bed. She'd loved once, had known true joy and had lost it when Mack died. Never did she expect to find that love again. She'd hoped to find some measure of caring with someone, but never to fall head over heels, butterflies in the stomach, deep love again like that. In truth, she hadn't really wanted to because the thought of losing again would hurt too much. But she had fallen in love again, she realized. That deep, right down to the bone, to the soul, kind of love.

"Oh? I spill my guts to you and that's all you've got to say?"

She grinned at him then, her heart filled with joy. She would explain to him later, tell him just how much he did mean to her. But for now, she simply said, "How about oh, I'm nuts about you, too?"

"That's better. I guess."

She laughed then and launched herself at him. "Then how about this? I'm nuts about you, Sheriff."

He kissed her hard and held her against him. "I've got to go before that foolish friend of yours gets herself into more trouble."

His words immediately sobered her and Maggie felt guilty for feeling such happiness when her friend had sounded so miserable on the phone. "Isn't there anything I can do?"

"Yeah. Remember where we left off. Because once I settle things with your friend, I want us to finish what we started."

Tess gripped the wheel of the car as she turned onto the dark road leading to Ginger's house. She had thought the place was spooky the first time she'd come in the late afternoon, when there had still been some daylight. Now, at half past eleven at night, it was flat-out creepy. Even a bright moon in the sky did nothing to dispel her unease. Driving slowly over the ruts in the road, Tess's heart pounded in her chest as she inched along, her headlights on full beam as she searched for the turnoff in the road that led to the house. Already tense, she jumped when the wind sent a tree branch swaying, brushing it against the side of her car.

Deep breaths, Tess. Deep breaths. There's nothing to be afraid of.

She repeated the mantra silently as she traveled farther down the road. At last, she reached the break in the trees and brush that signaled the turnoff. And she was grateful as she saw the lights burning in Ginger's house. For the life of her, she couldn't imagine why the woman would choose to live in such a remote place. Even if she got it rent free, she would never be able to spend a single night in the place.

Tess pulled her car up alongside Ginger's beat-up Toyota. After shutting off the engine and lights, she grabbed her purse and went in search of the other woman. When she reached the front door, she knocked and the door pushed open. "Ginger?" she called out, reluctant to cross the threshold.

She could hear a radio playing from somewhere in the back of the house. "Ginger? It's Tess Abbott. I'm here with the money."

Still no answer.

Growing uncomfortable, Tess pushed the door open farther and stepped inside. The place was a mess. Even in the dimly lit room, she could see dust balls in the corner and stains on the wood floor. The sheet across the windows used as a drape were a dull gray. Magazines, overflowing ashtrays and take-out containers with half-eaten food still in them littered the coffee table and floor. Clothes were thrown across an armchair. A coat lay in a heap on the floor. The work shoes she'd seen Ginger wearing at the restaurant were lying next to a threadbare sofa—as though she'd kicked them off when she'd sat down.

"Ginger? Are you here?" she called out again.

Sidestepping some of the clutter, Tess ventured farther into the back of the house. The rest of the place was just as dirty and cluttered as the living room. When she reached the kitchen at the very back of the house, she found dirty dishes in the sink, pots on the stove, a garbage can overflowing with trash, newspapers piled on the table and chairs. An open bottle of whiskey with a glass lay on the table. But it was a cigarette still burning in the ashtray and the open back door that put her senses on high alert.

Tess went to the door and looked out into the darkness. Several hundred yards of barren ground stretched between the house and the bayou. Thanks to the backdoor light she could make out the rusted remains of a child's swing set in the distance and beyond that she could see the water. How many times had she heard that expression about hairs standing up on the back of someone's neck? she wondered. Suddenly she felt the hairs on her own nape rising as she stared at the ghost of a child's plaything. All too clearly she remembered Spencer's story about the Arkansas family whose little girl had gone missing during the night.

Telling herself that she was being foolish, that Ginger probably just stepped outside for some reason, she descended the rickety steps. "Ginger," she called out. Walking slowly around the exterior of the house, Tess scanned the area. The sounds of the night surrounded her. A bird squawked in the trees that hung low over the bayou and the sound sent a shiver sliding down her spine. She heard the water splash and told herself it was a fish. When something slithered in the brush near her foot, Tess quickened her pace and moved farther away from the house.

"Ginger," she called out again and began walking toward the dock. But the farther away from the house she got, the darker it grew. Even the moon seemed to have ducked behind a cloud. Growing more uneasy by the second, Tess started to head back to her car to find a flashlight when she heard a moan.

Metsy Hingle

Her heart beating faster, Tess hurried toward the dock. "Ginger?" she called her name and heard another groan. She ran the rest of the way, and as the moon slipped from behind the clouds, it shone down on the dock. Tess's heart was in her throat as she recognized the brassy blond hair of the woman who sprawled on the dock, her hand hanging over the bayou.

Tess ran toward her, tripped over something and dropped her purse. Scrambling up to her knees, she saw the reason she'd tripped. It was a hunting knife lying there in the dirt and it was covered with blood. Quickly Tess got to her feet and ran over to the woman. "Ginger, what happened?" she asked and turned the woman over on her back.

Tess sucked in a breath at the sight of all the blood. She pulled Ginger's hand from her neck, saw that her throat had been slashed and heard the woman's gasps, the gurgles coming from her, as she attempted to breathe while blood poured forth.

"Oh my God. Don't move. I'll phone for an ambulance."

Ginger grabbed her arm. Her bloodied fingers held on to Tess's sleeve as she tried to speak. Tess leaned closer and tried to understand what she was saying, but she couldn't make out the words. "What is it you're trying to tell me?"

And then Ginger's grip went slack. Her head slumped. The sputtering and gurgling stopped. Horrified, Tess sat there for several seconds unsure what to do. Then she looked beyond the dock and saw beady red eyes in the dark water.

An alligator. When she saw the eyes moving toward the dock, she realized Ginger's bloody arm was still suspended over the water. Grabbing the woman's other arm, she began dragging her away from the water's edge and didn't stop until she saw those red eyes sink beneath the murky waters.

Shocked and scared, Tess tried to think. She had to get out of there, had to call the sheriff. Snatching her purse up from the ground, she ignored the sticky blood on her fingers and dug inside the bag for her keys. When she found them, she raced to her car. She was still trying to get the door open when she heard the sirens. Then she saw the flashing lights cutting through the darkness and two sheriff's cars come tearing up the road.

Sheriff Andy Trudeaux exited one vehicle. A deputy followed him. He ran over to her, stared at her bloody hands. "What in the hell happened? Are you hurt?"

"No. Not me," she managed to say. "It's Ginger. She's…she's dead."

Then he looked past her toward the dock where Ginger's body was lying. He rushed over to the dead woman and, a few minutes later when he came walking back toward her, his expression was hard and all business. "T-Boy, I want you to secure the crime scene and bag the weapon."

"Yes sir, Sheriff."

He pulled a notepad from his shirt pocket. "You want to tell me what happened?"

"I don't know. Ginger called me and arranged for me to meet her here. But when I got here, the house was open and she wasn't inside. So I came outside to look for her. And that's when I…that's when I found her. Like that, with her throat cut."

"She was just lying out there?"

"Actually, she was on the dock when I found her, but I dragged her farther inland because I saw an alligator in the water," she explained and was unable to suppress the shudder that went through her.

"Why did she want you to meet with her?"

"She said she needed to get out of town and she wanted money. She said she would tell me what she knew about my mother's murder and my father's trial if I would help her."

"And you didn't think there was anything wrong with coming out in the middle of the night and paying off the woman who helped send your father to prison?"

"I didn't say it was the smart thing to do," she told him, feeling some measure of control returning. "But if she'd have asked me to go to Timbuktu and bring her ten thousand dollars I would have gone. I want to know who set my father up and who killed my mother."

"Did you see anyone else?" he asked.

"No."

"I'm afraid I'm going to need you to come down to my office and fill out a statement. You can take your car and I'll follow you."

"Am I being arrested?"

"No. At least not yet. But if you know a lawyer, I'd suggest you call one and have him or her meet you at the sheriff's office."

Chapter Twenty-One

Spencer whirled around at the sound of Andy's office door opening, but was disappointed to see his sister, Nancy, standing in the doorway. Nancy was the attorney Maggie had phoned after getting Tess's call for a recommendation. He owed Maggie big time, he thought, for calling him and telling him what had happened. When Nancy stepped out and closed the door behind her, Spencer demanded, "Where is she? Is she okay?"

"She's fine, Spence," his sister told him. "She'll be out in a second."

As if on cue, the door opened again and Tess exited the room. She looked at Nancy and asked, "Did you phone him?"

"I did," Maggie confessed as she stood and went over to her friend.

"You didn't need to come down here, Maggie. You either," Tess told Spencer.

"I'm not sure you could have kept either of them away," Nancy said. "Particularly my brother. I thought Andy was going to have to lock him up to keep him out of that interview."

"I would have if necessary," Andy added as he exited the room. "If you should think of anything else or remember something later about what you saw or heard—and I don't care how insignificant you think it is—I want you to call me. All right?"

Tess nodded and took the card he handed her. She paused. "Sheriff, there is one thing, not from tonight, but from the first time I went to Ginger's place."

"You mean the time you followed her home and she accused you of trespassing?" Andy countered.

"Yes," she said. "There was someone else there with her. I never saw who it was. But I got the feeling she was afraid of whoever was with her. There wasn't any other car parked out front beside Ginger's. But there was a boat tied up by the dock."

"What kind of boat?" Andy asked her. "Can you describe it?"

Tess described it to him. "I don't know what brand or model or anything. It was just a boat."

"Doesn't Larry Gates own a boat like that?" Nancy asked.

"How would you know that?" Spencer asked his sister.

"Because Luke has been trying to convince me he should buy one so he can teach the boys to fish," Nancy explained, referring to her husband and twin sons.

"But the twins are only two," Maggie commented.

"My point exactly," Nancy said before turning her attention back to Andy. "But he's been pointing out boats to me every time we see one. Last week, we were leaving church when he saw Larry Gates trailering his boat and Luke pointed it out to me."

"Ginger went to see Gates," Tess told him. "Maggie and I saw them together and it looked like they were arguing."

"She's right," Maggie confirmed.

"I'll check it out," Andy said.

"Are you finished with Tess?" Spencer demanded, concerned because Tess's eyes had taken on a glazed look, which he suspected was due to exhaustion.

"For now," Andy told him.

Sorely tempted to take his friend's pistol and use it on the man for bringing Tess in for questioning in the first place, Spencer decided it was time to leave. "Then I'm going to take Tess home."

"But I have my car," Tess protested.

"I'll drive it back for you," Maggie offered. "I rode in with Nancy."

Tess hesitated a moment, then said, "All right. Thank you." Then she turned to Nancy. "And thank you for coming tonight."

"I was happy I could help. Although I must admit that I was expecting to meet you at my parents' next week over dinner and not in the sheriff's office," Nancy joked.

"Thanks, Nance," Spencer told her, not giving Tess the chance to say anything about the dinner invitation.

"No problem." And to Tess she said, "Call me if you need anything else."

"I will," Tess assured her. "And please, Nancy, send me your bill."

"Don't worry, I will."

"Come on," Spencer told Tess. "Let's get you home." And before she could argue with him, he gripped her arm and led her outside to his SUV.

Other than to respond with a simple yes or no when he asked if she was cold or wanted him to put on the radio, she remained silent throughout the drive back to the cottage. Once they'd arrived, he insisted on seeing her inside.

"It's really not necessary," she assured him.

"It is for my peace of mind," he told her as he unlocked the door and followed her in. "Do you want to talk about it?"

"No."

She kept way too much bottled up inside her, he thought, but he didn't have a clue as to how to get her to open up to him—especially not after what had happened between them earlier tonight.

"I'm okay now. You can leave, Spencer."

But he had no intention of leaving—not after what she'd been through. "I will, but first I'm going to draw you a bath," he told her and headed for the bathroom. While he wasn't at all sure a bath was the right prescription, in his thirty-four years of observing his mother and sisters, it seemed to be the universal cure-all for a woman.

Unfortunately, he thought as he turned on the taps, a bath wouldn't do anything for the knot he'd had in his gut ever since he'd gotten that call from Maggie telling him what had happened. When he had seen her at the sheriff's office, her clothes stained with blood, his heart had nearly stopped. Then when his sister, Nancy, had assured him that she wasn't hurt, that it was Ginger's blood, he'd been hard-pressed not to bang on the door of that room and drag her into his arms to make sure for himself.

"Is it ready?" she asked from the doorway. "I really want to get out of these clothes."

He tested the water, then stood. "Go ahead. I'll be waiting outside when you finish."

"Spencer—"

"Go take your bath, Tess. I know you don't want me here. But I need to be here."

To his surprise, she didn't argue further. She simply passed him and went into the bathroom, then shut the door.

Spencer stared at the closed door and speared his hands through his hair. Suppose she'd arrived at Ginger's place ten minutes earlier and the killer had still been there? He didn't even want to think about what might have happened to her. Because thinking about it made him feel ill. Even now, he thought as he sat on the bench at the foot of her bed, his blood ran cold when he pictured the scene his sister had painted for him of what Tess had witnessed.

He didn't know how long he'd been sitting there, lost in thought, before he heard the sound of the bathroom door opening. Spencer looked up. Tess stood in the doorway. The light spilling from the room behind her painted her dark hair the color of coffee. Her skin looked as smooth and pale as ivory. She wore a thigh-high pajama shirt of pale green. And that same glow from the bathroom that made her skin look so soft and beautiful made the shirt nearly transparent. The sight of her breasts, the dark rose of her nipples, had his breath backing up in his lungs and the front of his jeans growing tight. He averted his gaze only to find himself staring at those long bare legs. He drew in a breath and stood. "Feeling better?" he asked.

"Yes. The bath was just what I needed. Thank you." She looked back at the bathroom, a bleak look coming over her face. "My clothes—"

"I'll take care of them," he told her. He would burn the things, he promised himself. He'd already thrown out the bloodied jacket she'd had on, and he would do whatever else he had to do because he didn't want her to ever think about the horrors of what happened tonight again. "Would you like something to drink? Maybe some warm milk?"

She flicked off the bathroom light. "Actually, I think I'd just like to go to bed."

"Of course. You've got to be exhausted," he said and went over to ready the bed for her. He pulled off the throw pillows and piled them on the bench at the end of the bed where he'd been sitting. "I took some sheets and a blanket out of the linen closet while you were in the tub. I'm going to sack out on the couch tonight. So if you need anything, I'll be right outside the door," he explained as he pulled back the comforter and turned down the sheets.

"You don't have to stay on the couch," she said from right behind him.

With his own nerves still on edge, not to mention the hormones that had kicked in after seeing her, Spencer was in no mood to be pushed tonight. "It's not up for debate, Tess. I'm not leaving you alone tonight. Not after everything you've been through."

"Who said I wanted you to leave me alone?"

Spencer went still at her words. Straightening, he turned to face her. She looked soft and seductive, her mouth a temptation all by itself. Wisps of dark hair curled around her face, slightly damp from her bath. The flowery scent of her soap lingered and mixed with something exotic. The combination was erotic and played havoc with his fast-diminishing control. His emotions had been on overload since he'd received that call from Maggie. Hers had to be on the verge of shattering. She was reacting because of what she'd been through, he told himself. It would be unfair to take advantage of her vulnerability.

Then she moved closer, slid her hand up his shoulders, his neck and into his hair. When she pressed her lips to his chin, Spencer fought the urge to toss her to the bed. "Tess, I don't think you really want to do this."

"Don't I?" she whispered just before she nipped at his ear.

He held on to her shoulders as much to keep her from getting any closer as to keep himself from giving in. He closed his eyes, his breath labored as he tried to reason with himself and with her. "You've just been through a horrific experience. You saw someone die. Death has a crazy effect on a person's hormones. It leaves us with a need to feel, a need to…" His breath hitched as her mouth moved along his jaw, her fingers working the buttons of his shirt.

"I'm listening, Spencer. You were saying, it leaves us with a need to feel, a need to…"

"…a need to reaffirm life," he continued, paraphrasing the information from an article he'd read once about the effects of death on those who remained behind. "And the best way to reaffirm life, to prove to ourselves that we're still alive," he said, his breath ragged as she worked on the rest of the buttons on his shirt, her nails lightly scoring the flesh beneath.

She kissed her way down his chest and pulled the shirt free. Then she reached for his belt buckle. She looked up at him out of those liquid gray eyes as she unbuckled the belt. "…the best way to reaffirm life, that we're still alive," she prompted.

"Is for…is to make love."

She rose. Like a graceful cat, she stretched upward in one fluid movement, bringing her long, lean body against his longer and harder body. "Then reaffirm that we're alive, Spencer. Make me feel alive. Make love with me."

He kissed her. Taking his time, he tasted her, taunted her, taunted himself. Her mouth softened beneath him. But there was no questioning the heat that was there between them, an all-consuming passion that had been there, just under the surface, almost from the first day. Though it cost him, he lifted his head and asked her, "Are you sure this is what you want?"

A shudder went through her and when she opened her eyes, looked at him, for a moment he thought she might call a halt after all. But then she said, "Spencer, right now about the only thing in my life that I *am* sure about is that I want to make love with you."

He kissed her. Slowly, thoroughly, exploring every inch of her mouth until he had memorized every curve, every taste. And when he had his fill of her mouth—at least for now—he moved on to the rest of her. He kissed her jaw, her neck, tasted the hollow in her throat. And when he felt the rapid-fire beat of her pulse beneath his lips, Spencer felt a surge of need. Though it would probably kill him, he was determined to take things slow. He wanted to savor every moment, every touch, every sound from her. With that thought in mind, he began to unbutton her nightshirt.

By the time Spencer undid the last button on her nightshirt, Tess's nerves were screaming. After the horror of Ginger's death and the interview at the sheriff's office, she'd been so numb, she didn't think she could feel anything. And then she'd walked out of that room and seen Spencer. Her first instinct had been to throw herself into his arms.

And then she'd remembered. Some of the anger she'd felt toward him earlier reared its head again. But she hadn't been able to sustain it. She'd kept thinking of Ginger lying there dead. She thought of her mother, seeing her body that night so long ago. What if it had been her lying dead tonight on the dock instead of Ginger? She realized then that among the things she would regret most was that she had never made love with Spencer. That she had held herself—her heart—back from him. He was probably right, she admitted. On some level she did want to reaffirm that she was alive. But it was more than that. She wanted him. She wanted Spencer Reed. And whatever consequences came of this, she promised herself she would sort through them later. For now, all she wanted was him.

He eased the nightshirt from her shoulders. His knuckles brushed against her breasts. And when his palms slid along her ribs, the hunger she'd harnessed through those long, slow kisses snapped. Greed, sudden and selfish, shot through her. She clutched his shoulders, curled her nails into his flesh as he brought his mouth to her shoulder. His breath was warm against her skin, his hands firm, but gentle, as he held her. When he nipped the skin on her shoulder with his teeth, she shuddered.

"Did I hurt you?" he asked, lifting his head a fraction.

"No," she managed to get out through a throat that was dry with need.

"Good."

He took another bite, and then another, each one a little lower until he'd reached her breast. When he closed his teeth over the nipple, pleasure shot through her. She reached for him and when he stepped back, she nearly groaned.

"Wait," he told her. Lifting her, he set her on the side of the bed. Then he reached for her panties. With a slowness that drove her crazy, he eased them down her hips, along her legs and over her ankles. The brush of his knuckles along her hips, the glide of his fingers down her legs had sensations shooting through her like arrows.

"One of us is overdressed," she told him.

"I think I can fix that," he said, and there was no mistaking the hungry gleam in those blue eyes of his.

"Let me help you."

She reached for his belt and felt a surge of feminine power when he groaned. Once she had him free of his clothes, she simply had to touch him, had to feel him. She flattened her palms on his chest, swept them up his shoulders, around his neck, and drew his mouth back to hers. One kiss slid into another, each one more intoxicating, each one growing hotter than the one before it. He took them both down to the bed. And he kissed her some more, touched and teased her some more. Within moments she was hot and damp, and her hunger had escalated to violent urgency.

When she attempted to hurry him along, he said, "We're going to take this slow, Tess. Real slow. And by the time morning arrives, the only thing I want you to remember about tonight is me and this moment." Cupping her, he began to lazily stroke her with his finger, exerting just enough pressure for the ripples of pleasure to build then easing off before they exploded.

Nearly panting, she reached for him and tried to hurry him along. He caught her hand. Smiling, he said, "Patience, Tess. Patience."

But with each stroke, each touch, the ripples grew. Until the ripples became waves of pleasure threatening to crest over. All the while his mouth, his clever mouth, continued to minister more deep, slow kisses, followed by nips sharp enough for pleasure, but careful not to cause pain. And when she could stand it no longer, when her body was crying out for release, she pushed his hands away and rolled him onto his back. Closing her fingers around him, she smiled and said, "Let's see how patient you are."

Then she proceeded to drive them both mad. And when his patience reached its limit, he flipped her onto her back and filled her. She arched her back as he thrust into her. For long seconds he simply held her by her hips, held himself rigid. Then he began that slow maddening pace again. And when their bodies were hot and slick, and the anticipation and greed razor sharp, she clutched her muscles around him and then it was Spencer who was impatient. It was Spencer who slammed into her again and again until she felt herself toppling over and free-falling through space. And seconds later, she heard him cry out her name as he followed her.

When she awoke the next morning, Tess was alone. She eased up on her elbows, saw the dent in the pillow on the bed next to her and memories of the night flooded through her, warmed her. Refusing to regret what had happened, she grabbed her robe and went in search of Spencer.

She found him in the kitchen, hanging up the phone. "I'm beginning to think that phone is an appendage of your body."

He looked over at her, studied her face. There was an intensity in his expression, a warmth. "I think you know better than that. But you're welcome to come over here and check me out to be sure."

Tess blushed because she knew intimately each appendage of his body, as he did hers. Deciding to ignore the invitation, she asked, "Is that coffee I smell?"

"Sure is." He poured her a cup, but when she reached for it, he said. "It'll cost you."

"How much?"

"That's a loaded question, Abbott. And while I'm tempted to put a huge price tag on it, I'll settle for a kiss."

She kissed him and felt a flutter of longing as he pulled her against him and deepened the kiss. She could taste the coffee he'd drunk and it surprised her that after the night they'd spent she could feel that flutter of need beginning in her belly again. Judging from his arousal, she wasn't the only one. But instead of suggesting they go back to bed, he eased her away from him and handed her the coffee.

Tess took a sip and sighed. "You make great coffee, Reed."

"It's one of my many talents," he told her. "If you're hungry, I'll make you an omelet."

"Sounds good," she told him, and while she sat at the table, he went to work and within minutes he served her a fluffy omelet. "What about you?" she asked when he didn't serve a plate for himself. "Aren't you going to eat?"

"I already did."

"It looks good," she told him. And it tasted good, too, she discovered as she took several bites. Not until she saw him glancing at the clock on the wall for a third time did she realize that he was completely dressed, and that he seemed anxious. "Spencer, is something wrong? If it's about what happened last night—"

"What happened last night was incredible. It's also something that I want us to repeat a million times during the next fifty years."

"A million?" she teased, but she had to admit she liked the sound of fifty years of making love with Spencer.

"Maybe more," he told her seriously.

"Why do I have a feeling there's a 'but' coming here?"

"Because there is one. I spoke with Andy this morning. Larry Gates is missing. According to his wife, he didn't come home last night and his boat is gone."

Tess shivered at the memory of last night, of finding Ginger with her throat slashed. Of seeing all that blood. "You think he was the one who killed Ginger?"

"I think it's a good possibility. I don't know the reason yet, but I think it's connected to your mother's murder and your father's trial."

"Does the sheriff agree? Or does he still consider me a suspect?" she asked, recalling all too well the grilling Sheriff Andy Trudeaux had put her through the previous night.

Spencer pulled out the chair next to her and straddled it. "Andy knows you didn't kill Ginger Weakes. Unfortunately, you have motive and you were at the scene. And until he finds Gates, or whoever did kill her, he has to treat you as a suspect."

"I guess it's a good thing Maggie sent your sister there last night or I might very well have spent the night in jail. Do you think I should call Nancy and tell her I may need her services again?"

"Fortunately, for you, I know how to reach her at a moment's notice. So why don't we just wait and see if Andy is able to locate Gates and bring him in for questioning."

"All right," she said and took another bite of her omelet. But that worried look was in his eyes again. "Is there something else you're not telling me?"

"I won't make that mistake again," he assured. "But I'm worried about you."

"Why?"

"Because as long as Gates is out there, I think you could be in danger. I've got to go to Jackson. In fact, I should have already left by now. I've got a meeting at noon with my editor and then I've got to be at a press forum for five o'clock with the gubernatorial candidates. I'd like you to come with me. That way I'll know you're safe."

She considered it, recognized his concern. She had a few concerns of her own since last night. "I swore I wouldn't let whoever ran me off the road make me a prisoner by making me afraid of my shadow. I can't let what happened with Ginger last night make me a prisoner either. You have a job to do. So do I."

"Tess—"

"I promise I'll be careful. I'll keep the door locked and you have my word that I won't be making any more late-night trips to meet with a blackmailer." The grin she hoped her last comment would spark didn't come. "I'll be all right. And I could use a little time alone to try and see if I can figure out this thing with Pamela Caine. Please understand."

"I do," he told her. "But it doesn't keep me from worrying."

"I'm worried, too," she admitted. "But we're close. I know we are. If I had gotten to Ginger's sooner, we might even have the answers now."

"And you also might be dead," he reminded her.

"But I'm not. Now go meet with your editor, cover your debate and hurry back to me."

"You got that piece finished yet, Reed?"

"Keep your shirt on, Hank," Spencer told his editor. "I said you'd have it in time to make the next edition and you will. Now leave me alone so I can finish the thing."

The man grumbled the same thing he always grumbled, something about smart-ass journalists who cut their deadlines too close and caused their editors to get ulcers, then he pulled the door closed.

Spencer could have kicked himself for ever proposing 'The Road to the Governor's Mansion' series. Because here he was, halfway through the series, and he hadn't turned in the next article. He couldn't blame Hank for complaining or for reading him the riot act when he'd arrived at the office. But with all the stuff going on with Tess and then last night's events, his job hadn't been on his mind. Still, he'd made a commitment. So he went back to work.

He was just finishing up the article when the door to his office opened again. Spencer didn't even bother looking up this time. He continued to type away and said, "I told you I'd make the deadline, Hank. You coming in here every ten minutes to see if I'm done isn't going to make me work any faster."

"Just because I cut my hair shorter than yours is no reason to insult me by calling me names."

Spencer jerked his head up and stared at Phoebe Morris, the research assistant and fact verifier who had proved invaluable to him in the past. "Sorry, Phoebe. I thought you were Hank again."

"Last time I saw him he was at his desk chugging Maalox and taking your name in vain."

Spencer winced, knew he really did owe the man a sincere apology. Later. "So, did you have any luck?"

She plopped a file on his desk. "You owe me big time, Reed. And I don't mean lunch at McDonald's. Think big—like a weekend at a spa somewhere." She leaned over the desk, flipped the file open and withdrew a photo. "If the polls are right, that's a picture of the state's future first lady when she was a junior at Ursuline Academy in New Orleans."

Spencer picked up the somewhat grainy photo of an all-girl class in white shirts, plaid skirts and saddle oxford shoes. A red circle had been drawn around the face of a fresh-faced blonde. The name highlighted under the photo was Pamela Dupont. Who he knew was now Pamela Dupont Caine.

"You'll notice the name of the nun in the photograph with the girls," Phoebe told him.

"Sister Amelia," Spencer said, more to himself than to Phoebe.

"Moving right along, you may want to look at the next item," she told him. "It took quite a lot of persuading on my part, but I got the guy to fax me a copy of the transaction."

Spencer pulled out a copy of a sales receipt from a costume shop located in the suburbs of New Orleans for one "nun's habit" purchased ten months earlier. The transaction had been paid for by a credit card issued in the name of P. D. Caine.

"How on earth did you get this?" he asked, impressed.

"The guy working the register is a journalism student. I promised him you'd take a look at some of his stuff."

"Phoebe, I could kiss you."

"Save the kiss," she said as she headed for the door. "I'll take that spa weekend."

"Book it and send me the bill."

Once the door was closed, he finished off the article. After he hit the file-transfer commands, sending it on to Hank, he reached for his PalmPilot and located the cell number Pete had given him the last time he'd spoken with him. When he answered, Spencer said, "Pete, it's Spencer Reed with the *Clarion-Ledger*. Can you talk?"

"Not right this minute. But I'm scheduled for a lunch break in just over an hour."

"Is there someplace I could meet you? I've got a photo of someone I'd like you to look at."

"There's a place not too far from the prison where I eat lunch sometimes," Pete began.

"Great. I'll meet you there."

Just over an hour later in a restaurant located five miles from the prison, Spencer sat across the table from the security guard and watched as the man studied the photo he'd gotten from the press files of Pamela Caine.

Pete rubbed his fleshy jaw. "Well, she does look kinda familiar," he said.

"Do you think she could have been the nun?"

"Don't know. I mean, the nun was in that black outfit and I couldn't see her hair and she sure wasn't wearing makeup and jewelry."

"I know that, Pete. But try to imagine her with her hair covered up and without the lipstick." To help, he took the pen out of his pocket and drew a veil of sorts around the woman's face and hair, then colored it in with black ink. It was a poor imitation of a nun's veil, but he hoped it would at least provide the visual.

"Well now," Pete said as he looked at the results. "She does look more like Sister Amelia. Maybe if you could color over the necklace and dress the same way and make it look like one of them black dresses they wear."

Spencer ruined the rest of the photograph by drawing boxlike shapes from the neck down and scratched long black lines down it to try to achieve some semblance of a habit.

"Yep, I'd say that just might be her."

"Thanks, Pete. I really appreciate the help," Spencer said and, having left a tip on the table, he headed for the exit.

Okay, Mrs. Caine. Now all I have to do is figure out why you were masquerading as a nun, and what information you were going to give Jody Burns.

Because when he had those answers, Spencer told himself, he would know who killed Melanie Burns and framed her husband. He'd also know who had tried to kill Tess.

Chapter Twenty-Two

"This entire notion of yours about someone other than Jody Burns being responsible for your mother's death is not only stupid but it's a slap in the face to me and to your grandmother," her grandfather declared, his voice booming over the phone line as he continued to rant at her.

"I'm sorry you feel that way," Tess told him.

"Don't you even care that your grandmother has been sick with worry over you ever since she found out you were in that accident?"

"Of course I care. That's why I've spoken with Grandmother several times since then and she knows that I'm fine."

"She won't be when she hears about your little performance at Everett Caine's reception last night. Or didn't you think I'd find out what a fool you'd made of yourself accosting Everett and throwing out those ridiculous theories of yours in front of a room filled with people? I won't have it, Tess. Do you hear me? I won't have it."

She didn't need to see her grandfather to know that his face was red and that the angry flush would extend all the way to the roots of his silver hair. Nor did she have to see his face to know that his eyes, a darker gray than her own, were flashing with fire. "The choice isn't yours," she informed him. "Not everything is about you. This is about me. About my mother and my father."

"I suppose this lack of respect you're displaying can be attributed to the company you've been keeping."

"And what company is that?" she demanded.

"I'm referring to that bottom-feeding journalist Reed that you've been associating with. If you don't have the sense not to align yourself with a man like that, the least you could do is show some discretion."

Tess gritted her teeth. Determined not to lose her temper and say something she would regret, she struggled to keep her voice even as she said, "The only one who sounds like a bottom-feeder is whomever you have reporting back to you. I'm not a child anymore, Grandfather. Who I see is my business, not yours."

"That's where you're wrong. You are still my granddaughter and I won't have you embarrassing me any further. I'm arriving in Jackson this evening to make an appearance with Everett. When I'm finished, I'm flying directly back to Washington and you're coming with me. I'll expect you at the airport by eight."

"No."

"That wasn't a request. You're returning with me to Washington tonight." She heard his fist slap down on something. "I demand it."

"*If* I come home, it'll only be when I find out the truth."

"How dare you—"

Tess hung up the phone.

When her cell phone began to ring a moment later, she ignored it. She walked into the den and stared at the packet of photos on the coffee table. She'd put off the task as long as she could, Tess told herself. Sitting down, she picked up the envelope and removed the pictures from her mother's murder scene.

As she flipped through the pictures one by one, she found herself slipping back in time. Back to that time when she was four years old.

"I told you I've made up my mind and I'm not going to change it. So you might as well leave."

Tess woke up at the sound of her mommy's voice. It was her mommy's angry voice, she realized. The one she'd heard her using that morning when she and Daddy had been arguing about money.

"I'm not leaving until you hear me out."

"I already know what you're going to say and I don't want to hear it again. I'm going to get a job. Once I'm bringing in money, too, we'll be able to manage."

"And what kind of job are you going to get? Waiting tables? How do you think that's going to look? A senator's daughter slopping food in a restaurant?"

"I don't care how it looks. It's honest work and we need the money."

"And while you're working for peanuts, who's going to take care of Tess?"

"Tess will be fine. Lots of mothers work. There's no reason I can't, too."

"What's wrong with you? Have you forgotten who you are? Where you come from?"

"Please stop it," Melanie cried out. "Just stop it. I

don't want to argue with you anymore. This isn't your decision. It's mine. Why can't you accept that?"

Tess buried her head under the pillow. She couldn't bear to hear her parents fighting again. She knew Daddy didn't want her mommy to go to work. He wanted her to stay home and be a mommy. But Mommy had talked to her about it. She'd explained that they needed the money to pay for things like doctors and clothes and toys for her.

"Don't you turn away from me."

"Let go of me!"

Tess covered her ears. Crying now, she just wanted them to stop yelling, to make up like they had that morning, to kiss each other and play games.

Her mother screamed and Tess trembled. She heard glass breaking. *"Oh, my God! Melanie! Melanie!"*

Terrified, Tess pulled the covers over her head and sobbed and sobbed.

Maybe if she was a good girl, if she didn't get sick on the carpet again, Mommy and Daddy would be happy again. When the shouting stopped, she continued to lie there for a long, long time, her eyes growing heavy.

"Melanie? My God, Melanie!"

Tess jerked awake at the sound of her daddy's voice. She sat up in bed. She didn't feel good. Her throat hurt and she was hot. *"Mommy! Mommy!"*

But her mommy didn't come. Why didn't her mommy come? Mommy always came when she was sick. Grabbing her teddy, she climbed out of bed and ran down the hall to the den.

"Mommy?" she called out.

"Tess! Go back! Go back to your room," Daddy shouted.

"What's wrong with my mommy?" she asked as she stared at him holding her mommy. And then she saw the blood. On her mommy's head. On her daddy's hands and shirt. She saw the bookend in his hand, all red with blood. "Mommy!"

"Tess, get out of here," her daddy yelled. He threw down the bookend and grabbed the phone. "Operator, I need the police. My wife's been murdered."

Tess put down the photos with trembling fingers. As she did so, her eyes fell on the packet of letters from her father and she recalled the last one, the one he'd written to her on her twenty-ninth birthday. The letter in which he'd sworn to her again that he was innocent and that he would soon have the proof. That letter had been filled with love for her, as had all the others. It had also been filled with the hope that she would allow him into her life again. For her father, for the man who had never stopped loving her, she had to do this, she told herself. Regardless of what her memories told her, the man who'd written those letters could not have killed his wife.

So she picked up the photos again. And this time as she studied them, she avoided the photos of the body and concentrated instead on what else was in the photos. There were five shots—almost identical in composition—that encompassed the area next to the body and included a shot of the coffee table. She laid out the five shots side by side. Each pictured the big square wooden coffee table with the four glass panes inset. Two of the panes were broken and there were glass shards across the table. The grouping of photos that had been arranged in one corner had been knocked over. One photo lay on the tile floor, its frame cracked. One crystal candlestick with droplets of blood on it lay on its side atop the table. The mate lay shattered on the floor, the candles broken. The hardcover books had been scattered. One of her barrettes rested next to a jumble of magazines.

Each of the photos was the same, she thought. Going over each item one by one she noticed it—the silver foil gum wrapper that lay next to one of the books. Tess's heart nearly stopped as she looked at that wrapper. It was folded and tied into a knot—just the way her grandfather folded and knotted the silver wrappers from his chewing gum.

Tess tried to think back, tried to remember that awful night. Had it been her father's voice she'd heard? Or had she just assumed that any man's voice in her home would belong to her daddy? Even at four, she'd known her grandfather hadn't liked her father and that was the reason he and her grams never came to visit. So why had his gum wrapper been there?

Because he had been there that night.

With a sick feeling in her stomach, she picked up the phone and punched in the number at her grandparents' home. And when Elizabeth Abbott answered, Tess said, "Grams, it's Tess. I need to ask you something about the night my mother was killed. And I need for you to tell me the truth."

When Tess hung up the phone a few minutes later an icy calm had settled over her. She retrieved the number she'd called numerous times in her attempts to meet with Everett Caine. Only this time when his aide answered, she said, "This is Tess Abbott calling for Mr. Caine."

"I'm sorry, Ms. Abbott. He's at a press conference. He did say you'd be calling and that I should try to schedule you in to see him sometime next week."

"I need to see him today."

"I'm afraid that's impossible. After the press conference, he has a dinner engagement and then he leaves in the morning to begin a statewide campaign blitz before next week's election."

"Then I need you to give the lieutenant governor a message for me. Tell him I have the photo. Unless he wants to see it on the front page of tomorrow morning's newspapers, he'll see me tonight."

"But—"

"Give him the message and then call me back at this number."

Five minutes later when the phone rang and Tess answered, the woman said, "The lieutenant governor has asked that you meet him at his home this evening at ten o'clock. If you've got a pencil, I'll give you directions."

Seated at his desk, Sheriff Andy Trudeaux stared at the evidence spread out before him. It was nearly ten o'clock, almost twenty-four hours since Ginger Weakes had been killed. That made two deaths since Tess Abbott had showed up in Grady, and both were witnesses at her father's trial. Now a third prosecution witness and the man he suspected had killed Ginger was also missing. Yet he was no closer now to figuring out why than he had been that morning.

It was like a game of chess, Andy thought. And he considered each of the players. Jody Burns was the pawn. So were De Roach and Ginger. Melanie Abbott Burns had been the queen that had been captured and killed. Larry Gates was the knight. Was Caine the king as Spencer seemed to think? But if he was, what had been the motive? Where was the big payoff? The notoriety of winning a trial that helped jump-start his political career just didn't seem reason enough to justify murder. Yet with De Roach and Ginger dead, that left only two people—Gates who was now missing and Caine.

There had to be another player. But who? He came back to what had been troubling him the most—the missing photo and the negatives—and the fact that they had been in Rusty's possession. As much as he tried to figure a way around it and had not wanted to allow himself to believe it, Rusty had to have known, or if he hadn't known, he'd at least have had his suspicions. Why else take the photo and negatives?

He was missing something, Andy told himself. And whatever it was, it was in that photo. He picked up the photograph again, studied it for what had to be the tenth time in an effort to see what he was missing. When he still couldn't find what was eluding him, he grabbed the remote and turned on the television. The evening news came on, a recap of Ginger's murder headed the local news. Half listening, Andy continued to look at the photo.

"And today in our state's Capitol, Lieutenant Governor Everett Caine got a strong show of support from his longtime friend, Senator Theodore Abbott. The senator flew in from Washington this afternoon to speak at a forum of the state's most influential businessmen and businesswomen this evening."

The station went to a tape of the affair where the senator stood at the podium beside Caine. "My good friends, to ensure the continued prosperity of our great state for us, for our children, for our grandchildren and all generations to come, Mississippi needs a leader. Mississippi needs a strong man, a man of vision to lead us into the future and beyond. The man Mississippi needs is Everett Caine. I urge you to give him your vote in next week's election."

The senator stepped back. And as the assembled body stood and applauded and Caine lifted his hand in a victory sign, the senator slid a stick of gum into his mouth and began folding the wrapper, then tying it into a knot.

The television screen flashed back to the newscaster. "In other news today…"

Suddenly Andy stared back down at the photo of the Melanie Burns crime scene. And there it was—the missing piece—Senator Theodore Abbott's gum wrapper on the coffee table in his daughter's home. A home in which the senator had sworn never to have set foot in, and on a night when the senator had claimed to be nearly two hundred miles away.

Grabbing his hat and jacket, Andy exited the office. He called Spencer, filled him in on what he'd discovered.

"Have you told Tess yet?" Spencer asked him.

"I thought I'd leave that to you. This isn't going to be easy for her, Spence. The man's her grandfather."

"I know," Spencer told him. "I'll handle it. But I think it's something I need to tell her in person."

"That's your call."

"I'm in Jackson. Are you coming up here to confront Caine?" Spencer asked.

He would need to get a warrant, find out about jurisdiction. "Yeah, I'm going to confront the bastard. But first I need to make a stop."

Andy pulled his truck up the driveway leading to Rusty's place. When he reached the house where he'd spent so many hours, he was surprised to see his mother leaving. Andy got out of his vehicle and walked over to her car. "Mom, what are you doing here?"

"Rusty needed to see me about something," she said and Andy wished the lighting were better because he thought he could hear tears in her voice.

"Are you all right?"

"Yes," she told him. "I need to go."

"Mom—"

"Rusty's a good man, Andrew. Sometimes I think I never realized just how good a man he was and how much you and I depended on him. You remember that when you talk to him." And without any further explanation, she got in her car and left.

Dreading what was to come, Andy turned away from the sight of the taillights of his mother's departing car and went in search of Rusty. He found him sitting out back on the deck overlooking the water. For once, he didn't have a fishing pole in his hand. He just sat there staring out at the water.

He never turned around. As though he'd been waiting for him, he said, "I was wondering when you'd come."

"You knew that once you gave me the negatives I would figure it out."

"I counted on it. You were always smart as a whip, son. Even as a kid, you had a way of working things out in your head. Always looking for reasons, needing to balance things. It's one of the things that makes you a good lawman," he told him and Andy thought how tired Rusty suddenly sounded.

"Why, Rusty? You were always a good sheriff. You're the one who taught me the importance of being honest. Did you know all along that Jody Burns was innocent?"

"No. Truth is, at first I thought he was guilty just like everybody else. I didn't get suspicious until after the trial was over and he'd been sent to prison. You know me, always tidied up those files and reports. That's when I realized one of the pictures was missing."

"What happened?" Andy asked him.

"Gates claimed I'd misnumbered the pictures and Caine swore there'd only been eleven, not twelve like I said. Because it was such a big case, Caine had said they'd need the negatives. So I didn't have anything to check it against. When I asked to see the negatives, Caine told me they'd been lost. But I knew the man was lying. I hadn't misnumbered those pictures. I knew there had to be a reason that one was missing. I just had no way to prove it."

"So how did you get the negatives back?"

"That fool Gates gave him the wrong ones," he said, a hint of amusement in what was an otherwise grim voice. "The man was the worst deputy I ever had, never could get things straight, always in too much of a hurry. He was in so much of a hurry, he gave Caine the wrong negatives. I found the negatives from the Burns murder scene misfiled about a year later."

"Then why didn't you do something, Rusty?"

"I tried. I went to see Caine. By then Caine was the D.A. I told him what I'd found, that someone else had been there at the Burns home that night. That I thought he needed to reopen the case."

"What did he say?" Andy asked.

"He told me that if I knew what was good for me, I'd forget what I'd found."

"That's it? You let an innocent man sit in jail for twenty-five years because the man threatened you?"

"Yes."

"I don't believe you. You wouldn't do that," Andy insisted.

"I did."

"Why?"

"Because I made a mistake. I broke the law I had sworn to uphold and Caine found out about it."

"Hell, you don't even jaywalk. What law did you break?"

Rusty turned to face him then and the man seemed to have aged twenty years since he'd last seen him. It pained him to see this man he loved and admired, the man who had taught him to fight for what was right, to look so downtrodden.

"I deliberately lost evidence against a man who had been arrested for drug trafficking and the courts had to release him."

Suddenly it all clicked into place. "My father. When the charges got dropped against him, that's when he split on me and my mother."

Rusty nodded. "I was in love with Susan even back then. Your father knew it. Hell, I guess everyone knew it but Susan. Mick Trudeaux was a user. He was going to drag you and your mother down with him. He'd started using her little bookshop to run his drugs. He told me if I helped him get off, he'd leave the two of you. So I did it. And Mick kept his word. He left and never came back."

He'd done it to save him and his mother, Andy realized, and his heart ached for this man who was a father to him in every sense of the word. "Only, Caine found out about it."

"Yep. Gates found out first. And he told Caine."

"Is Gates the one who killed Lester and Ginger?"

"Caine wanted them shut up. Lester was a basket case. He thought the Abbott girl was here for revenge.

And Ginger, well, she was just as bad. It was only a matter of time before one of them broke down and ratted on Gates. So Caine had him take care of them."

"And Tess Abbott's accident?"

"Gates hired someone to do it. I don't know who. All I know is that Caine wanted her to stop digging. He probably used the same person to run her off that bridge that he sent to kill Lester."

"And Ginger?"

"Gates killed her."

"Where's Gates now?" Andy asked.

"Probably on his way to Mexico or somewhere far away. Caine was real unhappy that he'd botched the job on the bridge with the Abbott woman and he wasn't happy with the way he'd gotten rid of Ginger. I think Gates was worried Caine would be sending someone after him next, so he bolted."

"What about you, Rusty? Were you afraid Caine would send someone after you someday? Is that why you kept the negative?"

"I've never been afraid of dying, son. Only of living without your mother and you in my life. No. I kept the negative as insurance so that Caine could never do anything to hurt you or your mother."

"Me and my mother? How could he have done anything to hurt us? It was my old man who was dealing the drugs, not us."

"But your daddy used your mother's shop to traffic the drugs he was selling. Caine knew it. It didn't matter that she hadn't done it and that it stopped when he left. Caine said he would see to it that your mother lost the place if I didn't help him. She'd already lost the man she loved. All she had left was you and her shop. I couldn't let her lose that, too."

Jesus, what a mess, Andy thought. All these years Rusty had covered up a crime, allowed a murderer to walk free while an innocent man sat in jail. And it had all been because he'd loved them. "I'm going to need you to come in, Rusty, to make a formal statement. I'll also need you to testify against Caine."

"I'm ready," Rusty told him.

And that was why his mother had been there, Andy realized. "How much did you tell my mother?"

"All of it. I figured it was time I told her the truth. Just the way I taught you to do."

The icy calm that had settled over her after discovering it had been her grandfather at the house that night remained with Tess through the rest of the evening. And by the time she arrived at the lieutenant governor's home that night, that icy calm had given way to a cold rage. A rage toward Everett Caine for the part he'd played in destroying her family. A rage toward her grandfather for robbing her of not only her mother, but her father, too.

The house was a stately colonial seated high on a bluff. Accent lights showcased the manicured lawn and the well-tended gardens. After she parked her car in the circular driveway and mounted the steps, she rang the bell. She expected a servant to answer. Instead, it was Everett Caine himself.

"Come in, Ms. Abbott," he said, ever the genial host. "Why don't we go into my study and you and I can have a little chat."

Tess's impression of the house as she followed him was of a place that was cool, sophisticated and expensive. Very much like the man and his wife, she thought. He led her to a room with an antique desk, bookcases filled with law books and what appeared to be several first-edition classics. Wine-colored drapes in damask covered the windows. A photograph of the cool and elegant Pamela Caine sat on her husband's credenza.

He walked over to the built-in bar and asked, "Can I offer you something to drink?"

"No, thank you."

"If you don't mind, I think I'll have a brandy. It's been a long day," he said, acting as though not a thing in the world was wrong. He'd already removed his jacket and loosened the burgundy tie at his throat. The thick head of wheat hair remained perfect. So did the charming manner. He sat down in the chair behind his desk and cradled the glass of brandy. "Now, why don't you have a seat and tell me how I can help you."

Tess ignored the invitation to sit down. Instead, she removed the photograph from her purse and tossed it on the desk in front of him. "You can explain why that photo from my mother's murder scene was removed from the evidence file."

He flicked a glance at it, dismissed it. "If I remember correctly, there were several photos just like that one presented at your father's trial."

"Not like that one," she said, her voice deadly soft. "You'll notice the circle I've drawn around the gum wrapper on the table."

"What about it?"

"You and I both know whose gum wrapper that is."

"Why don't you tell me then," he said, and the amusement in his eyes only made the fury in her burn hotter.

"It belongs to my grandfather. When he quit smoking he began chewing gum. He has a nervous habit of tying the wrappers in a knot when he finishes with it.

Anyone who's known him for more than a few hours knows about his penchant for gum," she explained. "They also know about the wrappers. It's a joke of sorts on Capitol Hill. It's a fact that a fellow Ole Miss Law School alum would certainly know about one of the school's more famous and politically successful graduates."

"Suppose I did know?" Caine countered. "What does that prove?"

"It proves you knew it was my grandfather who was there that night at the house, that it was him I heard arguing with my mother. He was the one who hit her. Not my father. And it proves that you framed an innocent man. My guess is that when the news gets out, it's going to cost you the governorship."

"You'd be wise not to threaten me, Ms. Abbott."

For the first time since she'd arrived, she saw something other than cool arrogance in the man's eyes. "It's not a threat, Mr. Caine. It's a promise."

"In case you've forgotten, I'm not the only one you'll ruin if you leak this story of yours to the press. There's also your grandfather to consider."

"Oh, I haven't forgotten him. And my grandfather is going to have to answer for his hand in this."

"Just what is it you're hoping to accomplish by dragging all of this up now? Your father's dead. Destroying my career and your grandfather's won't do him any good."

"I owe it to my father to clear his name," she said. Because it was not only the truth. It was all that she could give her father now.

He slapped his glass down on the desk. "As much as I hate to disappoint you I'm afraid I can't allow you to do that, Ms. Abbott. You see, I intend to be the next governor of this state and I won't allow you or anyone else to get in my way."

"And just how do you think you're going to stop me?" she asked as she picked up the photo. "I've got the photograph."

"Which no one else is going to see," he told her, and when he lifted his hand, he was holding a gun.

A shiver of panic raced through her. She wished now that she had listened to Spencer and waited for him to come with her as he had asked. He snatched the photograph from her fingers and crushed it in his fist. Didn't he know that this wasn't the only copy? "How do you expect to get away with killing me?"

"The same way I got away with killing your mother."

Tess sucked in a breath. "But I thought…"

"That the senator killed her. So did he," Caine told her with a chilling smile. "Your grandfather called me that night, you know. Oh, he was blubbering like a baby, scared out of his wits. After your grandmother had told him that the two of you had left the hotel because you were sick and that Melanie had said she'd gotten a job at a restaurant, he was livid. So he went there to try to talk some sense into your mother. He tried to convince her to leave your father, to not make a fool of herself and him by waiting tables.

"The two of them got into a terrible fight. Your mother slapped him and ordered him to get out. And in a fit of rage he grabbed the bookend and hit her with it. There was blood everywhere and he thought she was dead. He was in a panic. So he called me and asked me to help him."

"So you concocted the plan to frame my father."

"It wasn't all that difficult. I made a call to Gates. He was more than happy to do me a favor."

"And in return, you helped finance his dealership," she added.

"It was a little expensive, but the investment paid off."

"And the others?" she asked.

"Gates handled them for me. He called the owner of the bar. For a few bucks, the man would have sold his mother. The same went for De Roach. And Virginia, well, the woman had the hots for your father, so getting her to go along was easy. She was told Jody would get off and then it would be her he'd turn to." He paused, then continued. "Your mother was the problem. She regained consciousness after I sent your grandfather back to Jackson."

"So you killed her?" Tess asked, both stunned and appalled.

"I couldn't let a little thing like her being alive ruin what was shaping up to be a very lucrative plan for me. Not only was I going to score a huge murder conviction, I was going to get a senator in my corner. A senator who not only has been generous in his endorsement of me as a candidate, but financially as well."

He smiled then, a truly evil smile that had Tess's blood turning cold. She tried to keep him talking, while she looked for something to use as a weapon. "But my father found out and he was going to expose you."

"Fortunately, Gates had a few contacts within the prison system. Most unfortunate about your father committing suicide like that when he was going to be a free man in just a few weeks."

"And how do you hope to explain away my death?" she asked as she spied a shadow at the doorway. Taking care not to alert Caine, she maintained eye contact with him and all the while she was praying that it was Spencer, that he had followed her there after he'd gotten her message.

"Why, everyone knows you're a distraught young woman. A room filled with people saw you verbally attack me at that reception. You've become overwrought and emotional since your father's suicide. Even your grandfather will attest to the fact that you haven't been yourself. Tonight when you came in here waving a gun at me, I had no choice but to defend myself."

"Spencer Reed knows where I am. He won't believe you."

"Everyone knows that Reed hates my guts. No one will pay any attention to what he says. Besides, he can't prove anything."

"My grandfather won't believe you. Neither will my grandmother."

He laughed. "Your grandmother is like my Pamela, she'll believe what she's told to believe. As for your grandfather, he'll believe me because he doesn't have a choice. I'm the man who saved his ass from prison. He wouldn't dare think of crossing me."

"Only, you didn't save him from prison. You were the one who killed his daughter," Tess accused.

"True. But that's our little secret and it's one I'm afraid that you, my dear, will not get to share with him or anyone else."

"That's where you're wrong, Caine," Theo Abbott said as he stepped through the doorway.

Caine whipped his gaze toward the doorway where her grandfather stood aiming a pistol at Caine.

In all the years she'd known him, Tess had never seen her grandfather look as cold as he did in that moment. His dark gray eyes were wintry. His face a mask of icy rage. "Grandfather, don't," she said.

"Listen to her, Theo. Put the gun down."

"All these years, you let me believe I killed my own daughter. And all the while, it was you who was responsible."

Panic danced in Caine's eyes. Sweat began to bead on his upper lip. "Think about what you're doing, Senator. You pull that trigger and you can kiss your career goodbye."

"He's right, Grandfather," Tess told him.

"Listen to her, Theo," Caine said. "We both have too much to lose for you to consider doing this."

"I've already lost," the senator told him as he pulled the trigger.

Caine grabbed his chest and a look of disbelief flittered across his face as blood began to seep through his fingers as he slumped in his chair.

At the sound of something hitting the floor, Tess looked at her grandfather again. He was holding the left side of his chest. Pain was etched across his face. "Grandfather," she cried out and raced over to him as he slid to the floor. "Hang on, I'm going to call an ambulance." Scrambling to her feet, she grabbed the phone. As she did so, she tried not to look at Everett Caine. His eyes were open wide, staring blankly, a surprised look frozen on his face.

"911 Emergency," a male's voice came on the line.

"I need an ambulance at Lieutenant Governor Caine's home right away."

"Give me your name and the nature of the emergency."

"My name's Tess Abbott. I think my grandfather's had a stroke. And you better send the police. The lieutenant governor…the lieutenant governor is dead."

Chapter Twenty-Three

Five days later. Jackson, Mississippi.

"Grams?" Tess knocked on the door of the adjoining hotel suite in Jackson, Mississippi, where she and her grandmother had spent the previous night. "I had some coffee and biscuits brought up from room service. I thought you might like some before we go to the lieutenant governor's funeral."

"That sounds good, dear. I'll be out in a few minutes."

"Take your time," she told her. "We don't have to leave for another forty-five minutes."

Walking back over to the dining table in the suite, Tess poured herself another cup of coffee and picked up the morning edition of the *Clarion-Ledger*. There on page one was the next installment of Spencer's feature "The Road to the Governor's Mansion." She stared at the headline:

A FINAL JOURNEY FOR CAINE
By Spencer Reed

Today Everett Caine should be in the last hours of his campaign, shaking hands and making speeches as tomorrow's governor's election approaches. Tonight he and his wife, Pamela Caine, should be meeting with their staff to make the final preparations in anticipation of a victory party. But Everett Caine is not making speeches or shaking hands today. Nor are he and Mrs. Caine planning a victory party. Instead of a celebration and a move to the governor's mansion, Everett Caine is making a final journey to what will be his final home. The lieutenant governor's road to the governor's mansion took an unexpected detour last week when the gun he and his good friend Senator Theodore Abbott were examining accidentally went off, killing Everett Caine.

Tess finished reading the article and took a sip of her coffee. She thought back to Pamela Caine's arrival at the house that night only moments before the ambulance and police arrived. While she had been stricken to discover her husband was dead, she had immediately taken charge and exercised damage control, spinning a tale about the gun accident. Any thoughts that she had had of correcting the matter had withered when the woman had squeezed her fingers and pleaded with her not to ruin the good things that her husband or Tess's grandfather had done. What surprised her the most was that she had gotten Spencer to agree to go along with her tale.

Spencer.

So much remained unresolved between them. With the media circus that had followed Caine's death and her grandfather's incapacitation due to the stroke, her grandmother had needed her. She'd kept vigil with her grandmother at the hospital and had been with her when the doctors had informed her that the senator had suffered a massive stroke. Not only had he lost the ability to speak, but he'd been confined to a wheelchair and needed constant care.

To make things easier on her grams, she had handled the media, dealt with his office and advised both the state Capitol and the White House that he would be unable to resume his duties as senator. Next week she would be helping her grams move the senator to their small home outside Jackson that they'd only used infrequently since the move to Washington. She would need to go to Washington and make arrangements to sell their town house. And she would also have to tell Ronnie and the station's black suits that she was not going to do the story on prison suicides. And at some point, she needed to have that sit-down discussion that Spencer had been asking her for.

At the knock at the door to the hotel suite, Tess pulled her thoughts from her musings. When she opened the door, the object of her thoughts was standing before her. "Spencer, what are you doing here?"

"I thought you and your grandmother might like a ride to Caine's funeral."

For a moment she was surprised he was going because of his hatred of the man, then she remembered his job. "I didn't realize when we spoke yesterday that you'd be going, but of course you're covering it for the newspaper."

"Actually, I'm not. I've already written my column for tomorrow's edition. My editor, Hank, is worried I'm sick because I wasn't meeting my deadline by the skin of my teeth for once." He glanced past her into the suite. "Is your grandmother still with you?"

"Yes, she's getting dressed. Please come in," Tess told him, remembering her manners.

When she closed the door behind him and turned around, he caught her by the shoulders and pulled her close and said, "I need this." Then he kissed her. The kiss was packed with need, with emotion, with desperation. When he lifted his head, she was feeling breathless. "I've missed you."

"I've missed you, too," she admitted. And it was true. She'd missed him more than she'd ever imagined she would.

"I know now is not the time or the place, but we do need to talk, Tess."

"I know. And we will. But first we need to get through Caine's funeral and I have to help my grandmother get settled and arrange for care for my grandfather."

"Yesterday you said she was going to move back to Mississippi. Does that mean you're considering leaving Washington, too?"

"I haven't made any decision yet," she told him honestly. "I'm flying back next week to put my grandparents' house on the market. And I need to meet with my producer and station management. As much as I love my job there, I'm not sure how happy they're going to be with me when I tell them I'm not going to run the story I promised them."

"What about clearing your father's name?" Spencer asked her.

"As much as I wanted to do that for him, I keep thinking of the people who would be hurt if everything were to come out. My grams, Pamela Caine, the former sheriff in Grady, Andy and his mother. Somehow the benefit to be gained by clearing my father's name doesn't seem to balance the damage it would do to innocent people." She sighed, rested her head on Spencer's shoulder. "Since Andy already has Gates in jail for killing Ginger, he'll be paying for what he did."

"And with Caine dead and your grandfather incapacitated, he doesn't have any leverage to use against them. Andy tells me Gates has been spilling his guts and they've already managed to pick up the hit man he hired to kill De Roach and to run you off the bridge."

"I'm praying that somehow my father knows and that he'll understand," she said, hoping that she was right.

"From what I've learned about him during this investigation, I think he will," Spencer told her. "I think he'd be proud of his daughter. I know I'm proud of you."

Tess lifted her head and looked into his eyes. "You do know that if you'd written the real story about what really happened that night at Caine's house, it would have been a career-making story for you. It still could be."

He shrugged. "There'll be other stories."

"Why *did* you go along with Pamela Caine's story about what happened? You never did say."

"For a lot of the same reasons you just gave. The scales didn't balance. Jenny's dead and nothing I do or don't do will change that. To expose Caine and what he did now wouldn't serve any purpose. A very wise woman tried to tell me that vengeance was a poor motive. It turns out she was right."

Tess couldn't help but smile. She touched his face. "You're a good man, Reed."

He flashed her that grin that she had found so infectious. "That's what I've been trying to tell you, Abbott. I just didn't think you were listening."

"Oh, I've been listening," she assured him.

Suddenly the smile on his face disappeared. His blue eyes went all serious. "Then I want you to listen to this, Abbott. I love you. I want you in my life."

"Reed—"

He pressed a finger to her lips. "Let me get this out. I want you in my life. I want to be in your life. I don't care if it's here in Jackson, or in Grady, or in D.C., or in Timbuktu. I want to be with you. I'm not expecting an answer right now. But I want you to know where I'm coming from."

Before she could respond, the door to her grandmother's bedroom opened and out walked Elizabeth Abbott. Dressed all in black with a pillbox hat atop her head, she held a black handbag. "Tess, dear, you didn't tell me we had a guest. Spencer, isn't it?" she asked and came toward them, a smile on her face.

"Yes, ma'am. It's nice to see you, Mrs. Abbott."

"Spencer came by to see if we'd like him to escort us to Mr. Caine's funeral."

"Why, I think that's a lovely idea," her grandmother declared.

Spencer beamed. "Whenever you ladies are ready," he told them.

"Why, I think we can go now, don't you, Tess?"

Tess glanced at her watch. "I thought you'd have some breakfast and that we'd just go to the funeral service, Grams." She didn't want to put her grandmother through the strain of the visitation at the funeral home as well.

Her grandmother took her hand and patted it.

"You're always so thoughtful, Tess. Just like your mother was. But I'm really not hungry and I'd like to go to the visitation and pay my respects to Pamela."

"Grams, you've been through a lot these past few days. Are you sure that's what you want to do?"

"I'm sure, dear." She turned to Spencer. "Shall we go?"

He offered her grandmother his arm and led them both from the suite.

"It looks like everyone in Jackson is here," Spencer remarked to Tess as they turned onto the street where the funeral home was located. Covering an entire city block, the stately-looking establishment with its black wrought-iron gates and curved driveway could have easily passed for a private estate. Instead, it was the grand send-off place from this life to the next.

When she spotted the news-station trucks along the street, Tess said, "Grams, there's a lot of media here. Why don't we just skip the visitation and go to the church."

"Tess, I've had to deal with the media all my life. It comes with being married to a politician."

"But this is different."

"She's right, Mrs. Abbott. Since the senator's stroke and Caine's death, your picture's been splashed across the newspapers a lot these past few days. There'll probably be a lot of reporters hounding you for an interview." He didn't bother telling her that because the senator had been reported as the one who'd "misfired" the gun that killed Caine, his own newspaper had pressed him to get an interview and that he had refused.

"As I keep telling my granddaughter, I can handle it," Mrs. Abbott informed him. "I truly am much stronger than either of you think."

"Tell you what," Spencer offered. "Why don't we drive around to the side entrance. That way we won't be in that crush going through the front."

"I think that's a great idea," Tess told him and the look in her eyes was filled with gratitude.

While the side entrance was better, one smart reporter had staked out the area. And she was waiting when Spencer pulled his SUV up to the entranceway and opened the door for Mrs. Abbott.

"Thank you," Elizabeth Abbott said politely as Spencer offered her his hand.

"Mrs. Abbott, how is the senator doing?" the newswoman asked as she stuck a microphone in her grandmother's face.

"He's doing as well as can be expected," Mrs. Abbott replied.

"Will you consider running for his unfinished term in the senate?"

"My grandmother has no further comment," Tess said firmly. "She's here to pay her respects to her friend Mrs. Caine."

"What about you, Ms. Abbot?" the persistent reporter asked. "Word is you're writing a tell-all book about your mother's murder."

"Then the word is all wrong," Tess informed her.

"Excuse us," Spencer said and he escorted both women up the stairs. "I'll park the car and meet you inside," he told Tess.

She nodded and disappeared inside with her grandmother. Ten minutes later when he went back into the funeral home Spencer was surprised by the number of people inside. Finally, he located Tess.

"Where's your grandmother?"

"She's talking to some politician's wife. She's over

there," Tess said, indicating the corner in the funeral parlor where her grandmother was engaged in conversation.

"Any more problems?"

"They have a few reporters roaming around inside here, but nothing my grandmother can't handle. She really is holding up through all of this remarkably well."

"You sound surprised."

"I guess I am," Tess admitted. "As much as I love my grandmother, I've always thought of her as…well, a little weak. She went along with whatever my grandfather wanted. But now, she seems so much stronger. This whole thing with my grandfather's stroke—I thought it would devastate her, that she might even fall apart. But she hasn't. She's been incredibly strong through the entire thing. She hasn't hesitated over making a single decision."

"I guess strong-willed women run in the Abbott family," he remarked.

She gave him a sidelong glance. "I'll take that as a compliment."

"It was," he told her and took her hand.

"Speaking of strong-willed women, what do you make of Pamela Caine?" she asked when they spied the widow at the front of a line receiving condolences from a throng of people.

"Personally, I think there's more there than meets the eye," he told her. "Do you still think she's the mystery caller?"

"Don't you?" he asked.

"I've been second-guessing myself a lot lately on that. I'm good at voices and I could have sworn she was the woman who called me. But when I asked her, she denied it. And when she pointed out that it would have been a foolish thing to do when she would have had so much to lose, I decided she was right. It wouldn't have made any sense."

"Did you ask her about buying that nun's costume?" Spencer asked, not quite ready to let the idea go.

"Yes. And she had a perfectly logical explanation. She bought it for a costume party and told me the date. I did some checking and there was an article in the newspaper about the costume party and it mentioned the Caines were there. She came dressed as a nun and her husband as a priest."

"Another coincidence," Spencer said.

"And you don't believe in coincidences."

"Nope."

"Then maybe it's time you start, Reed. Because I think, in this case, that's all it really was. A coincidence."

"It'll be a first for me," he told her. "But then, since I've met you, Abbott, I've experienced a lot of firsts. What's one more?"

Her lips curved softly. "I think we'd better go get my grandmother and head over to the church," she told him. "Later I'll let you explain to me what firsts you're talking about."

"I'll be happy to," he told her. And he fully intended to discuss the other firsts that he hoped to share with Tess.

"At least the crowd here at the cemetery is a lot lighter," Tess said more than two hours later as they stood at the grave site where Everett Caine's body was about to be laid to rest. The sun was still shining on the mountains of flowers sent from the funeral home to mark the final resting place of the onetime lieutenant governor and gubernatorial hopeful.

Despite her protests that she had paid her respects, her grandmother had insisted on going for the final ceremony at the cemetery. Once again, Tess found herself amazed by her grandmother's resilience and strength.

Tess stared over at Pamela Caine. Even in grief, the woman was the picture of beauty and grace, Tess thought as the woman stood bravely and watched them lower the casket of her husband into the ground. Dressed all in black in a slim-fitting sheath, the widow Caine's blond hair had been pulled back and styled in a chignon. A chic black hat sat atop her head. Silk hose and black Manolo Blahnik pumps, with a matching bag, completed the ensemble. She held a lace handkerchief in her hand and dabbed at hazel eyes bright with tears as the minister said a final prayer.

"Thank you for coming with me today," her grandmother told Tess. "You too, Spencer."

"You're welcome, Grams."

"I was glad to do it, Mrs. Abbott," Spencer told her.

"I only got to speak with Pamela for a second at the funeral home. I'd like to go pay my respects to her now. Will you come with me?" her grandmother asked.

"Of course," Tess told her and together with Spencer they joined the small line of those waiting to express their final words of sympathy.

As they waited at the end of the line, Tess thought about Pamela Caine again. Despite her assertion to Spencer about coincidences where Pamela Caine was concerned, it bothered her no end to think she'd been wrong about that voice, about the phrasing the woman had used.

The question that still puzzled her was, Why? They

edged a little closer, and when the three of them reached the widow, her grandmother hugged the other woman. "How are you holding up, Pam?"

"I'm doing okay. How about you, Elizabeth?" Pamela Caine asked, genuine concern in her expression.

"I'm fine. I've got my granddaughter and her young man. So I'm not the least bit lonely."

An odd comment, Tess thought. She stepped forward and said, "My condolences, Mrs. Caine. I'm sorry for your loss."

"Thank you," she murmured.

"My sympathy, Mrs. Caine," Spencer told her.

"Thank you, Mr. Reed. It was good of you both to come with Elizabeth."

Tess simply nodded.

"And I appreciate your discretion the other night. Both of you."

"I hope it makes things easier for you," Spencer told her.

"It does. And I trust now with Everett gone, all of us will have the justice that we deserved."

"I beg your pardon?" Spencer said.

"With Everett dead, you have the justice you wanted for your friend. And Ms. Abbott has justice for her father."

"What about you, Mrs. Caine? For whom did you get justice?" Tess asked her.

"Why, for me, of course."

"I don't understand," Tess said.

"My dear, I could forgive Everett many things. But he crossed the line when he got that girl pregnant. He had to pay for that. And now he has."

And as Tess stood there with Spencer and her grandmother at her side, Pamela Caine turned on her designer high heels and walked away.

New York Times **bestselling author**
Elaine Coffman brings you a tempestuous
tale of honor, betrayal and love lost and found....

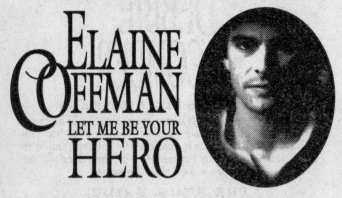

ELAINE COFFMAN

LET ME BE YOUR HERO

Claire Lennox, Countess of Errick and Mains, is a
powerful woman in a man's world. Confident and
courageous, she refuses to marry—ever again. Eight
years ago, when she was an impulsive young girl, she
lost her heart and her marriage to foolish pride.

Now, as desperate rivals plot to seize her title and lands,
one man is willing to risk everything to save her—her
former husband, Fraser Graham. As the noose of treachery
tightens, Fraser must decide if he will pledge his sword,
his strength and his heart to the one woman he has
always loved—or resign himself to losing her forever.

A "...lusty, tension-filled romance..."
—Romantic Times on The Highlander

Available the first week of November 2004
wherever paperbacks are sold!

MIRA®

www.MIRABooks.com   MEC2092

METSY HINGLE

66926 BEHIND THE MASK	___ $6.50 U.S.	___ $7.99 CAN.
66826 THE WAGER	___ $5.99 U.S.	___ $6.99 CAN.
66714 FLASH POINT	___ $6.50 U.S.	___ $7.99 CAN.

(limited quantities available)

TOTAL AMOUNT	$_____
POSTAGE & HANDLING	$_____
($1.00 for 1 book, 50¢ for each additional)	
APPLICABLE TAXES*	$_____
TOTAL PAYABLE	$_____

(check or money order—please do not send cash)

To order, complete this form and send it, along with a check or money order for the total above, payable to MIRA Books®, to: **In the U.S.:** 3010 Walden Avenue, P.O. Box 9077, Buffalo, NY 14269-9077; **In Canada:** P.O. Box 636, Fort Erie, Ontario, L2A 5X3.

Name:_____
Address:_____ City:_____
State/Prov.:_____ Zip/Postal Code:_____
Account Number (if applicable):_____
075 CSAS

*New York residents remit applicable sales taxes.
  Canadian residents remit applicable GST and provincial taxes.

MIRA®